A Nort

What Readers Have Said About

Murder on the Prairie: A North Florida Mystery
By M.D.Abrams

"M.D. Abrams has done an outstanding job in her first novel, *Murder on the Prairie*. The plot is fast paced and does not linger in the climax as it comes to an ending that leaves the reader waiting for the sequel. It has a spell binding plot and mixes it with intelligent thought about art and life and unforgettable characters. Definitely a good read!"

"Great book! I just finished reading it in two sittings because I didn't want to put it down. It flowed so nicely and grabbed and captured my interest."

"The book is marvelous! The plot is exciting and educational; the characters are well drawn and engaging; the story line is complex and moving along at a good pace. All in all--a very satisfying read."

"I don't know...the alligators, chiggers, snakes, have not made me any more likely to come to Florida. But, my curiosity is completely aroused about the prairie...the sink holes, etc., are giving me goose bumps - which I suppose is exactly what a mystery should do."

"One certainly does not have to live in North Florida to enjoy this new book! Anyone interested in mystery, ecology, and theater will thoroughly enjoy this first novel by M.D Abrams."

"It hooked me early on, and kept me going right up to the end. M.D. Abrams has written a book that kept me entertained, but that also worked my brain (HOW long ago did I read Chekhov?!)."

"Well-written with picturesque detail of the North Florida landscape, there's both substance and engaging characters in these real life situations."

i

Booklocker.com, Inc.
2006

A North Florida Mystery

Murder at Wakulla Springs

A North Florida Mystery

M.D. Abrams

Murder at Wakulla Springs

Dedicated to my friend Doris Bardon—a founding member of
Gainesville's Women for Wise Growth—and to all other community
activists who persevere to keep some portion of North Florida's
natural character for the benefit of all beings.

*Only when the last tree has died, the last river has been poisoned and
the last fish has been caught will we realize that we can't eat money.*
-Cree Indian proverb

Murder at Wakulla Springs

A North Florida Mystery

Acknowledgements

As a longtime South Floridian, I knew little about Northwest Florida. After moving upstate, I took advantage of the opportunity to explore parts of that region and have developed a deep appreciation for its natural beauty, old Florida charm, and places of outstanding significance. In this book, the town of Fairport and Graham Springs are fictitious but the Edward Ball Wakulla Springs State Park and the small fishing town of Apalachicola are actual places. All of the settings provide a context in which to highlight some of the major changes taking place in the region known variously as the Panhandle, Florida's Forgotten Coast, the Redneck Riviera, and more recently—for the purpose of real estate sales—Florida's Great Northwest.

I have spent years collecting information about issues relating to Florida's watershed but I am especially indebted to Kevin M. McCarthy (2004) for his beautiful book, *Apalachicola Bay* with illustrations by William L. Trotter; Tracy J. Revels (2002) for her well-researched, and highly readable, *Watery Eden: a History of Wakulla Springs*; the Tallahassee Film Society (2005) for *Wakulla Springs: A History in Film* with material from the Florida State archives; Jennifer Portman and Bruce Ritchie (2006), of the *Tallahassee Democrat* for their incisive series on Wakulla and other Florida springs; and Kathryn Ziewitz and June Wiaz (2004) for their masterful work, *Green Empire: The St.Joe Company and the Remaking of Florida's Panhandle.*

Other individuals contributed to my understanding of the locale and the story's action scenes. Among them were Dale Julian, of Apalachicola's Downtown Books; Captain Gibby Conrad's highly informative Apalachicola Bay eco-tours; the Apalachicola Riverkeeper organization; and the Florida Park Rangers who enthusiastically conduct the Wakulla Springs boat tours. Parts of the story relating to scuba diving were enhanced by generous interviews given by Wes Skiles, renowned diver explorer; Wuni Ryschkewitsch,

vii

a diver with forty years experience; and Jordan Gross, of Gainesville's Water World Dive Shop.

I owe a debt of thanks for the arduous job of critiquing and proofing my manuscript to Dorothy Staley, Anne Boches, and Chris Flavin. I am grateful to my writer's group for their continued support and encouragement. Special thanks to Claire Reishman, for allowing me to begin writing this book in the magical environment of St. Andrews-Sewanee, TN. Thanks also to dear friend Ron Kay for his creative marketing designs. Finally, I am profoundly indebted to Dorie Stein for her constant enthusiasm, support, and clever suggestions as I plotted my way through the story—t.t.e.o.t.

Gainesville, Florida
October 2006

A North Florida Mystery

Murder at Wakulla Springs

A North Florida Mystery

Murder at Wakulla Springs

Prologue

"Quite a crowd already," Alex said. He surveyed the cavernous lobby before signing the registration book.

"Oh, yes," replied the clerk. She wore a badge which read, "Wakulla Springs Lodge" with the name "Janice" above it. He suspected she was one of the young Florida State University students he had often seen working at the Preserve.

"Creaturefest is a very popular event. It's a fundraiser for Friends of Wakulla Springs put on by the Tallahassee Film Society. We're booked solid for the entire weekend," she said, leaning toward him. "My boyfriend and I always watch *The Creature from the Black Lagoon* on the Sci Fi channel."

"Really?" he replied absently, handing her his credit card as he continued scanning the lobby. Alex noted a number of people already dressed in 1950's boating clothes. Some wore hats decorated with small Creature dolls, while others wore rubberized replicas of the Creature's hands and feet. Their laughter made him regret the time he spent strolling around the waterfront, before checking into the lodge. He had done it to reorient himself. For just this one weekend, he wanted to experience peace and pleasure at Wakulla Springs rather than the turmoil it had recently brought him. The bitter controversy over his springs research had driven his wife and daughter away, and would possibly cost him his reputation as a scientist.

As he waited, he impatiently readjusted his Gill Man Creature suit which hung loosely draped over his arm like a deflated parade float figure. He was proud of his creation—made from an old diving wet suit and hood—and he hoped to be the only one wearing the full iconic outfit. Ever since he was a boy, Alex had loved to create and wear costumes. His father disapproved of the hobby, fearing Alex might one day become an actor...or worse.

Janice slid his credit card back across the desk and handed him a large room key. "Second floor with a view of the spring. So you're going to be the *Creature from the Black Lagoon?*" she said, peering over the desk at the slime green costume. "Cool suit. Have a great weekend, Dr. Hadley."

He thanked her, reached for his overnight bag, and walked up the marble steps near the reception desk. He couldn't help smiling as he turned the key to his room. He knew what to expect—the lodge was known for its old-fashioned simplicity, and the serenity of its natural surroundings. He entered the modest space and took a deep breath. He put his things down on the bed and was immediately drawn to the wide expanse of draped windows. He opened the drapes and stood looking out. An aura of peace descended upon him as he stared at the renowned spring through the broad expanse of lawn and moss-draped oak trees.

"This is just what I needed," he said, and felt a familiar sense of awe and intimacy for this seemingly ordinary pool of water. Alex had first-hand knowledge of its boundless depths and extensive caves. He was one of a privileged few professional divers to explore and map them. But, at this moment, he avoided any thoughts about the threats to Wakulla Springs once pristine waters.

Abruptly ending his reverie, he felt eager to join the company of others in the lobby, to swap stories about the making of the Creature movie. After a quick shower, and—dressed only in shorts, and a tee-shirt—Alex sat down and began pulling on the costume's web-footed pants. He pushed his left leg into the bottom, felt an odd crunch under the foot, and felt the first sharp sting.

Instinctively, he slid his hand into the lower portion of the suit. He experienced another stinging bite on his finger. He quickly withdrew his hand, and saw a small red fire ant crawling on it. Biting stings intensified on his feet and up his leg.

Panicky—his heart pumping wildly—Alex lunged toward the bed to get his Epi Pen. He tripped on the corner of the metal bed frame, landed on the floor, and cried out, "Holy shit!" then crawled over to the overnight case which lay opened on the bed. He tossed its contents searching for the epinephrine syringe. He knew he was in great danger when he realized it wasn't there.

"Impossible," he whispered, his throat dry from fear. "I know I packed it."

Still sitting on the floor, he clumsily tried to yank off the pants, but his swelling leg was stuck in the wet suit. His breathing became labored. His confusion and dizziness increased, and he knew he desperately needed to get help. He grabbed for the telephone on the nightstand, over-reached, and knocked over the lamp. Exhausted, Alex fell flat on the floor between the beds. In between violent wheezing spasms, he gasped for breath and flailed at the costume. The pain from his leg was excruciating. His face, eyelids, and lips were grotesquely swollen. In an almost dreamlike trance, he thought he heard someone knocking at the door. He tried to call out, but the swelling in his throat prevented it. Within minutes, he slipped into severe anaphylactic shock and unconsciousness. He lay still with one leg stuck in the Gill Man costume. Red ants emerged from the other leg of the costume, and blended into the rose-colored rug on which Dr. Alex Hadley lay dead.

Chapter 1

"Forgotten Coast indeed," I muttered as I drove along Florida's Highway 98 coastline which was dotted with new pastel painted stilt houses. They were lined up like lollipops along the Apalachee Bay on the Gulf of Mexico. After a weaving stretch of densely forested road, the sight of the bay had emerged like a shimmering gem in the late afternoon sun. I passed through Medart, saw the sign to Wakulla Springs State Park on SR 319, and promised myself a visit to the famed springs.

The cell phone jangled as I passed a narrow strip of beach along the shoreline. I pulled off onto the adjacent shoulder. I hated using the damn phone under any circumstances, and I was nervous using it while driving.

The ringing sounded insistent as I plucked the phone from my handbag and got out of the car. It felt good to stretch my legs after the four hour drive from Gainesville.

"Hey Lorelei, what's going on? I got a message at the plant lab you were looking for me."

"Jeffrey? It's about time you returned my calls. Don't you use your cell phone anymore?" I leaned against the car door and took a deep breath of the cool sea air.

"I've changed companies—my old cell stopped working. Anyway, my boss sent me to check out a lab at the University of South Florida in Tampa. I've been pretty busy."

"Knowing you, I'm sure you managed to get in some party-time."

He laughed, "I'll admit, I did get in some visits with friends. Hey, Louisa Monterosa asked about you."

"That's nice," I said, and wondered if the friends included his former lover, Eduardo Sanchez. It was hard to know where Jeffrey's sexual preferences were after the shooting which landed him in the hospital. He was always so secretive about his love life.

"So, Red, what's up?"

I scanned the sparkling blue bay and took another deep breath.

1

"What's up is that I'm on the road to Apalachicola. I'll be there for about six weeks—in a play," I said. The bay air held only the faintest fishy odor. No one was on the little beach except an occasional seagull running along the water's edge as the waves ebbed and flowed. "Apalachicola? How lucky can you get? It's one of my favorite towns."

"Yes, mine, too. Bill and I..."

"Lor? Are you okay? It's been a while since we've talked. Have you started dating? You need to find someone your own age. Someone passionate crazy about you. You do remember what passion feels like, don't you?"

It was the same tune Jeffrey had been singing since he showed up in Gainesville two years ago.

"Of course, I remember. I suppose you mean someone like you."

"Not so passionate anymore," he said. "Besides, I'm focused on my doctorate. Life's not quite as exciting as it used to be."

"Exciting? If that's what you call it when you got shot in the head and nearly died on me? Anyway, the reason I was trying to reach you was to let you know I was leaving town for a while. Just in case..."

"In case what?"

"I don't know. I guess I just feel better if friends know where I am. I'm counting on this time away to be peaceful—so I can figure out what to do with my life."

"Without Bill? C'mon, Lor, you know..."

"Please Jeffrey, don't tell me again how much better off I am without him."

"Okay," he said, and lowered his voice, "I know it's been rough, but you'll pull through it. Is there anything I can do to help?"

"Just stand by. You may get a late night call or two. By the way, let me get your new cell number."

He gave me the number, and I jotted it down on a gas receipt.

"So what's the play?" he asked.

"Renee's directing her own adaptation of Ibsen's *An Enemy of the People*. I'm going to play the wife. It's not much of a part, but..."

"You're kidding me."

"Okay, wise guy. I get it. The new widow playing an old wife."

"Sorry, Lor. You're breaking up—are you on your cell?" he asked. "You're not driving now are you? I remember that road. It's pretty narrow in spots."

"No, I've stopped along the beach," I said, feeling comforted by his concern. "It's so unpopulated, Jeffrey. There's some development, but it still looks like old Florida. I can even see shrimp boats moving out to the gulf."

"Maybe I could make time to come up and visit you for a couple of days. See the play and..."

I knew what he had in mind, but I still felt too vulnerable to entertain the idea of Jeffrey bunking in with me. "You're welcome to come up, but you'll have to find your own place to stay."

He said, "Hey, I just thought of something. I have a friend around there. I've kind of lost track of where he lives, but he's cool— a geologist and an environmental policy wonk. Graduated from USF. We worked together once in Tampa."

"How can I find him if you don't know where he lives?" I asked, thinking it would be nice to get to know someone local.

"Good point. Let's see, last I heard he was working for FPIRG—the Florida Public Interest Research Group. You could ask around. Wait a minute...he's a diver, he used to teach at a dive shop in Carrabelle. You'll like him, Lor, and if you get lonely..."

"What's his name?" I asked.

"Hadley. Alex Hadley. Just tell him I said to take good care of you."

"Thanks, Jeffrey. I'll do it."

Before getting back into the car, I picked up a broken conch shell from the grass. I lifted the shell to my nose, and touched the hard outer part to my tongue, before dropping it back on the ground. The taste triggered childhood memories of the beach.

Along the coast, on the way to Eastpoint, I was shocked by the amount of storm damage. A boat had settled on top of a building, other buildings were off their foundations, fish packing houses lay in ruins, water front restaurants were closed, and one dilapidated store had a sign, "We have not moved." Many of the destroyed properties had "For Sale" signs on them. Hurricane Dennis' storm surge had made a wreck of the area.

I drove past the bridge to St. George Island and through East Point, which looked pretty much intact. I was surprised to see condos and a marina in this town prized as a fishing village. I finally crossed the bay causeway and the John Gorrie Bridge. It exited right in the heart of town.

It had been years since I visited the Panhandle. Bill and I had stayed at the quaint Cape San Blas Inn on the St. Joseph Peninsula. We enjoyed solitary walks across the wild dunes and the white sandy beaches. I planned to revisit the areas where I had once been happy.

The town of Apalachicola looked like I remembered it. The historic Gibson Inn stood at the foot of the bridge. Its spacious porches and Victorian trim lived up to the claim in its brochure which described Apalachicola as a "Victorian fishing village." I drove two blocks, lined with small stores and restaurants, and turned right down Avenue E. The old fashioned marquee displayed "Dixie Theatre" in large letters. It was where our play would be produced. I parked and got out of the car.

A petite old woman was reading a poster at the theatre entrance. She wore a small red suede hat with silk flowers on the brim, and carried a matching bag.

"What a great old theatre," I said, walking up alongside her and taking in the old fashioned ticket booth.

"Oh, yes. It's a real treasure. The Partingtons have done a remarkable job of restoring it." She glanced at my car then back at me. She had a bright and curious look. "Are you driving through or vacationing?"

"I'm here for the play. I'm going to be in it," I said, gesturing toward the poster. "I hope you'll come to see it."

"Really?" she said, glancing back at the poster. "I like Ibsen, but I don't know this play. Will I like it?"

I laughed. "I hope so."

"I try to see all the plays and films at The Dixie. Did you know this theatre's been here since 1913?"

4

"No, I didn't. I guess I'll learn more about it when we start rehearsals tomorrow. I've only just arrived. By the way, I'm looking for this address on Water Street." I showed her the address on the contract Renee had sent me.

"Oh, my dear, it's just around the corner." She pointed toward the bay. "Water Street is the next block down. Turn right, and it's a little ways before the big Apalachicola River Inn. You can't miss it."

I thanked her and returned to my car. It was approaching dinner time, and I noted a quaint looking café across from the theatre. It appeared to be open. Turning on Water Street, I found the address at a small entranceway next to the Bay Street Fish Market. The apartment was on the second floor.

Not an attractive location, I thought, but a definite advantage to be on the water, and it was a short walk to the theatre. I parked the car under a shady magnolia and grabbed one of my suitcases. The faint smell of disinfectant permeated the narrow stairwell. I wondered what I would find in apartment 2A—my home away from home. The door was open.

I put my bag down. The apartment appeared to be clean—something a traveling actor is apprehensive about since some of our colleagues have been known to leave messes behind. The bedroom and bath were small, as was the kitchen which had a pass-through to the living-dining area. The furnishings were spare but tasteful. I pulled the small glass-topped dining table across the wooden floors and arranged it and two chairs under the windows facing the bay.

I returned to the kitchen to examine the contents of the refrigerator and cabinets. The refrigerator contained a small platter of cheese and crackers covered in plastic wrap with a hand-written note that said, "Welcome." There was no signature.

"How thoughtful," I said.

I leaned against the kitchen sink suddenly feeling weary and slightly depressed. I spied a wall phone next to the pass-through. "No," I thought, "I'm not going to give in this easily." Next to the phone was a menu for Sophie's Café—the one across from the theatre. It was time to get acquainted with the locals and grab something to eat before tonight's "meet and greet" at the theatre.

As I left the apartment, a large black cat attracted my attention with several squeaky meows. He was sitting at the front of the door to Apartment 2B. As I paused on the landing, I heard a soulful operatic aria coming from inside. I stooped to pet the cat and wondered who my opera loving neighbor might be.

Chapter 2

I took a leisurely stroll along the wharf. Purple night clouds were moving in across the darkened water. Turning onto Avenue E, I looked into some of the antique and gift shops. It had become chilly outside.

I opened the door to Sophie's Café, and the aroma of fresh baked bread lured me inside.

"What are you making? It smells delicious," I said to a tall middle-aged woman who was arranging the baked goods. She wore her thick black hair pulled back into a bun, and a slash of gray ran down the middle.

The woman looked up and I was struck by her eyes. They were slightly protruding and the pale blue-green color of the water I had seen earlier in the day. She smiled as she continued arranging the fruit-filled cookies.

"Just some Rugalla and these," she said, pointing to a pan of stuffed triangle-shaped pastry. "They're my own version of pot pies to go...they called them pasties in London. Today I've filled them with ricotta cheese, spinach and a secret ingredient. Would you like to try one?"

"Definitely," I said, looking up at the whimsical painted menu on the wall behind the counter. "And a latte as well, please. I'll eat here."

"Sit anywhere," she said. "I'll bring."

"Are you from England?" I asked, making conversation while she arranged the sandwich on a plate with a sprig of parsley and several slices of green apple. I couldn't quite place her accent except that it was clipped, like the British accent.

"No, actually I was born in Israel, but I lived in London for a time."

"How interesting," I said, paying her at the cash register. I walked to a small table near the window with a view of the theatre.

"You're an actress," she said, bringing over the plate.

"How can you tell?" I asked, glancing across the street to the theatre.

"The way you carry yourself. And," she chuckled, "I saw you earlier—across the street. I know there's a new play starting rehearsal tonight."

Small town, I thought. Everybody notices when a stranger arrives. "A couple of your fellow actors have already come in today. If you don't mind, I'll sit with you for a few minutes. There's not much business at the dinner hour." She eased down opposite me. "Oy. Too much standing."

"Umm, this is just as delicious as it smells. Is there curry in it? I'm going to be your best customer."

She nodded and smiled in a maternal way that made me like her right away. I knew she had to be Sophie, the owner of the café.

"So, let me guess," she said. "You'll be playing Dr. Stockman's wife. Am I right?"

"You know the play?"

"Oh, yes. I've read it and I've seen it on stage in London. I'll be interested to see how you do it. It might create quite a stir around here, but I like that. Sometimes, Apalachicola gets a bit too sleepy for my taste."

"You think it won't be well received here?" I asked, sipping my latte and studying this sturdy looking woman.

"It's about truth-telling...and upsetting people's dreams. Not a very popular subject anywhere."

The sound of a Chinese wind chime caused her to look up as two new customers entered the café.

"Excuse me," she said, returning to the counter.

"Lorelei!" It was Renee. She rushed toward me with a man in tow. He was tanned, boyishly handsome, and wore a tee shirt with *Riverkeeper* across the front. He looked to be in his late twenties or early thirties. Renee bent down and hugged me. "Lorelei Crane meet Mike Pardo. He'll be playing Dr. Stockman, your husband."

Mike and I shook hands. I liked his firm grip and rough hands...very unactor like, I thought.

"Please join us," she said, pointing to a larger table across the room.

8

I moved my things, and they returned with plates of food. Sophie followed with their drinks.

"So, Lorelei, when did you arrive?" Renee asked.

"About an hour ago. I loved the drive."

"You've seen the theatre," she said, nodding in its direction across the street. "Isn't it perfect?" She took a few bites of her sandwich and kept on talking. "It's a more intimate space than the Tuscawilla in Gainesville, but we'll have smaller audiences, too. Apalachicola's population is only about ten thousand—isn't that what you told me, Mike?"

He nodded, but didn't take his eyes off me.

Renee continued, "December wouldn't have been my choice for a serious play like ours, but it was the only open date they had, and I've been dying to do it." She glanced at Mike Pardo.

He finished his sandwich, and said, "I've been looking forward to meeting you, Lorelei. Renee says you're a very good actress. Have you checked into your apartment yet?"

"Oh, yes" I said. "It's clean, and it has a great view of the bay. Perfectly adequate though I probably won't be spending much time there. Where are you from, Mike?"

"Mike's a local actor," Renee said.

He shrugged. "More local than actor. As you'd imagine, there's not much work for an actor around the coast. I own a boat, and I do eco-tours of the Apalachicola Bay."

That explains his tan, I thought. "Maybe you'll take me out one day. I'd love to see the bay area. I've only explored the beaches on the gulf side."

A shadow passed over his face. "Well, we've got a lot of big issues about the bay right now, and…"

"C'mon you kids," Renee said. "Let's get over to the theatre. You'll have plenty of time to get acquainted later."

"Ms. Scalia, shall I bring over the coffee and pastries around ten?" Sophie asked as we approached the door. "That's when I close up."

"Please, Sophie, call me Renee. And, yes, ten o'clock will be perfect."

9

It was dark when we left Sophie's, and there was a cold breeze off the bay. I wished I had worn a jacket and hoped the theatre would be warmer.

Renee was right, the theatre was small. It didn't appear to hold more than a hundred people. The large stage was set with a long table and chairs, and a couple of bare-bulb standing lamps provided the only light. We were the first to arrive, and Renee gave me a tour of the backstage. Unlike the stage itself, backstage was small and cramped.

By the time we returned, the cast had assembled and were chatting with one another. I didn't recognize anybody and wondered if I was the only out-of-towner.

A young woman with a buzz-cut hairdo introduced herself as Liz Regis, our stage manager. After passing out schedules, contracts, and copies of the script, she announced, "Friday, December 2nd is the final rehearsal—technical and dress combined—and we open on Saturday, December 3rd. That gives us just four weeks of rehearsals. I know it's a tight fit for those who are driving down from Tallahassee, but you need to be here and ready to work by 5:30 every evening, except Mondays, and from 10 am to finish on the weekends. Questions about the schedule?"

She paused while everyone looked over the handouts. Next, Liz asked us to briefly introduce ourselves.

When that was done, she said, "Now, here's your director, Renee Scalia."

"Thanks, Liz," she said, smiling at each of the actors. "I hope you all are as excited as I am to do this play. In a little while, I want to get your impressions of it. But, first, please note the change of setting. We will not be in a coastal town in southern Norway, but in a coastal town in our own southern Georgia—a place called Eden Springs."

"Is that a real town?" asked one of the actors.

"No, it's pure fiction, but if it reminds you of Warm Springs, Georgia you can use that as a tag. What made me feel called to do *Enemy* is how contemporary the issues are. Consider that Ibsen wrote it in 1882—and, by the way, it was published in November so we're celebrating the 123rd anniversary of the play. How many of you have already read or acted in this play?"

All hands went up.

She said, "I'll recap the plot anyway, in case it's been a while since you read it. *Enemy* is about a town that turns on its doctor scientist when he attempts to publicize his research findings about a local spa. The town leaders are afraid his information will jeopardize their plans for improving the economy."

Mike Pardo said, "Since I'll be playing the doctor, I'd like to know what you think Ibsen's message was. How scientists can become obsessed with their pursuit of truth, how easily the public can be manipulated, or something else?"

A couple of the younger actors responded and were split on their views. I listened and began to wonder about the role of Dr. Stockman's wife. In my recent reading of the play, she struck me as an unrealistic character—too supportive of her husband and willing to allow her family to be destroyed. The more I thought about Dr. Stockman, the more I leaned toward the idea it was a play about a man who was obsessed and self-absorbed.

The man playing Dr. Stockman's father-in-law asked, "Ms. Scalia—Renee—you haven't told us yet if you've changed the time in which the play is to be set. Will it be staged in modern time, or in the original time period?"

"Oh, it does call for modern staging, don't you think?" she replied. "In fact, I've just been to the Goodman Theatre, in Chicago, where they're doing Ibsen's *Dollhouse*. Rebecca Gillman's adaptation put Nora in a modern condo, and she shopped at a Whole Foods store! So, yes, and when you see the costumes and set-design, I think you'll be very pleased with my adaptation. In fact, it's time to show you what our artistic designers have come up with so far."

The costume and set designers got up to display their sketches. There was more talk about the staging and characters until Sophie showed up with carafes of coffee, hot chocolate, and pastries. Everyone swarmed around the goodies, and I had a chance to talk to a couple of the actors. They were theatre students at Florida State. Like many of the student actors I've worked with, they were excited at the chance to work with equity actors in a classic drama.

It was after ten when everyone began to leave the theatre.

Mike Pardo came up and said, "How about I walk you back to your apartment? It's pretty safe around here, but I'd like the company."

"Sure, we can talk some more about the play."

We walked back to Water Street, talking about how the evening went. When we arrived at my building, Mike held open the door and started to follow me up the stairs.

I turned and said, "Goodnight, Mike. See you tomorrow."

There was a silly grin on his face as he passed me on the stairwell and stood looking down from the top step.

"What are you doing?" I asked, beginning to feel defensive.

He smiled and said. "I live in 2B. We're neighbors. Goodnight, Lorelei Crane. I hope you sleep well." With that, he inserted his key and entered his apartment.

As I walked into my place, I reconsidered my living arrangements—handsome leading man, black cat, and soulful music? This should be an interesting run, I concluded.

Chapter 3

Late Sunday afternoon Homer McBride called from Gainesville. The cast was on a dinner break, and I was studying my script at a table outside of Sophie's Café. The weather was perfect—sunny, but cool enough for a sweater—and the bay breeze made me glad to be near the water.

"Lorelei, am I disturbing you? Are you in the middle of something?"

"Homer? Why no, you caught me during a break. How nice to hear from you." I said, surprised at just how glad I was to hear his voice.

Alachua County Sheriff's Detective Homer McBride and I had become friends over the past year. We had met at the beginning of the Paynes Prairie criminal investigations. We'd had lunch together several times and went to the movies on a couple of Sunday afternoons—not official dates, but just as friends. He was easy to talk to and always had a funny story to tell about some of the dumb criminals he had encountered. Homer was in his mid-forties and what some might describe as a man's man. He was about five nine with a rugged build—just shy of stocky—square jaw and dark features. When I let myself, I found attractive...but that's as far as it went.

Homer said, "Look Lorelei, I know you're just starting rehearsals, but I wonder if you could do me a favor."

"Sure. What is it?"

"I'm going to be at Wakulla Springs tomorrow, and I'd like you to meet me there if you can get away for an hour or so."

"Luckily tomorrow's my day off, and I've wanted to see the springs. I think it's about an hour's drive."

"So you'll come?"

"Sure. Did you finally get some vacation time?"

He chuckled. "I haven't had a vacation since the wife and I separated a couple of years ago, and she took the assignment in Europe. Anyway, I'll be staying at the lodge. How about meeting me for lunch...on the State's tab?"

"Sounds good. But what are you doing out of your jurisdiction, detective?" I wanted to prolong our conversation. It felt good to talk with someone from home. I already felt as though I'd settled into a different world.

"It's official business," he said. "May turn out to be something I could use your help with, but I'll tell you about it when I see you. Oh, did I mention I enrolled in Florida State's Master's Program in Criminal Justice?"

"No, you didn't. I'm proud of you." I was still mulling over his comment about needing my help with a case, but I knew he wouldn't discuss it over the phone.

McBride countered, "I'm proud of you for getting out of town for a while. It'll do you good."

"I hope so. Does the FSU program mean you'll be commuting back and forth to Tallahassee for classes?"

He laughed. "Sure, my department would be crazy about that. No, it's mostly online. Looks like I'll learn a lot of computer stuff. Pretty snazzy."

"You sound excited about it." The lightness in his voice surprised me since not much got Homer McBride pumped up.

"I guess. After twenty-five years in law enforcement, it'll be good to learn something new. So, I'll look for you around noon. You've got my cell and pager if you run into any snags."

"Mind if I join you?" Mike Pardo stood at my side as I closed the cell phone.

"No, sit." I replied. "I thought I'd run into you at the apartment this morning when I was unpacking my car. You must be an early riser."

He slouched in the chair and rubbed his face. "I usually get down to the dock around dawn. I piddle around, get the boat ready for the day...you know, a sailor's work is never done." Mike smiled, and in the bright sun, I saw just how white and straight his teeth were. Either expensive orthodontist work or good genes, I thought.

"I did meet up with your cat in front of the fish store. What's his name?"

"The large black one?"

I nodded.

"He's not my cat. He just visits me from time to time."

"Does he have a name?"

"I call him Clarence," he said. "After the Duke of Clarence."

"In Richard III?"

"Yes, I once played the role. It's my favorite Shakespearean play."

"An odd choice for a boat captain. Didn't Clarence drown?"

Mike tipped back his head, and his face looked convincingly filled with grieve, as he intoned, "Oh Lord! me thought, what pain it was to drown! What dreadful noise of water in mine ears! What sights of ugly death within mine eyes!"

I applauded. "Yes, that's it. Well done."

"It's a nightmare I've shared," Mike said, unsmiling. "But a great soliloquy, don't you think?"

"It is."

I was impressed with his heart-felt rendition of the lines, and wondered if he once had some terrifying incident in the water, but instead I asked, "How long have you lived in the apartment?"

He drew a long breath. "A few years. I kind of like the simplicity of it—turn-key is the expression. I'm out on the boat a lot, and sometimes I spend weeks in Tallahassee whenever I can get an acting job. What about you?" he asked, giving me an appraising glance. "I picture you in a big house in Gainesville—husband, kids, the whole thing."

During the previous night's "meet and greet," I had revealed little about my personal life—nothing about my marital status—and spoke only about my theatre experience. I wasn't ready to divulge my life history. My personal goal in leaving Gainesville was to re-invent myself.

"You've got the wrong picture. Actually, I'm going to love being on the water," I said, closing the script, and getting ready to leave. "And I agree with you about the simplicity thing. Anyway, break time is up," I said, pointing to the large-faced watch on his wrist. "Let's get back to the theatre."

Mike frowned, and as we left the café said, "You like to be mysterious don't you, Mrs. Crane? I'm quite harmless, but I could use some company. There aren't many adults in our troupe, and we do live across the hall from one another. How about dinner tomorrow night? I'm a decent cook."

As he held open the theatre door for me, I was charmed by his earnestness.

"Of course, Mike. I don't mean to be unfriendly. Dinner would be nice, but let's do it another time." As we entered the dark theatre I wondered why such a handsome and agreeable young man would lack for companions."

The next day, I drove to Wakulla Springs. I spotted McBride as soon as I entered the lodge. He greeted me with a large smile and a handshake.

"Lorelei, thanks for coming. I've reserved a table for us." He took my elbow and led me into the long dining room.

After we had been seated and placed our order, I said, "This place is so beautiful. I can't believe I've never come here before." I looked around at the crystal chandeliers, the marble floors, and the large windows looking onto the tree filled grounds. Are the rooms as attractive and ornate as the lobby and the dining room?"

He shrugged. "It's kind of old fashioned for my taste, and much too quiet." He paused and gave me a look that brought a flush to the base of my neck. "I'm glad to see you. Do you think you'll be okay in Apalachicola—away from your friends?"

"An actor's life," I sighed, and felt touched by his concern. "Yes, Homer, I think it's going to be the best thing for me. I'm glad to see you as well."

"Look we've only got an hour or so. I have to be back in Tallahassee by two. I'm going to ask you to do me a favor, but first I want to fill you in on something."

McBride became all business in a way that reminded me of the first time I met him when he interviewed me about Jeffrey's shooting.

"Oh," I said, taking a sip of water, "I'm disappointed you don't have more time. What's going on?"

16

"Me, too. Look, I'm working a homicide case—on special assignment with the Florida Department of Law Enforcement." He had my full attention. "Why'd they bring you all the way from Gainesville?"

"I used to work for the FDLE while I was going to college. They wanted someone on this case from outside the area. I guess my name came up—I've got friends there—you know how that happens."

"So will you be stationed in Tallahassee?"

"Stationed?" he smiled at my word choice. "No, I'll be heading up the investigation from Gainesville. Most of the investigative work will be done by the local Sheriff's Office with some assist from the Park Patrol Service."

"I see," I said, intrigued by McBride's assignment. "What's so special about the case that requires an out-of-town detective? Can you talk about it?"

He looked around to see who was sitting at the nearby tables, absently pulled a pack of cigarettes from his jacket, caught my look, and shifted them to an inside pocket.

"I see you still haven't stopped."

"Yeah, the stress don't stop either. To answer your question, I can tell you that I'm on the case because FDLE thinks—if it turns out to be murder—it will become a major political potboiler. They don't want it to spill over to the Capitol. They want the investigation to be credible with as little visibility as possible. I figure they'll also want an outsider to dump on if it doesn't go well." He made a dismissive gesture and shook his head. "Sometimes friends in high places can become your worst enemies."

Lunch was served, and our conversation became more personal.

"How's your son doing?" I asked.

McBride's face brightened. "Just great. I'm going to try to get him home over Thanksgiving."

"How does he like boarding school? It's somewhere in Tennessee, isn't it?"

"St. Andrews-Sewanee. It's fairly expensive—his mother and I are chipping in for it—but I'm confident they'll straighten him out.

From everything he's told me, the instructors care about the kids, he's excited about his classes, and he loves being in the mountains."

"I'm glad for you."

"How about you? You're looking good—no obvious scars or bruises. You okay?"

"I'm holding it together. Coming over here to do the play's the best thing that's happened to me since Bill's death."

McBride reached across the table and placed his hand over mine. It was a strong, comforting hand. Our eyes locked, and for the flicker of a moment we seemed to communicate our mutual sorrow...love, grief, loss...life's whole platter. The moment ended when he looked away and removed his hand from mine. I shivered, and looked out the window. "Homer..." I began, and stopped while I searched for words to thank him for his sympathy...or whatever it was we had just shared.

He motioned the waiter for the check. "Sorry, Lorelei," he said, pulling a credit card out of his wallet and handing it to the attentive waiter. "I can't stay much longer. When I asked you to meet me, I didn't know they'd book me up the way they did."

I said, "What can I do to help you?"

He leaned forward. "Let me tell you why I wanted to meet you. Like I said, the locals will conduct a routine investigation into the death. The problem is—the victim was involved in such a hot political issue people around here are going to be very cautious about talking to officials. And if we find it was murder..."

The way he looked at me made me sense what was coming next.

"That's where you come in, Lorelei. That is, if you're willing." He gave me an apologetic look.

"What do you want me to do?"

The waiter returned, McBride signed the bill and put the credit card back in his wallet. "I talked to Delcie this morning. She's got a new client—someone in Atlanta. His company is biding on property near a town called Fairport. It's in this area. He wants her to check out the political scene before his company makes the final bid. They suspect some shenanigans—the group that owns the property is vague about some land use issue. Delcie's client wants her to investigate—

all low-key—find out what's happening. They don't want any surprises."

I listened, and wondered what Delcie's client had to do with McBride's investigation. "What's the connection? How do I fit in?"

"Delcie mentioned she was going to ask you to make the inquiries for her client while you're here. The connection may be that the dead man was from Fairport—he was some kind of local agitator. I need someone who can ask questions about him without people getting defensive. It fits. You were damn good about getting information in the Paynes Prairie case. I want you to do it again."

"You want me to nose around? Looking for...?"

"So far, just check out the local scene. There may be some link between Delcie's client and the man's death...it's a small town. Find out what's been happening there. Get the details from Delcie. Be creative, Lorelei, maybe pretend you're an out-of-town realtor."

"Pretend?" I said, and laughed. "Homer, I've been pretending all my life. I made a career of it, didn't I?"

He smiled, "I never thought of it that way, but I guess that's what you actresses do." He let his gaze shift around the room— checking to see who was seated at nearby tables. It was a very large room with few tables, and even though the food was excellent, there were few lunch customers.

"Well there's a bit more to acting than that," I said. "So you said the man who died came from Fairport? I saw the sign on my way here. Okay, I guess I can do it. I'll have some time during the week to check around. But, you haven't told me the man's name."

McBride's attention returned, and a glint of sunlight from the nearby window made his hazel eyes look almost deep green matching the color of his shirt. "Hadley," he said. "Alex Hadley. He was some kind of environmentalist—right up your alley." He eyed me as he took a sip of his coffee. Shoving the mug aside, he added, "His body was found here—in the lodge—two days ago. That's all I can tell you right now." He left the dining room before I could say anything more. I sat in stunned silence. Alex Hadley—the friend Jeffrey wanted to me look up? Almost too much of a coincidence, I thought.

Chapter 4

As I was leaving the lodge, I noticed a small truck parked on the grass at the edge of the parking lot. A sign painted on its side said Florida Department of Law Enforcement Crime Forensics.

I drove back to Apalachicola, and my mind swirled with what McBride had told me. It was almost too coincidental to be believed, and I wondered how I would break the news to Jeffrey. I also reflected on the brief tender moment Homer and I had shared...it deepened my feelings toward him.

When I saw the sign to Fairport, I pulled off the road and called Delcie. Delcie Wright had worked for McBride, as a sheriff's deputy, up until about six months ago. She inherited some money from an uncle, quit her job at the sheriff's office, and opened her own private investigation firm. Delcie and I had been friends since college when we took acting classes together.

"Discreet Inquiries." It was Delcie's voice.

"Hi, Del, it's me."

"Lorelei? How are you, girl? You doing okay over there? I hope you're eatin' lots of shrimp and oysters."

I laughed, Delcie loved seafood. It was all she could talk about when I told her of my decision to take the acting job in Apalachicola. "I guess I'm okay. I'm parked along the road that leads to Fairport, and I've just come from a very interesting lunch with..."

"McBride. So, he's filled you in?"

"I suppose. You two are just determined to get me into the private investigation business, aren't you? Or do you think I just need to keep busy?" Since Bill's death, Delcie had been encouraging me to study for a P.I. license and come to work for her. "Take your mind off your troubles to snoop into other people's," she had said. In fact, it was McBride who first suggested the idea about a year ago.

"Well, the detective thinks you'd be good at it," she said. "So do I. And if it helps fill the time...you know I've been worried about you."

I could picture Delcie, sitting at her desk, with her long legs stretched out on an open drawer. She was a beautiful African-

American woman who could have become another Haile Berry if the times had been right.

"You're a good friend, Delcie, but telling me I'd be a good snoop isn't much of a compliment."

"C'mon, Lorelei, you know…"

"Yeah, I'm good at changing roles. McBride suggested I pretend to be a nosy realtor, and find out everything that's going on in Fairport. Isn't that what you wanted for your new client? Who is it, by the way?"

"You'll never guess—a name out of the past…Luther T. Williams."

"Your old Luke?"

"One and the same. I haven't heard from him in three years, and presto—he pops back into my life and offers me an assignment. He's paying damn well to boot!"

"Have you seen him. Is he still married to…"

"No and no," Delcie said.

"Oh, my, that's fraught with possibilities, isn't it?"

"Don't know, but it sure struck me strange that he'd call like that…and he was all business-like. Said an old friend told him about me starting my own private investigation business."

"Do you think…"

"Honey, I'm not thinking about anything but making the rent. But know this, if that man thinks he can just sugar his way back into my life by giving me a job…"

"C'mon, Delcie. You loved him."

"Yeah, well that was then. Anyway, I need to tell you what he asked me to look for. Where are you? Do you have something to write on? There are some names…"

"I'm in my car near the turn off to Fairport. Hold on a minute, and let me get a pen." I rummaged through my bag for a pen and something to write on while trying to hold the cell phone to my ear. "Do you think Luke will be coming to Gainesville?"

"Don't know and don't want to think about it right now. So far, it's like I said, strictly business."

"Okay, I'm ready…"

"Gotta go, Lorelei, my other line just lit up. Call me back and I'll give you the names."

When the call ended, I took a deep breath, and thought about Delcie and her old boyfriend, Luke. She was devastated when Luke told her he was going to marry a woman he'd met in Atlanta. Delcie and Luke had gone together, off and on, for more than ten years, and she always assumed that he would someday ask her to marry him. I liked him very much and thought they were a great couple—both of them were as handsome as movie stars. Now I wondered what his story was and whether or not his investigative assignment was a ruse to connect with Delcie again.

During the half hour drive back to Apalachicola, I considered how to tell Jeffrey about his friend Alex Hadley. He needed to be told, yet I was afraid Jeffrey would see it as an excuse to come to visit me—to be on the scene—and that was something I didn't want.

I stopped at Sophie's for coffee. The café was empty, and I found Sophie sitting at a table by the window. She had a far-away look and seemed startled when I came in.

"Cloud-gazing?" I asked. It was mid-afternoon. Dark gray storm clouds had begun to form over the bay.

"Lorelei, I'm glad to see you," she said, her face brightened as she rose from the table. "Let me get you something to eat."

"Just coffee, thanks. But if you have a minute, I'd like to talk." The look on my face must have communicated my mood.

"Something bad happened," she said, as if it was expected, and she wiped her hands on her apron. "Of course, we can talk." She made a sweeping gesture indicating the lack of other customers, and moved behind the counter.

She returned with two steaming mugs of coffee and some small pastries. The pastries smelled of fruit and sweet dough as if they just came out of the oven. "Come sit," she said, motioning me to follow her back to the table by the window. "Tell Sophie."

"A friend of mine—my first husband actually—suggested I look up a friend of his while I'm here. I just learned his friend died— a couple of days ago—at Wakulla Springs."

"Oh, my," Sophie said, putting both hands to her cheeks. "Died? Diving? Those caves…"

"No, I'm not sure how it happened. It may even be…well, my problem is telling Jeffrey. I know he'll come here, no matter what I say, and I don't want to see him right now."

There was a pause as we both sipped the hot coffee. She seemed to reflect on my concern as she picked up the plate of pastries and offered them to me. I declined.

"You said he was your first husband? You're married again?"

"That's just it. I'm feeling very vulnerable right now. My second husband, Bill, died just six months ago, and I've been in a kind of daze."

Sophie gave me a sympathetic look and placed both of her hands on mine—they were large veined hands, and comforting as Homer's had been earlier. "So, you don't know if you should tell this Jeffrey about the death of his friend, yet you think he should be told."

"That's it," I said. "One of the reasons I came here is to get closure on Bill's death."

She shook her head. "How did he die, if I may ask?"

I turned away, and watched a young couple reading the playbill in front of the Dixie Theatre. I hadn't intended to tell my story. Yet Sophie was someone whose warmth and empathy were hard to resist. "A brain aneurysm. He was at a conference in Miami. They found him in the morning—when he didn't show up for his presentation. It was a shock. He was only fifty-six."

"Oy vey," Sophie said. "It's terrible when someone dies so unexpectedly. It takes a long time to get over the grief and the shock—so many things left unsaid."

Yes, I thought, not to mention the distressing way in which he was found…alone, naked on the couch in his suite, and an empty bottle of wine with two glasses on the table. It was never determined who had been in the room with him.

"Truth is, our marriage had been in trouble, but we were trying to revive it. At least I thought so. Anyway, Bill and I used to come here—to the beach—in the early days. It's where I want to say goodbye to him, and get on with my life."

"And you don't want your first husband to interfere, am I right?"

"Yes."

"This is a good place for goodbyes, Lorelei. We're surrounded by water—the bay, the gulf, and the river. Water has a transformative effect you know—it washes away and it purifies. It's the reason I came here...to live in such a spiritual place."

"I guess that's why I was drawn to come here as well."

"Sometime, if you like, I'll tell you more about the sanctity of water. Growing up in the Middle East, I have a special appreciation for it."

"I'd like that," I said, and looked at Sophie with growing admiration. "So, about Jeffrey? What would you do?" I asked.

She lifted her shoulders and spread out her hands in a shrug. "Death makes its own announcements. He'll find out about his friend, one way or another. It's not necessary for you to be the messenger."

"Hmm, you may be right," I said, though I was still uncertain how I could talk to Jeffrey without telling him. "Guess I'll just see how it plays out." My gaze returned to the window. The young couple was gone, and a small red truck pulled up in front of the café.

"How are rehearsals going?" she asked. "The other actors who come in here seem happy. Ach, excuse me, Lorelei. It's my delivery." She picked up our empty mugs and returned to the counter just as a young dark-haired girl backed through the door carrying a large carton of supplies."

"Shalom," the girl announced. Sophie smiled and returned the girl's greeting as she took the box and placed it on a table behind the counter.

I went to the cash register to pay for the coffee, but Sophie waved me away as she started checking a bill the young girl handed to her.

"Thanks, Sophie—for everything," I said, and left. She waved back.

I returned to my apartment and sat at the table overlooking the bay. I thought about Sophie's advice. Yes, I guess I could let Jeffrey learn about Alex Hadley's death from someone else. If I left my cell phone off, I wouldn't have to talk with him. I could collect my

messages and call back whomever I wished. At last, I thought, I see
the benefits of a cell phone.

I called Delcie. The windows were open, and the impending
storm brought in the fresh sea air. It overcame the aroma of fish from
the market below.

"Hi Del, can you talk now?"

"Lorelei, yes. Sorry to have cut you off, but I've been waiting for
a call and that was it."

" Luther T.?"

She responded with her deep-throated laugh. "As a matter of
fact, it was, Ms.Snoop."

"Hey, don't make fun of your new assistant! Now, what's the
deal. You said you had names."

"Right. He told me the names of the key players in Fairport.
They're the ones he doesn't quite trust. See what you can dig up
about them...how they feel about his company's purchasing the land,
and how they think the locals will react. You know, that kind of
thing."

"Okay, who are they?"

I opened the notebook I used for my notes about the play.

"The mayor's name is Pete Stigler. A good old boy who owns a
lot of land around town. He also owns the town's funeral home. Then
there's—get this—Mona Lavender."

"You're kidding? That's the name of a flower, isn't it?"

"Yeah, but according to Luke, she ain't no flower-type. She's the
Director of something called the BSRC...Beautiful Springs Resource
Council. It's made up of a group of the big landowners, the
newspaper editor—all the town's powerbrokers, if you can call them
that. Anyway, he's met Ms.Lavender. She's a tough cookie so don't
be taken in by the baby blues and bottle blonde."

"Are most of these people realtors?" If so, I was thinking I
would not pretend to be a realtor, but I could be shopping for
property. Not such a far-fetched idea

"I'm not sure, but they do own most of the land around the town
including the spring that Luke's company hopes to buy."

"There's a spring? What's it called?"

"Graham Springs, in Liberty County."

"And your boyfriend's company wants to do what?" Knowing the sensitivity surrounding water issues in north Florida, I suspected I was about to discover something key to Delcie's assignment.

"I'll tell you, Lorelei, but he made me swear I wouldn't let it get out. So don't you tell anybody else. Promise?"

"Okay, I promise. Tell me." The secrecy made me recall McBride's assertion that there might be a connection between the death of Alex Hadley and Delcie's new assignment in Fairport.

"He told me they want to set up a water bottling plant at Graham. He said bottled water is a real growth industry now, and they expect to market the water in Atlanta and other cities along the east coast."

"And the secrecy, I presume, is that people in Florida—north Florida in particular—get out their shotguns at the threat of someone proposing to take their water to other areas."

"That pretty much sums it up, Lor. So you can see why he needed to have a low profile scan of the situation."

"Uh huh. I'll keep a low profile all right 'cause I sure don't want to stick my nose into that hornet's nest."

"Just keep me posted on what you find out. And keep track of your expenses, and I'll reimburse you."

"I'll tell you, Delcie. I'm not real happy about helping Mr. Luther T.'s company, but since McBride asked me help out, I'll do it."

"Thanks, Lor. He promised we'd share the information. Hey, be sure and eat some oysters for me. Take care. And call if you get lonesome."

Chapter 5

It rained well into the evening, and I stayed in my apartment studying interpretations of Ibsen's *An Enemy of the People*. The scientist physician, Dr. Stockman, faced opposition from his friends—which he perceived as a systematic betrayal—for his insistence on exposing the town's health threat. An acquaintance, who was a boat captain, Captain Horster, stood by him, and provided Stockman with a place to hold a meeting. Many townspeople showed up, but—roused by the Stockman's own brother who was the mayor—they refused to listen to the doctor's warning. Afterwards, they publicly declared him to be their enemy and attacked his home and family. The attacks only strengthened Stockman's resolve to remain in the town and continue to expose the health threat.

I wanted to understand Stockman, and I wanted to figure out his wife's motivation. She was caught between a wild-eyed idealist husband and a wily old codger of a father. Her main concern was to protect her children and herself from a return to the poverty from which they had just emerged. Yet, her husband, oblivious to all but his own quest, ignored her pleas for moderation.

Was Katherine Stockman simply a nineteenth century version of the "stand by your man" type of woman's nonsense? As I analyzed the role, I needed to dig for more depth in her character. Who was she before she married Stockman? How did she manage when they lived as penniless missionaries in the wild North? What shaped her loyalties, her sensibilities?

By nine o'clock, it had stopped raining, and I decided to get some fresh air. When I got downstairs, I found Mike Pardo drinking a bottle of beer in front of the building. He asked me to join him on a walk along Water Street. I agreed and we strolled along the wharf. There was no one else in sight.

After a long silence, Mike finally said, "I love the air after a storm, don't you? For me, it's like being out on the open water."

I didn't respond. I wondered if I had made a mistake in joining him when I felt so wrapped up in my own thoughts about the play and the day's events.

He touched my arm, and stopped walking.

"You're awfully quiet. Something wrong?" We stood under a street lamp, the light was muted by the after rain mist. Mike's concerned look provoked a slow stream of tears and a feeling of loneliness. It was one of those sudden waves of emotion I had experienced since Bill's death.

I took a deep breath and said, "Just thoughtful—preoccupied is more like it. Rainy nights..."

"And Mondays always get you down?"

"Something like that," I said. "To be honest, I'm a bit depressed by the play, and about the death of someone I had hoped to meet. Sorry for being such lousy company."

"Hey, why do you think I was standing outside? I've been feeling the same way. My apartment started to close in on me."

I looked at him more closely. He looked tired...unlike how he had looked yesterday.

"You said someone died?"

"He was a friend of a friend, and yes, he lived around here—in Fairport," I said.

"Fairport? What was his name?"

"Alex Hadley."

Mike's body stiffened. He looked stricken. "Not Alex. Oh God, what happened? I didn't hear anything about it."

"So you knew him?" I asked.

"Of course I knew him. He was a kind of hero around here. He stood up to the big developers and the local politicians who supported them. God, I can't believe it."

He stood shaking his head as if to rid himself of the news. "C'mon, let's sit down over there," he said, pointing the building across the street. "Tell me everything."

We walked up the steps of the Grady Building—the renovated historic ship's chandlery—and sat down on an ornate wrought iron bench on the porch.

"When did he die?"

"It happened the day before yesterday—Saturday. At the Wakulla Lodge."

"How did it happen?"

"I don't know," I said. "My ex-husband was friends with Alex and asked me to look him up while I was here. Yesterday, I met with a detective friend from Gainesville. We met at the lodge, and he told me about it."

"A detective? The police are involved? What do they think happened?"

"Like I said, I don't know. I gather there's some political angle. They're trying to keep a low profile about it. Maybe that's why you haven't heard. Did Alex have enemies?" I asked, thinking about McBride's suspicion.

Mike gave a mirthless laugh. "Enemies? Yeah, I'd say Alex pissed off quite a few people. But not enough to..."

"Does he have a family?"

"Yes and no. He and Jennie were estranged. She hated all the confrontation he generated. Jennie went home to her father after their little girl was almost run over by some rednecks. They pulled some nasty stunt at their house—the kid wasn't hurt, but it gave Jennie a scare."

"I'll bet it did. Fairport sounds like a dangerous little town."

"Yeah, life in small towns can sometimes get mean. Anyway, I used to meet Alex at Nature Conservancy meetings in Tallahassee. We'd go out for a beer afterwards, and he was always talking about his wife. I think they loved each other. But, I could understand her frustration. Alex's battles made life pretty difficult for them."

We sat without speaking. When he bent down and rested his head in his hands, I wanted to touch him and let him know I understood his grief. But I didn't, and in a few minutes, he sat back up.

"Jesus, Lorelei, it's tough to lose a good man like Alex. There aren't that many around here who'll stand up for what they believe."

"It's beginning to sound like our play," I said.

"Maybe that's what got me down. That play—it's too close to home. I've been fighting to preserve our own Apalachicola Bay. My Dad spent his life as a fisherman here, and I see developers buying up as much of the waterfront as they can get their hands on. After the last

29

hurricane, it was like the gold rush. People were buying distressed property to build condos and God knows what." Mike waved a hand in disgust. "Hey, I don't want to bore you with my shit. Do me a favor?"

"What?" I said, seeing the worried look on his face in the shadows of the street lamp.

"Let me know if you hear anything more about Alex. I'll get on the phone and try to find out for myself, but if your friend tells you anything…"

"Sure, Mike. In fact, tomorrow I'm going to the dive shop where Jeffrey said Alex worked."

"Horse's place in Carrabelle?"

"Horse?"

"That's his nickname. His real name is Alec Stern. He'll tell you how he got it. He's a great storyteller."

"So you know him, too?"

"Of course, he and Alex were very tight. Solid guy, although there have been some nasty rumors about him lately. Why are you going to see him?"

I wondered if I should confide in Mike. I still didn't know much about him, but instinct told me he was trustworthy.

"I've got kind of a side job. Please don't tell anyone."

Mike gave me a bemused look. "You're a narc?"

I laughed. "Be serious. I'm checking up on some things for a friend in Gainesville. It's about a land deal in Fairport that may have a connection to Alex. That's all I can tell you," I said, and stood to leave.

"Well, Lorelei Crane. You've turned out to be a very mysterious woman. Un-actress like." He took my hand. "I'd like to get to know you better—maybe have a glass of wine, or dinner."

"Let's go back," I said, removing my hand from his. "I'm very tired."

Once upstairs, Mike said, "See you tomorrow…at rehearsal. I'm a pretty good cook, you know. I'd like to treat you to my special cuisine."

I nodded, thinking, don't push it, Mike. I'm old enough to be your auntie. "Sleep well, see you tomorrow."

I undressed and got into bed. As I lay there, reflecting on the evening, I decided Mike might turn out to be a good friend. And, if he was also a good cook, so much the better. The whirr of the ceiling fan lulled me to sleep.

It was a cool sunny morning as I drove back along the coast to Carrabelle. The water glistened in the sunlight. I had a new appreciation for the road as it wove through a patch of Tates Hell State Forest. I had asked one of the cast members about the strange name. He told me the legend of a local man named Cebe Tate. Sometime in the 1800's, he had wandered into the forest and got very lost. For days he was attacked by mosquitoes, biting flies, and snakes. When he finally emerged at Carrabelle, he told everyone he'd been to hell. The name stuck.

The dive shop was easy to find. It was on the gulf side of the road. A small single story pink stucco building with a weather-beaten sign out front said, "Stern's Dive Shop: Rental Equipment and Repairs, Gear, Boat Tours, Instruction." The rusting hulk of a shrimp boat sat on the side of the building along with empty bottles, cans, and fishing gear.

There were no other cars in the lot. When I entered the store it looked a mess—a jumble of equipment. A long table in the center aisle was stacked with dive masks, lights, water proofed bags, and items I couldn't readily identify. Dive suits and vests were hung in a display along the wall with a rack of dangerous looking spear guns. On the walls were faded pictures of watery caves and gulf reefs. An unexpected aroma of coffee permeated the air.

"Can I help you," a hoarse, deep-throated voice called out, and I turned to see a large man with a pony-tail hunched over on a stool in the corner nearest the front window. He had a plastic coffee mug in his hand.

I was momentarily startled by his presence and blurted out, "Mr. Stern?"

"That's me," he said, and I detected an amused glint in his eye. "What can I do for you? You looking for gear, instruction…what?"

I approached closer. "I'm a friend of a friend of Alex Hadley's and…"

"Alex?" He almost choked on his coffee, and slipped off the stool. He looked angry. When he stood up, I saw just how large he was, maybe six-two or more. He wore a faded tee shirt, cargo shorts, and orange flip-flops. "What about Alex?" he asked, still scowling. He had a large face with the deep creases you see in longtime cigarette smokers and people who've spent too much time in the sun.

"Have you heard?" I replied.

"That he's dead? Lady, the grapevine out here's faster than email. Are you a cop?"

"Me? Why no. What makes you think that?"

"I figured they'd be here pretty soon. Alex worked for me—part-time. He was a dive instructor. So if you're not a cop, why're you here?"

What to tell him? He looked like a man who'd heard every phony story there was so I stalled. "I guess you knew Alex pretty well since he worked for you."

He gave me a suspicious look. "You didn't answer my question. You said you're a friend of a friend of Alex's? Who's the friend, and what's your name?"

"My name is Lorelei Crane, and the friend is Jeffrey Waterman. He asked me to look up Alex, but before I could, he was dead. I wanted to know more about him before I break the news to Jeffrey. They haven't been in touch for a while."

He studied me, and his face relaxed. "Alex was a dive instructor here for about three years…and a good friend."

"Have you heard anything about how he died? My friend will want to know," I said.

"No more than was in the paper—and that wasn't much. Supposedly he died at the lodge getting ready for the Creaturefest. They say he had an allergic reaction to a bite or something. It's got people really curious."

"Did he have a lot of friends around here?"

Stern shook his head. "Don't take this wrong—me and Alex were tight—but he wasn't the most lovable guy in the world. He could be a real pain in the ass. Thought nothin' of telling people what he thought no matter whose toes he's stepped on. Brutally frank, you know the type."

"Would anyone have wanted to harm him?" I asked, and immediately knew it was the wrong question. Stern eyed me apprehensively as he took a sip from his coffee mug. "You sure you're not a cop, lady? Cause you're beginning to sound like one."

"Oh no, actually, I'm an actress. Look, Mr. Stern…"

"Horse is how I'm known around here."

"Okay, Horse. Here's the deal, my friend Jeffrey's one of those anal people. He's going to ask me a ton of questions about Alex Hadley's death. So, I'm just trying to anticipate every angle…you know."

He slammed his mug on the counter, took my arm and swiftly shoved me toward the door.

"What? Mr. Stern. Horse. Hold on…you've got me all wrong."

"You may be an actress, lady, but I can tell you're shittin' me. I don't take shit from nobody. So you can just be on your way."

The door was open, but I stood my ground. "Please, just hear me out before you jump to any conclusions. I'm also a friend of Mike Pardo!" The mention of Mike's name had the effect of stopping Horse from throwing me out of his store.

"Hell, why didn't you say so in the first place?"

I touched my arm where his fingers had probably left a bruise.

"Sorry I got rough with you. Guess I'm stressed out right now. C'mon." He took my arm more gently and ushered me back into the store. "I'll give you a cup of coffee, and you can tell me what you're after."

Chapter 6

"How do you know Mike?" Horse asked, handing me a bottle of cold water from his small refrigerator.

We were sitting at an old wooden card table in the back of the dive shop. The room seemed to be a combination kitchen, storage room, office, and—noting the camp cot under a bank of shelves—home away from home. It had a damp and musty odor even though a wall air-conditioning unit was turned on.

"We're in a play together, at the Dixie Theatre in Apalachicola. That's why I'm here. My home's in Gainesville."

He leaned his chair back and said, "I always think of Mike as a boat captain. I forget he acts sometimes. Interesting fellow. How long have you known him?"

"Days," I replied, bluntly, giving him an apologetic look.

"I didn't buy your cockamamie story about the anal boyfriend. I'm an old con myself. What did you really come here for, Lorelei? If that's your real name?"

"It's my real name. And, to answer your question, I honestly did come here so I could answer Jeffrey's questions about Alex. But, I'm also making inquiries for other friends. They want to know about Graham Springs, and…"

"Alex's research." The front legs of his chair hit the floor, and with his face was close to mine he said, "Right?"

"Something like that. But you yourself said people are curious about his death."

"People are always curious when someone dies suddenly. The story in the papers may be true, or not." He pulled on his sun-bleached blonde gray pony tail. "Guess we have to wait till the cops tell us something."

"Do you think something else happened? And if it wasn't an accident…?" I asked.

"Did Mike tell you about the meeting Alex had in Fairport a couple of weeks ago?"

"No," I said.

"Well, you mentioned Alex's research on Graham Springs. Whatever he found out worried the town elders. In fact, they wouldn't even let him have his say at the city commission meeting."

"What happened?"

"A few of us chipped in to rent a beer joint outside of town, and invited the people in town to come hear what he had to say."

"You said a few of you?"

"Yeah, me and some of Alex's beer drinking buddies."

"Did Alex get to present his findings?"

"No. Only a dozen or so people showed up. Some roughnecks—including that piece of rural shit, Buster Stigler, the mayor's son—made such a ruckus that everyone left before Alex said much."

"What was it that was so controversial?"

"I don't really understand it all myself. He never did want to tell us anything specific. Just like Alex to be secretive. Anyway, he did say what he found would have a bad impact on both Graham and Wakulla Springs. Said he'd prove the expert at Florida State was all wrong. There was a flap about it—it's been in the local papers. In fact, another one of my dive instructors—Rick Lucas—works for the professor Alex was arguing with."

"Really? This Rick Lucas, how can I get in touch with him?"

Horse reached behind him and grabbed a clip board. He scanned it and said, "Rick should be here this weekend. You could see him then. Or, I guess you could see him in Tallahassee. He's generally there during the week. Works in the office of a Dr.Matos...Hubert Matos. Rick's always quoting him about this or that. "

I took a small notebook out of my handbag and wrote down the names. "Do you have a phone number for Lucas?" Horse gave me both Rick's home and work numbers.

"What's he like?" I asked.

"Rick?" He tilted his head, pursed his lips, and hesitated before answering. "He's very smart. Very ambitious. An excellent diver—served in special ops with the Navy Seals. You don't get much sharper than that."

"You don't much like him, do you?" I ventured.

Horse laughed, "Now, why'd you say that?"

"Do you like him?" I persisted.

"Do I like Rick Lucas?" He sighed before responding. "Hell, sometimes Rick can be charming—women like him. But Rick's the moodiest dude I've ever met. You don't want to get him angry. Other than that, yeah, I guess we get along all right."

"Anybody here?" A voice called from the front of the store.

"Sounds like I got a customer," Horse said. "Not too many of them during the week." He rose and started back into the store.

I noticed a copy of the *Wakulla News* on the chair next to me. I picked it up to see the article about Alex Hadley's death.

"Mind if I stay here and read the article about Hadley?"

"Help yourself."

It was a small article on the inside page. As Horse had said, it didn't say much about how Alex had died. It mentioned academic degrees, and his role with the Florida Public Interest Group and his activism on behalf of North Florida springs. It also identified his next of kin, Jennie and their daughter Clare Hadley.

I returned the paper to the chair and went back into the store. A young man was sifting through the gear on the center table. Horse was back on his stool next to the front window.

"I'll leave you my cell phone number," I said. "I'm staying in an apartment across the hall from Mike—on Water Street." I took out my pad, wrote down the cell number and handed it to him.

"Mike's building? I stayed there when I lost my roof in Hurricane Earl a few years ago."

"So Mike owns the building where I'm staying?"

"Yeah, he's a great guy," he said, offering his hand. He paused for a moment, still holding my hand, and, in a low voice said, "Look, Lorelei, I really cared about Alex. Let's stay in touch, you know, and let me know if you find out anything. Maybe I can help you in some way."

"Thanks, Horse, I'll remember that," I said, and left.

It was about noon when I reached the turn-off to Fairport. I decided to look the town over and have lunch there.

Main Street consisted of the City Hall and a group of small retail and service businesses, and a couple of empty stores. Brightly painted green wooden benches, and concrete flower urns sat in front of the city hall and Herb's Diner. It looked like an effort to pretty-up the town for tourists. On this Tuesday, there was no one walking around, although a dozen or more cars and trucks lined the three block strip.

When I entered the diner, I felt self-conscious as every head in the place swiveled around to look me over. The word *outsider* seemed like a hunk of flashing neon on my forehead. A middle-aged, dark-haired waitress waved to me from behind the counter.

"Just sit anywhere, honey. We're not busy today."

I sat at a booth near the front window and picked up the one page menu. The day's special was oyster stew. I learned a long time ago, that ordering the daily special was the wisest choice in small restaurants because it was the most likely to be fresh and a dish the cook liked to make.

The waitress came over—wearing a nametag that said Linda Mae—and greeted me with a friendly smile. "Where you from, sweetie?"

"Gainesville," I replied.

"I got a cousin up in Gainesville," she said. "Comes down for huntin' season in Tates Forest."

"Not Gainesville, Georgia. I'm from Gainesville…you know—University of Florida—Fighting Gators."

She looked around with a smile, and I saw I had again drawn the attention of several patrons. "Honey, this here's Seminole Country. The only gators we like is in our swamp or in our stew."

I put up my hands in surrender. "I get it, and speaking of stew, how's the oyster stew special? It's not too salty is it?" I asked.

"Well, Mayor Stigler here says it was real tasty," she nodded to the older of the two men in the opposite booth. He gave me a brief but pleasant smile. The young one stared at me with a degree of belligerence probably provoked by the other man. He looked like he might be the mayor's son—ruddy complexion, in his mid twenties, with a greasy looking mop of black hair. He had one of those barbed wire tattoos on his upper arm. If he was the mayor's son, I remembered the epithet with which Horse had described him.

"All right, I'll have the special and a glass of unsweetened iced tea," I said.

She nodded and left.

"So you're from Gainesville?" the mayor asked in a slow drawl. He ran a hand over his nearly bald scalp and added, "Gotten pretty crowded there, hasn't it?"

"Yes, like most places in Florida, it's growing too fast."

The younger man mumbled something that I couldn't make out, and used his fork to make stabbing gestures into the pie crust left on his plate.

The mayor blew his nose into the paper napkin, bunched it up, and dropped it on his plate. He had a smile that didn't match the cold look in his eyes. In an instant I decided I would not trust this man. Something about his face wasn't right. He had thin tight lips, a wrinkled forehead that told me he was a worrier or a schemer, and a receding chin. I considered myself an expert on faces.

"What brings you up here?"

Okay, Lorelei, this is your entrée into Fairport, so keep it simple.

"My husband and I used to vacation up here. We always talked about buying some property…you know, for retirement maybe even investment. It's so lovely and unspoiled, at least it was."

"Well, well," the mayor said, moving to the edge of the booth and turning to face me. "You're in luck. I own a considerable amount of property around here. Would you be interested in coming over to my office in City Hall after lunch?"

I checked my watch and decided I had another hour of so before I needed to return to Apalachicola to prepare for rehearsal. "Yes," I said.

"In a half hour then…at one? By the way, my name's Stigler, Pete Stigler. And what's your name?"

"Crane," I said. "Lorelei Crane."

"Then I'll look for you at one, Mrs. Crane." He reached across the table and impatiently poked the young man in the arm causing him to drop the fork. "C'mon Buster," he said, and turned. "This here sullen boy is my son and only heir...God help me."

Buster gave his father a disdainful look, slid out of the booth, and headed out the door without speaking. The mayor nodded in my direction and followed him out. I watched through the window and saw Buster get into a large black pick-up truck. He backed out and took off so fast I could hear the squealing tires. The mayor stood watching, shook his head, and walked away in the opposite direction.

After lunch, I found Linda Mae at the register. I said, "Your mayor seems real nice, but what's the deal with his son?" I gestured toward their booth and the pie plate with pieces of crust scattered across the table and onto the floor.

"Buster? Them two's always fightin' about something." She lowered her voice and said, "Buster's girlfriend works here summers. She told me, he's been naggin' his poppa to give him some land near Graham Springs. Wants to set up a rental business—you know, tubes and rafts, and such."

"And his father won't do it?"

She looked around to see if anyone was nearby. "He's a decent mayor all right, but when it comes to anything to do with his property he can get real mean. Told Buster he'd have to stand in line with a lot of cash same as anyone. He knows Buster don't have the money to buy land, and that the boy wants it real bad."

Another customer approached the cash register. Linda Mae gave me a look, and said, "Thank you. You come back and visit us again now, hear?" She handed over my change and turned her attention to the customer behind me.

I left Linda Mae a big tip, hoping I could count on her as a helpful source of local gossip. As I walked toward the City Hall, I thought about McBride and Delcie and realized they were right about my so-called "snooping skills." In fact, I had to admit I was beginning to find this assignment quite interesting.

Chapter 7

Once inside the quaint City Hall, I looked for the mayor's office. I passed the office of the Beautiful Springs Resource Council (BSRC) and noted the name, *Mona Lavender, Executive Director*, painted on the beveled glass door.

The door to the mayor's office had a sign that said, "Please knock before entering." I did, and he greeted me at the door.

"Come in, Mrs. Crane. Have a seat." The room was spacious and tastefully furnished. He gestured toward a small grouping—sofa, and a round oak table with chairs—and said, "I hope you don't mind, but I invited my colleague, Mona Lavender, to join us. She's in charge of what passes for our Chamber of Commerce—the Beautiful Springs Resource Council. Ms. Lavender and I own some property together."

No sooner did I choose a chair, than Ms. Lavender made her entrance. She was taller than the mayor—a large woman with casually styled short blonde hair surrounding a horsy shaped face. The hair color was what I expected from Delcie's description. What most surprised me was how she swept into the room with such a dramatic flair she reminded me of the old time actress, Loretta Young. Young had been a favorite of my mother's, and when I was a child, she made me watch every rerun of her weekly TV show.

"You must be Mrs. Crane," she said, in an accent I guessed to be upstate New York. She extended her hand. "Mayor Stigler tells me you're interested in purchasing land in this area."

When she sat down opposite me I caught a flowery scent that was lighter than the makeup she wore. The mayor sat down between the two of us.

"Yes, we just happened to be talking—in the diner—and I mentioned my interest in property."

"Lovely," she said, with a glance at the mayor that suggested they had caught a "live one." "Are you here alone or with your husband?"

"My husband died recently. It was our dream to buy something up here for our retirement." It was a lie, but sounded plausible enough.

"I see. I'm sorry. I'm a widow, too," she said, bowing her head for the appropriate moment before resuming a business-like tone. "And what did you have in mind...how large a piece were you thinking of? Something with a house, or...?"

I wanted them to believe I was a good catch, so I continued weaving my story. "I inherited a large sum of money and what with the stock market..."

"Oh, yes," Stigler weighed in with eagerness, "and Florida land is a popular investment these days. They're not making any more of it, you know."

"So, you could afford a large tract?" Ms. Lavender asked, ignoring the mayor's practiced joke.

"Yes, and something near water, but I don't want to live on the gulf because of the hurricanes. Maybe near a river or a spring. I hear there are lovely springs in the area."

"Have you heard of Graham Springs?" Mayor Stigler asked.

"Yes, I think so. In fact, wasn't it mentioned in the *Wakulla News* today? Some environmental activist from Fairport just died. The article mentioned his work at Graham Springs."

I watched the effect of my words. Pete Stigler's body noticeably stiffened, and he cast an anxious glance toward Mona Lavender. Her gray-blue eyes returned his glance with a steely look.

"Yes, poor Dr. Hadley," she said. "He had a heart attack or something, wasn't it? I haven't read the paper yet. Have you, Peter?" I knew she was lying—a sharp business woman like her would want to know the news at the start of the day. I began to suspect I had met a fellow actress in Ms. Mona Lavender. It was her Loretta Young carriage, her carefully enunciated speech, and the studied expression of sympathy. She was good at it.

The mayor shook his head and started fidgeting with some property description sheets on the end table. I could see beads of perspiration on his forehead. At last he said, "In any case, let's not trouble Mrs. Crane with our little local dramas. I've brought these descriptions for you to look at." He shoved the sheets toward me. "Perhaps we could go out and take a look at the ones that interest you."

I checked my watch. "Actually, I have to get back to Apalachicola. I have rehearsal tonight and..."

Ms.Lavender looked at me with renewed interest. "Oh, so you're an actress? Are you going to be in the new play opening at the Dixie?"

"Yes," I replied. "And I really must leave now or I'll be late." I stood and they followed me to the door. "If it's all right, I'll take the descriptions with me and arrange another appointment."

Mayor Stigler returned to the table, slipped the sheath of papers into a folder, and brought them to me. "That would be fine, Mrs. Crane. Here's my card. Call me when you're able to come back."

Ms. Lavender stood at the door with her arms crossed, flashed a practiced smile, and said, "And when you do come back, I'll introduce you to some of the wonderful things our Resource Council does. We're very proud of our work in this area." That was probably as close to gushing as the cool Ms. Lavender ever came...if that was even her real name.

I waved goodbye and walked out of the building. Once outside, I scanned the bank of free real estate and tourist magazines on the curb. I took one of the free tabloids and glanced at it as I walked back to Herb's Diner where I had left my car. The headline said, "Local Activist Defies City Council." There was a picture with Alex Hadley's name in the caption. It was my first look at the man I had spent the last couple of days learning about. The photo was blurred, but it showed him standing in front of a small group of people on the steps of City Hall. The paper had come out last Wednesday—four days before Alex died. I tucked the paper under my arm and hurried to my car.

Back at my apartment, I heard my cell phone ring just as I sat down to read the tabloid article. It was McBride.

"Lorelei? How's it going? Sorry I had to rush away from lunch. I'd like to meet you again...when we have more time to talk."

"I'd like that too, Homer. I've already met the owner of the dive shop where Hadley worked, and some of the Fairport people whose names Delcie gave me."

"Good," he said. "Look, it's starting to look like Alex Hadley's accidental death was no accident."

"Wow, that's what you suspected, wasn't it?"

"Forensics found red ants and traces of what they think were sugared pieces of apple in the foot of the costume. The manager said they've never had a report of red ants in the rooms before."

"Ants? You think someone deliberately put them into the costume?"

"Don't know. Apparently the guy had just come out of the shower, and maybe couldn't get to his shock kit fast enough. We're still working on it."

"Horse Stern—who owns the dive shop—said people are curious about Alex's death—as though they didn't believe the newspaper account."

"Interesting," he said. "Lorelei, I'm coming to Tallahassee later this week. By that time, I should have more information. Can you meet me at the lodge again on Friday?"

"It'll have to be lunchtime, Homer."

"All right, that'll do. Eleven thirty in the lobby?"

"Okay. Now, you want me to tell you what I've found out so far?"

"I'm impressed you've already done some checking."

"Oh, yes. I've even met some of the cast of characters…with emphasis on the word characters."

"Tell me, and we'll see how well your description matches up with local law enforcement." McBride said..

"Well, first thing this morning I met Horse Stern—improbable name but a solid guy, I think. He and Alex were close friends. He's suspicious about Alex's death. When I asked him who might have had a grudge against Alex, he mentioned the mayor's son—Buster Stigler."

"Fairport's Mayor Stigler?"

"Right. Apparently, Buster and friends broke up a meeting and kept Alex from discussing his ideas about Graham Springs. I've met the young man, and I can tell you he's one angry fellow."

43

"Tell me more," McBride said, in a voice that suggested he was writing it down.

The aroma of garlic and ginger wafted through my open window. Mike's cooking, I thought, as my taste buds started acting up. I picked up the newspaper.

"I'm looking at an article in the Fairport paper about how Alex confronted the city council and was practically thrown out of the meeting. It had to do with Graham Springs. Seems the council accused him of starting rumors that would have a negative affect on property values. Wait a minute, I'll read it to you."

"So it got nasty?" he said. "When did this take place?"

I scanned the article for a date. "Two weeks ago. The council met on Monday, October 30th. The paper just came out last Wednesday. I'll bring it to you."

"And Hadley died on the 12th," he said, as if to himself. There was a long silence.

"Look, Lorelei, I've got a meeting with my boss in ten minutes. Give me the gist of what else you found out. Leave the details for when we meet."

I took a moment to reflect on the day. "Horse mentioned a couple of other people you might want to check out. Dr. Hubert Matos at Florida State, and his assistant, Rick Lucas. Matos and Hadley were apparently at odds over springs research. Rick Lucas is also a part-time dive instructor at Stern's. I'm going to meet him this weekend. I can give you his number."

"No, that's all right. We learned about the feud from some of the Tallahassee FPIRG people Alex worked with. What else?"

"Do you know about Pete Stigler and Mona Lavender?" I asked.

"Just that they more or less run things in Fairport."

"I met them today. They're my new best friends—very interested in selling me a large tract of land. I suspect they'd do anything to make a juicy deal."

"Real estate vultures? Hmm, that assessment won't give Delcie's client much comfort. See what else you can find out about them."

McBride sucked in a breath.

"Are you smoking again, Homer? I thought you were trying to quit?"

"Trying, yes, I'm trying. It's like the old joke where the drunk says, 'I know I can give up the booze...I've done it often enough.'"

I was sympathetic to McBride. "So, that's about it. I'll try to dig up something more concrete on the 'vultures,' and I'll see you on Friday. In the meantime, I've got to start some serious work on the play."

"When's the opening again?"

"Saturday night, December 3rd. I'm saving a ticket for you."

"We'll see. Take care, Lorelei. I appreciate what you're doing. I'll let Delcie know what you told me...that is, unless you want to call her yourself."

"I probably will," I said.

We said goodbye, and I heard the knock on my door.

"Hi, Lorelei. Anything new about Alex? I heard about the article in the *Wakulla News* today...not much information." Mike stood in the doorway looking concerned.

"No news," I said, "though I did meet Horse Stern. Quite a character."

"That he is. Hey, how about an early supper before we go to rehearsal?"

"I could hardly resist after the way you've tempted me with the aromas," I said, glancing at the brown stain on the shoulder of his Florida Gators tee shirt.

He looked down at the stain. "Teriyaki sauce. I guess I got carried away with the whisk."

"Early supper? What's on the menu?" I asked.

"Wild Alaskan Salmon—basted in Teriyaki sauce, obviously—fresh asparagus, and cous cous with ginger and garlic. Are you up for it?"

"You're on, Chef Pardo. Can I bring something?"

"Nope, just your appetite. Come over in an hour. Rehearsal starts at five-thirty."

I passed the hour by arranging all of my play materials on the glass table in front of the window. It was a mindless task, but I wasn't focused enough to buckle down to reading. I wanted to talk with Renee about the role of Mrs. Stockman, and we were all still on book anyway. Instead, I gazed out the window and thought about Alex Hadley.

I held up newspaper photo of him and tried to imagine what he was really like. It was hard to tell from a one dimensional black and white news photo. All I could see was a squareish face — wide nose and maybe a dimpled chin. He wasn't smiling, and the ball cap he wore shrouded his eyes. From his tight tee shirt, it looked like he had a muscular build—probably a swimmer's body. Compared to the people standing around him, he appeared shorter than most. It surprised me. I always expect heroes to be tall. I put the paper back down on a chair and realized I was able to tell very little about Alex Hadley from that photo. I wondered if I'd ever get to meet his wife.

I called Delcie, and she answered on the second ring.

"Hi, Del. Lorelei snoop, here. Are you sitting on the phone or what?"

"No, Ms.Snoop, I am not sitting on the phone, but I am glad to hear from you. Have you found out anything yet?"

"I've met the mayor and his sidekick, Mona Lavender, but all I did is set the stage. I've got them drooling over my so-called large inheritance, and desire to buy a retirement estate. I'm going to get with them again later this week. I'll know more then."

"Just don't make them suspicious. Remember, Luke only wants to know if they're on the up and up…if he can go ahead and present the deal to his management."

"I understand, but as McBride's probably told you, there's the matter of Alex Hadley's death which may be tied up with the deal."

"I know. So be careful. Don't mistake the slow drawl for slow thinking. Some of those rural folk can be more cunning than any city slicker. Especially when they're hungrier."

"I got it, Delcie. Anyway, I just wanted to check-in. It's nice to hear your friendly voice."

"How are rehearsals going?"

"Good, the play's beginning to shape up."

"Well, have fun. Stay in touch."

"I'll call you later in the week," I promised.

By now the aromas from Mike's apartment set off alarms in my taste buds. As I showered and dressed for the evening, I thought about the people I had just met. Some might prove to be as interesting, and possibly as vicious, as the characters in Ibsen's play. I'd baited the hook with Mayor Stigler and big Mona—as I now thought of her. That would give me the chance to get information about the water bottling plant Luke's company proposed. It would also allow me to visit Graham Springs and inquire into the reasons for so much controversy—reasons that may have led to murder.

Chapter 8

When I entered Mike's apartment I smelled delicious cooking aromas. I was immediately attracted by the walls that were covered with art—modern abstracts, and beautiful land and seascapes—some by famous artists like Winslow Homer.

"Wow, I didn't know you were an art connoisseur in addition to all your other talents. This is an impressive collection," I said, walking around the room.

"Don't be too impressed. Most of them are just well-framed good prints. I was in the framing business for a while right after I got out of college. Why don't you sit down, Lorelei. Let me get you a glass of wine."

I sank into a maroon leather couch that faced the bank of windows overlooking the bay. "Thanks, I'd like that."

Mike's furnishings were eclectic, rather like the man himself. They were a mix of tropical rattan and traditional wood. A low-lying walnut entertainment center covered the side wall. It held a CD player and CD's, an array of magazines and books, and framed photos.

I called out to Mike, "When I first moved in, I heard some plaintive music coming from your place. It sounded familiar. Do you remember the piece?"

He replied, "May have been *The Pearl Fishers* by Bizet. I've been playing it a lot lately."

I picked up one of the photos and studied it. It looked like a typical family shot with Mike and several other people standing around a seated older couple—presumably his parents. Mike stared out at the camera with a happy smile on his face and his arm draped around an attractive looking dark-haired woman. His sister, I wondered?

"Nice family photo," I said. "You may be the only human being I know who doesn't have an oversized TV set in their living room."

He returned with two glasses of wine and cast a sad glance at the photograph as he slipped a Diana Krall CD into the player.

48

"Don't be too impressed about the TV," he said, sitting in a chair across from me after handing me a glass. "I've got one in the bedroom."

I noticed he had changed out of his stained tee shirt into a Hawaiian shirt and chinos. He was quite good looking, I thought, and was immediately reminded of Jeffrey when he was younger. I couldn't help wondering about Mike's love life.

"For Gator games, no doubt," I replied, and silently admonished myself for a brief moment of lustful thoughts. "By the way, where's Clarence? I haven't seen him since I arrived."

"Clarence isn't my cat. He just visits me sometimes because I give him fish. I'd like to have a cat, but I like my freedom better. I think Clarence shares my view about remaining unattached. Do you have any pets?"

"We have a cat. He's being cared for by neighbors while I'm away."

"Now that we know one another so well," he said with a look of amusement, "here's a toast to new friends."

We leaned toward one another and clinked glasses.

"To new friends," I repeated, taking a sip. "Umm, this is wonderful. What is it?"

"It's an organic wine from California. A Syrah." He leaned back and casually stretched out his legs. "Dinner will be ready in a few minutes. In the meantime, tell me about your visit with Horse."

"Ah, Horse. At first he thought I was a police officer and nearly threw me out of the store."

Mike laughed. "Sounds like Horse. He doesn't have much respect for law enforcement—or any authority figure for that matter. He's had his share of bad experiences with them."

"I suspected as much, but I convinced him I was a friend—using your name, by the way—and he talked more freely."

"What's his take on Alex's death," Mike asked.

"He's skeptical…about it being an accident."

"Really? What does he think?"

"He didn't really say. By the way, I didn't want to ask him, but how'd he get the name Horse?"

49

"Oh, just from the old tune by the group *America*...remember 'the horse with no name?' Anyway, back to Alex. The accident does sound strange. Everyone knew he always carried an Epi Pen." Mike looked thoughtful for a moment.

" I've also been checking out the town of Fairport."

He gave me an admiring smile. "You certainly are getting involved. Do you think it wise? Especially if there was foul play involved?"

"Foul play?" I smiled at the theatrical phrase. "Look, let's not talk about this stuff. I'd like to know more about you."

He gave me a silly grin. "Like what's a nice boy like me doing alone in a small town like this? I'm afraid we don't have time for much in the way of life stories, do we?"

"I guess not," I said, "but, I do want to hear it sometime."

He looked at his watch, sniffed the air, and got up. "Smells like dinner is ready. Right on schedule. C'mon, Lorelei, have a seat at the table." He disappeared into the kitchen.

"Have you ever seen a copy of the Fairport tabloid?" I asked.

Mike brought a platter of food to the table. It was beautifully presented, and he served with flair.

"What about it?" he asked.

"Hmm, I just wondered." I tasted the fish. "Mike, this is wonderful. No more questions. I just want to savor this beautiful dish."

We ate in silence broken only by the soft grunts of pleasure that food lovers make.

Finally, when I had cleaned my plate, I said, "The paper had this diatribe against Alex Hadley for attempting to get the City Council to pay attention to his ideas about the springs."

"Coffee?" he asked.

"No thanks, I'll be drinking enough of it tonight."

"Sounds like the Fairport rag." He started to clear the table, declining my help, and returned to the small kitchen as we continued to talk. "I'm not surprised it came out against Alex. The editor is a complete toady. No, I take that back. He's a treacherous toady—kind of reminds me of the guy in *Enemy*. He's done more flip flops than a skate-boarder. He's in with all the council members, and they're into selling land. It's become the most popular sport in the Panhandle these days—buying and selling land."

"What about a water bottling company at Graham Springs? Do you think they'd be interested in that?"

"I can't imagine they would be," Mike said. "The springs are kind of sacred...they'd want to make money from it; not drain it. But then, nothing that group did would shock me."

I watched Mike doing dishes at the sink in the small kitchen. His perspective was very interesting. And, if he was right, I wondered why they were stringing Delcie's client along.

Mike came out of the kitchen. "Are you ready to walk over?" he asked.

"I am. Let me just get my bag, and I'll meet you downstairs. Mike, thank you so much for this marvelous dinner. You can cook for me anytime."

He bowed, took my hand and kissed it. "Mrs. Stockman, I must say you deserved a decent meal...for putting up with that crazy doctor husband of yours."

We both laughed, and I went back to my apartment to get my stuff before joining him. I needed to push back my thoughts about Hadley and Fairport. It was Ibsen who demanded my immediate attention.

I spent all my time working on the script. Renee had helped me deconstruct my scenes as Katherine Stockman—admiring wife and devoted mother—who was torn among her loyalties...to her husband, her children, her father, and to her own sense of truth and justice. She also played the peacemaker, trying to bring the two brothers—Dr. and Mayor Stockman—closer. Renee thought she showed a modicum of spunkiness for the times.

Wednesday afternoon, Mike showed up for rehearsal looking surprisingly haggard. He said he was busy taking tourists out on the bay and tending to other business. On our walk home together, we only made small talk. He promised to take me out on his boat on the following Monday.

Thursday morning, I awoke ready to make another trip to
Fairport. I called Pete Stigler's office and arranged to meet him and
Mona Lavender after lunch. Before our appointment, I also planned to
drop by Herb's Diner, and see if I could pump any more information
from the waitress, Linda Mae.

The sky was overcast, and I hoped the rain would hold off long
enough for what I expected to be a tour of Graham Springs. It was a
little before noon when I pulled up in front of Herb's Diner. I could
see Linda Mae through the plate glass window and was relieved it
wasn't her day off.

"Well, hey there. Glad you liked the food well enough to come
back," she said, ushering me to the same booth where I sat earlier in
the week.

She stood with her order book ready, as I picked up the menu. It
was a simple choice. "I'll have the special, Linda Mae," I said,
looking around to see only a few customers seated toward the rear of
the diner.

"Iced tea—unsweet—right?" she asked.

I smiled and nodded.

When she returned with the tea, I said, "I'm going out looking at
property around here today. Where do you think would be the best
place to live?"

She placed her hands on her hips, her head tilted slightly, and her
lower lip protruded as she considered my question. "First I'd say
around Graham Springs. But it's very pricey. Then there's some real
nice land near the forest."

"Well, I wouldn't want to be in one of those exclusive type
communities with lots of big houses. Is there much development
around the springs?"

"Actually, no...at least not yet. The city council's started trying
to get money folk to buy, but I ain't seen it. They been acting like
they was the St. Joe Company or something. Think they're going to
get rich retirees from up north, but it's the same old people coming in
here for lunch everyday...'cept a few tourists, like yourself."

"Gee, I'm surprised they'd have a problem. People usually like to live near water. I know I do. Is there something wrong with the water around here?" I asked.

Her face took on a frown, until a light bulb went on. "Course, you're referrin' to that whole thing with Dr. Hadley…God rest his soul."

"Oh, I read about him in the paper. You knew him?"

She nodded. "Him and his wife and little girl used to come in from time to time. I always used to think they was a nice family."

"Until?"

"Well, he took it on himself to cause a lot of trouble around here. Dividin' people against one another, and trying to scare us about the springs. You really should be asking the mayor all this. I only know what folks around here was talking about."

"What kind of things were people saying? If you don't mind telling me."

"No, it's all right. Everbody who lives here knows about it. Dr. Hadley was tellin' everyone—those that'd listen—about some shenanigans goin' on. He said the Resource Council was going to sell out to some huge corporation that wants to take our spring water."

"You mean a water bottling plant?"

"Something like that."

"Would that be a bad thing, do you think?"

"Well, that's where all the arguments started. Dr. Hadley and some in town thought it'd ruin not just our springs, but might even affect Wakulla."

I found it fascinating that, of all the people with whom I had spoken, it was Linda Mae who gave me my first clues about the firestorm Alex Hadley had ignited. No wonder Delcie's client was concerned.

"What do you think? Could Dr. Hadley have been right?"

She slipped into the booth, and in a conspiratorial voice, she said, "Alls I know is that Dr. Hadley didn't own any springs property. He didn't have anything to gain by trying to stop it being used. But others do, and now he's dead. That's all I got to say."

Before she could slip out of the booth, the mayor's son, Buster, came into the restaurant and walked right over to us.

"You spreadin' your usual gossip, Linda Mae?" He said, plunking himself down in the booth across from mine. "You best not be bad-mouthing me or my daddy. It's got you into trouble before."

Linda Mae's eyes widened, and she bolted up and headed back to the kitchen.

I was concerned about her and said to Buster, "You scared that poor woman, and she wasn't doing anything more than talking to me about all the nice places there are to live around here. Why were you so rough on her?"

"I seen you in here a few days ago, didn't I?" Buster asked. "You're the lady from Gainesville wantin' to buy property. Right? My Daddy told me about you."

"Yes, I plan to look at some property with your father and Ms. Lavender."

"Well, don't bother looking at Graham Springs. The old bird won't sell; none of them will. I've been tryin' to buy a piece of land daddy owns so's I can set up a tourist business. He won't sell it to me, and I'm his kin."

"I don't know," I said. "Both he and Ms. Lavender led me to believe the property is for sale. I understand there's even a corporation making an offer...for a water bottling plant."

Buster pounded his fist on the table. "So she's been tellin' you that Hadley bullshit?" he asked, casting an angry glance toward the kitchen. "There ain't goin' to be no bottling plant, and you ain't goin' to get our springs property!"

"First of all, Linda Mae didn't tell me anything about Hadley's idea. I learned about it from someone else. Secondly, why do think Alex Hadley would talk about a bottling plant if he didn't have a reason?" I felt like I was prodding an angry bull, but I hoped it would result in new information.

Buster began shredding his paper napkin with a fork. "Hadley was just trying to stir things up so he could make a name for himself up in Tallahassee. Typical tree-hugger."

54

"And now he's dead. Quite a coincidence, wouldn't you say?" I said, returning his hard stare.

He held the fork in midair, narrowed his eyes, and appeared to be sizing me up with more serious interest. He dropped the fork and it clattered as it hit the table. "What's your angle, lady? Why you in here askin' me and poor dumb Linda Mae a bunch of questions about Hadley? I saw you two talking up a storm before I even came in. And it wasn't about the tuna casserole, neither."

I didn't respond, turned my attention to my iced tea and kept my eyes forward. I might have pushed too hard, I thought.

"You gonna answer me or not? What's with all the questions?"

"Look, I have no angle, as you put it," I said, in a voice designed to defuse the tension. "I'm simply trying to find out about the town in which I may someday retire. That's not the least bit unusual. And, yes, if there is property for sale at a nearby springs..."

"How many times I got to tell you...it ain't for sale! So why don't you just go back to Gainesville and buy land there. I hear they have a bunch of springs in that area. Don't start messin' with something that ain't yours to have."

I didn't want to get Buster any angrier than he already was and said, "Look, I'm sorry you're so upset. I just came in here to have lunch." I looked back at the kitchen and, fortunately, Linda Mae was approaching with my tuna casserole.

Buster poked his finger at her, and said, "Linda Mae, I don't care what this here lady says, you got a big mouth. It's gonna seriously get you hurt one day." He picked up the menu and ordered, "Give me a burger, fries and a large Pepsi. And don't forget the extra ice."

He's impossible, I thought, casting a reassuring glance at Linda Mae who gave me a worried look and headed back to the kitchen.

I started eating and out of the corner of my eye saw Buster slump down into the booth and stare into space. The actress in me was fascinated by what he was thinking and how he had gotten to be so mean.

Chapter 9

"In here, Mrs. Crane," Lavender said. She and the mayor were in her office, and I had nearly passed it when she called to me through the open door.

The office of the Beautiful Springs Resource Council was anything but beautiful. A conference table practically ate the room and was surrounded by mismatched chairs. The table was littered with newspapers and real estate flyers and a collection of *Florida Trend* magazines. The one redeeming feature to the decor was the enlarged photographs of Graham Springs, Tate's Hell State Forest, and the gulf...mostly the part with condos. The room reeked of a sweet smelling air freshener not unlike the scent I remembered Mona wearing the day we met.

"Good, I see you wore sturdy shoes," she said, giving me the once-over. She gestured to the wall photos. "Beautiful part of Florida, isn't it? I wanted you to have a view of the different areas and the kinds of properties that are available. As you can see, depending upon your taste, there is a range of settings for your retirement home."

"Nice to see you again, Mrs. Crane," the mayor extended his hand. "The property over there on the coast has gotten exorbitant since Hurricane Dennis. Lots of speculators. We think we can find you something you'll like. Shall we get going, Mona? I know Mrs. Crane only has a couple of hours to give us."

"Please, call me Lorelei. As I've told you, I'm really most interested in being near springs."

Stigler gave Mona Lavender a look that said, "I told you so."

"All right then, let's go. We'll take my car," she said.

We drove away from town in Mona's baby blue Mercedes and turned onto an unpaved sand packed road. Mona did most of the talking. She chatted about this and that area of the county and described some of BSRC's accomplishments.

"We were the ones to get the county and state DOT to clear some of these roads so there'd be access to land. And we monitor what goes on here, as well."

"Got the sheriff to get rid of a methamphetamine operation back in the woods there," Stigler said. "In my time, it was moonshine."

"That's what I'm talking about," Mona said. "Not many towns keep an eye on what goes on around them. We're out to attract quality people, like you, to buy this beautiful land. Right, Pete?" She turned to the mayor who was leaning forward from the back seat.

"That's right," he replied. "Oops, you missed the turn-off."

Mona backed up and parked. "We'll walk from here," she said. We started through a shrubby area, with the mayor in the lead.

"It's not far," Mona said. "Now this is the type of property you'd be buying if you want to live near springs. It's mostly pine, magnolias—some beautiful old live oaks—and lots of scrub. Easy to clear for a house pad."

"How big are the lots?" I asked.

Stigler responded, "There are various sized lots. Would you want something as large as 25 acres?"

"Maybe. What's the price range?"

Mona paused and said, "See if you like it first, then we'll talk about price later. Oh, here we are."

I was amused by her reluctance to discuss prices.

We were standing on the edge of what appeared to be a large pond with almost turquoise colored water.

"This is Graham Springs?" I asked, looking at a disappointing body of water.

The mayor laughed, "Oh, no. This is a little feeder spring. It's just one of the properties for sale."

"But I thought we were going to Graham?" I said.

Mona glanced at Stigler and said, "The property at Graham is…well, there's sort of a bid on it already. We'll have to wait to see if it comes on the market again."

Bait and switch. I should have known they'd try something like this. I turned to Stigler. "Look, I talked with your son today, and he said you own the Graham Springs property. He also told me he wants to buy some himself, but that you'd never sell it to him."

"I don't know what that young man was thinking. I've told him over and over again that he couldn't have that property. It's become an obsession with him."

Mona had walked a distance from us, and pointing across the pond, she shouted, "Now this piece right here has a lot of promise. See the lovely tree canopy on the other side, and see how clear the water is. Well, it'd be easy enough to get rid of the algae. Anyway, you could put a house pad right over there."

As though reading my mind, the mayor said, "Look here, Mrs. Crane, I hope you don't think we're trying to deceive you. You shouldn't listen to anything my son says. Ever since his mother left, he's gotten a lot of weird ideas into his head. Sometimes, I try to protect him from himself, and it just makes him madder at me."

"May I ask who is the intended buyer of the Graham property?"

"I'm afraid I'm not at liberty to say."

"Is it a company that wants to build a water bottling plant? I think I should know that before I consider buying land on a tributary spring."

I could see Pete Stigler puffing up like a penguin in distress. "Honestly, Mrs. Crane. You shouldn't pay attention to local gossip."

"So Alex Hadley's accusations were wrong?" I asked.

By this time, big Mona had returned, and took in the distress shown by her colleague.

"What's going on?" she asked. "Pete?"

"Apparently someone has filled Mrs. Crane's head with all that Hadley claptrap."

"It's not true," said Mona, quick to the defense. "Hadley was a troublemaker. Whatever anyone's told you about his alleged charges…well, they're flat out false. Even the city council wouldn't listen to him."

I wondered how far I should pursue the subject and decided to take another tack.

"I would still like to see Graham Springs. Is it nearby?" I asked.

The mayor looked at his watch. "It's not very far, but by the time we walk around it might make you too late," he said, relieved to be off the topic of Hadley. "But we'd be happy to show it to you. We're very proud of it."

"Named after Florida Governor Bob Graham. When he was governor, he sponsored the purchase of Wakulla Springs for a Florida Park Preserve," Mona said, on our way back to the car. "The legislature also allocated funds to buy up some of the land around our spring for a preserve. It's enhanced the value of the surrounding property. You'll see."

I heard loud thunder and saw streaks of lightening shoot down on the road ahead.

"Oh, my," Mona said, "It looks like we'll have to postpone our visit." The sky darkened, the wind began whipping the shrubs, and the rain started pelting down. "This storm's not going to let up anytime soon."

After we had turned around and were on the blacktop, I said, "It's obviously upset you, but if I'm going to invest some of my life's savings in property around here, I think I deserve to know more about the controversy involving Graham Springs. Someone told me there's a Dr. Matos at FSU..."

Mona gave me a quick phony smile, took a deep breath, and said, "You might as well tell her, Pete. I don't see why this damn thing doesn't just go away. It's such a nuisance."

A nuisance that may have caused Hadley's death, I thought. Big Mona would probably think a major hurricane was a nuisance if it interfered with a land sale.

"It wasn't so much a controversy as simply an academic quarrel," Stigler said. "You know how scientists are...they all have their pet theories."

"Okay, and the quarrel was about what?" I asked.

"Dr. Matos—who, by the way, is an expert on springs hydrology—believed Graham Springs wouldn't be affected in any significant way by development."

"And it wouldn't impact Wakulla Springs?" I asked.

Stigler responded, "Matos assured us that Graham and Wakulla are not connected. Hadley disagreed. So you see, it was a tempest in a teapot."

"Excellent description, Peter," Mona said, with a finality suggesting that the subject had been put to rest.

"I'd like to believe your assurances, but I think I'll have to make some inquiries on my own." I intended to put them on notice, and it had its effect. They both seemed to get huffy, and I could feel a chill in the air all the way back to town.

By the time we returned to City Hall, the rain had let up, but the sky remained ink black and threatening. Mona, Pete and I—we were now on a first name basis—agreed to meet again on Monday.

I started back to Apalachicola. The rain resumed in earnest as I passed Carrabelle Beach and entered the two lane stretch of road that ran between Saint George Sound and Tate's Hell Forest. I idly considered the "horrible experience" Cebe Tate had that resulted in the unusual name for both a forest and a swamp.

My windshield wipers were on high, but there were times when I was able to follow the road only by checking the white line down the middle. It was nerve-wracking, and my back and shoulder muscles were painfully tense. I hated driving in these blinding tropical downpours.

I slowed to thirty miles an hour and noticed the glare of high beams in my rear view mirror. Someone had pulled up right behind me.

"Damn," I said. "Why's he getting so close?" My anxiety level increased, and I put the emergency blinkers on. I wanted to be sure the driver could see me.

My head jerked forward as I felt a sharp bump in the rear of the car. I resisted the impulse to brake—fearing a skid—and gripped the wheel tighter. Again I checked the rear view mirror.

"What the hell? Who's back there?"

The rain kept beating down—sometimes in almost horizontal sheets—and the wind made me struggle to hold the steering wheel steady. I looked back and forth from the road stripe to the rear view mirror. The headlights continued to shine through a watery blur.

Whoever it was, they were still on my tail. I began to feel panic and started taking gulping breaths.

"Shit! Why don't you just pass me if you're in such a God-damned hurry?" I blurted. I was afraid to brake for fear I'd be hit again.

Did I dare even take my foot off the accelerator to slow down? Maybe then he'd pass me. It didn't look like there were other cars coming along the other lane. At least I couldn't see their headlights through the downpour.

My car lurched forward again! Another hit? I couldn't believe it. This time it felt even more forceful.

"Okay you bastard," I muttered." You trying to play chicken with me?"

Now I felt certain the first hit had been no accident. I pictured a couple of good old country boys having some rainy day fun with an out-of-towner. I recalled my license tag holder said Florida Gators with an Alachua County plate. "Boys will be boys," I could almost hear some local judge saying when I brought their dumb asses to trial.

What should I do? Are they going to hit my car again? Nothing like this had ever happened to me. I glanced at the rear view mirror, and realized the reflected headlights were too high for a car. It must be a truck or an SUV, I thought, and it seemed tied to my rear bumper. What could he be thinking? Another hit like the last one could make me skid off the road. Was that the intention?

I shivered at the thought.

Several moments passed. The headlights continued to shine in my rear window creating a watery glare. Still close behind me, they started flicking their high beams off and on.

"So you want me to get out of your way? And just where the fuck do you think I can pull off?" I said, glancing out the driver's side window. I couldn't make anything out through the driving rain, but I knew I was on the coastal part of the road. I remembered this stretch ran alongside a narrow grassy shoulder and had about a six foot drop down to the beach.

The driver kept madly flicking his headlights. My heart pounded faster as I tried to think what to do.

I didn't see any oncoming traffic, and I decided to move into the left lane even knowing it would be dangerous given the low visibility.

I hoped he would just pass me, and I'd move back to my side of the road. I could almost picture him and his buddy grinning as they drove by.

I thought of my daddy's warning when he taught me to drive. "If you must pass, be sure to stay in the opposite lane as little time as possible. You can never tell when a car's going to turn onto the road in front of you," he said, "and bam!" The loud clap of his hands was imprinted in my memory.

I was sweating heavily. I took one hand off the wheel long enough to turn up the AC and punch the defrost button. Then I craned forward trying to see if there were any headlights coming from the opposite direction. There weren't.

"Now or never, Lorelei," I said.

I eased into the left lane—trying to avoid a skid—and drove alongside the narrow coastal shoulder.

"Please God, let them pass."

My car lurched again—this time it took a hit on the passenger side.

I was losing control of the steering. I glanced to the right and caught a glimpse of the large black vehicle as it passed. I could just barely hear the horn through the thundering deluge.

"Holy shit! He tried to run me into the water."

The rear end of my car swerved.

It all happened so fast. Instinctively, I hit the brakes.

My head slammed against the side window, as the car went into a dizzy spin. I had the sensation I was flying, then the car stopped, and my head snapped back against the headrest.

When I recovered from the shock, I looked out the windshield and found myself staring across the road. It was disorienting until I realized that my car had slid backwards... perpendicular to the highway. The rear end had landed in the sand, and the car leaned against the embankment like some child's toy.

Still dazed, I sat for several minutes, in an almost vertical position, lying against the back of the seat. Finally, my head cleared. Lorelei, check yourself out, I thought. Any injuries? Anything broken? I felt along the side of head where I had bumped against the window. It was a little sore. I wriggled my toes, moved my foot and legs and made a systematic inventory of my body. No pain. Good. "Jesus, I've got to get out of here," I said. I feared the tide might pull the car out with it. I remembered the time, when my boyfriend and I parked on Daytona Beach. We were so busy making out, we didn't pay attention to the afternoon high tide—at least not until we felt the car moving. Fortunately, we got out, but the car had to be towed from the surf.

I turned off the ignition and tried to open the door. It was so heavy—weighted by the tilt and increased gravity—I had to slowly twist myself around to push it open with my feet. The door finally gave way, and I was terrified when I felt the car begin to shift to the side.

"Please don't roll over," I said, as I carefully edged myself through the opening, and dropped to the sand. Quickly I rolled out of the way of the car...just in case.

I kneeled on the sandy beach—shivering and drenched—but I thanked God I wasn't injured. I stood up helplessly staring at my car. I regretted not grabbing my handbag and cell phone, but I was afraid to try and reach back inside for fear it would dislodge from its perch.

"Shit, shit, shit," I said, climbing up the sandy embankment to the road. I hunched my body against the rain, and hoped to flag down a passing vehicle.

Great, I thought. How often had I extolled the isolation of this coast? Now I'm going to have to walk all the way to Eastpoint in this downpour unless I find a house along the way. I started shaking. Pneumonia came to mind, and—thinking of the large black truck that caused my predicament—Buster's name popped into my head.

Chapter 10

I walked along the grassy shoulder, shivering and reliving the frightening experience that put me out in the downpour. I tried to concentrate on putting one foot in front of the other in what felt like an endless journey.

The staccato honks of a car horn made me look around. I saw a small red truck parked across the road. The driver was waving at me and shouting for me to come over.

"Get in," he said, after I ran across the road. He reached over and opened the passenger door.

Hesitating, even in the downpour, I looked at the driver. He appeared scraggly, and—in a moment of paranoia—I wondered if he was the one who pushed me off the road and was now picking me up to rape or murder me.

He must have seen my fear and said, "C'mon, lady. I ain't goin' to hurt you. You must be the one was in that car back there on the beach."

He had a soft drawl and kind eyes. I climbed in and was immediately relieved to be out of the rain. The cab smelled of fresh wet hay.

"That's my car," I said, wrapping my arms around myself to stop the shivering. "Can you give me a lift to the nearest telephone?"

"You wanna use my cell phone?" He reached into a compartment on the dash and handed me a phone. "Go ahead. I already reported it to the Sheriff's Office. You all right? You need to go to a hospital or anything?"

"No, I'm fine. Thank goodness. But I could use a towel...I'm afraid I'm dripping all over your seat."

"No problem. There's an old gas station a ways up here. I'll pull over, and get you something to wrap up in. By the way, I stopped to check if anybody was in the car. I grabbed your handbag and cell phone—it's on the floor behind my seat. Didn't want it to fall into the wrong hands, you know what I mean?"

"You're an angel," I said, and glanced behind his seat for reassurance that my things were there.

My rescuer had long greasy looking hair and tattoos covered his arms. At first glance, he was just the kind of guy from whom I ordinarily would not accept a ride, but the look in his eyes had made it feel safe...they were kind of sad and sympathetic.

He pulled off the road under the canopy of an abandoned service station, and reached behind the seat. "Here's your bag and phone. Was going to turn it in when I got to Eastpoint."

I bent over with choking sobs. The tension of the accident, the kindness he was showing me, and the sudden realization that someone had intentionally tried to hurt me welled up and spilled over into a deluge of tears as streaming as the rain outside.

"It's all right, m'am. You'll be all right," he said, lightly touching my shoulder. "It's pretty scary running off the road like you did—especially in a heavy storm—easy for a car to hydroplane like that. Lucky you went off where you did or you'd of been torn up on those rocks."

My tears subsided, and I wiped my face with the large bandana he handed me. I didn't tell him it wasn't a skid, but a person who pushed me off the road. All I wanted to do was to get to a safe place...and get warm.

"I got a towel somewheres back here," he said, getting out of the truck and looking in the space behind the seats. "Dammed if I can find it."

"Look, if you'll just take me into Apalachicola I'll report in to the Sheriff's Office and get someone to drive me back to the car. Can you do that? I'd really be grateful."

"Sure, lady. I'm heading through there anyway...going to Port St. Joe. Here, let me put the heat on...maybe it'll stop you shivering."

As the cab of the truck became warmer, my shivering subsided. The rain turned into a light drizzle as the man, who introduced himself as Lonnie, drove me back to my apartment. I tried to give him money, but he wouldn't accept it. He just wished me good luck and said he was glad to help out.

Angels come in many wrappings, I thought as I headed up the stairs. Mike stood on the landing outside his door.

"Wow, what happened to you, Lorelei? You look like a drowned rat! Forgive the comparison."

"I'll tell you all about it if you give me twenty minutes to shower and get into something warm. I had an accident just the other side of Eastpoint. Can you give me a lift back to my car?"

"An accident? Are you all right?" He stepped in front of me for a closer look.

"Yes, and no. Listen, just wait for me. Twenty minutes."

I stepped around him and opened the door to my apartment. Once inside, I stripped off my wet clothing and got into the shower. I completely immersed myself under a blast of hot water—my body was getting warmed at last—and once again the tears poured out. I felt utterly alone...and scared. I thought of Bill and how comforting it would be to have him hold me in his arms and reassure me that everything would be okay. "Oh, Bill...Bill."

I pushed away my thoughts of comfort. They were an emotional indulgence I couldn't afford.

"Scared...terrorized," I said, stepping out of the shower. "That's what the crazy bastard wanted me to feel." I reminded myself that I would see Homer tomorrow, and knew he'd know what to do about the incident.

Mike drove me back to my car, and I told him the story about the truck I believed had intentionally pushed me off the road. I didn't speculate on the reason for the incident, and I didn't mention my suspicion that Buster Stigler was the driver. I had no proof whatsoever.

When we arrived at the scene, a Franklin County sheriff's deputy was standing next to his patrol car, and a tow-truck was pulling my car up from the beach. The rain had stopped, but the sky was still overcast.

"One of you own this vehicle?" the deputy asked, as we approached.

"It's mine, officer."

"What happened? Did you skid or what? It was a bad storm."

"Actually, I want to report that I was forced off of the road."

"Forced?" he repeated, looking incredulous. "May I see your driver's license, please." I showed him the license; he took down the information and said, "Will you please explain your statement, Mrs. Crane?" He prepared to take notes.

"I was driving back from Fairport—when the downpour was heaviest—and a large vehicle, I think it was a truck, started to bump my rear fender. At first I thought it was accidental. You know, like he just didn't see me ahead of him. God knows I had trouble seeing. Anyway, I put on my flashers, and he hit me again. I knew if I tried to pull over the shoulder would have been mud, and I was afraid of skidding. So, I moved into the other lane—to get away from him— and that's when he finally shoved me off the road. You see where I landed."

"Could you identify the vehicle that hit you?" he asked.

"I just caught a quick glimpse. It all happened so fast, and with the rain..."

"What did you see?"

"A large black truck," I answered, remembering what Buster's truck looked like the day I saw it at the diner.

"That's it? That's all you saw?" he asked. "What about the driver? Did you get a look at him?"

I shook my head.

The deputy looked skeptical. I knew I hadn't given him much to work with.

"Okay, Mrs. Crane. At least you don't seem to be hurt. We'll get your vehicle back up on the road. You may be able to drive it or not. They'll tow you if you need it. Here's my card. If you think of anything else about the accident, call me."

He handed me his card, nodded to both me and Mike and started down the embankment. He began talking to the tow truck driver.

The tow truck finally pulled my car back up on the road.

Mike said, "Let me get in and see if works." He started it without a problem and drove a short distance along the shoulder before backing up. "Seems okay."

The tow truck driver completed a form using my automobile club card, handed the card back, and left. The deputy also returned to his patrol car and drove away.

"Look, Lorelei," Mike said. "You've had quite a shock. Are you sure you can drive back to town? We could always just park it somewhere and get it later."

"I'll be fine, Mike. Don't worry. "

He grasped my shoulders and studied my face. "All you have to do is to follow me back. Let's go to Sophie's. It's almost time for rehearsal, and you could use some of her good minestrone soup and a glass of Israeli wine. She keeps a bottle in the back. That'll settle you."

I smiled at his prescription, but thought he was probably right. Soup and wine would be both relaxing and comforting.

I nodded, got into my car, and numbly followed Mike all the way back into Apalachicola.

Sophie looked up and gave us a questioning glance when we walked into the café. "What's happened? Lorelei, are you all right?"

"She's been in a car accident," Mike responded, as he took my elbow and led me to a table.

"I'm just a bit shaken, Sophie," I said. It was the understatement of the year. "Mike suggested I get some soup and wine to settle me. We've got rehearsal in a little while." I looked at my watch to see we had only forty-five minutes.

"Certainly, I'll bring you a bowl of minestrone. I only wish it was chicken soup, but I don't make that until tomorrow."

"How about a glass of that Israeli wine from your private cellar?" Mike asked.

"You get the wine, and I'll get the soup," she said to Mike. "You know where I keep it."

In a few minutes, the two of them provided me with enough food, drink, and caring to dispel the loneliness I felt earlier.

"You both are wonderful. I can't tell you how much better I feel now," I said, as I finished eating. "I'm ready to take on Dr. Stockman and his whole damn town!"

Mike laughed. "See, Stockman's wife is sturdy," he joked, pounding his chest in a Tarzan imitation.

"But you're her reckless husband," Sophie responded. "I know. I just reread the play. Renee gave me a copy of the script."

"That's the first time you've described me as reckless. I'm crushed," he teased Sophie.

"My darling young friend, I only wish you were a bit more reckless in real life. It would do you good."

They exchanged guarded looks.

I saw that Mike was still looking as tired as he had the night before. Sophie's comment seemed to deflate him, and he slumped a little in his chair.

"Arrogant is how I see him. My dear husband here thinks he knows what's best for everyone." I reached over and poked his arm in a teasing way. "And, I have to say that Mike's almost too convincing in the role. Makes me wonder about you, Mr. Pardo. How much is acting?"

He put on a fake smile and responded, "It's all an act, isn't it? Just like life."

Sophie cast him a sympathetic look and returned to the counter as other customers wandered in for afternoon coffee.

Mike sat up and let out a resigned sigh. "Are you ready to talk about what you really think happened back there on the highway?" he asked in a low voice. "I don't mean to get into your business, but I do know people around here. I may be able to help."

I continued sipping the fruity wine as I debated telling Mike the whole story...what Linda Mae confided at Herb's Diner and my subsequent run-in with the mayor's son, the bait and switch land visit pulled by Mona and Pete Stigler, and—finally—the so-called car accident. I decided it was a situation for me and McBride to figure out. Besides, I thought, Mike didn't look like he needed anything more to worry about.

I put my hand on his. "You're a dear, but I'm sure you've got enough going on without my extra-curricular adventures. Frankly, I didn't notice until now, but you look worn-out."

He shrugged. "I'm always bushed when I have to juggle my numerous gigs."

Is that all there is to it, I wondered, and said, "Look, Mike, don't worry about me. I appreciate your offer to help, but I can take care of it."

He looked doubtful, cocked his head, and continued to stare at me with watery blue eyes and a half-smile that made me feel like cradling him in my arms.

"As you wish. Just know I'm around if you need me."

When Sophie came back to the table she was smiling. "Listen you two. I just talked with Renee, and we decided to have a Thanksgiving dinner here for the cast members who'll be in town. It's a potluck. I'll provide the turkey and dressing. Everyone else can bring something to go with it." She looked at Mike. "And I'm sure you'll be bringing the wine, yes?"

"Of course, aren't I the town Bacchus?" he replied with uncharacteristic self-mockery.

"It sounds wonderful, Sophie," I said. "Count me in for…a fresh cranberry sauce. I'll make my mother's recipe."

Mike looked at the clock. "Let's get going, Lorelei. As you often remind me, your friend Renee isn't very tolerant of tardy actors."

Chapter 11

On the way to meet McBride, I drove past the section of road where my car had been shoved off onto the beach. It was eerie to see it on such a sunny day. The water was glittering and blue—indistinguishable from the sky when my eye traveled to the horizon. It all seemed so innocently serene. This part of Highway 98 was one of the few remaining Florida coastlines where you could actually drive along the water without being surrounded by buildings. I loved it.

When I pulled into the parking lot at the lodge, I saw McBride talking to a deputy standing next to a Wakulla County sheriff's car. McBride spotted me and waved. I got out of my car and joined them.

"Lorelei, this is Deputy Thompson, Wakulla Sheriff's Office."

Thompson touched the brim of his hat.

"Deputy, this is a friend of mine, Mrs. Lorelei Crane, from Gainesville."

The deputy looked at me thoughtfully for a moment and said, "Crane. Aren't you the lady who reported being pushed off the road yesterday...on that stretch of 98? I saw the Franklin County report this morning."

McBride turned swiftly, "Lorelei, is that true?"

"Yes, it's true," I replied, and turned to Homer. "I'll tell you about it at lunch."

"Sir, I think you'd better warn the lady about asking too many questions about the case around here," the deputy said. "Like I just told you, it's a hot potato right now. Got a lot of people stirred up—for a lot of different reasons."

I was stunned that Deputy Thompson knew so much about me and my activities. The next thing he said surprised me even more.

"Mrs. Crane, this here's a big county, but there aren't that many people in it. Everybody pretty much knows everybody else's business."

"But, who told you I...?"

"There's no secret to it. I had lunch the other day at Herb's Diner in Fairport. The waitress there's..."

"Linda Mae?" I asked.

"That's right, Linda Mae. She's my sister."

"Your sister?" I repeated, astonished by the connection.

"That's right. She told me about a lady from Gainesville asking a lot of questions and meeting with the mayor." He looked at my red hair, and gave me the once over, and said, "From her description I figured you must be that lady."

He spoke with the kind of condescension that good old boys reserved for interfering women. I regretted not having thought to wear a wig during my snooping assignment. I turned to see McBride's reaction, but he had stepped back, smoking a cigarette and watching the two of us with interest.

"Well, I have to give you a warning," I replied, with a dose of tartness reserved for male chauvinists. "The mayor's son, Buster, was very abusive to your sister. You should be worried about how he threatens her. I know I am."

"Oh, don't waste your time worrying about Linda Mae and Buster. They've been at it since high school."

Right, I thought, he's been bullying her since high school is more like it. And we all know how that can escalate. Deputy Thompson's willingness to brush off my concern only intensified my dislike for the man.

McBride rejoined us.

"Well, I'll just be on my way," Thompson said. "Detective McBride, we'll sure call you when there's anything new on the case."

McBride waved to him, peeled the paper off his cigarette, and crumbled the tobacco on the ground.

He took me by the arm. "I thought we agreed...low profile," he whispered harshly as he steered me into the lobby.

Once we were seated in the dining room, he said, "Okay, what happened? Who bumped you off the road? You weren't hurt were you? You don't seem to be any the worse for wear."

"Which question should I answer first," I said, smiling at the mixture of concern and irritation. "No, I'm not hurt—physically, at least. Though I'll tell you, at the time I worried my car might be washed out to sea."

He smiled and said, "Always so dramatic. So who did it? Do you know?"

"I think it was Buster Stigler. At least the truck I saw looked like his."

McBride gave a low whistle. "The mayor's son? Why would he want to run you off the road?"

"I had a set-to with him at that Herb's Diner...where the deputy's sister works. I had lunch there yesterday, and Buster didn't like it that Linda Mae was filling me in on the local gossip about Graham Springs and Alex Hadley. He was also angry at his father for thinking of selling me property near the springs. Apparently, it's a big issue between them."

"And you think that's why he rammed you?"

"Not entirely, though everything I've learned about him suggests he can be violent. Anyway, what Linda Mae was telling me about Alex Hadley explained why the BSRC members were so upset by Hadley's protest."

"Yeah, yeah. They thought he'd ruin the reputation of the springs. I know about that. Well, look, one of my investigators will have a talk with Buster boy. I'll tell him to be sure to take a look at his truck fender, as well. When it's over, he'll know we're watching him. He works here at Wakulla...a groundskeeper or something. Anyway, I'll try to keep him away from you."

"He works here?" I said, surprised to learn that Buster actually had a job. "Thanks for the protection. And what's with this Deputy Thompson? Is he helping you any? Frankly, I don't like his attitude."

"Never mind about Thompson. For now, he's useful."

I was about to ask what McBride meant when the server came to our table to take our drink order. We both ordered the special—the fried oyster platter. Fried oysters were always my weakness in the bay area, and I was sure the lodge restaurant would give me a generous order.

McBride took out a container of mints, offered me one, and popped a couple in his mouth. "I'm impressed with what you've already found out. But I don't like it one bit if you've goaded one of the locals into attacking you. We'll talk about that later."

I asked, "What about Hadley's death? Have you found any new evidence?"

He nodded. "We're pretty sure it was murder. Very clever, I might add."

"The red ants in his Creaturefest costume?"

"Right. Everyone we've interviewed has been surprised that he didn't have one of those—what'd they call them—Epi Pens close by. They say he was almost obsessive about keeping one close at hand."

"And you didn't find one?"

"Nope."

"How could anyone have placed the ants in his costume to begin with? Surely he would have seen them crawling around if they'd been in there a while."

McBride took a sip of water and cautiously looked around the room. "The deputies found his car unlocked. When they interviewed the park personnel, one of the rangers said he talked with Hadley down at the waterfront. He remembered it because they had a manatee in the lagoon that day, and Hadley was pretty excited about it. It was right before a boat tour so he fixed the time accurately."

"Manatees? Here? Wow, I've got to get on one of those boat tours."

McBride continued, "We know he was down there more than a half hour before he registered at the lodge. Since his car was unlocked someone could have easily got into it, placed the ants in the costume—along with the apple to keep them interested—and removed the syringe."

"But that sounds more like someone took advantage of an opportunity rather than something planned, doesn't it?"

"No, it wasn't by chance. Someone knew he'd be here, and must have been watching for him," McBride said. He stopped talking when the waiter brought our lunch.

"Anything else?" the waiter asked.

McBride ordered coffee and we started eating. He didn't speak again until we each had devoured a section of the oysters that were piled high on the platter.

"You can have my fries," I said, proud to exert at least some degree of restraint.

"No thanks," McBride replied and patted his stomach. "You're not the only one who has to watch the scale."

The coffee arrived, and McBride took several sips. "Okay, where was I? Yes, you suggested it was a crime of opportunity. Yet too many people knew a lot about Hadley's habits. Everyone we interviewed admitted to knowing Hadley never locked his car, he always carried one of those syringes, and that he loved costumes and was certain to be dressing up for the Creaturefest. He'd done it before."

McBride stopped to stab a few more oysters.

"So do you know who was at the Creaturefest?"

He nodded, but continued eating.

"Homer, slow down on the oysters."

"I can't," he grumbled, his mouth full. "I love the things, and don't get 'em like this back in Gainesville." But he finally did stop…just short of emptying the platter. He wiped his hands on his napkin, took a deep breath, and said, "Okay, here's the deal, Lorelei. We've got a bunch of suspects. All of them had the opportunity, but none with an unusually strong motive. That's where you come in."

"Me? I thought you just wanted me to find out what was happening in Fairport. And I think I did. I haven't yet told you…"

He interrupted with a wave.

"I know. The Buster thing, and your meeting with the Fairport Chamber of Commerce."

"It's the 'Beautiful Springs Resource Council'"

"Same thing. Anyway, so far we know three people—connected to Hadley—who were on the scene around the time of the murder." McBride ticked them off on his fingers: number one is his friend, Richard Lucas. Two is his father-in-law, Clifford Rinehart—who actually found the body. And three, Dr. Hubert Matos, the water expert that Lucas works for. We're checking to see if any of the folks from Fairport attended the Creaturefest."

I leaned back in my chair, and looked at McBride. "Anyone could have collected red ants—they're all over the place—and put them in his costume."

"You've got it."

"So, where do you begin?"

"We've already interviewed the three I mentioned. Now, tell me more about this Buster kid."

"Hot-head is the first thing that comes to mind. Mean, angry, sullen...you get the picture? Part of a group who disrupted a public meeting Hadley tried to have."

"Yes. From that description, I can see why you thought he might have attacked you. We'll be talking with him."

"Well, don't ask that Thompson guy to do it. He's as sensitive as a rock."

McBride gave me a patient smile. "Will you get off that subject?"

"Okay, what do you want me to do?"

"I'll take care of young Stigler. I'd like you to check out Lucas. Something about him doesn't ring true. You're an expert in reading faces and people's motivations. I'd like to know what you think of him. He's real smooth."

I thought a moment, remembering what Horse had said about Richard Lucas. "The dive shop owner described Lucas as charming, very smart, and very ambitious."

"Maybe that's why he rubs me wrong," McBride said. "I'm used to dealing with criminals who are mostly dumb."

He leaned back in the chair, put out his arms and braced his fingers behind his neck in a stretch. It was one of the most unselfconscious gestures I'd seen Homer make, and it made me smile.

"What?" he said.

"Nothing. Did you know that Lucas was also a Navy Seal...in special operations, I think?"

McBride straight up. "We haven't dug that far yet. Look, can you make some excuse to meet him? I'd like your impression."

"I think so. He gives dive lessons at Stern's on Saturdays. I've always wanted to learn how to dive."

"This guy—Horse Stern—he's another one. I didn't have much luck talking to him."

"Oh, he's a good guy," I said. "Just very cautious...especially when it comes to law enforcement."

"I'll bet," McBride responded.

"Really, Horse is cool. I'll call tonight and arrange to meet Lucas. He'll go along with me."

McBride gave me an embarrassingly admiring look. "You're some woman, Lorelei Crane. But then I've always thought you had a lot of spunk. I told you that before, didn't I?"

"You did that, Detective McBride, and I still consider it quite a compliment coming from you."

"Hmm," he said. "Any chance you'd be willing to meet me in Tallahassee one night—when you're not rehearsing? I'd arrange a hotel room for you so you wouldn't have to drive back at night. I know a really nice restaurant, and..."

I took a deep breath. He had taken me off-guard, and I didn't know if I was ready to take our relationship to another level. "I don't know," I said. "Let me think about it. You're going to be spending Thanksgiving with your son, Bobby?"

"Yes, how about you? Are you coming back to Gainesville? You could join us."

"No, it's too long a drive for one day. There's a potluck with the cast, and...I'd rather not be home for a holiday."

"I understand, holidays are hell when you've lost someone you loved."

What a rare piece of sentimentality from Detective McBride, I thought. I wondered again about his wife, and how permanent their separation was. Once before I had asked about her, and he changed the subject.

The waiter brought our check, and McBride insisted upon paying. "Still on the dole," he said. "By the way, have you spoken to Delcie?"

"Yes, I called her last night and told her about my visit to Fairport. It confirmed what her client had suspected...there's something they're hiding. I'll be going back next week and maybe learn more."

"Good," he said. "You sure you have time for all this. Doesn't your director mind you being away so much?'

"It's not away. I mean, I show up for rehearsals. I've pretty much memorized my part—it's not a very demanding role. No, if I weren't helping Delcie and you, I'd just be walking on the beach feeling sorry for myself."

He smiled. "We don't want you doing that. Though a walk on the beach sounds like something I could use."

"Well, come on over sometime. You seem to be in the neighborhood often anyway. It's just another hour's drive to Apalachicola."

"I just might do that," he said and looked at his watch.

We left the restaurant, and he walked me to my car. Once I was seated, McBride leaned in the open window.

"Listen, Lorelei. I know you tend to get caught up in things. Probably an actress thing, but I want you to be very careful. Someone you've already met or will meet has committed a murder. Once a person does that, it's easier to do it again."

"I promise, Homer. I'll be careful."

"Stay in touch. I want to hear after you meet Lucas. And no more surprises like the deputy telling me you were run off the road yesterday. He's right about one thing—this case is a hot potato. I think it'll turn out there's a lot of money involved, and who knows what else."

"Don't worry about me," I said, and patted his hand. "I'll call you tomorrow."

He bent in and kissed me on the check. "Take care."

I pulled out of the parking lot with my heart pounding. I couldn't believe it, Homer had actually kissed me, and I felt like a silly school girl. I looked in the rear view mirror and saw him lighting a cigarette as he stood and watched me drive away.

Oh, Homer, I thought, am I really ready to have a romantic relationship with you?

I stopped before entering the main road, and checked my cell phone. There were three messages from Jeffrey. I'm going to have to call him back, I thought. There were also two other messages: one from Renee, and one from Sophie. That's strange, I thought, what could have happened?

"We can't find Mike," Renee told me the moment I walked into Sophie's café. Renee and Sophie stood side by side looking worried. "He was supposed to come in early for rehearsal," Renee said. "We were going to talk about some notes I gave him. When he didn't show up, I came here. We thought he might be with you."

"No, I've just gotten back in town. He hasn't called?" I asked. Renee looked at her watch. "He's almost two hours late. I've tried him on his cell and his home phone, but there was no answer."

"He didn't come in this morning either," Sophie added. "I asked him to pick up some oysters for me on his way back from the dock. I called down there but no one has seen him."

"Has this happened before—Mike just not showing up?" I asked Sophie.

She hesitated before answering and seemed to be considering what to say. "Mike is a considerate young man, and under most circumstances he would call if he wasn't going to show up."

"Most circumstances?" Renee and I asked at the same time.

Sophie looked embarrassed, she brushed her hands along the sides of her thick braided hair and said, "Look, ladies, I don't know how to say this without breaking a confidence, but sometimes Mike has a bit too much to drink."

"Oh, Jesus," Renee said, throwing her hands in the air. "Don't tell me my leading man is an alcoholic."

Sophie reached out and touched Renee's shoulder. "Oh no, I didn't say that. It's just that Mike has had some difficulties, and now and again...how to say? It gets too much for him. You know what I mean?" she said, looking at me. "But don't worry, he's not a drunk. Believe me, I know drunks."

Renee said. "Okay, we'll just have to find him."

"Let me try the apartment first," I said. "If he doesn't answer the door, I can get in. I know where he hides his key."

"Ay," Sophie said, "don't be too hard on him, Lorelei. Maybe you can help him. You both suffered tragic losses."

"Help him? What loss? He struck me as an upbeat and uncomplicated guy."

"It's not for me to tell you," she replied, and began clearing tables.

I left to return to the apartment.

After knocking on Mike's door for several minutes, I went back downstairs and found his hidden key wedged at the bottom of his mail box. I returned to the apartment and opened the door.

"Mike," I called. "Are you here? It's Lorelei."

There was no answer, but I quickly absorbed the scene. The air was stale. When I went to open the windows, I saw half a sandwich and a torn open bag of chips on the table. An old Karen Carpenter song was playing on the CD machine. I turned it off. Pages of the script were scattered on the coffee table, and a large empty vodka bottle sat on the floor next to it.

"Mike, we're worried about you. It's Lorelei," I called out again, as I went into the bedroom.

I found him entangled in bed covers, unshaven, and sound asleep. I gently shook his shoulder and said, "Wake up, Mike. It's Lorelei."

"Lorelei?" he said, half opening his bloodshot eyes. "I was dreaming about you. You were rescuing me."

From what, I wondered, but this wasn't the time for dream analysis. "Mike, you need to get up, and into the shower. You had us worried."

He mumbled, "You worried about me? What a wifey thing to do."

"C'mon," I said, tugging at his arm to pull him up. "You need to get into the shower. I'll make some coffee."

He got up, awkwardly pulling the covers around his waist, and stood looking at me.

"That way, to the shower," I directed, and gave him a little push.

When Mike joined me in the living room, after showering and getting dressed, he looked gaunt and embarrassed. I fed him several cups of coffee and a slice of heated-up pizza I found in the refrigerator.

After his third cup, he leaned forward, head in hands, and began to cry.

"Mike, please. What's wrong?" I said, feeling myself on the verge of tears as I witnessed his sorrow.

"Can't," he said, between sobs. "Can't talk. My head feels like its going to explode…I need aspirin or something."

I retrieved some aspirin from the bathroom cabinet and gave it to him with some orange juice—food, caffeine, and vitamin C were the only hangover remedies I could think of.

He stopped crying and began staring at the photograph on the entertainment center. I looked at my watch. We were already half an hour late for rehearsal.

"C'mon, Mike. Do you feel well enough to go now?"

"Don't know. It's too hard. You go on."

"Please," I said. "It's okay. We all lose it sometimes."

He gave me a weak smile and said, "All right, I'll go. I guess you need your leading man. But no more coffee. I'll take a Coke with me. When I was in Australia, they called it 'Black Aspirin'—good for a hangover—it's the bubbles or something. I hate to think what Renee's going to say when her two leads walk in late."

"Don't worry about Renee," I said.

He gathered up his script and cast a quick glance again at the photograph. The cause of his distress was connected to one or more of the people in the photo.

"Let's go," Mike said.

On the way to the theatre I said, "Mike, do you know a Rick Lucas by any chance?"

Mike stopped dead and gave me an incredulous look. "Know him? He was once my fiancée's boyfriend. What about him?"

"I'm going to meet him tomorrow—at the dive shop—and I wondered what he's like."

Mike looked concerned. "Lorelei, he's a total bastard. I don't know why you'd want to meet him, but please be careful. Charley was afraid of him. That's why they broke up. She didn't trust him." It was the first I learned of Mike's fiancée. I had a hunch she was the dark-haired girl in the photograph. I would ask about it when he was more stable.

As we continued to the theatre, I said, "Rick was friends with Alex Hadley, right?"

"Friends?" he said, in a mocking tone. "I don't know how Horse described it, but I'm not sure I'd call them that. Rick is very competitive. If he could undermine Alex—like he discredited his ideas about the springs—he'd do it. Rick would try to deflate you sometimes when he had nothing to gain by it. That's just Rick...he's like a scorpion. He'd sting you even if you were trying to save him. I'm not sure Alex saw through the guy, but I think his wife did. I got the impression she didn't like him either."

"Why?"

"She once mentioned to me that Rick kept Alex from getting a job with Matos. She said Alex knew about it, but didn't really care since he had no respect for Matos. Something about where he got his research money, I don't know."

"That's interesting," I said, glad now I had asked about Rick. It made me both cautious and interested to meet the character who seemed to stir such mixed feelings in people. We entered the theatre and I said, "Well, here we are. Chin up."

Mike groaned. "You'd better cue me well, Lorelei. My brain feels like a pound of grits, and my head's still throbbing like a kettle drum in a high school marching band."

Chapter 12

I awoke on Saturday morning thinking about Jeffrey. I had finally returned his call the night before. He was furious with me. "Why in hell didn't you call me as soon as you found out about Alex?" he demanded. "I had to hear about it from a friend in Tampa. And why haven't you returned my calls? What's going on, Lorelei?"

I tried to make him understand I was busy with rehearsals, investigating a land deal for Delcie, and spending reflective time alone. Actually, it wasn't entirely true. I intended to take walks on the beach and try to think about my life without Bill, but I hadn't found time yet to do it.

Jeffrey wasn't buying my excuses, so I said, "The real reason I haven't returned your calls was the fear you might just show up here once you heard about Alex's death. I didn't think I could deal with you along with everything else."

He protested and said he never intended to intrude on me. "Remember, Lor, I was the one who first urged you to take that job. I knew you needed time away."

It was true. Jeffrey was the first one I had told about Renee's offer. He did encourage me to accept it. I had forgotten that, thinking it was only Delcie I had confided in.

He said he would be going to Tampa for Alex's memorial service the following Tuesday. "He was such a great guy," Jeffrey said. "We got to be drinking buddies and commiserated with one another about our work situations. He had just started with the water management district. He hated it as much as I hated working for the damn developers—we both felt like we had sold out. Jesus, what a waste."

"It's a shame the two of you didn't stay in touch."

"Yeah, I'll miss him anyway. You know what I mean...just knowing I'll never see him again. That hurts."

I did know what he meant. It was the same dull and desolate feeling I experienced long ago when I lost my dad, and now when I thought about Bill. The mosaic of my world was broken. Sometimes I tricked myself into thinking Bill was just gone on a long business trip. Denial had its merits.

I apologized to Jeffrey for not returning his calls, and he seemed mollified. We ended the conversation with my promise to check in with him from time to time.

"I worry about you, Lorelei," he had said in his sweetest voice. "Please take care of yourself."

I assured him I would, but I didn't dare tell him I knew about the real cause of his friend Alex Hadley's death, nor about my involvement with McBride's investigation.

I telephoned the dive shop and talked with Horse.

"I wonder if you'd do me a favor?" I asked.

"What kind of favor?" The echo in his voice sounded like he was talking in the bathroom. You never know where people are when you call them on their cell phones.

"I'd like to take a dive lesson from Rick Lucas. Does he have any openings today?"

There was a long pause. "You really want to take a lesson?" he asked. "You didn't mention it before."

"Yes, it's something I've always wanted to do. When I was at the shop, and I heard how much experience Rick Lucas has...I thought I might as well do it while I'm on the coast. Can you arrange it?"

"I guess so," Horse said. "The first lesson is more or less an introduction. Shouldn't take more than an hour or so. Wait a minute, and I'll check the schedule."

While I waited for Horse to return to the phone, I sat at the table looking out at the bay. It was a beautiful fall morning, and the crisp air made the distant shrimp boats stand out on the horizon like pop-up pictures in a children's book.

"Lorelei?" Horse said returning to the phone. "Yeah, I probably can fit you in if you can get down here right away. Rick doesn't have a student until later in the morning."

"Great," I said. "I'll be over there by ten. And, Horse, can you do me another favor."

"What is it?" He sounded wary.

"Don't tell Rick I was in there asking about Alex Hadley."

"I can't lie to Rick," he said. "Hell, he's been one of my best dive instructors for years."

"But I thought you'd want to help find out what happened to Alex."

"I do, but it stops with lying to a friend. I don't pull that shit."

"All right," I said. "I really don't have anything to hide."

What struck me first when I met Rick Lucas was his almost effeminately chiseled angular face—Greek, I thought—and short black hair salted with gray. I guessed him to be in his late thirties. He greeted me the moment I walked into the shop.

"Mrs. Crane?" he said, extending his hand in a firm grip.

"Yes, and you're Rick Lucas?"

He was about six feet tall and had a nice smile marred only by a discernable gap between his two front teeth.

"Horse will give you the paper work to fill out while I gather up the equipment."

I joined Horse at the front counter, and registered and paid for the first lesson. He acted cool, saying nothing about our earlier conversation.

I walked to the back of the store where Rick was assembling gear.

He said, "Horse tells me you're an actress."

"That's right." I stood watching the precise way he lined up various pieces of diving equipment on a wooden table.

He gave me the once over. "Size ten?"

I nodded as he selected a wet suit and hood from the nearby rack.

"I heard they were doing an Ibsen play over at the Dixie theatre," he said, returning to his task. "What role are you playing?"

"I'm playing the wife of the protagonist. Do you know the play?"

"I think they did it when I was in high school," he replied, gathering dive equipment from different parts of the store. "Something about a crazy doctor, isn't it...the play?"

"Not so crazy...more like arrogant," I replied, following him around.

"Horse has you down for an introductory lesson. Let's go outside. Here, would you carry this for me?" He handed me a pair of flippers, a snorkel, and a weight belt, and led the way out of the shop carrying the rest of the gear.

We walked around to the back of the building where we deposited the equipment on a battered mosaic stone table with concrete slab seats. A rusted oxygen tank was leaning against the building. As he arranged the gear, I sat down and observed him more closely. He was completely focused on placing each piece of equipment in a certain order. Obsessiveness was probably a good thing in someone who's going to take you into the deep, I thought.

Finally, looking satisfied with the arrangement of gear, he sat down next to me. "Before I begin, I need to know a little about you," he said. "I know you're an actress from Gainesville, but I don't know much else. I must say, Horse didn't prepare me for how beautiful you are. Do people tell you how much you look like Susan Sarandon?"

"It's the red hair," I said, feeling flattered by the comparison. "Thank you."

"How did you find out about the dive shop?"

He fixed me with a sharp stare while he awaited my response. His eyes were arresting with small black pupils embedded in a large yellowish-green iris...for some reason they reminded me of a leopard—which fit perfectly with the elegant way he moved his body.

I wondered if Horse had told him about inquiries, and decided to stay as close to the truth as possible. "My ex-husband wanted me to meet his friend, Alex Hadley, and he told me I could locate him through the dive shop. That's how I first came here."

"So you know about Hadley? His death, I mean."

"Yes, I heard."

His eyes took on a clouded look, and he glanced out toward the bay. "It was a terrible thing...Alex's death. He was my friend, you know." He said it like a badly acted line from a play.

"So Horse told me. I'm sorry," I replied, remembering Mike's comment that Alex and Rick were more competitors than friends.

86

"I'm disappointed that I didn't get to meet him. I heard he was a great guy."

"Great?" His lips curled into a small smile. "Yes, maybe that's true," he said, with an oddly vacant look on his face. He began mindlessly moving some of the smaller items around like they were a puzzle.

Neither of us spoke for several moments, then he snapped out of his reverie and said, "What made you decide to take dive lessons? You'd have to be an adventuresome woman."

I shrugged and gave a lighthearted laugh. "I know it sounds impulsive, but I've always wanted to learn how to dive. Part of my natural curiosity being an actress you know…to have many different experiences."

He was staring at me as though he might find the answer to his question if he looked at me long enough. Rick Lucas was handsome, but his studied gaze was intimidating. I remembered Mike's comment that his fiancée had been afraid of Rick. I could see why. I picked up one of the face masks and started examining it.

"I've done some snorkeling before," I said. "My husband and I used to come here…to Indian Pass, actually."

He glanced at my hand to see the wedding band that I still wore. "Is your husband with you in Apalachicola?"

I put the mask down. "No, he died…about six months ago."

"I'm sorry to hear that. It must be hard for you to come back here again." There was a note of genuine sympathy in his voice. I relaxed a bit and realized I had absorbed some of his tension. "I don't know yet. How about you…are you married?"

"God, no. I've got an old man living with me—my father—and I don't think any woman would put up with him. He's my albatross," he said, with a dark look. "Besides, I'm so damn busy—between the university and diving—I don't have the time for romance."

"Ah," I said. "What do you do at the university?"

"I'm a researcher in the Department of Geology. Anyway, let's begin, shall we?"

It was the abrupt finish to our getting acquainted session. Something seemed to have made him cross.

"First off, I want you to learn about the equipment we'll be using," he said. "It will give you an appreciation for what you've set out to learn. For starters, you say you're already familiar with the face mask from your snorkeling experience. The one you just picked up is for skin diving. It's what we call a low volume mask," he said, picking it up to show me. "And, you can see the pocket for your nose so it can fit tightly over your face. We're going to begin with skin-diving so you'll be using a mask like this, and these fins—have you used fins before?"

"Yes."

"Good. After I see what kind of swimmer you are, and what you can do under water, we'll move right on to scuba instruction. Does that sound all right?"

I nodded.

"Now, I'll just show you some of the equipment we'll be using later."

He gave me a lecture on the differences between skin diving and scuba diving equipment and told me about the different agencies that provide certification. He showed me each piece of gear as he described it—weight belt, regulator, pressure gauge—and other gear. It took well over an hour, and I was impressed with his authoritative presentation...and a bit overwhelmed by it.

When he finished, he must have read my expression. He looked amused as he asked, "So, Mrs. Crane, are you still convinced you want to get certified in scuba? Skin diving is a lot less complicated."

What could I say? I'd gone this far to engage him, but I had no intention of donning all that gear and plunging into the deep. I didn't feel that adventuresome. I only planned to spend a couple of hours getting to know Rick Lucas, and then find an excuse to back out.

"Definitely," I said. "I definitely want to get certified in scuba."

"Okay then. Help me back in with the gear, and we'll set up an appointment for next week. Be sure to bring your swim suit. The second phase of training will take about six hours. We'll be using a swimming pool near the shop."

Rick gave me a dive manual to study. Horse was involved with a customer when I left the dive shop, and we only waved goodbye.

On the way back to Apalachicola, I thought about my first impressions of Rick Lucas and what I would tell McBride. Rick had confirmed what I heard about him from Horse—good looks, charm, and competence. McBride had said he couldn't read him—that he was too smooth. That was probably the impression he would have given under the circumstances of their meeting.

I tried to analyze my feelings about him. For one thing, I didn't see why he would find me a threat, yet I sensed a certain tension and cautiousness in his reaction to me. Was it something about me that Horse had told him? On the other hand, he openly expressed his feelings about his father and pretended to have feelings about Alex. It was the occasional vacant look I found creepy…like something deep inside of him was disturbed.

In short, I knew Rick Lucas was far too complicated a man to assess in a one hour meeting. I also knew that whatever it was I felt lurking beneath the surface could make him a dangerous adversary— a scorpion was the word Mike had used to describe him.

Chapter 13

"So you're telling me you didn't get any further with Lucas than I did?" McBride asked.

I was back in my apartment, talking to him after returning from the dive shop.

"No, he's a complicated guy."

"Who am I talking to? Surely not *The* Lorelei Crane who claims to be the master of character motivation? C'mon, give me more than 'he's a complicated guy,'" McBride said, sounding half teasing.

"And you give me a break," I retorted. "Seriously, what I meant is that people have differing views about him. Mike Pardo, my actor friend, says he's abusive and untrustworthy. Horse Stern describes him as charming—which he is. I just haven't pealed the onion yet, but rest assured, I will."

"Pealed the onion?" McBride repeated. "Is that some kind of acting jargon?"

"You know what I mean." He was still teasing me, but I rather liked this side of Homer McBride. "Look, I have a longer diving lesson scheduled next weekend. It'll give me a chance to learn more about him."

"A diving lesson?" he whistled in surprise. "I didn't take you for the athletic type."

"I'm not, really. I have done some snorkeling before, and I thought it would be a good way to get Lucas relaxed with me. Besides, I might like it. You never know."

I stood in front of the windows. I couldn't get enough of the bay view. It was so fascinating to watch the changes in the light and hues at different times of day. The pelicans and seagulls were crowded next to each other on a nearby pier like targets in a carnival shooting gallery.

McBride said, "Well, from what you've told me, I wouldn't go into any deep water with the guy. At least not until we know more about him."

He had a point. "Actually, we're just going to snorkel in shallow water—don't worry." It always pleased me when Homer expressed his concern. "Is there anything new with the investigation?"

"We've got too many people who had the opportunity to slip ants into Hadley's costume," McBride said.

"You mean, Rick Lucas and his boss weren't the only ones Hadley knew who were at the Creaturefest that Saturday?"

"That's right. The whole Fairport gang was there—the mayor, his son, the Lavender woman. And, of course, there's Hadley's father-in-law. Remember, he found the body. I'm still trying to figure out where he fits in."

There was a long silence, and I could just picture McBride tapping an unlit cigarette on his desk. He was right though; there was a confusing array of suspects.

"Problem is, any one of them could have done it," he said. "There's nothing to picking up a pile of ants. When you think about it, it was a hell of a weapon…no prints, no clues. They all admit they knew Hadley had a serious allergy."

"So now you think it wasn't planned?"

"Not sure. Too many things had to be in place: Hadley leaving his car unlocked while he walked around the spring, the costume on the back seat. I'm beginning to wonder if your hunch was right…someone saw an opportunity, and went for it."

"The question is who that someone was, and why they'd want to kill Alex Hadley," I mused, and started making a list on the notepad I kept on the windowsill:

1. *Rick Lucas,*
2. *Dr. Hubert Matos,*
3. *Mayor Pete Stigler,*
4. *Buster Stigler*
5. *Mona Lavender,*
6. *Cliff Rinehart*
7. Unknown

McBride said, "By the way, I'm going down to Hadley's memorial service on Tuesday. I'll be interviewing the widow and her father, Cliff Rinehart."

"Is there anything I can do in the meantime?"

"Yeah, find me someone with a good motive for murder."

"I thought that was your job, detective," I joked.

"I'm working on it. Have you talked with Delcie recently? Did you ever find out what had her client so nervous?"

"No. Other than the bid from Delcie's client, I still don't know why the BSRC group is acting so funny about the springs property. I'm going to make another real estate appointment with them."

"It might be helpful," McBride said. "My gut tells me Hadley's death is tied up with something about those springs. He got people in Fairport stirred up, and then—boom—he's dead. Deputy Thompson said his men couldn't find anything useful at the Hadley house."

"What about his office?"

"He didn't have another office."

"Did they check his computer?" I asked, thinking about all the research Bill had on his.

"They picked it up. Our guys are scanning it now. I'm not sure they'd even know what they're looking at."

"Okay," I said. "I'll try to find out more about what's going on in Fairport, and I'll call Delcie."

Neither of us spoke for a moment, then McBride asked, "Thought any more about meeting me for dinner in Tallahassee? I'll be over there on Monday. I'm going to the university to talk with Lucas and Matos again. I want to hear what they have to say about the alleged springs controversy. I'm also curious why they were attending a Creaturefest last week."

"Good luck," I said. "Homer, I'm sorry, but I'll have to take a rain check on dinner. We don't have an evening off next week. We're holding rehearsal on Monday to make-up for Thanksgiving."

"Thanksgiving already? Okay, Lorelei, a rain check it is. But just a reminder about Lucas."

"Yes?"

"Stay out of the deep end of the pool."

"Don't worry, Homer, I'll be careful."

I sat at the table for awhile reflecting on our conversation. I glanced down at my list of suspects. I put a star next to Buster

Stigler's name because, so far, he was the only person I knew to have shown violent tendencies. Could he have been angry enough to kill Alex Hadley believing the property he hoped for would be threatened by Hadley's research? Dumping ants into someone's costume seemed an almost childish prank...easily thought of by a sullen young man like Buster. In Hadley's case the prank was deadly.

I looked at my watch and knew I had to get ready for rehearsal. As I showered, I kept thinking about McBride's gut feeling...that Hadley's research findings might point a finger at the murderer. Having been an academic's wife, I was certain Hadley had backed up his research. It had to be somewhere in his house, I thought. Maybe I could find it, where the sheriff's deputies had failed.

I imagined searching the house and immediately thought of Horse. He would probably be familiar with the place...they were friends. He might even have a key. I quickly got dressed and called the dive shop. I briefly told Horse my idea, and asked if he'd help me.

"Now that's something I can do for you," he replied. "But what do you expect to find that the police haven't picked up?"

"I don't know exactly. Maybe something they overlooked. It's worth a shot."

He hesitated, "I think you're on a wild-goose chase, but—what the hell—it can't hurt to have a look around. Alex and Jennie always left the back kitchen door open...said they lost the key. Maybe we could still get in that way. When do you want to do it?"

I thought a moment, "Not today, I'm on my way to rehearsal right now. Tomorrow?"

"Sunday's a big day here," he said. "But I could do it after I close the shop around seven." He paused and added in a wistful tone, "I haven't been over to the house since Jennie left."

I pressed, "Name a time and place. I'll meet you."

Horse replied, "It just dawned on me, there'll probably be crime scene tape around the place—or someone posted there. Maybe it's not such a good idea. What if I call Jennie and ask permission?"

"Please, Horse, my intuition tells me Alex's research caused his death. If it looks too risky, we'll turn back. But we've got to do it as soon as possible."

"I just don't welcome an encounter with Deputy Thompson, or any of his boys. We're not exactly friendly. I guess if we go after dark we might get around the yellow tape without anyone being the wiser." I sighed in relief. "Thank you. So let's meet around 10:00 P.M. My rehearsal should be over by nine, so I'll have time to get there."

"Okay, Lorelei, ten o'clock in the parking lot of the old Methodist church in Fairport. It's a block away from Alex's house. We aren't as likely to be noticed if we walk along the back field."

"I know the church. I'll be there," I said.

I was struck by Horse's comment about Deputy Thompson. I'd have to ask him about the man who gave me such bad vibes.

As it turned out, rehearsal ended early, and when I called Horse he agreed to meet me at eight thirty instead of ten o'clock. It was already quite dark when I pulled into the church parking lot. I was barely able to make out Horse's van in the shadow of a vapor lamp. When I got outside, I smelled frost in the air and was glad to have worn my lined jacket.

Horse stepped out of the van. He was dressed all in black and wore a heavy knit fisherman's sweater, and cap. It occurred to me he might have had prior experience with this sort of caper—perhaps a too playful word for breaking into someone's house.

"We'll walk through the pasture behind the houses," Horse instructed. "I hope you wore your hiking shoes."

Actually, I did have on the hiking shoes I'd purchased last year when I was searching the Prairie on an evening not unlike this one—except that night's excursion had been complicated by severe thunderstorms and other frightening events.

Horse held a small flashlight beam behind him so I could follow as he made his way from the back of the church. We walked through tall grass, and he motioned me to stop when dogs began barking nearby.

"They're probably penned," he muttered.

I stepped closer to Horse, hoping he was right.

Someone shouted at the dogs and the barking gradually stopped. We proceeded along the pasture fencing.

"There, the Hadley's house is right up there...on the rise," Horse whispered.

I saw the outlines of the house. It was an average sized, one-story ranch-style house. As we moved into the back yard, I spotted a child's swing set. The grass was uncut, and there was a small overgrown kitchen garden. It made me sad to think about the life that had once filled the now deserted house.

"Jennie loved to grow herbs and veggies," Horse said. "Got the green thumb from her dad."

There was no police tape, but there was a shiny new lockset on the kitchen door. Horse tried it anyway. It didn't open.

"What now?" I whispered.

"There's a door into the garage. Follow me." Horse led the way around to the side of the house to another door. It had a cat door at the bottom, and lattice panes of glass on the upper part.

"Let me borrow your jacket a minute," Horse said.

I obliged, and he wrapped his hand in it, and punched a glass pane out of the door. He reached in, unlocked it, shook the glass off of my jacket, and gave it back. I took it gratefully. I had begun to shiver either from the night air or the realization of what we were doing, or both.

"This way into the house," he said softly, as I closed the door behind us.

We made our way through a garage and laundry room. I followed Horse into the kitchen, but I tripped on the threshold. I tried to break my fall by grabbing at a nearby table, and a large fruit bowl crashed to the floor.

"Shit," I said, between clenched teeth as I landed on my knees.

He took my arm and helped me up. A muffled noise came from the front of the house, and there was a thump like a door being shut. We froze.

My first thought was it must be their cat. It has always comforted me to think nighttime house noises are made by cats. My heart pounded faster when I realized it could also be another person. Horse still had such a tight grip on my arm it began to hurt. I pulled away.

"A burglar?" I whispered.

"Ssssh," he replied. "Whoever it is, I don't aim to get shot." He doused his flashlight. We huddled together against the kitchen doorway in dark silence for what seemed a very long time until there were no further sounds. The kitchen smelled sour, like when a refrigerator's been turned off, and the door's left open.

Horse said, "You stay here while I take a look around."

"Oh no, I'm coming with you."

I stayed close behind him as he slowly moved down a long hallway. He flashed his light into the bedrooms, a bathroom, and the living room.

"Doesn't look like anyone's around," he said, leading us back to one of rooms which appeared to be Hadley's office.

I breathed relief and said, "Thank goodness. Wouldn't it be weird if someone else were snooping around the same time as us?"

"Maybe not so weird," Horse said.

"What do you mean?"

"Nothing, forget it. Anyway, here's his office. You want to look around, right?"

"Yes, can I have the flashlight?"

I was eager to get started, and I let Horse's cryptic comment pass. He handed me the light and sat in a chair at the large computer desk situated under a window. McBride had told me the deputies had taken the computer. Only the monitor and cables remained. The desktop held a couple of framed photographs of a lovely blonde-haired woman, and a laughing little girl.

"That must be Jennie and his daughter…?"

"Clare," he replied.

I sifted through the desk drawers, but nothing captured my attention. I shined the beam on two four drawer file cabinets, topped by bookshelves which were loaded to the ceiling.

"Hey, the bottom file drawer is open," I said, walking over to look at it. It had been left half way out and was so crammed with folders there was no way to tell if anything was missing. I wondered if it was Hadley, the police, or someone else who had left it open.

"Anything useful?" Horse asked.

"Not yet."

I briefly looked into the other drawers, but it was much the same thing. The folder labels referred to old water management district reports, conference proceedings, Florida Public Interest Research Group newsletters, and the like. It would have taken me days to comb through the contents of Hadley's files, and I had the feeling he wouldn't have kept the controversial research among them. I scanned the rest of the office. The floor was stacked with books, magazines, and reports.

"Any ideas?" I asked, turning the light on Horse. His hand rose to block the glare, and I quickly lowered the beam.

"Check the credenza," he said, pointing to the wall opposite the file cabinets. "He used to put keepsakes in there. Stuff his father left him."

On top of the low credenza were a group of framed photos. I picked up one of Horse, and two men in swim suits with dive masks in hand. One of them I recognized to be Rick Lucas.

"Here's a photo of you and Rick? Is that Hadley, too?" I showed it to Horse.

"Yeah, that's us."

I studied it for a moment. Other than the newspaper photo, it was the first time I got a good look at Alex Hadley. He was taller than Horse and Rick, and had the muscular body of a swimmer. His face held a sweet crooked smile and I was struck by how carefree he appeared. There were more photos, awards, and certificates hanging on the wall above.

I opened the credenza doors, and several items spilled out onto the floor.

"Was he always this messy?" I asked, picking up a small book, an old pair of binoculars, and what looked like a divers watch.

"Don't think so. Why?"

"Well, it almost looks like stuff was just shoved in here."

Horse got up and bent over the credenza for a look.

"Oh no, Alex never would never have left it like that. Somebody's been messin' with his stuff."

"The sheriff's deputies?" I asked hopefully.

"Maybe."

"You really do think someone else was in the house, don't you?"

"Well, if there was, you're crashin' into the table would of scared him away."

"I hope you're right," I said, and remembered the sound of a door slamming shut.

Horse said, "Look, stay here. I'm going to look for another flashlight in the garage. That way, we can both look around…save time."

Reluctantly, I handed him the flashlight and sat down where he had been seated. It felt scary sitting in the pitch dark, and the air around me started feeling thick. When Horse didn't return in a few minutes, I got up and felt my way back into the hall.

"Horse?" I called, hoping he was on his way back into the house. No answer.

I remembered the bathroom was next to the office. I inched my way along the dark hall until I felt the opening. Bathrooms are pretty much laid out the same way, and I thought I could use it even in the dark.

I entered the room and felt my way along past the sink and a long counter. In the dark, your senses become more acute—especially if you're wary—and just when I felt the cool porcelain of the commode, I heard the shower curtain rustle.

Someone else was here.

Instinctively, I started backing out of the room.

There was a ripping sound as the curtain was torn from its hooks. I heard a grunt.

A body crashed into mine, and wrapped the shower curtain around my head and body with such force and suddenness I didn't even cry out.

I felt myself pushed to the floor.

My head bumped against something hard, but it was cushioned by the bunched up curtain.

A foot glazed my right ankle as my assailant apparently stepped over me on the way out.

"Ouch! You son of a bitch!" I cried in a voice muffled by the curtain.

The bathroom door slammed shut.

Dazed, I began struggling to untangle myself. I pulled the top of the curtain away from my face, sat up, and took several deep breaths before pulling myself out of the folds. It was like trying to get out of a sleeping bag in a small tent.

My head was throbbing as I stood up. I leaned on the counter to catch my breath and felt my feet entangled in the folds of the bunched up shower curtain. I finally freed myself and stood in the bathroom doorway.

"Horse, where the hell are you?" I yelled, no longer caring who heard me.

My breath was ragged, and I leaned against the door jam hoping for a reply. I kicked the shower curtain aside and found the commode again. It took a few moments before my body relaxed enough to use it, after which I sat there, my head in hands, trying to calm down.

On wobbly legs I left the bathroom and started back down the hall to the kitchen. What is taking him so long?

Oh, Jesus, I thought, when it occurred to me that whoever attacked me might also have run into Horse on the way out. I inched my way toward the kitchen straining for any sound. My mouth was so dry it hurt. Get a kitchen knife, I thought, just in case.

"Lorelei?"

I nearly jumped out of my skin at the sound of Horse's voice.

Chapter 14

"Lorelei, are you all right?" Horse said, shining his light on me. "What happened? Did you fall again?" He was taking in my obvious distress and disheveled appearance.

I shook my head and jerked his arm down to get the glare of the flashlight off me. My breathing was still irregular.

"Sorry," he said.

"What took you so long?" I asked, a bit sullenly. "Didn't you hear me calling you, for God's sake?"

He took my arm and led me back down the hall to Hadley's office. "I was in the garage, and I didn't hear you. Sit down." He took another flashlight from his jacket pocket and handed it to me. "Here, I found one for you. Do you want some water?"

We pointed our lit flashlights to the floor. The reflected glow placed us both in eerie looking shadows.

"No, just stay here." I said, still shaken by my encounter in the bathroom.

"Tell me what happened. Are you hurt?" Horse asked.

"In a minute," I said, leaning over to put my head between my legs. I held the position until I felt my breathing slow, and I was able to speak without gulping for air. "Somebody was hiding in the bathroom. When I went in there, he jumped me, wrapped me up in the shower curtain and took off." I reached down to massage my bruised ankle. "Whoever it was nearly broke my ankle on their way out."

"A man or a woman?" he asked.

"That's a funny question. A man, I think. Though now that you mention it, it could have been a woman. Either way it was someone strong. I didn't have a chance to fight back before I got tangled up in the damn shower curtain."

Horse hunched down in front of me. "But you're okay, right? No harm done."

"Are you kidding?" I said, really annoyed that Horse dismissed my assault so quickly. "I have a bruised ankle and maybe lost a year of my life from stress. It was damn scary. Let's just finish looking around and get out of here. This place is giving me the creeps."

"Look, whoever was here has gone by now. I'm sure we've scared him or her away."

"I sure as hell hope so," I said, "though I'd like to return the kick."

"It'll go faster if we split up. That is, if you feel okay doing it."

"Yeah, I'm okay, and I really want to get out of here."

Horse said, "You take the master bedroom, and I'll have a look around the other bedroom and the living room. I want to check to see how someone else got in here."

I entered the master bedroom, and except for the unmade bed, the room had the same stale, unlived in feeling as the rest of the house. I didn't like being in a stranger's bedroom—especially a stranger who had been murdered.

I checked all the drawers and night tables. Nothing unusual jumped out at me. I entered the walk-in closet, shut the door, and was relieved I could finally turn on a light in the windowless room.

There was a maze of shoe boxes and luggage on the upper shelves. One side of the closet was obviously Alex's. Very few things were left hanging on Jennie's side. It appeared she expected to be gone for a long time.

With the closet door closed, the room felt close and musty. The task of searching through all the belongings seemed overwhelming, and a repulsive invasion of privacy.

"C'mon, Lorelei, get over yourself. Just think of it as a wardrobe room," I said aloud, attempting to overcome my squeamishness.

I sat down in the middle of the floor and started systematically scanning every quadrant of the room. Where would I hide something in a closet? Nothing I saw looked out of the ordinary. Finally, my gaze reached the closet floor.

That's when I saw the corner of a gray box behind a pile of hiking gear. I crawled over to the spot, shoved everything away, and pulled a small fireproof security box into the center of the closet floor. Bingo! I thought. It had a combination dial, and it was locked. I picked up the heavy box and left the closet. Even with the aid of my flashlight, it took a few moments to readjust to the darkness as I hurried back to the office.

"Nothing seems disturbed, but the front door is unlocked," Horse said, as he followed me into the room. "It's just a button lock. Anyone could've used a credit card to pop it open."

"And he or she didn't find what they were looking for," I said, pointing my flashlight beam onto the security box which I had placed on the computer desk.

"Where'd you find that?" And with a chuckle, Horse added, "Compliments of the inept Deputy Thompson, I take it."

"Hidden on the floor of the bedroom closet. What's the deal with you and Thompson anyway?"

"It's a long story," Horse replied. "Now we have to get this baby open. Under the circumstances, I don't think Jennie would mind."

Mentioning Jennie gave me an idea. "Do you know their little girl's birthday?" I asked.

"Sure, let's see. I used to come to all her parties...uh, she's a Christmas baby. Yes, December 23rd."

"What year was she born? Let's see, yeah, it was the same year as we went on that dive trip—when we took the photo. December 23, 2001."

I immediately started turning the dials 12-23-01, and the lock clicked open.

"Brilliant," he said.

"Lucky," I retorted.

The security box contained the expected items: birth certificates, insurance policies, copies of health and mortgage documents, a few pieces of old jewelry, and some American Eagle gold coins.

"What's this?" Horse picked out something that looked like a cigarette lighter.

"Thank you, Jesus," I said in my best preacher voice, and took the object from him. "This little thing is what they call a travel or flash drive." I took it out of its case and showed him the USB plug. "Plug this into a computer port and it contains enough memory to hold several books. Or, if we're lucky, a lot of research."

"The mother lode," he said. "I'll be dammed. I just can't keep up with all this new technology. That thing doesn't look any bigger than a Bic lighter."

"I wouldn't know about it either, but my husband carried these things around with him to conferences. They were always lying on his desk."

The mention of Bill brought a sudden sting of tears. It came out-of-the blue and hit me in the pit of my stomach. There is no more husband, I thought, feeling the shock of truth.

"Lorelei?"

"I'm okay. I'll put the box back in the closet where I found it, and let's get out of here."

We made our way out of the house and took the same path back to our cars.

"What are you going to do with that thing?" Horse asked. We were standing next to my car in the church parking lot.

"I don't have a computer in my apartment, but I'm sure Mike does."

"Hmm," he said, rubbing his hands together for warmth. It had gotten very chilly, and we could see our breath as we talked under the church's vapor light.

"This drive could be an important piece of evidence."

He gave me a weak smile, "Lorelei, if it is as important as you think, you've just trashed it."

"What do you mean, I 'trashed it'?"

"I've had some experience with the law—enough to know that evidence gotten illegally can't be used. Why don't you give it to me. I'll put it in Hadley's locker, at the shop, and say I just found it."

"Shit," I said, thinking, of course, I knew that. I took a deep breath. "No, I'm going to keep it for now. It may at least point out the killer's motive." I touched his sleeve. "That's worth something, isn't it?"

Horse said, "Yes, but if whoever was in the house with us finds out you have it, it could be dangerous. Please, Lorelei, I'd feel better if you let me take it to the shop, like I said."

"No, I'm going to keep it, but I appreciate your concern. I want to thank you for coming with me. I don't think I would have done this alone."

"Yeah, breaking and entering is one of my former trades," he gave a rueful laugh. "It was like old times."

We parted at the church parking lot, and I drove back to my apartment. It was around midnight before I got to bed. I lodged the flash drive squarely under my pillow—as though it were a diamond. Hard-won; carefully kept.

I slept deeply, but awoke with a start at eight o'clock. After twenty minutes of yoga, I had breakfast, showered and dressed. It was time to see what prize we had captured the night before.

I knocked at Mike's door and announced myself. The door opened slowly, and Mike stood inside wearing stripped pajama bottoms and a tee shirt.

"Lorelei? What's got you up so early?" He brushed his hair back with one hand.

"Can I come in?"

He looked bleary-eyed. I couldn't tell if it was from sleep or drinking or maybe a bit of both.

"Sure. If you don't mind that I'm not quite up and dressed yet. I do have some coffee brewing."

I followed him in and sat down at the dining room table. A copy of the script and various materials about Ibsen were spread across the table.

"I was up pretty late trying to get a better grip on Dr. Stockman. I didn't hear you come in. By the way, where'd you disappear to so fast after rehearsal last night?" He started to clear the table. "Here, let me get all this stuff out of your way."

I put my hand on his arm. "Just leave it, Mike. My dining room table looks about the same."

"So what happened to you?" he asked. "I was hoping we could have a beer or something."

"I had some business to take care of," I said. "Do you have a computer?"

"Business on a Sunday night in Apalach?"

"Apalach? Is that what you locals call it?"

He nodded.

"So, do you have a computer or not?" I persisted, trying to circumvent his inquiry.

"Yes, I have a laptop. Why?"

"Could I use it?" I took the small drive out of my sweater pocket and showed it to him.

He gave me a curious look. "Sure, I guess so. What's on that? Your script?"

"No, just something I want to check out. And I may want to email a friend. You do have email, don't you?"

Mike laughed. "Lorelei, it may surprise you to know that I have all the bells and whistles on my computer...including DSL."

"Great, where is it? Can I use it right now?"

"Wow, you certainly are Ms. Business this morning. Follow me," he said, with a chuckle.

He led me into his bedroom, which was on the opposite wall from mine. I noticed his apartment was a mirror image of the one I occupied, but larger. He had apparently added a deck and enclosed it. The bedroom furnishings were military style—navy with brass fittings, and a maroon bed cover. Pictures of sailing vessels hung on the walls. It looked like the furniture might have been from his childhood bedroom. The laptop was on a desk under the window. Mike flipped it open, and turned it on. The computer booted up with a Winslow Homer screen saver.

"Here you go. I guess you know how to navigate it. I'll get you some coffee. Make yourself at home."

"Thanks, Mike," I said, as he left the room.

I couldn't wait to see what was on the disk. I plugged it into the back of the computer, and the E drive icon appeared. I clicked on it, and saw the title: "Dye-Tracer Study: Graham Springs."

I opened the file to what looked like a chemistry report. There were a various numbered experiments, detailed lists of chemicals, numerical tables, and graphs. I continued scanning through the report hoping to find something intelligible that would explain a threat sufficient to cause Alex Hadley's murder. Finally, I gave up looking at the data and closed the file.

"Dammit," I said, as Mike returned to the room with a steaming mug of coffee.

He handed it to me, and sat on the edge of the bed nearby.

"Problems?"

"I can't read the damn thing. Do you know any chemistry?"

"Chemistry? No. First course I took nearly caused me to flunk out of college. Ask me about astronomy, or even a bit of geology, and I'm your man. Otherwise, I'm strictly an arts guy."

I swiveled the chair around to face Mike. The morning sun streaming into the room lit up his face. He suddenly looked so young. And, I thought, so handsome. Our eyes locked, and a spark of electricity zipped between us. I shuddered and looked away.

"Speaking of chemistry," he said provocatively, and touched my hand.

I pulled away and said, "Mike, this is serious."

"What's on the disk that's got you so uptight?" he asked, straining to look at the screen.

"It's research that Alex Hadley did before he died."

"Oh, I see what you mean about the chemistry. How'd you get the disk anyway?"

"Don't ask," I said.

He frowned and stared at me for a moment. "You think this has something to do with his death?"

"I do."

"Okay, I won't ask where you got it, but what are you going to do with it?"

"That's why I want to use your email. I'm going to send the file to my friend Jeffrey—my first husband, actually. He and Alex were friends. They once worked together. Jeffrey will be able to interpret the data or find someone who can." I turned back to the computer to send the file.

"If it's a lot of data, I think you'd better zip it."

"How do I do that?" I asked, feeling Mike's warm breath as he bent over me.

"Here, let me show you."

106

I slid my chair aside, and he hunched over the computer for several minutes. I felt a flush of warmth from his closeness and the fresh laundered smell of his tee shirt. He obviously had just slipped it on before answering the door.

"Do you know Jeffrey's email address?"

"Yes, I'll send it to him at the university." I moved back to the computer, and typed in the address. I entered "Confidential" in the subject line and inserted a short message asking him to analyze the data a.s.a.p.

"Done," I said, and breathed a sigh of relief, as the message disappeared from the outbox. I removed the flash drive and pocketed it.

I turned back to Mike, who was sitting on the edge of the bed. He gave me a sexy smile.

"Now, about that chemistry question," he said.

"Forget it," I said. "I'm old enough..."

"I know...but you are my stage wife, after all."

I rolled my eyes, got up, and carried the coffee mug back into the kitchen. Mike followed me.

"So how about getting together after rehearsal tonight?"

"Maybe. It depends."

"On what?"

"On what I hear back from Jeffrey. But thanks for your help, Mike. I'll see you at the theatre."

I left before he could protest and returned to my own place. Once inside, I leaned against the closed door. "That was a close call, Lorelei," I said to myself. "That boy could really hook you if you let him."

107

Chapter 15

Much as I dreaded it, I knew I had to tell McBride about my discovery. I also knew I'd have to fudge a bit when he pressed me for the source of the information. Otherwise, my straight arrow detective might feel pressure to charge me with a crime. He was in Tallahassee when I finally reached him on his cell phone.

"And you said you simply found this computer drive...where exactly?"

"Well, it wasn't me actually. It was Horse who found it—in Alex's locker at the dive shop. You know, when he went to clear it out."

Oh boy, I thought. Lorelei you'd better hope that Horse will stand by you with your improvised story. But it was his idea, after all.

"Uh huh, and did it ever occur to Horse—or you for all that—that anything of Alex's would be evidence? He should have called Deputy Thompson before removing anything from that locker."

"He and the deputy aren't exactly the best of friends, and I think Horse maybe didn't want to tangle with him again. You know, since he missed finding the drive when he searched." Good story, I thought.

"Dammit, Lorelei, you know what I mean. That drive could be material evidence. Now it may be worthless. Did Horse find anything else in the locker?"

"Nothing much. Just some diving gear."

As though speaking to himself, McBride said, "Why in hell would he leave a computer drive in a dive shop locker? Lorelei, where's the thing now?"

"I've got it."

"Great. So much for the chain of evidence. Well, just bring it with you when we meet. Are you free Wednesday? I'll be over in Tallahassee again, and we can meet at the lodge."

"Yes, I can be there," I said, hoping to hear from Jeffrey by then and having the chance to redeem Homer's confidence in me. "Are you still going to Tampa for Alex's memorial tomorrow?"

"Yes," he replied.

I said, "I'm curious about what the Rineharts will have to say. And how did your meeting with the professor go?"

"I haven't been to the university yet," he said.

"I'm going to make another appointment with the folks in Fairport. I was supposed to see them today."

"Right," he said. "Sorry, but I need go now. So, I'll see you around noon on Wednesday. Bye."

After the abrupt end to our conversation, I called Delcie.

"Where have you been, Lor? Didn't you get any of my messages?"

I looked at my cell phone and saw there were four messages. I quickly scanned them to find two from Delcie, one from McBride, and one from a number I didn't recognize. "I guess I haven't looked at my cell for awhile. Sorry, Del."

"Forget it. I'm sure you're wrapped up in the play. I know how you get."

"Usually, but this time I'm feeling detached. My part doesn't excite me much, and Renee seems satisfied so..."

"So what are you doing then?"

How much should I tell Delcie, I wondered. "You know, I'm spending some of my time working for you and McBride."

"No surprise, but he hasn't updated me. By the way, I saw Luke this weekend."

"You did? So things are heating up with you two again?"

"No, he flew in for a one-day workshop—some start-up company at the Progress Center in Alachua. We had dinner together."

"And?"

"No 'and'."

"Are you disappointed?"

"A little, but then I didn't get my hopes up too much in the first place."

"Good."

"Luke asked if there was anything new on the Fairport inquiry. Is there?"

"I'm going to make another appointment with them for Wednesday. Did McBride tell you he thinks Alex Hadley's murder may be related to something going on in Fairport?"

"No, like I said, McBride doesn't confide in me. He seems to trust you a lot more. Is there something going on with you two?"

"I'd tell you if there were. Oh, he's asked me to dinner, but I've turned him down. I'm not sure I want to get that friendly with the detective."

"Smart move, girlfriend. You know he's married, and the grapevine has it he's still tough on women. I wouldn't trust him as a romantic partner, if I were you. Hey, are you coming home for Thanksgiving? You know there'd be room at my mom's table for you."

"Thanks, dear, but I'll be staying here. We're having a potluck at the local café. I think I need to spend some time with the cast outside of rehearsals. Besides, I want to take some walks on the beach...where Bill and I used to go."

"Hmm, I understand." She paused for a moment and added, "Anyway, let me know if you find out anything in Fairport. I'd like to touch base with Luke again before Thanksgiving."

I laughed, "Still keeping those hopes alive, are you?"

"Well, you never know. Sometimes it's presence not absence that makes the heart grow fonder."

"I'll call you," I promised.

It was almost ten o'clock when I finally reached Mona Lavender. I apologized for not being able to meet today, as I had promised. We made an appointment for Wednesday morning, and I told her I had a luncheon date at noon.

"No problem, Mrs. Crane," she said, all business. "We can cover a lot of territory in a couple of hours. I'll set out an itinerary for us."

"Will Mayor Stigler be with us?"

"I don't know. I'll have to check with him. Would you like him to join us?"

"Yes, I would. I have some questions about the future growth of Fairport that I'd like to ask him."

"I'm certain I could answer your questions, but if you insist."

110

"It's my preference," I said.

"Nine o'clock then?"

"Yes, at your office. And remember, you promised to take me to Graham Springs."

I settled in at the dining room table to review the play materials, but my mind kept wandering. Would there really be anything on that drive that pointed a finger at Alex Hadley's murderer? Who else was in the Hadley house last night? Was my mugger a burglar, or someone looking for the same thing I was? What are the BSRC members hiding, and how can I flush out more information from them when we meet on Wednesday?

I kept trying to refocus my attention on the script as more and more questions popped into my mind. I wanted to know more about Deputy Thompson, and if it was really Buster Stigler who ran me off the road last week. Questions popped into my mind like cards in the old black fortune balls you shook to reveal different answers.

"Stop it," I said aloud. "Forget the Hadley character, and get back to Mrs. Stockman. Renee may be satisfied, but a satisfying performance isn't a very worthwhile effort."

Ah, back to the seminal actor's question: what did my character want, and what obstacles was she facing? Obviously, she seemed to want a comfortable home and stable life for her family after suffering the privations of living in the mountains. The obstacle? The obvious one was her husband's stubborn arrogance. There was also an internal obstacle—her own pride in his intelligence and integrity. Her pride and loyalty are what made her stand by him in the face of losing everything she cherished.

Did I have it right? I became mesmerized staring at the placid bay waters, and my mind drifted. And what's Lorelei's motivation, I wondered? Why is she getting deeper and deeper into a murder investigation about someone she didn't even know? What does she want?

I needed to clear my mind, and got up from the table. I went into the kitchen and put on the kettle for tea. I had a packet of Chai tea. Its spicy flavor and aroma would help me concentrate.

"Shit. Horse!" The thought was a bolt out of the blue. I had to warn him about the story I told McBride. I called the dive shop.

"Dive Shop. Go Noles," he answered, and I was once again reminded that this was FSU Seminole territory.

"Horse? It's Lorelei."

"Oh, how'ya doing this morning?" His voice dropped to a conspiratorial whisper. "Find out anything in that little computer thing?"

"Not yet. But, I'm calling to warn you."

"About what?"

"I talked with my friend, Detective McBride."

"Detective? Shit, Lorelei...you never told me about a detective."

"Don't get so upset, he's just an old friend—from Gainesville. Anyway, he's involved in the Hadley investigation."

"I thought Thompson..."

"Deputy Thompson is leading the local investigation. McBride's working out of Tallahassee."

"Jeez, FDLE's involved?" He sounded frantic. "And this friend of yours is he your boyfriend, or what?"

"He's not my boyfriend, we're just friends. I helped him out on a case last year, and he asked me to let him know if I learned anything around here."

"So, you've been snooping for the cops? Why the fuck didn't you tell me earlier? I knew I shouldn't trust you the minute you gave me that dumb story about your ex-husband."

"Calm down, Horse. There's nothing to worry about."

"This detective friend of yours, did you tell him about last night?"

"I'm not stupid. Of course, I'm not going to talk about it. I'd be incriminating myself, wouldn't I? Besides, I'm an actress, remember? I'm good at telling stories."

"Don't kid yourself. Anyway, how the hell do I know I can trust you now?"

"Look, Horse, I..."

"Just keep your mouth shut, or we'll both get fried."

He hung up.

"Damn, Lorelei, you botched that one," I said aloud.
I rang him back, but the line was busy. I guessed he was mad enough to take it off the hook.

I left my apartment around noon, and decided to have lunch at Sophie's. The café was busy. When Sophie noticed me standing in the doorway, she ushered me to a table near the kitchen. Menus and bills were scattered on it along with a copy of the local newspaper.
"Here, this is my table. Sit." She scooped up the papers and put them on a chair. "Where have you been? I haven't seen you since last week—when Mike was missing."
I sat down. "Oh, I've been working on the play, and...you know."
She peered down at me, looking as though she could read my face. "So, lunch?"
"Yes."
"Try the special...Tofu Ruben. You won't even know it's not corned beef."
"Sold," I said. "And a café con leche."
"Latte," she corrected.
When she returned with my order, she sat down. "Oy," she heaved a sigh, and said, "So, tell me, Lorelei. How is Mike doing? I haven't seen him either."
I munched on the sandwich before answering. "Delicious. I don't think I've tried tofu like this before. I don't miss the meat at all."
She nodded approvingly.
"About Mike? He seems to be fine. We haven't talked much about his little drinking bout. By the way, he did mention having a fiancée. Charley, I think."
"Charlene," Sophie responded, and a dark look crossed her face.
"What happened to them? I get the impression they're not together anymore."
She shook her head. "She died. It was tragic."
"She's dead? How?" So that explains it, I thought, remembering Mike saying that we both had suffered losses.

"A boating accident," Sophie said. She pursed her lips and shrugged as she got up in response to a call from the woman who was minding the front counter.

I finished the sandwich, and glanced at the newspaper Sophie had moved to the chair. The headline read, "County Commissioners Place Moratorium on Building."

It was a long article describing the response to a rash of developers who were bidding to buy distressed waterfront property in Franklin County with the intention of building large scale condos and hotels.

The article also mentioned the St. Joe Company. St. Joe was the former paper company—associated with the same Ed Ball who once owned Wakulla Springs—which owned almost a million acres of property in the Panhandle. About half their land was within 10 miles of the gulf coast and included water front, forest, and wetlands. The company was now in the development and real estate business.

The scale of the new company's vision troubled many who lived in the region, along with the fact that St. Joe's activities made them a catalyst for fast-paced growth—the "growth machine" as it was called. One pundit described St. Joe's expansive plans as a "Shermanesque march across the Panhandle."

A St. Joe spokesperson argued that development was inevitable—given the population growth in Florida and the natural beauty of what they were dubbing "Florida's Great Northwest." In their favor, their developments were well-planned, and often with environmental sensitivities. They allocated seemingly generous amounts of land for preserves and conservation.

"Déjà vu," I said, thinking about the recurring fight in Gainesville to stop development on the edge of Paynes Prairie. Now, I was aware of another Florida land boom. Major development was happening in one of the last parts of the state where nature prevailed. The gulf coast's seafood industry was already reeling from the shock of regulatory policies, hurricanes, pollution, and reduced water flow in some areas.

I knew that insuring slower and more sustainable growth depended on local groups banding in coalitions. The Panhandle

Citizens Coalition was one such group mentioned in the article. Companies, even those with good intentions—like St. Joe—would always look to their major shareholders interests first.

When I finished the moratorium article, I noticed a headline at the bottom of the front page: "Investigation Closes In Activist's Death." I picked up the paper and avidly read the article. It stated the Wakulla County Sheriff's Office had no new leads in the Hadley case and had finished interviewing persons of interest. It gave a brief bio on Hadley, and mentioned the memorial service in Tampa. The article ended with a quote by Deputy Thompson that left me in shock:

"At this time, we still believe Dr. Hadley's death to be accidental, and expect the case will be closed at the conclusion of the coroner's inquest."

"You're shaking your head at the news?" Sophie said, returning to the table. "I don't blame you."

"No, I've just read something incredible about Alex Hadley's murder investigation."

"Oh, the man who died at the Wakulla Lodge? You said murder? I didn't know he was murdered."

"Apparently neither did the Wakulla Sheriff's Office. Sophie where can I get a copy of the paper?"

"Here take this one," she said, perplexed.

"Thanks," I said, folding the paper and tucking it into my bag.

Sophie said, "Did you read about the building moratorium? It's created a stir. Personally, I'd like to see them make it permanent. My taxes are already going up too high. If it continues, I'll be forced out, and they'll put in a Starbucks."

I sympathized with Sophie, but I was still thinking about the Hadley article. It made me think of Horse. "Sophie can I use your storeroom for a few minutes? I need to make a call and I'd like some privacy."

"Sure," she said and started clearing the table.

I entered the small well-provisioned storeroom and stood at the back door while I tried calling Horse. I had to warn him about the concocted story I gave McBride.

"It's Lorelei. Don't hang up," I said, when I heard his voice.

"Why not?" he asked. I could almost feel the anger coming through the phone.

"Take it easy, will you? I've called to warn you about something, or we'll both get into trouble."

He grunted. "Like I trust you to keep me out of trouble?"

"Please, Horse. Just hear me out."

"Okay, shoot."

I told him what I told McBride about finding the computer drive in Hadley's locker at his shop.

"Jesus, Lorelei. Now you want me to perjure myself?"

"You were the one who came up with the idea. Anyway, it's better than being charged with breaking into his house, isn't it?"

"I don't know. I could say Jennie gave me the okay. I did want to contact her."

"Too late, Horse. You've got to back me up on the story."

"I don't know. I'll think about it," he said, and hung up.

Despite his anger, I felt sure that Horse would stick with me. What choice did he have, after all?

I left the storeroom, gave Sophie a hug goodbye, and paid for lunch. It wasn't until I was entering the theatre that I remembered what she had said about Mike's fiancée dying in a boating accident. How terrible, I thought, especially since Mike was a boat captain. I knew, at some point, I would have to ask him about it. I also wondered what McBride would have to say about the article with the surprising quote from Deputy Thompson.

Chapter 16

I yelled, "Mike, help!" as I ran out of my apartment and banged on his door.

He opened the door. "Lorelei? What?" he said, pulling me inside.

I collapsed on his sofa, and started to cry.

"What happened? Is someone in your apartment?" He grabbed a boat hook from the wall and started for the door.

"No, no. I don't think anyone's still there. But someone was. Go look. Please."

In a few minutes he returned. "Jesus. Somebody's really trashed the place. All your stuff..."

"I know. Come back in there with me, will you? I've got to see if he got it."

"What?"

"The flash drive. That must be what he or she was looking for. C'mon," I said, grabbing Mike's arm for support. I was really shaken. Nothing like this had ever happened to me before.

We went back into my apartment. All the lights were lit. "In the bedroom," I said, pulling him along with me.

The bedding had been torn off the bed. We looked everywhere. The flash drive was gone.

"McBride's going to kill me," I said, standing in the middle of the living room.

"Kill you for what? Christ, this isn't your fault."

"Should I call 911 or the police?" I said. "Their number's on the side of the refrigerator."

"I'll get it." Mike went into the kitchen and found the number for the sheriff's department. He dialed and handed me the phone.

I took it, and began shaking as I spoke. "I'd like to report a break-in, a burglary."

They told me someone would be there within fifteen minutes. While we waited, Mike helped me look around the bedroom one more time. The sheriff's deputy arrived, but we still hadn't found it.

"I don't know," I said to most of the officer's questions.

"Well somebody sure was looking for something," the young deputy replied as he surveyed the apartment. "I'll turn in the report. If you think of anything that's missing, you call us." He handed me a card.

"I will, sir. Thanks for coming so quickly."

He touched the tip of his hat and left.

I stuck the card alongside the telephone where I had already placed a card from another Franklin County deputy, the one I obtained when I was run off the road on the way to Eastpoint. I was beginning to get a collection. I wondered if they'd soon recognize a pattern and label me a crank.

"C'mon, I'll help you straighten things up," Mike said. "Could of been they were just looking for jewelry or cash. Sometimes there are transients along the waterfront. This part of Water Street is pretty deserted at night. Maybe we'll still find your drive tossed out in the street. Anyway, I copied everything on it."

"Oh, thank goodness you did, but it's not the same thing as having the original, is it? As for your theory, I didn't bring any jewelry with me. I didn't bring anything of value, really—except for my wedding ring, and I'm wearing it."

"Well, let's just get the place back in order, and I'll make you a stiff drink at my place. We'll figure something out."

We spent the next half hour restoring my temporary abode. Articles had been pulled off the bathroom and the kitchen shelves, and the bedroom drawers had been emptied along with clothing I had left in my suitcases. It appeared to be an act of pure viciousness— even my play materials were scattered all over the living room floor. Whoever did it not only stole Hadley's data drive but obviously meant to send me a message. The message I got was that someone knew who I was and what I doing...other than acting. I felt thoroughly violated. And I was scared.

After making my apartment presentable, we returned to Mike's place and once again I collapsed on his couch.

He fixed me a drink. "Here. It's Weller's bourbon. Just sip it. It's a magic potion with the power to transform even the worst case of nerves—I save it for hurricane season."

"Thanks, Mike," I murmured, taking a sip and feeling the liquid slide smooth and warm all the way down. "Hmm, it's good," I said. "I don't know what I'd have done if you weren't here. I was so frightened when I saw the apartment."

"I don't blame you. I'm just glad you weren't there when they broke in."

That thought hadn't yet occurred to me, but it brought back memories of the mugging I received in Hadley's house. My guess was that the two incidents were connected, and the person or persons who did it knew exactly when I wouldn't be at home. I took a couple more sips of the bourbon and began to feel more relaxed.

"I really don't know what I'm doing in the middle of all of this," I said.

"What do you mean?"

"I think I need to figure out how and why I've gotten so involved in Alex Hadley's death. It's ironic, actually. Here I am trying to work out Mrs. Stockman's motivation, and I don't even understand what the hell I'm doing."

He laughed as he sat down next to me on the couch. "I guess that's why we're actors. It's easier to get into someone else's life than to figure out our own."

"Maybe, but lately I feel like I'm an observer—a member of the audience—watching my own life play out."

Mike moved closer to me and said, "Detachment's one way to deal with the pain, isn't it?"

I gestured to the bottle of liquor. "And that's another way, right?"

"You got me there," he said, lifting his glass in a toast. "Different strokes..."

"Mike, I had lunch at Sophie's today. She told me your fiancée was killed in a boating accident. Is that her in the picture?" I nodded toward the family photograph.

He stiffened following my glance. "Yes, that's Charley."

"Tell me about her...about the two of you. It'll distract me from being afraid."

He took a long swig of his drink and gave me a questioning glance. "You really want to know?"

I said, "Yes," and slipping out of my shoes I pulled my feet up under me on the couch.

There was a long silence while he stared at the picture.

"Charley and I were college sweethearts. We got pinned during our senior year, and we decided to marry after graduation. Her family decided otherwise. You know the usual complaint, 'you're too young.' They wanted me to establish myself before they would consent. Bottom line, they were wealthy and very socially conscious. I came from a family of fishermen."

"What'd you do?"

"Charley wouldn't go against her folks. Instead, after college, we moved to Atlanta and lived together for a couple of years—much to her parent's displeasure. Then my dad died, and I had to move back here to take over his seafood business."

"You own the store downstairs?"

"Yes, and some other properties around town." He paused, and said, "Charley got a job in Tallahassee—at Florida State—there wasn't anything for her to do in this town. It was there she met Rick Lucas."

"She dumped you for him?"

"Not really. When we left Atlanta we had agreed to date other people for a while. She just made a bad choice. Rick started getting abusive, and Charley came running back to me—I realized how much I missed her. We got engaged, and then..."

Mike started to choke up, and he stopped talking. I could tell he was trying to control his emotions.

I moved closer, and put my arm around him. "It's okay, Mike. You don't have to go on, if it's too much. I understand." I felt tears stinging my eyes as if his pain had pierced through to my own. "Really, it's okay," I murmured again, as if talking to myself."

"No," he said, pulling away. "I have to talk about it. I want you to know."

He took another sip of whiskey, put it down on the table and turned to me with a shattered look. I could barely hear him when he said, "Lorelei, I killed her."

"What?"

"It happened on Thanksgiving weekend. It was overcast and stormy weather was predicted. Against her protests—Charley wasn't much of a water person—I persuaded her to go out for a short ride on my boat. I wanted to show off the new boat, and I wanted her to see the waterfront property I had inherited."

"You were trying to impress her."

"Yes, I guess so. A storm came up—it can happen pretty quick out in the gulf—and I was having trouble handling the boat. A big wave dragged Charley overboard...I couldn't see her for the driving rain."

"Oh, how awful," I said, immediately remembering his sorrowful soliloquy about drowning.

"Her body washed up on shore over at Eastpoint."

"How long ago did this happen?"

"It'll be seven years."

"Oh Mike, I'm so sorry."

"I know," he said, standing. "You'd think I'd be over it by now, but..." He picked up the bottle and placed it in the cabinet along the wall.

"You don't want any more of this, do you?" he asked, as an afterthought.

"No. But, do you want to talk some more? Tell me about her." I said, looking at the photograph.

"What is there to say? I loved her. I haven't been able to get close to anyone since."

"You still blame yourself for the accident, don't you?"

"I guess so. Sophie's talked to me about it so much—she's a really kind woman, you know—but the guilt."

A long silence was permeated with sadness. My heart ached for Mike...and for the reawakening of my own grief.

"Is there anything I can do to help?" I asked.

He gave me a soulful look, "Sleep here...with me. Will you, Lorelei?"

"Mike, I..."

"We don't have to do anything, you know, sexual. We can just keep each other warm...and safe from our demons."

I wasn't eager to return to my violated apartment, and Mike looked so fragile. "All right, Mike. Just this once."

He led me into the bedroom, and handed me a pajama top. I changed in the bathroom. When I returned, the bedroom was lit only by the glow of the full moon streaming across the bed. Mike was already there—sitting up in the bed.

I got in beside him. He held me in his arms, and stroked my hair without saying a word. Silent tears rolled down my face as I remembered how good it felt to be held with such caring.

His hand gently touched my face, and he said, "Don't cry, Lorelei. You're so beautiful. He wouldn't want you to be sad."

I thought he's right. Bill would tell me to move on with my life. I turned my head and kissed Mike on the cheek. "Thanks," I said. "You're very sweet, you know."

His lips touched mine, hesitated, and pressed harder. I responded to his kiss with unleashed ardor. My pent up need for intimacy surprised me.

Mike's hand reached into my pajama top and gently caressed my breasts. I felt my nipples harden.

We were both breathing hard.

"Mike, you said..." I began to push his hand away, my brain overcoming the response of my body.

"Do you really want me to stop?" he asked, in a husky voice.

I could feel the heat from our bodies as he moved his body closer.

It's been so long, I thought.

"No," I said, twisting against him as our embrace tightened, and we slid down on the bed, locked together as one.

I awoke to the aroma of bacon and coffee. The sun was shining, and I heard Mike in the kitchen. I quickly got into my clothes and joined him.

He kissed me. "Good morning, Lorelei. I hope you slept as well as I did."

Mike appeared unusually cheerful, and even youthful, I thought ruefully. I took a deep breath. "Hmmn, you sure know how to wake a woman up. Everything smells delicious." I picked a piece of bacon from the plate and started to chew on it.

"Yes, I slept wonderfully—thanks to you." I gave him a meaningful look, which he returned with a sweet smile.

"Was my apartment trashed or was it only a nightmare?"

"Probably both would be the correct answer," he said. "Have a seat. How do you like your eggs...fried or scrambled?"

"However you like yours," I said. "I like them both ways."

He gave me a mug of coffee.

"So, any ideas who broke into your apartment last night?"

I wrapped my hands around the cup, and walked over to the windows that faced the bay. As usual, I was amused to see the pelicans and seagulls snuggled up on the pier below. Did they ever leave?

I said, "Yes, I have an idea about it, but, it's too beautiful a day to deal with that." I was beginning to conclude that Buster Stigler, and the BSRC had something to do with all of my encounters. They definitely seemed to be hiding something, and Buster was angry and impulsive enough to be talked into anything that required brawn. Even Mona Lavender seemed capable of it. I would tell McBride about it on Wednesday.

Mike brought the plates of food to the table, and we sat down to eat.

"Thanks for...last night," he said, and paused. "and for listening to my sad story. It's so easy to talk to you."

"I'm glad you were able to talk about it. I understand now why it's taking you a long time to get over it. Such a tragic accident."

"Lorelei, I want to know more about you. You haven't told me anything about your husband's death."

I shuddered at the thought of exposing the story of Bill death. "You know, Mike, it still too early for me to talk about it. I'm sure you understand."

Mike nodded. "Then how about spending the day with me?"

I didn't have anything scheduled. "What did you have in mind?"

"I'd like to take you out onto the bay—give you a personal eco-tour."

"Lovely," I said. "I'd like that. I have a couple of phone calls to make, but I can be ready by ten."

"Good, I'll pick up some sandwiches from Sophie's and meet you at the dock."

Mike gave me directions to his boat, and I returned to my apartment.

Everything in the apartment appeared normal. I made one more futile effort to find the flash drive. I called Jeffrey and was eager to hear if he had received my email. His phone was turned off. I realized he had probably gone to Tampa for Alex's memorial service. I tried McBride, and got voice mail. I left a message telling him about the article quoting Deputy Thompson. I didn't want him to know about my break-in until I saw him. He'd only be worried—or mad, or both.

Next, I thought of calling my mother, but remembered she wouldn't be home from her cruise until the weekend. Despite the evening spent with Mike, or maybe because of it, I began to feel depressed. I chided myself for having sex with him. I didn't want that kind of a relationship now and vowed I wouldn't let it happen again. It was a night when both of us desperately needed each other. It was a one time thing, I thought. I hoped Mike wouldn't expect otherwise.

"Get up, and get moving, Lorelei," I instructed myself.

I showered and did some yoga before dressing for the day. At nine-forty five, I left for the dock feeling invigorated and looking forward to a day on the water.

Mike was waiting for me dockside at the Scipio Creek Marina. He helped me down into the boat. It was a small flat-bottomed boat with a bimini canopy.

"I hope you put on sunscreen," he said. "It's deceptively cool out on the water, but the sun…"

"Excuse me, Captain," I said, noting the captain's hat he wore. "But I was raised in South Florida. I know about sun."

"Right," he replied, looking apologetic. "I guess I'm used to warning Yankee tourists."

He revved the engine, and we slowly backed away from the dock.

Mike was standing at the controls, and I sat on the bench next to him.

He maneuvered the boat along the shoreline. It was populated with seafood packing companies and derelict boats…one was half-sunk in the water.

"It looks so dilapidated," I said. "The fishing industry is in trouble here, isn't it?"

"It isn't what it used to be in my dad's time, but we still produce about ten percent of all the oysters sold in the country. We've got a thriving industry in mullet, grouper, blue crab, and shrimp, of course. But you've seen the shrimpers when you passed through Eastpoint."

"Yes, but I also saw packing houses destroyed by Hurricane Dennis. And then I read about all the land speculation and the St. Joe development plans."

Mike shrugged, "I know," he said, steering into the open bay. "It isn't St. Joe's developments I worry so much about; it's all the other stuff that will follow."

"Like strip malls, chain stores, and high rise condos," I said.

"Yes, but also as we move from agriculture to development more lawns and golf courses will be fertilized, and…"

"Meaning more run-off into rivers and springs," I said, thinking about the mats of algae I'd seen covering portions of the springs.

"And there goes the quality of water for every living thing and purpose." He handed me a pair of binoculars. "You might see an osprey or an eagle around here. The grasses and reeds are an important part of the estuary."

"Estuary? I know the term but refresh my memory."

"Basically, it's a body of water where fresh river water combines with sea water—the gulf in this case and the Apalachicola River. It's an essential spawning ground for fish, shrimp, and a whole host of marine animals. The cleanliness of the bay is also the reason why we have some of the best oyster beds in the world. There are several estuaries in the Panhandle, but Apalachicola Bay is the largest in the contiguous United States...something like well over 200,000 acres."

"Wow, that's impressive. You know, I've yet to have my first oyster dinner in town."

"We'll have to remedy that. We've got some great restaurants, but I'd start with Papa Joes right here at the marina. It's a landmark. The seafood's as good as you'll get anywhere, and there's a sign over the entrance that says, *It Ain't Easy.* Coming from a fisherman's family, it always makes me smile."

"I'd love to try it," I said. Then pointing to the railroad trestle running across the river, I asked. "What's that about?"

"That's the old Apalachicola Northern Railroad. Around the turn of the century—when the oyster packing business was booming—it used to make fresh oyster runs to Atlanta. Around that same time this was a huge lumber town—cypress especially. Underwater there's a fortune in trees and lumber fallen from the barges heading up north. Some people make a business of what's called 'deadhead logging.' The cypress is especially valuable."

"Amazing," I said. This was a world I never knew existed.

"There were timber mills all over the region, and turpentine extraction as well."

"Do you think there'd still be some of those industries upstream of Graham Springs?" I said, wondering if Alex Hadley had found out the springs were polluted.

"Could be a small turpentine mill, but I'm not sure if any of them are still in business. I'd say there are toxins—from old St. Joe Paper—still leaching into the water all around here." He steered the boat close to the shore, and said, "See that tree there—the one with the broad leaf? That's an Ogeeche Tupelo."

"Tupelo honey?" I asked.

"Yes, the tree grows here, on some small rivers in Georgia, and on the Yangtse River in China. That's where the beekeepers have to place their hives. "

"No wonder the honey so expensive."

"Uh huh, but they say it's healthier for you than other kinds. You can get some while you're here."

"Tell me more. Apalachicola's history is fascinating. I can't recall learning anything about it in school."

Mike casually steered the boat midstream. There were no other boats in sight. "The railroad had killed the cotton shipping industry—that was the big thing around the time of the Civil War. Believe it or not, our sleepy little town even had foreign consulates because of the importance to Europe of cotton shipping. We were the third largest port in the country. Then seafood, which has been sold commercially since before the war, became our next big industry."

"Sounds like the area's been very adaptable."

"So far we have been, but we've got problems that aren't easy to solve."

It was chilly under the canopy, and I climbed out onto the sunny deck. "I realize how little I really know about Florida," I said. "I think growing up in south Florida keeps you ignorant about the rest of the state north of Orlando and Disneyworld. Even Gainesville and North Central Florida were different, but this area...you know, when you drive the Interstates all the time, you don't learn much."

Mike took a deep breath and seemed to relish the fresh bay air. "Glorious, isn't it?"

"It sure is," I replied, stretching my legs out on the warm deck and leaning against the canopy pole for support. "Tell me about the problems you mentioned?"

Mike frowned. "There are tremendous demands on water—especially from the growth in Atlanta. Believe it or not, their water needs impact both the quantity and quality of water that flows into Apalachicola Bay. The watershed combines three rivers that flow down from the north. And I haven't even said anything about the damn U.S. Army Corps of Engineers which keeps on dredging the river like it was a major navigable channel...which it isn't!"

"Interesting," I said.

Mike continued, "Solving the watershed problems has created such huge political, economic, and environmental battles they call it the Tri-State Water Wars—Alabama, Georgia, and Florida. We're not just talking about any water fight like the one down in Tampa. The Apalachicola River and Bay are of major environmental and economic significance. By the way, the Apalachicola is the largest river in Florida. Bet you didn't know that either."

"No, I didn't."

"This is the second largest estuary reserve in the U.S. with more biodiversity than almost anywhere else. It's been designated as a National Estuarine Sanctuary, and that's forced the three states to work together to protect it."

I was impressed by Mike's knowledge and his passion.

After a few minutes, he sidestepped the wheel and moved closer to me to look at me.

"What?"

"I don't know. It's the way you look sitting there in the sun— your hair shining like bronze makes you look like a goddess."

"Oh my, what a compliment," I replied, reflexively pushing my hair back off my face.

"I guess I've had enough of playing tour guide. I'd rather just enjoy the day with a beautiful woman. Do you mind?"

"No, I don't mind. But what you've told me about the bay has wetted my interest. I'd like to learn more about it and the whole area. Can you recommend a book or two?"

"I wouldn't know where to begin, but we have an excellent bookstore, Downtown Books. They're real friendly, and they carry all sorts of good stuff about the area. They'll show you some books that might interest you."

He returned to the controls and steered the boat into a narrow channel of the river under a thick canopy of trees.

"Just finish the story about the water wars. Did the three states settle their differences?"

"Hell, no. One time, the governors locked themselves up in a hotel room to come up with a compromise, but even that didn't work.

Some of the issues have gone up to the Supreme Court, and you can imagine the political maneuvering in Washington."

"What a shame. The whole state's changing so fast."

"Not the whole state," he said, and flashed a bright smile. "Now, Ms. Crane, how about a cold beer and a gentle ride through the swamp? If you want to see Florida as it's been for thousands of years...this is the place."

"I thought it was politically incorrect to use the word swamp. Isn't it called wetlands?"

"A swamp is a type of wetland with woody plants and trees. This feels almost primeval. It just sinks into your bones. Can you feel it?"

I tried to absorb the atmosphere. He was right, it did feel as though we were drifting back to some primitive time. "Perfect," I said, "but don't bring us closer to the bank and the alligators."

"You scared of gators?" he asked, grinning.

"That's a long story," I replied as I slid back into the cabin, opened the cooler, and brought out two cold beers.

We glided through the brackish water, listening to the sounds of the birds, and the constant buzz of insects in the dense tropical canopy. From time to time, Mike would point to a turtle sunning itself on a fallen log, or a white heron standing majestically on a jutting piece of bank. We didn't speak. The utter solemnity of nature's beauty filled my heart with an almost painful feeling of unity and connectedness...it was an extraordinary experience.

Chapter 17

I got up early Wednesday morning and did my exercise routine. Yesterday's boat trip with Mike turned out to be a relaxing and spiritually satisfying experience. He was an easy companion, and there was no pressure from the previous evening's tryst. We simply enjoyed each other's company. Rehearsal went smoothly, and the day had ended on a positive note.

While showering, I began to feel tense about my meeting Mona Lavender and Mayor Stigler. This might be my only chance to find out what they were hiding—why they tried to stonewall me about Graham Springs. I normally don't like confrontation, and prefer to use more subtle strategies to achieve my goals. Some people might call it manipulative, but I think it a more civil strategy.

I arrived at Fairport City Hall punctually at nine. Big Mona and Pete were waiting for me in Pete's office. We exchanged greetings and set off immediately. This time, Pete took his car, a Cadillac Escalade, and they seated me in the front passenger seat.

"We're going to Graham Springs, right?" I asked.

"Yes, we're going to the springs," Pete responded.

"I'd like you to tell me more about this controversy between Alex Hadley and Dr. Matos. Specifically, what impact it had that got you all so upset with Hadley?"

"You tell her, Mona," Pete said. I had the feeling they had rehearsed the subject.

She said, "Hadley was spreading the rumor that development at Graham Springs would have a disastrous effect on Wakulla Springs. He never backed up his claim. We came to believe it was nothing more than a hoax. Some wild eyed attempt to keep growth from taking place in the area. You know how desperate some of these environmentalists can become."

"And, thank God, the investigation into his death is almost over," Pete said. "It's put a cloud over the whole town. Did you see they're calling it an accident?"

I turned in my seat to face Mona. "I read that in the paper. But Hadley was a respected scientist. They usually can back up their claims."

Mona said, "That's just it, the most real authority on hydrology in the region is..."

"I know," I said, "It's Dr. Matos at FSU."

"Yes, Dr. Matos. When we asked him about Hadley's claim, he dismissed it. He said his own research showed no connection between the two springs. His research associate, Dr. Lucas, even made a presentation to our council on the subject."

"And that's why you saw Hadley as a trouble-maker?"

"Exactly. For some reason, he either was trying to stop any development at the springs, or maybe he wanted to drive down the price of property so he could buy it himself. He liked to dive at Graham."

"I wonder what development you think he was trying to stop?" I asked, sounding only mildly interested.

Mona and Pete glanced at one another in the rear view mirror.

"Go on, tell her," he said.

She took a deep breath, and said, "We do have some development ideas for Graham Springs."

"We? Who is we?" I asked.

"The Beautiful Springs Resource Council, of course."

"I see. You mean the council owns the spring's property?"

"Initially some of us owned parcels, but we've agreed to pool our acquisitions."

"So, is there really any property left for sale at Graham Springs?"

Mona paused again. "Well, yes and no. It depends upon how much we sell to another buyer who's interested in a rather large parcel."

"This doesn't happen to be an Atlanta company, by any chance?" I said.

Both Pete and Mona did a double take—first at me then at one another in the rear view mirror."

Mona spoke first, "That is highly confidential." I witnessed her face morph from fear to anger as she demanded, "Who told you about it?" To my surprise, she actually punched Pete in the shoulder from behind. "I'll bet it was that blabbering roughneck son of yours! Isn't there any way we can be rid of him?"

Pete said, "It better not be my damn son, but I've been wondering what he's up to. He's been walkin' around grinning like he's got some big secret. It's not like him."

Mona turned to look out the side window. I could tell she was steaming mad.

I thought, it would serve you right, Buster, if I let you take the heat. But instead I said, "Oh, no. It wasn't Buster."

Mona's head swiveled around. "Then who? Just how much do you know?" she demanded again.

"I'm not at liberty to say." There, I thought, so much for you and your confidential deal.

Her eyes narrowed. This was the witchy edge to her otherwise smooth veneer. She seemed to be considering another way to get me to reveal my source, but I steered the conversation in another direction.

"So that's it? You were afraid Alex Hadley's findings— whatever they were—would sour your deal with this big client?"

"Yes," Pete admitted, turning off the main road onto a narrow and bumpy gravel road that appeared overgrown with brush.

"But why all the secrecy about who the prospective buyer is?" I didn't want to reveal I already knew why. That Luke's company wanted to set up a water bottling plant, and that it was certain to ignite a political firestorm.

Big Mona shot Pete a negative look warning him to say no more.

"Well, let's just say folks around here are already uptight about forest clear cutting and land speculation. They'd really be worried if some big out-of-state company was to own a hunk of one of our springs," he said. "Here we are, Graham Springs." He stopped the car, and we got out.

Pete led the way down a small sandy path through the woods until we reached the opening onto the spring. It was serene and beautiful, as I had expected it to be. The dark blue-green water, shimmering in the sunlight, revealed tall grasses beneath the surface. We stood at the edge which, like a beach, had a shallow sandy bottom. Looking beyond—along a heavily wooded area—the water was deeper and darker. I took a deep breath of the fresh earthy aroma of trees and water and saw a bright red cardinal swoop across the surface.

"Lovely," I said. "How big is the spring?"

Pete glanced around and pointed to the water on our right. "The spring pool is about two hundred feet in diameter. As you can see, it's quite shallow here, but at the other end it drops to about fifty or sixty feet.

"It looks relatively clear," I said, but glancing to the other bank I saw a green mat covering part of the surface.

"You've got hydrilla and maybe some kind of algae," I said. "We've got similar problems on our prairie marshland in Gainesville. The park rangers are forever trying to get rid of it."

Ignoring my comment, the mayor exclaimed, in a voice that reflected genuine emotion. "It's beautiful here, isn't it?"

"Yes, it is," I said. "Too bad there has to be any development in areas like this."

"It is private property," Mona said, defensively, swatting at a mosquito that buzzed around her face. "Why shouldn't we be able to enjoy it...as long as it's not ruined?"

I felt certain a nearby water bottling plant would ruin the springs. It was hard to imagine such an industry exploiting such a place. Yet I knew one of the springs north of Gainesville had a water bottling plant. It wasn't at all uncommon now that bottled water was America's drink of preference.

"If I understand correctly, you and the BSRC pretty much own all the land surrounding the spring?"

"About sixty acres," Pete said, stooping down to sweep his hand through the water. "The National Park Service owns some where it borders on the Apalachicola National Forest." He stood, touched the water to his lips, and said, "Constant seventy degree temperature. Just perfect."

"Do you think you'd be interested in buying if something becomes available?" Mona asked.

I was thoroughly enchanted by the scene, and I walked further along the edge to get a view from another location. "Definitely," I said. "When will you know about your other buyer?" I found myself actually considering the purchase, until I remembered that Hadley's research might result in the state acquiring it.

"Soon, I think," she said. "It will be anytime now, don't you think so, Pete?"

Pete didn't respond. He strolled along the edge of the spring, looking up and down into the surrounding tree canopy as if conducting a survey.

"He's always creating imaginary parcels for sale," Mona explained.

Drooling over dollar signs is more like it, I guessed.

"There are no problems with the water quality, or getting permits to build or anything? No chance of someone showing up with Hadley's findings?" I asked, pointedly.

"None whatsoever," Pete said, walking back toward us.

Mona nodded agreement. "Don't think it rude—may he rest in peace—but Alex Hadley's theories went with him to the grave. Didn't they?"

Did I see her wink at Pete, or was it just a twitch in her eye as she swatted at another mosquito.

"What's the price per acre?" I asked.

"That will depend on a number of factors. Right now, I'd say it'll be starting in the neighborhood of fifty to sixty thousand an acre." He checked with Mona who nodded back with a satisfied look on her face.

"Isn't that kind of steep for raw land in this county?"

Mona looked affronted at my objection. "My dear, surely you understand that land for sale near a beautiful spring like this has become a rarity in Florida. People from up north will think nothing of that price."

"I guess you're right. I'll give it some thought," I said.

We returned to the car and headed back to Fairport. No longer listening to their chit chat, I had learned enough to figure out the game the two of them were playing, and I definitely caught a whiff of greed. Always a good motive for murder.

I drove on to the Wakulla Springs Lodge to meet McBride for lunch. He was waiting for me in the lobby.

He put his hands up to ward off my question, "I got your message about Thompson's statement. Just remember you can't always believe what you read in the papers."

"So, it isn't true?"

"I'll tell you about it later," McBride said, as he led the way into the dining room,

The hostess seated us at a table for two against the window.

"So, how'd it go with the Fairport realtors? Pick up anything new?" he asked.

"Nothing but the dollar signs in their eyes. Boy, they're practically drooling over the chance to sell the Graham Springs land."

"Well, I've got some news. An FBI check revealed your Mona Lavender has a bit of a record."

"For what?"

"Seems she was involved in a pyramid scheme in upstate New York about sixteen years ago. Somehow it was connected with the mob, and that's why the bureau was on it. They never were able to pin anything solid on her, but she's in their files—under a different name, as you'd expect." He paused, and added, "You don't look as surprised as I thought you'd be."

"I always thought there was more to her story—there's something real hard behind that fake small town friendliness. I recognized a fellow actor right away, but the mob? That part is a shocker."

McBride looked weary.

"What's going on with you, Homer? You look like you haven't had much sleep."

He rubbed the back of his neck. "All this traveling back and forth from Gainesville triggers my insomnia. It's a real pain. I miss my desk," he said, with a mock boyish sulk.

"Poor Homer," I said, and patted his hand. "How did the memorial service for Alex go? Did you learn anything from his wife or father-in-law?"

Before he could answer, the waiter came to the table and recited the luncheon specials. He took our orders and left.

McBride stared out the window.

I followed his gaze. You could see through the tree lined expanse of lawn all the way down to the lagoon.

"It's sure peaceful here, isn't it? A hell of a place for a murder."

I said, "I don't know, check out the vultures on the beach. I'm sure they have a human counterpart in the vicinity."

He snickered. "You're right about that. Hey, you know what they call a group of vultures?"

"No."

"A wake. A wake of vultures."

Sometimes McBride really surprised me with stuff like this. "How'd you learn that?"

"My son told me. He read it in a book somewhere."

We stared at the large black birds. Some had their wings outstretched—sunning themselves like any tourist would do.

Our food arrived. My salad was huge, and I was delighted by the delicious corn bread that came with it. It had the slightly sweet taste I preferred. The food at the lodge, billed as traditional southern cuisine, was plentiful and delicious.

"About the Rinehart's?" I reminded him, as I dug into my lunch.

"Oh, yeah," he said, taking a sip of water. "Mrs. Hadley's father, Cliff Rinehart, says he came up to give Hadley an ultimatum. Apparently, his daughter and granddaughter have been living with him ever since they left Hadley. The daughter's been real unhappy, wanted to go home, but was afraid."

"Afraid?"

McBride finished a bite of his hamburger and said, "Yeah, apparently some of Fairport's fine citizens had gotten nasty with them. Didn't like what Hadley was stirring up."

"Fries?" he asked, shoving his plate toward me.

I pushed the plate back. "Love to, but no thanks," I said. "I heard the same story from Horse. Hadley's daughter was nearly run-over by some hooligans. I'll bet Buster Stigler was involved."

He nodded. "Anyway, Rinehart apparently never did get along with Hadley. Thought his son-in-law was an arrogant, selfish...you know. So when his precious daughter started getting depressed over their separation, he drove up to Fairport. Found out Hadley was at Wakulla and intended to have it out with him. That's when— according to him—he found Hadley dead."

"How'd he get into the room?"

"Says he got the maid to unlock it. Gave her some cockamamie story."

"Do you believe him?" I asked.

"I'm keeping an open mind. He wouldn't be the first father to want to kill his son-in-law. He was seen hurrying down the back steps near Hadley's room, and he didn't even report what he found until he was on his way home."

"You think he got in there when Hadley was in the shower and put the ants in the costume?"

"Don't know. Could have been they were put there while the costume was in Hadley's car, or in the room. Rinehart's a hobby gardener, and he did know about Hadley's allergy."

I laughed, "C'mon, Homer, you told me everybody knew he had a serious allergy problem. It doesn't take a gardener to know that ants bite! You're reaching on that one."

McBride shrugged and looked chagrined. "Maybe, but something about the guy's story didn't hold up. I've got to think about it some more."

"What about Buster Stigler. You told me he does landscape work here. I'd pick him as a more likely suspect."

McBride nodded. "Don't worry, he's on my list. Like I said, there are plenty of suspects to go around. By the way, I ran into Jeff Waterman at the memorial. He asked me if I'd heard from you."

I thought about the data I had sent to him. "Speaking of Jeffrey, you know that drive I had of Hadley's?"

McBride put his hamburger down, and said, "Had?"

"I tried to call you about it but…"

"About what?"

"It was stolen from my apartment in Apalachicola. I was at rehearsal Monday night and someone broke in and took it. They trashed the place."

"Did you report it to the sheriff's office?"

"Of course, but don't worry. I had emailed a copy of the contents to Jeffrey to evaluate. He should have it when he goes in to work today."

McBride put his head in his hands. "Jesus, Lorelei…I really worry about you. You're not trained to handle this kind of stuff." He looked up and asked, "Did they at least get any prints? Do you have any idea who might have done it?"

"No, all the deputy did was take down the information and tell me to call if I found anything missing."

"Shit," McBride said. "You see the connection, don't you? Whoever took the drive may be afraid of what Hadley found. They could be involved in his murder."

I felt guilty about duping McBride and messing up important evidence. I watched as he absently took out a pack of cigarettes, tapped one out of the pack and tamped it on the table. He put it and the pack alongside his plate.

Finally, he looked up at me. "So? Who broke in? Could it have been Stigler's son?"

"I thought it might be him. Did your men find any evidence that he was the one who bumped me off the road?"

"No, unfortunately, his truck was all spit and polish. There wasn't even so much as a scratch on the bumper. One of my guys did put a bit of fear into him—let him believe he was a person of interest in the Hadley murder. That should have been enough to scare him into behaving but maybe it didn't take."

"I would think so," I said, and started buttering a piece of corn bread and handed it to McBride. "Go ahead and eat it, Homer. You didn't even finish your sandwich."

I found myself sounding like Sophie. I could almost hear her saying, "Eat, eat, you'll feel better." He ate the corn bread and stared out the window.

I wondered how I should admit to McBride that my apartment thief was probably the mugger who attacked me at Hadley's house. I was beginning feel ensnared by my own lies—*oh what a tangled web we weave when first we practice to deceive.* A line from Shakespeare, I guessed.

McBride signaled the waiter and ordered coffee.

I weighed the implications of lying to him about the flash drive and decided to take the plunge. "Actually, Homer, I have a confession to make. I hope you'll forgive me." I told him the entire story about Horse and me entering the Hadley house, my being mugged, and finding the drive in a security box. He listened with his head down. I sensed his mounting anger.

When I finished my story, he took a sip of coffee, and gave me a hard look. His voice was measured, "You do know you risked being arrested for breaking and entering. And your friend Horse risked even more. He's already got a record."

"For what?" I asked, not surprised given Horse's attitude toward the law.

"Drugs—in California. Heroin, to be specific. Guess that's how he got his nickname."

"So both Horse and Mona Lavender have had criminal records."

"Yup," he said. "If you'd scratch around enough, you'd find a lot of people who have moved to Florida to get away from their old lives."

McBride cocked his head and grinned suddenly. It was unexpected. I was prepared for a blistering lecture. "It's my fault. I never should have gotten you involved in this investigation. First, someone tries to bump you off the highway, then you tell me you've been mugged, and now there's this burglary. I've put you right in the middle of things, and it's getting dangerous." He picked up the lone cigarette, replaced it in the pack and signaled again for the waiter.

I felt so relieved by his response, I wanted to reassure him. "Please don't worry. I'll grant you I've had some scares since I've been up here, but it's nothing I can't handle. I've got friends in Apalachicola, including a great neighbor in the adjoining apartment. He's really been there for me each time…"

"He?" McBride said, looking curious.

"Mike Pardo. He's in the play. A sweet young guy. He knew Alex. In fact, his deceased fiancée once dated Rick Lucas."

"Ah, Rick Lucas," McBride said. "There's a man we should get to know better."

"That's right. You were going to meet with Lucas and Dr. Matos on Monday afternoon."

"I met with them all right. Got a bunch of gibberish. When I tried to find out about their beef with Hadley, they got technical on me. Anyway, I did learn that Dr. Matos has a research grant from some forestry products company."

"Do they own a mill upstream from Graham Springs?"

"Could be."

"My friend Mike told me there used to be turpentine mills in the area. He thought there still might be a small operation going. If there is, it would be a source of pollution for the springs."

McBride said, "Which might help explain why Matos claims to be certain Hadley's allegations are wrong. He's got an interest to protect."

The check arrived. "It's on me. Least I can do is feed you lunch since you won't have dinner with me," he said.

"Now, Homer. It's not that I won't. You know I'm in rehearsals every evening."

As we left the dining room, he took my arm. "Seriously, Lorelei, you and I need to have a little talk. Let's go outside."

"Where you can smoke," I said, teasingly.

We left the lodge, walked down to the waterfront, and found a nearby park bench. I was glad to be out of doors. Even the vultures didn't disturb me. McBride pulled out his pack of cigarettes, lit one, and inhaled, and coughed.

"Too much fresh air, or are your lungs protesting?" I asked.

He gave me a serious look. "For two cents, I'd tell you to stick to your play, and forget about the Hadley case."

"But..." I protested.

"But," he repeated, "You've already established relationships, and I have to admit you're in a useful spot here. I think once we find out who had the greatest stake in Hadley's research, we'll have our man."

"Or woman," I added, thinking about Mona Lavender.

"The Lavender woman? You think she could have mugged you and broken into your apartment?"

"It's possible. Especially now that I know about her background. Mona Lavender seemed relieved by the news that Hadley's death was an accident, and when she and Pete Stigler took me to the springs they seemed positive their Hadley problem was solved. Did you know the BSRC members own about sixty acres around the springs?"

"The mayor told me," he replied.

"They have a lot of money riding on the sale of the property."

"A pretty good reason to want to keep things status quo," McBride said.

"Look, Homer, I'm willing to continue. Whoever they are, they've really got me angry...you should have seen my apartment. They even stomped all over my play materials. That was just nasty."

He looked amused. "Got you riled up? Not a good thing to do to a red-head," he said, as he field stripped his cigarette, and scattered the tobacco on the lawn. "Okay, Lorelei, as long as you're mindful of the risks involved. That's why I wasn't upset about Thompson's news release. Everyone will let their guard down a bit, and we can sort things out easier."

"Tomorrow's Thanksgiving, and I'll be with the theatre company. You're still going to spend it with your son?" I asked.

"That's right. We may go fishing."

"Oh, and don't forget I'm going snorkeling with Rick Lucas on Saturday. Anything special you want me to find out?"

McBride thought a moment. "See if you can get a better fix on him and Hadley, and what he knows about Hadley's research."

"All right, I'll try."

We walked up the path to the parking lot. At the edge of the lot, McBride stopped.

"I want to show you something,"

We were standing in front of a Florida Heritage Landmark sign, *Wakulla Springs Archeological and Historic District.* I started reading it aloud.

"The location is significant as it represents relationships between human culture and natural resources from the settlement systems of the Paleoindian period to the recent historic past, a period of nearly 15,000 years. There are 55 recorded archeological sites located on the property..."

McBride listened for a few moments, and said, "No, Lorelei, that's not it." He stooped down and pointed at the ground next to the walkway.

"It's this. A hell of an ant colony. And a convenient one, too."

I stood next to him and looked down at the site. There were several busy ant mounds the color and consistency of cornmeal.

"We're pretty sure this is where the killer scooped up the ants. We're testing the sand from this mound to see if it's a match with what was found in the boot. Looks different from other places around the lodge."

I tried picturing the scene as it might have taken place the day Hadley was killed. There must have been a lot of people walking around waiting for the Creaturefest to begin. This was a perfect spot to pause and read the historic marker. The killer must have stooped down—like he or she was tying a shoelace—and quickly scooped up some ants—maybe using an empty soda or coffee cup from the concession stand. Then there was a piece of apple dropped into the cup to keep the ants busy until they were emptied into the foot of Hadley's costume. Easy and unobtrusive.

McBride stood up, brushed his hands together and walked around the side of the building to a staircase leading to the second floor. I went back to finish reading the historic marker.

...Evidence of visits by Spanish and other European explorers has also been found. Late nineteenth and early twentieth century use included heavy timbering and naval stores activities and until the 1930's it was a favorite place for picnics

and political rallies. The acquisition of the area by Edward Ball in 1934 resulted in its development as an attraction, but one which focused on the preservation of wildlife and conservation of natural features. The construction of Wakulla Springs Lodge was completed in September 1937. It is a fine example of the use of Mediterranean Revival architecture in an elegant yet restrained application of the style such that it does not detract from the natural surroundings. The district was listed on the National Register in 1993.

When he returned I said, "This Edward Ball did something very good here."

He put his hands on my shoulders, and looked at me with such tenderness I hoped, for a wild moment, he was going to kiss me. Instead, he said, "C'mon, Lorelei. Maybe another time we can come back like tourists." He took my arm and we started walking toward my car.

We stood next to the car and McBride said, "Call when you hear from Waterman about Hadley?"

"I will," I said.

"And remember what I told you before...be careful with Lucas. Something about the guy really gets under my skin."

I nodded. Before getting into the car, I wished Homer a Happy Thanksgiving. I reached up and hugged him. We held onto to each other for several moments, and I felt disappointed when he pulled away. I wanted more.

Chapter 18

I tried calling Horse on the way back to Apalachicola. When he answered, I hurriedly said, "Horse, this is Lorelei. Please don't hang up again. I've got to talk with you."

"Yeah, what's so important?"

"I've just talked with my detective friend, and I told him the truth about how I got the flash drive."

"Shit, Lorelei," he whispered. "You really want to get me thrown in jail. What'd he say?"

"He was angry, but basically he's letting it pass. You won't have any problems with him. He doesn't really have any evidence, does he?"

There was a long pause, and I heard Horse chuckle.

"I guess you're right there. Sorry I got so ticked with you before. You should have told me you were working with a cop."

"I apologize, Horse. I really think of him more as a friend. It didn't occur to me to tell you." It was a half-truth, but I needed to regain Horse's trust.

"So, was what we found of any use?"

"I don't know yet. I couldn't understand the research so I sent it to a friend. I haven't heard back from him yet."

"Let me put you on hold a minute, Lorelei, I've gotta take this from Rick."

He clicked off. While I waited for Horse to return on the line, I drove past the spot where my car had been pushed off of the road. It reminded me of Buster, how his father described his changed attitude, and Mona's apparent dislike for the young man. I wondered what Buster was up to. Could it have been he who broke into my apartment? But what would he want with Hadley's research?

My thoughts were interrupted when Horse came back on the phone. "Okay, Lorelei. Rick asked me to remind you about your dive lesson on Saturday."

"Yes, I remember. Anyway, Horse, I wanted you to know our adventure is now out in the open. You won't need to lie for me."

Horse said, "I was dumb to get involved in the first place. I sure don't want to see any more jail time." I heard him take a deep breath. "Well, what's done is done. Gotta go, there's a customer here. See you Saturday."

I continued on to Apalachicola, and remembered it was the eve of Thanksgiving. I had some shopping to do. I stopped at the Piggly Wiggly and picked up a bag of fresh cranberries and a couple of oranges to make mom's orange cranberry relish to bring to the Thanksgiving dinner tomorrow.

Back at the apartment, I started the relish. I found a small food processor in the back of the cabinet and was able to finely chop the orange segments—peels and all—with the cranberries. I mixed in about a cup of sugar and put the mixture on top of the stove to simmer. That was Mom's secret...cooking the mixture, and refrigerating it to gel over night.

As I was about to take a shower, my cell phone rang.

"Lor, it's Jeffrey."

"Well, it's about time I heard back from you."

"I turned my phone off during Alex's memorial service. Guess I forgot to turn it back on until today. I got your message, but I wanted to wait until I had something before calling you back."

Half dressed, I sat down on the bed. "Did you decipher the research?"

"Yes, and I've had the data looked at by a friend over in the Center for Natural Resources."

"Do you know what Hadley found that caused so much commotion?"

"Didn't you read his conclusions?" Jeffrey asked.

Impatiently, I replied, "Jeffrey darling, if I could have understood the file, I wouldn't have had to send it to you."

"All right, I'll give you the short version. Alex performed a tracer study that, according to his data, demonstrates a connection between Graham and Wakulla Springs. The dye he placed in Graham took under two weeks to show up at Wakulla. My friend, who's also a diver, thought the connection might have been found during one of the diver mapping expeditions of Wakulla. But she said they haven't traced all of Wakulla's water sources."

"Okay, so there is a connection to Wakulla."

"My friend—who knows Dr. Matos—told me that Matos published a paper on North Florida springs in which he dismissed Graham as a sinklake of little magnitude. In other words, Matos said Graham didn't flow to any other body of water, and there was no connection between it and Wakulla."

"Alex's findings were just the opposite. But is that so unusual? A difference of opinion between scientists."

"Given the proximity of the two springs, my friend was surprised when she read Dr. Matos' conclusions, but he has a national reputation in this field. Florida springs are in the spotlight right now. Wakulla's a first magnitude spring—one of the largest in the world—and lots of agencies are trying to deal with the sources of its pollution. If Dr. Matos says a nearby spring doesn't pose a threat, well then..."

A light bulb went off in my head. "Well then, development, or even a water bottling plant at Graham wouldn't be a problem."

"Probably not," Jeffrey said.

"Wow, Jeffrey, this is really important."

"You think Alex's findings are related in some way to his murder?" he asked.

I stood up, excited that some of the pieces of the puzzle were falling into place. "I do, and I'm sure Homer McBride will think so, too. A lot of people around here have a stake in this."

"Including Dr. Matos," Jeffrey said.

"Yes, of course," I said, and I couldn't help wondering if Dr. Matos was part of the BSRC land partnership. "Did you find out anything else of interest?"

"Just a minute, Lor. Let me scan through some of this. I think there is something more."

I paced the floor, waiting for Jeffrey to respond. I stopped in front of the long mirror on the back of the closet door and was pleased with what I saw. I pulled in my tummy, stretched to my full five feet seven inches and thought, not a bad body for an old broad. I flashed a Hollywood smile.

"Yes, here's another one of Hadley's conclusions," Jeffrey said. I closed the closet door and sat back down on the bed to listen.

"Apparently when Alex did a dive in Graham Springs, he found a place where there was a large fissure in the rock at the top of the cave. When he tracked the location of the fissure to where he thought it was above ground, he found a low lying area near the edge of the spring. Water was pooling there, and he guessed it soaked into the cave below."

"Get to the point, Jeffrey. What does this have to do with anything?"

"It's all in his conclusions if you would have read that far, Lorelei." He sounded annoyed.

"Sorry for being so snippy with you. I'm just anxious to learn why Hadley was such a threat to so many people here."

Jeffrey said, "The point is, Alex warned that any extensive building on, or even near that site might cause the cavern to collapse. If it did, then the water flow would be blocked, and eventually it could flood the whole area."

"Oh, my God. If anyone had even an inkling about this...it's no wonder they wanted to shut him up. Development at Graham Springs might not only be a point of pollution for Wakulla, but a potential flood zone as well."

"At least that's what Alex believed," Jeffrey said.

"Listen, Jeffrey, can you write up what you just told me? I'd like you to take it, along with a copy of the file I emailed, to Detective McBride at Alachua Sheriff's Office? I'll tell him you're bringing it."

"I can do that."

"You're a life saver. I owe you."

"Really? When will you pay up? I could be over there in five or six hours."

"C'mon, Jeffrey. We both have jobs, and you know how I get before an opening night."

"Promises, promises. Same old Lorelei."

"Hey!"

"Just kidding." There was a pause, and I felt the question coming before he even asked it. "So how are you really doing, Red? The holidays are here. It's gotta be pretty tough being alone."

"I'm keeping really busy, but I haven't taken time yet to think much about myself or my life...such as it is."

"You're a strong woman, Lorelei. I guess it just takes time to adjust to the shock of loss," he said. It was the new Jeffrey talking. The one who had been through a near death experience.

"It helps to have friends like you. I love you Jeffrey Waterman," I said, and I meant it. I had come to appreciate Jeffrey in a whole new way since his brush with death last year, and I was finally willing to take some responsibility for our divorce.

"I love you, too. Now, I've got to run. I'll get all the stuff over to your detective. Keep in touch, and let me know how this thing turns out."

"I will, dear. Goodbye."

I called McBride and left a message on his voice mail. I said Jeffrey would be delivering some important information to him, and I wished him a happy holiday again. Next, I called Delcie.

"Lorelei? I'm glad you caught me. I was just headed to mom's in Jacksonville. What's up, girl?"

"What's up is that I've discovered more about why Luke has been getting static from the BSRC in Fairport."

"No kidding, tell all," she said, and I could hear the excitement in her voice.

"I can't tell you everything right now. It's too complicated. I've arranged for a report to be delivered to McBride."

"McBride? I thought you were working for both of us. C'mon, give it up."

"Okay, Del, here's the bottom line. According to Alex Hadley's research, Graham Springs has new levels of pollution, and it is connected to Wakulla Springs. No one's going to permit anything like Luke's company wants to build. But it's not conclusive. A springs expert at Florida State has published a different opinion. I think it will all be cleared up when McBride solves the Hadley case."

"How'd you find all this out? Luke will want to know," Delcie said.

"Is he going to be at your mom's?" I asked.

"Well yes, I was going to tell you before you dropped this news on me."

"I'm glad, Del. I really am."

"Me too, maybe there's still hope for us." She paused. "But tell me more."

"Just tell Luke what I said, and after Thanksgiving, get a copy of the report Jeffrey's going to give Homer."

"Jeffrey?"

"Yes, I emailed a copy of Hadley's research to Jeffrey for interpretation. He's checked it all out, and he's going to give McBride a report." I didn't tell Delcie about the theft of the flash drive. That would have alarmed her and taken more time to explain.

There was a long whistle and Delcie said. "You really earned your stripes on this one, Lor. I never expected you'd come up with anything like this. Luke and I will owe you big time."

"Yeah, yeah...I notice you didn't say anything about a monetary reward."

She chuckled, "How about a home-cooked gourmet southern dinner with an expensive bottle of wine?"

"Gourmet southern? Isn't that an oxymoron?" I teased. "But, you know my weak spot. As soon as I get back to Gainesville, I'll expect you to spend at least three days cooking for me."

"You got it," she said. "And Lor, thanks. Luke's going to be very glad to get this news. It may even make him a bit sweeter towards me." She gave a salacious little giggle, before saying, "Oh, I'm sorry, honey. I'm so thoughtless. You must be feeling blue what with the holiday and all. How're you holding up?"

"Jeffrey asked me the same question. I'm all right. I'm busy, and since I'm away from home...well, the truth is I feel like my life's suspended...somewhere between Mars and Venus," I said, and laughed. "Guess that sounds silly."

"No, going away was good for you. How's the play coming?"

"Oh, it's coming well enough. I'll be glad when rehearsals are over. I'm kind of bored with them. It'll be more fun when there's a live audience."

"How about if I drive over for the opening? It's the first weekend in December, right?"

"Uh huh. Oh, I'd love you'd to be here, Del. You could stay at the Gibson Inn. It's a really classy old place right in the heart of town. You'd like it."

"Fine. I'll make a reservation," she said.

"Delcie, I hope you have a great Thanksgiving. Tell Luke hello for me."

"I thought you hated him," she said.

"Only when you did. Love you."

"Love you, too," she replied.

Talking with Delcie made me feel homesick, and wishing I was spending the holiday with my friend and her family. I needed to be fussed over...and loved.

Chapter 19
Thanksgiving

I awoke with a feeling of despair so heavy that I lay in bed, my body inert—eyes closed—unable to face a new day. Instead of looking forward to Thanksgiving, which has always been my favorite holiday, I dreaded it. It took all my energy to force myself up. I staggered into the bathroom, ran a bath, and threw in some aromatherapy beads. I hoped a good soak and the fragrance of eucalyptus would help lift my spirits. I made some Chai tea, took it into the bathroom with me, and placed it on the floor next to the tub.

Lying in the tub, with my head propped against an air pillow, I sipped the spicy aromatic tea. My thoughts drifted back to last Thanksgiving. I pictured Bill nervously hovering over me as I set the table for our guests. I half smiled as I remembered giving him one task after another—as you would a child—just to get him out from underfoot.

Our guests were the half dozen of his students who remained in Gainesville during the holiday. As we planned the menu, we had talked about whether or not to have wine at dinner. It was always a conflict for him since some of the students were underage. Yet, ultimately we agreed that for those who wanted it, a glass of wine would add a touch of festiveness.

I began crying as I imagined him at the head of the dining room table. Closing my eyes, I pictured his tall good looks, and the boyish lock of pale blonde hair that fell across his forehead as he bent down to carve the turkey—all the while dispensing quips about the economics of the turkey industry. He told them how the growers were gobbling up their profits—and made other silly jokes to set the students at ease. It always amazed me how utterly charming and spontaneous Bill was with his students—a chameleon so unlike the introverted, conservative man he was when we were alone.

I took the washcloth to my face and pressed the warm water against my eyes. Instead of stemming the tears, I began sobbing and keening my sorrow into the cloth. I slipped under the water, and briefly wondered if I could will myself to drown. When I came up for air, I realized the bath had gone cold. I began to shiver.

"Get a grip, Lorelei, and stop being so dammed dramatic. Drowning yourself in the bath? Are you crazy?" I got out of the tub and wrapped a large towel around my body. "Get dressed, get out, and cheer up—you're still alive."

Who in hell put that message in my mind? Was it you, Bill? I thought about the times when I had lain in bed at night, unable to sleep, and feeling desperately lonely. I talked to him then, and sometimes I could almost sense his response. It was comforting, but lately I had trouble remembering exactly how he sounded.

As I stepped out of my door on the way to Sophie's, I ran into Mike. He had, in tow, a cooler on wheels. It was the kind you could pull along like a suitcase. I guessed it was filled with bottles of wine and beer.

"Lorelei, how're you doing? Ready for the feast?"

"Yes, I guess I am," I said, somewhat startled.

"Let's walk over together."

I hesitated, still feeling in a funk, but I tried to hide it. As we started our walk along the waterfront, Mike said, "God, this is the kind of day that makes you glad to be alive, isn't it?"

I thought his comment a bit ironic after I had considered drowning myself only hours before. I looked up at a cloudless deep blue sky and knew what he meant. It was one of those gorgeous fall Florida days. The temperature outside was about seventy degrees, and it was sunny. I inhaled the fresh bay air and agreed, "Yes, I guess it is a good day to be alive."

Mike turned, alerted by the uncertainty in my voice. "Has something happened?" he asked. "You seem kind of different. Sad. Is it something going on in your other life?"

"You mean, my life of mystery?" I said, and smiled for the first time that day. "Oh, the tangled web I've woven..."

"To deceive," he replied. "Scott."

"What?"

"Sir Walter Scott—Marmion. 'Oh what a tangled web we weave when first we practice to deceive.'"

"Huh. I guessed it was Shakespeare."

Mike stopped and turned to face me. He dropped the handle of his cooler, crossed both hands over his heart, and recited:

O! many a shaft, at random sent,
Finds mark the archer little meant;
And many a word, at random spoken,
May soothe or wound a heart that's broken!

"Also Scott. My high school English teacher made us memorize verse. After I read Ivanhoe, I took a liking to Sir Walter." He picked up the cooler handle, and we continued walking. "Holidays are hard, aren't they, Lorelei? I know. I always feel a melancholy myself thinking about Charley. But I try to jack up my spirits. As they say—fake it till you make it."

I could have hugged him, but I had my hands full carrying the relish dish. "Well, I'll get through it. I spent the morning doing yoga and meditating. It always helps—as have your soothing words, at random spoken."

"Good. Let's just have a nice time today. How about it? I've got some premier booze here, and knowing Sophie, there'll be plenty of great food."

"Agreed," I said, as we reached Sophie's. We walked through the door to the café. The air was filled with rich aromas.

"Attention everyone. The stars have arrived, and we can eat." Sophie said, clapping her hands together.

Mike and I followed her to a makeshift bar set up in the corner of the café. He started to unload bottles. I placed my relish dish on a table covered by a white cloth and decorated with colorful gourds. My taste buds came alive at the sight of all the dishes and the complex mingling of their aromas.

Renee said, "C'mon you two, sit down and let's have a toast before we begin the feast."

A dozen or so cast members were seated at tables pulled together in banquet style. Mike brought several bottles of chilled wine to the table, and we sat down.

Renee lifted her glass. "First a toast to my brave and wonderful cast. It's long been my dream to produce this Ibsen play, and you're making my dream come true." She turned to Sophie, who was busy arranging dishes on the table behind us, and said, "Next to Sophie Vatine, who has nourished us in every way and made us feel welcome in Apalachicola." Sophie gave a short bow. "And last, in no way least, to our dedicated producer, Dixie Partington—actor, impresario, and—along with her father Rex and his wife, Cleo—the family who restored the historic Dixie Theatre and brought it back to life."

When Renee finished her toast, there was an explosion of conversations and laughter. Mike raised his glass to me and said softly, "And here's a toast to my leading lady…a woman who is intriguing in every way."

I felt my spirits lift amid the warm and festive atmosphere.

Sophie stood at the head of the table, hands on her hips, and announced, "Enough drinking and talk for now. It's time to eat. Come. Before everything gets cold."

There was a quiet hum of conversation while we enjoyed the Thanksgiving meal. When people started back to the serving table for dessert, Mike raised his glass in a toast, "Here's to Dr. Stockman, Ibsen's hero who said—in the modern vernacular—take your job and shove it."

Everyone laughed.

"But was he a hero?" Renee asked. "Or was he simply an arrogant scientist who said 'shove it' to his family and community as well? We've been struggling with that question, haven't we?"

I thought of Alex Hadley. He, like Ibsen's Stockman, allowed his family to suffer and—however ill conceived the BSRC plan for development—tried to stop his town from realizing economic opportunities from Graham Springs.

"Let's put the question back to you, Mike. You're our own local hero. How about it?" one of the actors said. "You're the guy who's running all the eco-tours, working with Apalachicola Bay and Riverkeepers. Would you be willing to undermine the local tourism and seafood industry if you believed the bay was badly contaminated?"

Mike pushed his chair away from the table, leaned back, and took a moment before speaking. "Truth and consequences...is that it? You all know I've given Stockman's position a lot of thought. But I think there were other ways he could have handled the situation. If he'd been a bit more diplomatic and realized the impact of his actions...he could have accomplished something productive rather than destructive."

Sophie said, "But then, they wouldn't have called him an enemy of the people...and Ibsen wouldn't have a play."

Renee said, "Sophie's right, in a way. Ibsen did set the play up as a kind of literary debate, didn't he? Pure scientific truth versus pragmatism. In fact, in the late 19th century creating this kind of social polemic was called Ibsenizing."

"But it's not simply a literary convention," I added. "Since I've been in the Panhandle, Ibsen's plot has taken on a whole new reality. Do you all know about an environmental scientist, Dr. Alex Hadley, who lived in Fairport?"

Someone said, "Wasn't he the guy that died over at Wakulla Springs at the Creaturefest? Some kind of accident or something?"

"Yes, he's the one," I replied. I wasn't going to challenge the cause of Alex's death. "He was a Dr. Stockman. Hadley conducted research about a spring near Wakulla that upset some of the leaders in Fairport. His family was threatened, forced to leave town, and it ruined his marriage. Like Dr. Stockman, the city council kept him from announcing his findings in a public forum. They were afraid he'd spoil their real estate development plans."

"Unbelievable," someone said.

Renee chimed in, "And that's why I've been so passionate about wanting to do this play. It was published in 1882, but it's amazingly contemporary. As Lorelei just told us, the issues are still relevant. People don't want to hear the truth if they have a stake in believing otherwise."

Conversations broke out around the table and gradually drifted from the subject of the play. Mike got up and brought back more wine. A couple of actors, across from me began to talk about their memories of other Thanksgiving dinners away from home. Their stories were poignant and had the effect of making me feel drained. It was dark outside, and when I looked at my watch, I realized we had been eating and drinking for several hours. It was time to leave.

"Mike," I whispered. "I'm going to go home. I'm beat."

"I'll walk you," he said.

"No, you don't need to do that."

"I want to," he insisted. "I can come back afterwards. They'll all be in their cups by then. It's probably a good idea for me to take a break."

I rose from the table, thanked Sophie, and said my goodbyes to everyone.

As Mike and I walked back to the apartment, I said, "They called you a local hero. You must be well-respected around here, not that I'm surprised."

"And I found it interesting that you brought up the case of Alex Hadley. Just how involved are you in all that Fairport stuff? You haven't told me anything since we emailed the research to your friend in Gainesville."

"Not tonight, Mike. I'm really bushed. It's been an emotionally exhausting day for me."

"Gottcha," he said.

He walked me up to my apartment door. When I turned to tell him good night, he took me in his arms and tried to kiss me.

I averted my face, and gently pushed him away. "No, Mike. I can't do this...not today," I said, and thought, not when Bill is still too much with me.

"Okay, can't blame a guy for trying," he said, a bit lamely. "Good night, Lorelei. Sleep well."

Stepping into my dimly lit apartment was like stepping back into my depression. I undressed and got into bed, wanting the day to end. As I lay there, I tried to picture me and Bill walking along the shore at Indian Pass. Eventually, I drifted into sleep.

Chapter 20

By 8:30 the next morning I was on my way to meet Rick Lucas for my second dive lesson. I began thinking about how I would get Rick to answer McBride's questions without creating too much suspicion. McBride wanted to know more about Rick's relationship with Alex Hadley, and how much he knew about Hadley's research.

When I pulled up to Horse's dive shop, I was grateful the sun had come out and it had gotten warmer. I had dreaded the idea of going into the water if it had been as cloudy and cool as when I left Apalachicola.

I entered the shop, and Horse said, "Rick's out back waiting for you. He's loading gear." He gave me a sullen look, and I guessed he was still angry about my relationship with McBride.

"Loading?" I asked.

"Yeah, you're going to a local pool. You didn't think we'd let you out in the gulf without training, did you?"

"Of course, I completely forgot."

He didn't look up as he pretended to be sorting items on a sale table and asked, "Heard any more from your detective friend about our little adventure?"

"No, but I told you, there's nothing to worry about," I said, knowing it wasn't quite true now that I knew about Horse's criminal record.

I walked back outside to look for Rick. His black pickup truck was parked at the side door. He looked up as I approached and then finished securing a couple of brightly colored oxygen tanks at the back of the truck.

"Morning, Mrs. Crane. Ready to get wet?" he asked, repeating Horse's line. He looked more cheerful and relaxed than when I first met him. Despite the chilly morning, he was dressed in shorts, flip flops, and a Florida Seminole tee shirt.

I glanced up at the sky. "I'm ready as long as the sun stays out."

I had my swim suit on under my jeans, sweat shirt, and wind breaker. I must have looked more like I was going snow skiing than swimming. Rick looked me over and gave a faint smile.

"Oh, you'll warm up. The pool's heated and I've got plenty of exercises for you to do."

"Where are we going?"

"Over to the country club. They let us use their pool in the winter months. C'mon, hop in. I'll just be a sec. I need to see Horse before we leave."

He went inside, and I looked more closely at his truck. No, I thought, this isn't the same one that ran me off the road. That one didn't have an open bed. I would have noticed the difference. Yet, when I glanced toward the back of the shop I saw a truck topper that looked like it belonged to Rick's vehicle. I walked around and saw an FSU parking decal and a bumper sticker that said: *My wife told me she'd leave me if I didn't cut down on my diving. I'm sure going to miss her.* I returned to the cab and got in.

Rick opened the door and slid into the driver's seat. He brought with him an almond like fragrance from some sun screen he must have put on while he was inside.

He poked his head against the windshield, and said, "Clear blue sky. A perfect day for diving lessons." We pulled away from the shop, crossed the main highway, and headed north on a county road.

As I expected, the cab of the truck was immaculate—unlike my recollection of Jeffrey's truck which was crammed with old fast food wrappings and reeked of stale beer.

"Did you read the material I gave you last week?"

"Gee," I said, "I think it's still in my car. I'm so sorry...what with the holidays."

"It's okay. I'll be going over a lot of skills today. You can read the manual later, and there's a video I'll loan you."

I felt relieved, and I was glad he didn't seem to take my failure for lack of interest.

We drove in silence and arrived at the country club within minutes. It was a small single story pink stucco building that attempted elegance by classical architectural features—phony Grecian pillars and a stained glass rose window above the entrance. It was the kind of design that became popular in tract homes in the

1990's. Rick parked along the side of the building near a gate leading to the pool. We got out.

"Can you give me a hand here, Mrs. Crane?" Rick began unloading equipment.

"Please, it's Lorelei," I said, coming around to the back of the truck.

"All right, Lorelei. Take the cooler, and I'll get the rest of the stuff. Oh, you can change in the women's shower area. They've left it open for us."

I walked through the fence gate and entered the pool area. It was average size and had a scattering of lounge chairs and tables with umbrella stands but no umbrellas. I deposited the cooler next to one of the tables, and headed toward the sign leading to the showers. When I returned—stripped down to my bathing suit, but still wearing a windbreaker—Rick had unpacked his cargo bags and had all the equipment beside of the pool. He was sitting on a lounge chair and gave me an appraising look as I approached.

"Did you put on sun screen?" he asked, offering the tube.

"Yes, I did. Thanks."

"Good," he said, as I sat down. "Now, let me go over what we'll be doing today. You're only going to be here a couple more weeks, right?" He fixed me with a sharp look, and I had the feeling there was more to his question than his failing to recall how long I'd be there.

"About three more weeks...until the play closes. Why?"

"Nothing, really," he said, "it's just that we usually do two separate pool lessons with a class in between."

He had mentioned this during our first lesson. He said, since it was private instruction, he could compress the classes into one at the pool and one in open water.

"You said we'd be doing six hours today. Isn't that a lot of time in the pool?" I asked.

He laughed. "Oh, we'll take breaks, don't worry. It'll be strenuous, but you look like you can handle it." Rick walked to the pool's edge and said, "Here's the plan. First, you'll do a swim test. After that, we'll review the gear—in the water—and I'll demonstrate how to use it. I'll demonstrate the basic skills for scuba, and you'll

practice a lot. Like I said, we'll take several breaks." He pointed to
the cooler next to the table. "I've brought some snacks."

Good, I thought. I knew how hungry I got after any amount of
exercise. I had only a light breakfast at Caroline's Dining Room
before leaving town.

Rick rubbed his hands together. "Let's begin. You'll need to
shed the jacket, won't you?"

"I guess so," I said, taking it off, and feeling myself shiver at the
still cool temperature.

"First, I'd like you to show me how you swim. Just do a few
laps."

I entered the cold water, shivering, and did several total dunks
before beginning the laps. When I had gone back and forth several
times, I looked up at Rick and he nodded his satisfaction.

"Now, I need to see if you can survive in the water without
swimming. Please tread or float, whichever, for about ten minutes."

"Ten minutes? That's a long time." I said, hanging onto the side
of the pool beneath him.

He squatted down and gave me an admonishing look. "Not long
if you're unable to swim and waiting for rescue."

I treaded water for a few minutes and then switched to floating
on my back. I let the water cover my ears, and slowed my breathing
as I watched the clouds drift in the morning sky. Rick was watching
me from the edge of the pool. He seemed to be in his own meditative
state, and for a moment. I found it hard to believe that this handsome
and elegant looking man could be a suspect in a murder, but I
remembered Delcie's comments about not being able to tell
murderers by their looks.

I dropped my legs and bounced up at the shock of his touch.

Rick had entered the water and stood next to me. "That's
enough," he said. "Do you meditate?"

"Yes, I do yoga breathing exercises."

"Good. Relaxed breathing is critical in diving. I'm sure you
won't have any problems achieving neutral buoyancy."

"What's that?" I asked.

"We'll cover it later. We can skip the snorkeling lesson since you told me you've gone snorkeling before."

"Yes, with my husband."

"Okay, let's get out of the pool, and put on scuba gear."

During the next couple of hours, Rick taught me the underwater signals, how to use the pressure gauge, and clear the regulator. Finally, he gave the signal to get out of the water.

I climbed out of the pool in my wet suit, and though I was feeling tired, I didn't mention it. The break would be a good time to find out more about Rick Lucas.

He brought the cooler to the edge of the pool, and we sat dangling our legs in the sun warmed water. He offered me a bottled water, some fruit slices, and one of many high energy bars he kept in an airtight bag. I took the water, and a bag of fruit.

"There's a lot more to scuba than I realized," I said.

"The water's a foreign environment—sometimes hostile—so you need a lot of skills."

"Yes, I can see that now," I said.

We sat in silence for a few moments. The water in the pool was sky blue, and the tile side panels had a playful motif of water mammals—porpoises, whales, and reef fish of many different colors.

"You're a good teacher," I said, knowing a bit of flattery generally loosened people up to talk. "Was Alex Hadley as good a diver as you? Horse told me you were a Navy Seal."

Rick noticeably stiffened at the mention of Alex, and I could sense the air between us change. "What made you think of Alex Hadley?" he asked, scowling.

"I don't know. I guess that the two of you were scuba diving instructors. You were good friends, right?"

"Yes," he said, giving me a probing look. "We talked about him last week. Is there something else you want to ask me?"

"Nothing really. I guess since he was a friend of my ex-husband, I just wanted to know a little more about him."

"Uh huh," he said, staring into the water. He was obviously unwilling to volunteer any more about Alex Hadley.

During the long silence, I considered how to get Rick to open up. I remembered the mention of his father had evoked an emotional response during our first meeting. If I could learn more about this relationship, I might better understand Rick's motivation and behavior. It might also help me gain his confidence. I couldn't go back to McBride with another excuse like "he's a very complicated man."

"So, how was your Thanksgiving? Did you spend it with your father?" I asked.

Rick grunted, a snicker crossed his lips, and he took a long sip of water. "No thanks-giving is more like it. Spending the day with my old man is like being tied to a post and whipped."

"How dramatic," I said. "If it's that bad why don't you move out?"

Rick shook his head. "Move out? Like I haven't sworn to do it a thousand times. But, as crazy and mean as the old geezer is, I promised my mother before she died I'd look after him. When I got out of the service and he had his first stroke, I took him in to live with me."

"That's very commendable of you," I said, and meant it. This was a different Rick Lucas than the one Mike or Horse described. He seemed more human. "Usually it's the other way around."

"What do you mean," he asked.

"I mean, usually it's the parent who promises to look after the child."

He shrugged. "I guess in most families it's that way." He stood, and stretched his neck and shoulders. I watched his face become contorted as he said, "I've been looking after myself since grade school. The old man did nothing for me, but make me work out in the fields till dark. And then slap me around if I didn't finish my homework, or if I got a bad grade in school."

"How awful. It's so cruel to treat children that way. It affects them for the rest of their lives. It's already hard enough being an only child," I said, knowing it from my own experience. "The expectations can feel crushing."

"Hard if you have a mean S.O.B. for a father," he said. "Excuse me, I'll be right back." He turned and walked to the men's shower room.

When he returned he said, "Ready to get back in? We've still got a lot to cover."

We dove back into the pool. He had me review the skills we worked on earlier. Then he demonstrated regulator recovery, mask clearing, and buoyancy. Once again, he was very impressed with my relaxed breathing and told me I could easily achieve neutral buoyancy—the ability to rise and sink in the water by means of breathing. He called it the Zen of breathing.

We were in deeper water when he signaled that we take another break. As we rested at pool's edge, I munched an energy bar and began to feel an odd camaraderie with this moody man.

"You seem to be enjoying yourself," he said. "Not too tiring, is it?"

"Not exactly a walk in the park, but I feel energized by the swimming. I wish there was more to see than the bottom of the pool."

"Next week—you're free then, aren't you?"

I nodded.

"We'll go into open water and practice the skills you've learned today."

"Where will that be?" I asked.

"Probably near the dive shop…if the water's calm. So what else have you been doing besides rehearsing? Any sightseeing?" he asked in a surprisingly conversational tone.

"Actually, I've been looking at property. I love the area."

He tore open an energy bar, took a bite, and asked, "What area?"

Casually, but with calculation, I replied, "Graham Springs, actually. I've fallen in love with the place."

He raised his eyebrows, but didn't respond.

"Do you know it?" I asked.

Rick took a deep breath and looked at me as though he had just solved a puzzle. "That's your real interest in Alex Hadley, isn't it? I guess someone's told you his bogus theory about the springs."

"I've heard something about it, and the conflict it caused between you."

"Conflict?" he said, giving me a cold studied gaze.

"Something about his research contradicting the findings your Dr. Matos had published? It wasn't clear. What's it about? Can you tell me?"

The tension between us returned, and I sensed I was metaphorically moving from the shallows to deeper water with Rick Lucas.

He looked away and said, "What can I say? It was an academic matter. A difference between experts. Happens all the time."

It sounded like the same line Mona and the mayor had given me. Rick was blowing me off, we both knew it, but I wasn't going to give up so easily.

"Not exactly the way I heard it," I said, trying to keep things on the light side. "People I talked to in Fairport mentioned the dispute. They said Alex was stirring up a lot of trouble. For one thing, he claimed Graham Springs was connected to Wakulla. That would have a lot of implications for land sales, wouldn't it?"

"Bullshit," Rick said. "He couldn't prove it."

"No? Then why'd he keep trying to persuade people? I'm only asking because I may buy a piece of property there."

Rick stood up, and nervously paced the edge of the pool. "Who knows why Alex did what he did. Dr. Matos found no link between Graham and Wakulla. If you knew anything about Alex, you'd know he could sometimes be an arrogant bastard."

Rick became more agitated, and I half-regretted stirring him up. Yet I knew I had to continue to probe.

"Alex had all the answers," he continued. "Alex was the most daring and skilled cave diver, the most ingenious researcher...frankly, he was just a big pain in the ass!"

He stopped suddenly, and stood over me. His face flushed with anger. Perhaps seeing my surprise at his outburst, he realized he had gone too far. He shrugged, took a deep breath, and cracked his knuckles.

"Sorry," he said, regaining control. "Guess I'm just all wound up—what with the investigation and all. You don't know what a career killer it can be to have cops questioning everyone about you at the university."

"Not a problem," I said. "But I'm confused about your description. Weren't you friends?"

"He might have said otherwise, but I was his friend."

I wondered if Alex betrayed him in some way. There were always at least two sides to every relationship story. Maybe I'd only been getting one of them.

Rick said, "Look, do you want to learn to dive, or do you want to interview me about Alex Hadley? If you want an interview, make an appointment at my office." With that, he started back into the pool.

I had no choice but to follow him. Yet I had the same anxious feeling that Rick Lucas was unstable. At one moment he was helpful and open—sharing his feelings about his father—and at the next, he abruptly closed down.

Rick seemed to calm down by the time we began the final segment of my training. We practiced good buddy and rescue skills for open water. By the time we got to the final emergency skills—using the extra regulator they called octopus, and the single breath up—it took an effort to swim up and back in the pool.

When I returned poolside with my gear, Rick was packing things up. I offered to help, but he suggested I relax while he finished loading the cargo bags.

"Rick, I'm sorry I upset you asking so many questions about Alex Hadley and the springs. I suppose that's what ruptured your friendship."

He kept putting the gear away and spoke in an almost sing song voice...as though he'd rehearsed his response. "Like I told you, Alex was headstrong. He didn't believe in compromise. Dr. Matos and I wanted him to share his research with us—so we could collaborate—but he acted like we were his enemy."

"Did you ever try to get him to explain?" I asked in a neutral tone. "Could there have been another reason he wouldn't share his work with you?"

Rick stopped packing and froze for a moment. I knew instantly I had crossed a dangerous line. Within moments he was in front of me. He leaned over, bracing himself on the arms of my chair, so close I caught the scent of chlorine on his body.

"Who the hell are you? Why do you keep at me about Hadley?" he asked. His voice was low, almost snarling. His eyes flashed in anger.

I squirmed and glanced around even though I knew there was no one else in sight.

"C'mon tell me, how do you know about Alex's dye tracer work? I'm thinking you're more interested in talking about me and Alex than scuba diving. Who sent you here?"

"Please," I said, "you're scaring me, Rick." I pushed him away, and he backed off—still glaring at me.

It had been risky to mention what I knew about Alex's research. Despite the fact that my heart was racing, I feigned surprise and went on the offensive.

I said, "Why are you so paranoid? Sure I'm curious about Alex. I guess one of the realtors must have mentioned the research."

Rick's eyes narrowed as though he was trying to see through my response. Then, as suddenly as he had attacked, he stood back, took a deep breath, and forced a smile. "All right, Lorelei. Sorry if I frightened you. Like I told you, I'm a bit stressed by the whole thing. You understand."

"I can see that," I said, gathering the remainder of the gear to help carry it to the truck. "I've got to get back for rehearsal."

On the drive back, Rick asked, "By the way, you said the Fairport realtors told you about Alex's research. Did they actually show you any...reports or other documents?" His tone was off-handed, but I noticed his face looked strained.

Dammit, I thought, I may have woven one of those tangled webs again with the realtor story. It could be checked. "No I've never seen any documents. It may not even have been the realtors. I've talked to quite a few people about the springs ever since I considered buying property there."

He pulled up next to my car. "Here you are, safe and sound."

"Shall I help you unload the gear?" I asked.

"No, I'll do it. You have to get back." He reached behind my seat and pulled out a manila envelope. "We'll meet here at nine am next Saturday. Here's the video I mentioned. It'll help if you review the material I gave you and take a look at the tape. Next week's your last lesson."

"Thanks, Rick. I'm really looking forward to it."

"Right," he said, and gave me an intensely curious look as though he was still trying to read something in my face to help him decide if he could trust me. "Take it easy."

Chapter 21

On the drive back, I puzzled over the morning I'd spent with Rick Lucas. His psychological make up seemed even more complicated than I'd thought. Even considering his stress, as a result of Hadley's murder investigation, I suspected he was typically pretty emotionally volatile—probably as a result of his childhood. Still, I was impressed by his willingness to care for an invalid father whom he said he despised. The question remained...was this a man who could commit murder?

I drove slowly to avoid following too close to the large flat bed truck that had pulled onto the road ahead of me. It carried a huge pile of pine tree trunks. It was a common sight on North Florida highways. It always made me a little sad to see those tall stately trees unearthed, and frequently on their way to becoming pulp.

I returned to thinking about Rick Lucas. Yes, I supposed—if sufficiently provoked—he could become violent. The sly way Hadley was killed didn't seem to be his style. Inserting red ants into a costume wasn't a very macho method of killing. I could see it as a juvenile act of vengeance on the part of a Buster Stigler, or even a crafty act by Mona Lavender, or Hadley's gardener father-in-law. But Lucas had been a Navy Seal. He had the strength and cunning to use more direct ways to kill.

This line of thought gave me goose-bumps. It made me worry that if Rick was the murderer, I had already come too close to provoking him. And why did he ask if I had seen documentation of Hadley's research? Did it mean neither he nor Dr. Matos was certain about what the studies contained? Or if they knew—given the controversy—did they want to make sure the information was suppressed? Were the stakes for Lucas and Matos big enough for them to break-into Hadley's house and my apartment?

The lumber truck pulled onto a side road, and I hit the accelerator. The challenge in understanding Rick Lucas's motives was similar to what I did in analyzing a role for a play. The critical question—the one over which all actors often agonized—was what does my character want? It was what both McBride and I had discussed—motivation. Many people had a motive for wanting to silence Hadley, but for which of them was the need so desperate as to drive them to murder?

When I returned to my apartment, I got ready for rehearsal. I realized it was time for me to shelve the Hadley drama and get my head into Ibsen's. Before doing so, I put in a call to McBride.

"So you didn't drown," he said. I heard a TV playing in the background and guessed Homer was at home.

"No, I didn't. Actually, Rick said I would make an excellent diver. I have something called Zen breath."

"Use Certs," he quipped.

I laughed at the lame joke and asked, "What are you watching?"

"Some show about China. You know they have very little crime there. I'd be out of a job."

"Or working for the secret police."

"Hey," he protested. "What do you take me for?"

"Sorry."

"Okay, so what did you find out about our boy Lucas?"

"He's definitely got some serious issues and a hair-trigger temper. For a while there, I was nervous about being alone with him."

"What happened?"

" I asked if he had ever confronted Hadley about his secrecy."

"And?"

"And, I made the mistake of mentioning the dye tracer studies. That made him really suspicious. I think I covered myself. Anyway, he seemed to calm down."

"Are you scheduled for another lesson with him?" McBride asked.

"Yes, I have one more next Saturday."

"Cancel it," he said.

"Cancel it?"

"Yes, I don't want you alone with him again."

"Oh, I don't seriously think he would hurt me. He's just stressed out."

"He should be. There's a new development in the case. I don't want you taking any more chances."

"What new development?"

"I can't discuss it now. By the way, thanks for getting Waterman to drop off the copy of Hadley's research report. I've put it out for another opinion. If it checks out, it may be useful."

"You're welcome. But when can you tell me about this new development?"

"Meet me at the Wakulla Lodge for lunch on Monday. It's your day off, right?"

"Yes. At noon?"

"That's good. And Lorelei, be careful. You've made yourself very visible asking a lot of questions. Someone might think you've gotten too many answers."

"Can't you even give me a hint about what's happened?"

"You'll hear about it soon enough."

For the second time that day, I felt a shiver of apprehension. "Oh, I'll be careful," I promised.

The evening's rehearsal went on until the wee hours of the morning. Mike and I fell in step to walk home together.

"So how do you think the play's going?" I asked as we were leaving the theatre.

"Well enough, but…"

"What?"

"Sometimes I see this kind of confused look in your eyes, and I wonder if you'll be on cue."

"Honestly, Mike. I'm still struggling with Mrs. Stockman. She's so…submissive."

"That's a hard role for you, isn't it?" he said.

"It is. Maybe on closing night I'll just slap you when you make one of your particularly arrogant statements."

He laughed, "Oh, a little surprise like that would get everyone charged up."

"Of course I won't do it. And right now, all I can think about is sleeping late."

"I feel the same way," Mike said. "I've got no eco-tours booked today. By the way, now that you've gotten to know the notorious Rick Lucas, what do you think of him?"

We had turned onto Front Street, and—despite the dim lighting—I saw a couple sitting close together on a bench at the waterfront. It was a romantic scene that made me feel melancholy.

"So," Mike said, "what'd you think about Lucas?"

I slid my arm through Mike's and said, "He didn't seem to fit all of your stereotypes. He has a temper, but there's also something vulnerable about him. Did you know he takes care of his invalid father?"

"Vulnerable? Like a python," Mike said and made a face. "Leave it to a woman to..."

"Oh, c'mon now," I said, and snuggled closer to him, hoping to push back my feelings of loneliness.

Mike suddenly grabbed me by the shoulders. He put his face close to mine, and whispered, "Lorelei, don't tell me you're falling for Lucas' charm—it could be fatal, you know."

I broke Mike's grip and started walking ahead into the darkness. It was the second time in a day I had been lectured to about Rick Lucas, and I didn't like it.

"Wait a minute, Lorelei," he said, catching up with me, and taking my arm. "Sorry I came on so strong, but I care about you. I don't want to see you get entangled with the likes of..."

"Please, Mike. I'm really quite tired. I appreciate your concern, but I'm perfectly capable of taking care of myself."

We walked the rest of the way in silence. When we reached the top of the landing, Mike took my hand, and gave me a sweet look. "How about breakfast or brunch, whatever time you get up?"

I shrugged. "It depends when I get up. Come to think of it, I'm going to spend the day at Cape San Blas."

"Then how about meeting me at Sophie's before rehearsal?"

"That's possible. Anyway, I can't think straight right now. I've got to get to bed."

He leaned forward and kissed me lightly on the lips. "Goodnight then, Lorelei."

It was almost noon when I awoke. I dressed quickly, and headed to the beach on Cape San Blas. It was less than an hour's drive from Apalachicola with hardly any traffic. It was another sunny day and relatively warm. When I arrived at the Cape, I stopped and bought a sandwich, a bottled drink, and a copy of *The New Yorker* magazine at the general store across the street from the Cape San Blas Inn. Bill and I had stayed there for one idyllic weekend early in our marriage.

I parked at the beach, grabbed an old aluminum sand chair and beach towel from the trunk of my car, and trudged across the dunes to a relatively unpopulated spot. There were only a few other people on the beach, and I was grateful for the solitude. After getting settled, I started to do some centering yoga postures. There was a gentle breeze off the gulf, and the sounds of seagulls overlaid the laughter of children who were playing further down the beach along the water's edge.

My breathing began to synchronize with the sound of the waves rolling onto the shore, and—with my eyes closed—I called up the memories of our stay at the Cape. Images began to drift in and out—walks we took along the shore at daybreak and dusk, intimate candlelit dinners on the back porch of the Inn, and the languorous lovemaking in our room during the heat of midday. I pictured the room, in cool white, and the sun streaming through the wooden Venetian blinds. It made us feel as though we were on a tropical island.

I became hypnotized by my memories, the warm air and sounds of the rolling surf. I began to feel hungry, slowly ate lunch, and spent the rest of the afternoon alternately napping and gazing at the water. *The New Yorker* remained unopened on my lap. By late afternoon, a chill in the air warned me it was time to leave. I gathered my things reluctantly. The day left me with a feeling of spiritual release. I felt Bill's presence. For the first time since his death, my anger dissipated, and forgiveness toward him began to feel possible.

I headed back to town feeling refreshed and relieved of the tension that had been building over the past few days. I looked forward to the excitement of the play's opening. It was only days away.

172

Late that afternoon, I walked over to Sophie's. It was an hour before rehearsal was scheduled. When I entered, Mike was seated at a table with a couple of our fellow actors. Sophie greeted me from behind the front counter.

"Lorelei, how nice to see you. What's a matter, you don't like Sophie's cooking no more? I haven't seen you in days."

"Nothing of the kind...I love your cooking. Truth is, I've been mostly eating frozen dinners. I have to watch my weight before a production, or I won't fit into the costume. It's the middle age thing."

Mike looked up and hailed me over to his table.

I greeted everyone and sat down. We chatted about how the play was going and speculated on how many people would attend opening night. I ordered the soup and sandwich combination and coffee. From time to time, I caught Mike staring at me, and it made me feel a little uncomfortable.

As we started walking to the theatre, Mike took my arm and drew me down to a street bench near the entrance.

"Lorelei, I was thinking, how about spending the day with me tomorrow? The weather is so perfect, I'd like to take you out on my boat again. We could go out into the gulf."

"I'm sorry, Mike. I've already made plans."

"You have?"

"Yes, I'm going to have lunch with my friend at Wakulla Springs."

"The detective?"

"Yes," I replied.

"Are you...seeing him? Socially I mean?" Mike said, disappointed.

"No, nothing like that," I replied. "It's about...well, you know."

"Alex Hadley."

"That's right."

"And why are you still involved in all this?"

I couldn't tell if he was genuinely puzzled, or being sarcastic. In either case, I didn't
have a ready answer. Instead, I looked at my watch, and said, "We'd better go in. Renee will give us the evil eye if we're late."

As we walked into the theatre, Mike said, "I have to tell you, I don't understand this whole thing you've gotten into. Isn't one drama enough for you?"

I didn't respond, though silently I had to agree with him. I hadn't figured it out either. The Hadley case and my renewed involvement with McBride were inexplicably fulfilling. No, maybe not fulfilling, more like intensely distracting...and a little dangerous.

Chapter 22

Mid morning, I left to meet Homer. I decided to take a new route and turned onto State Road 319 to Wakulla. It passed through the towns of Sopchoppy and Crawfordville. One of the actors had told me about a great bookstore in Crawfordville, and I had left early enough to stop there. I found the Tattered Pages Bookstore and bought a mystery recommended by the owner. Local writer Glynn Marsh Alam set her novel, *Dive Deep and Deadly*, at Wakulla Springs though she chose to call it Palmetto River. I was eager to read it.

I drove on to the lodge, and when I pulled into the parking lot I noticed the familiar Florida Department of Law Enforcement truck parked where I had seen it before. Uh oh, I thought, not another crime at the lodge. McBride rushed to meet me as soon as I entered the lobby. He had been sitting on a couch in front of the huge fireplace.

"Lorelei, you look great," he said, as he took my arm and led me into the dining room. "I've been thinking about you." He gave me a long warm smile, and I felt a little shiver of pleasure.

"I'm glad to see you too, Homer," I said. "I can't wait to find out what's happened."

"You saw the FDLE truck outside?"

"I did," I said.

At McBride's direction, the hostess seated us at one of the window tables for two at the furthest end of the dining room. No one was seated around us.

We ordered, and I said. "Tell me. What's happened?"

"Buster Stigler is dead," he replied, in a flat tone watching my reaction.

"What?" I was stunned.

"Yup. Looks like an accident. Happened right here on one of the trails. Hit a ditch, and his tractor rolled over on him. Broke his neck."

"When?"

"Sometime late Saturday afternoon. That's why I couldn't tell you anything when we talked. I didn't know much about it myself."

"Oh, my God. Buster dead. I can't believe it."

"The park ranger called Deputy Henderson, and he called me."

The news was so creepy. I had been thinking about Buster on Saturday as I drove home from Carrabelle. It was probably not long before the accident occurred.

"What does this do to your list of suspects?" I asked.

"Shortens it," McBride replied.

Impatiently, I said, "You know what I mean, Homer. I had Buster down for the murder and all the things that happened to me."

"Still could be. We'll have to see how this thing unfolds. I'm waiting for the Medical Examiner's report. Until then we can't be certain what really happened."

"Oh," I said, still feeling shocked by the news.

"Anyway, I want you to be extra-cautious in your dealings with those people in Fairport."

"You think it wasn't an accident, don't you?"

"I don't think anything, yet. But when a person of interest in a murder case suddenly has an accident… I just want you to be on guard."

We ate in silence. There was so much to consider. I was picturing the brash Buster Stigler when I first met him in the Fairport diner. I couldn't help feeling sympathy for his father and his girl friend.

"So how's it going?" McBride said, shoving his plate aside.

"What?" His question startled me out of my thoughts of Buster.

"The play. You're opening this week aren't you?"

"Oh, yes. It's going well. I hope you're still planning to come."

The waiter cleared the table and delivered the check.

"Homer, you didn't make me drive all the way over here just to tell me about Buster and ask about the play. You could have done that on the phone. What else is on your mind?"

He gave me a long appraising look. "I'll admit, I wanted a chance to see you again."

"I'm flattered," I said pleased by his response.

"And I'm still stymied about this whole Graham Springs dispute. I know it's an important piece of the puzzle, but I can't figure who had the most to lose or gain by Hadley's research."

"You mean the strongest motive for murder?"

He nodded. "What bugs me is I'm still seen as an outsider around here, and I have to count on the locals to give me information."

"Do you think you're not getting it all?"

"Right."

"So how can I help?"

"Stigler's funeral is scheduled for Wednesday. I'd like you to attend, and…"

"You want me to check things out for you?"

"Yes, that's it. You're good at sizing up people, and you've already established some relationships."

"Okay, I'll go."

"It starts at eleven o'clock at the Methodist church."

I know the one, I thought, and remembered the cold night that Horse and I parked in the church lot before we broke into Hadley's house.

"Thanks, Lorelei," McBride said, and looked relieved. "I'm going out to take a look at the accident scene. Wanna come with me?"

"Is it far?" I asked.

He looked down at my open sandals. "Don't you carry any other shoes with you? You know, in case you get stuck and have to really walk somewhere?"

I smiled at his practicality. "I never think about it. But I'll be okay."

"One of the park rangers will drive us out there."

McBride paid the bill and excused himself to make a phone call. I wandered into the gift shop. It had an old-fashioned soda fountain that was practically a block long. The other half of the store was devoted to racks of Florida tee shirts, post cards, and colorful souvenirs—stuffed alligators, manatees, seashells. I could imagine how busy the fountain and shop might be on weekends, and especially during the hot summer months when families came to swim at the springs.

I wandered to the back of the shop and found a variety of interesting books. I picked up one called *Watery Eden: A History of Wakulla Springs*. I browsed through a few pages. It looked interesting and would serve as a nice complement to the mystery novel I had just bought. I was excited to have something to read about the local area, and it would be a pleasant change from the Ibsen script.

By the time I paid for my purchase, McBride hailed me from the lobby. A park ranger, in a green uniform and wide brimmed hat, was outside talking to some tourists. She leaned against a Florida Park Service golf cart. When she spotted McBride, she waved us over. Her metal badge said "Jackie Werner, Park Service Specialist."

McBride introduced us, and we climbed into the cart. I sat in the front, next to the ranger. McBride sat behind us on the seat that faced backwards.

"My boss said you want to go out to the accident on the Hammock Trail."

"That's right," McBride said.

The ranger looked at my sandals and said, "It's kind of mucky out there right now. You might not be able to walk around much."

"I'm okay," I replied, and hearing a snort from McBride, I reached back and stuck my elbow into his ribs.

The ranger drove off the main road onto a narrow sandy tract called the Sally Ward Trails.

"I guess this leads to the Sally Ward Spring," I said, recalling a picture I'd seen in the lodge dining room.

"It does, eventually," the ranger said. "But we're only going as far as the Hammock Trail."

"Does the Sally Ward Spring flow into Wakulla Springs?" I asked.

"We don't think so. Actually, no connection has been made between the two even though they are only a mile apart."

"Interesting," I said, thinking about the disputed connection between Graham Springs and Wakulla. Dr. Matos and Rick Lucas maintained there was none, and those two springs were even further apart. Maybe they were right after all.

It was a bouncy ride, but I enjoyed being out of doors and loved the fresh smell of the woods.

The ranger slapped her arm and said, "Any other time of year, you'd be really bothered by the mosquitoes. In fact, see that small tree over there?" She pointed off to the right. "It's a Wax Myrtle tree. The Indians who inhabited this area used to rub themselves with the bark to keep the mosquitoes away."

We arrived at the accident scene which was surrounded by yellow police tape. The small green tractor that Buster had been driving lay on its side just off the trail. A couple of uniformed FDLE agents were placing stakes around it and taking measurements of the area.

McBride jumped off the cart saying, "Lorelei, you stay here."

I obeyed, and noticed the muddy ground and the pools of water near the tractor.

"Easy to see how he could have toppled," the ranger said. "All the rain we had a week ago washed out some of the trail. Guess that's why Buster was out here with the tractor...rebuilding the trail."

I watched McBride light up a cigarette while he directed his questions to one of the forensics men.

"So you knew Buster?" I asked, still watching McBride.

She replied, "Not that well. I'm usually down at the dock, and I don't see the landscape guys that much."

"What was your impression of him?" I asked, looking more closely at the ranger. She appeared to be in her forties, and her tanned face had a relaxed agreeable look—like she laughed easily.

"Buster? Seemed like an okay kid, though I don't think I ever saw him smile. Maybe he had problems at home, I don't know."

"Did you know his father is the mayor in Fairport?"

She looked surprised. "No kidding, I hadn't heard that. But I'm kind of new here myself."

My gaze returned to the accident scene where one of the investigators was gesturing in what appeared to be a recap of the accident. The other agent stood by, frowning. When he started talking to McBride and pointing to the tractor, he made hand gestures of different angles as though disputing the account of his colleague.

"Is he your boyfriend?" the ranger asked, looking at McBride. "He's quite a hunk."

I blushed, "No, he's a friend. We happened to be having lunch together here, and he invited me to tag along."

"Oh," she said, looking first at Homer and back at me. "Too bad."

I let it go, and within a few minutes McBride trudged back up to the cart. His shoes and the cuffs of his pants were wet and muddy.

"Okay, Ms. Werner. We can go back now. Appreciate the lift."

She gave a small laugh and said, "I'm afraid you'll have to see a bit more of the trail. If I turn around here we'll wind up with the tractor."

"Fine," he said, as the cart jerked forward.

I gave Homer an inquiring look. I wanted to know if he'd found out anything significant. Of course he wouldn't talk about it in front of the ranger. He shrugged, and ran his hands through his hair. It was a gesture I had come to know, one that reflected his frustration.

Ranger Werner said, "When there's a heavy rain like we had, we often have to close this trail."

"Was it closed on Saturday?" McBride asked.

"I don't think so, but I am surprised Buster was out here then. I didn't think he worked weekends."

"Really," McBride said, but asked no further questions.

The ranger dropped us off at the lodge and made a brief pitch urging us to take the boat ride around the springs. McBride thanked her again.

"So?" I whispered. "What do you think?" We were standing at the entrance, in front of the large rocks which held plaques about the springs and the lodge itself.

"Think? I think I need a damn new pair of shoes!" he said, looking down and stomping his feet.

I hit him lightly on the shoulder. "You know what I mean."

"Do you realize that's the second time you've poked me within the last hour. I could have you arrested for assaulting an officer."

I laughed. "Homer! Tell me what you learned out there. No joke."

His face clouded over, he took out a cigarette, tamped it on the back of his hand, and returned it to the pack. He said, "Okay, here's what I think. I think the M.E.'s going to determine that Buster Stigler didn't die just from falling off a tractor."

I sucked in a breath. "You don't mean…"

"Yup, I do mean. This case is heating up."

"How do they think he was killed? Was he shot? Are there footprints? Any major clues?"

"Won't know for sure until we get full forensics."

"Any ideas about who might have done it?"

"Until all the evidence is collected, I'm not counting anyone out."

This was classic McBride…unwilling to share information just when you were most interested. I thought for a moment. Surely Buster's father wouldn't be a suspect. But maybe his girlfriend, or even Mona Lavender would be. Mona detested Buster. It was unlikely that Rick Lucas or Dr. Matos would have been involved. Or it could be someone completely unknown to us.

"Homer, what about Buster's girlfriend? And you haven't said anything about Alex Hadley's father-in-law. Have you cleared him yet?"

McBride waved his hands to hold back my questions. "Like I said, no one's off my list." He stepped closer, gave me a concerned look, and took hold of my arms. I felt a shiver of electricity, and though he didn't say anything, his eyes registered the connection. "Lorelei, remember what I told you. You've got to be very careful now. Whoever is responsible for Stigler's death is becoming desperate."

"Surely, you have some clue."

"I have a few hunches about the case, but hunches aren't proof. That's why I need you to attend the funeral. You can help by remaining safe and alert." He looked at his watch. "I've got to get back to Tallahassee. I'll be in touch."

He turned and abruptly walked to his car. As I watched him pull away, I thought, what are your hunches, Homer? Who should I be most afraid of? I regretted not pressing him harder to divulge his list of suspects. It left me wondering about everyone. Maybe that was his intention, I thought.

I had some time to kill before I had to be back in town. Since I'd already invested in two books about the springs, I decided to act on the ranger's suggestion and take the boat tour. I walked down to the dock, paid my admission, and was just in time for the next tour.

It was amazing. I was on one of the electric boats along with about thirty other people. As we cruised from the spring pool onto the Wakulla River, we were treated to the sight of tall old growth cypress, covered with Spanish moss, which lined the banks, and sat amid stream with their knees protruding. They looked eerily primeval. The boat came within touching distance of alligators, turtles, spread-winged Anhingas, a variety of other wading birds, and ducks, but they seemed undisturbed by us. Thanks to the canny tenacity of Ed Ball, an above water fence—downstream—kept jet skiers and boaters from interfering with the park's river wilderness. It was a paradise. I understood why the Indians called it "mysterious waters," and Revel's book was named, *A Watery Eden.*

We cruised back to the spring pool along a densely wooded channel where *The Creature from the Black Lagoon, Tarzan* and other films had been made. This was the seemingly unremarkable pond I had seen from the lodge restaurant. Our guide said it was one of the largest and deepest freshwater springs in the world. Wes Skiles, an explorer diver in the Wakulla 2 Project led a team that reached the furthest distance achieved at the time—4,400 feet at depths surpassing 300 feet with a massive cave system. I was delighted to learn one huge cave with a rectangular vertical boulder standing in the middle reminded him of the movie *2001 A Space Odyssey*, so he named it "Monolith Room."

Glass bottomed boats used to show off the pristine quality of the water—clear to about 150 feet—which once brought film makers to shoot underwater scenes. Now there were few days during the year when the water was clear enough for the glass boats. The major problem with Wakulla, however, was not just tannic acid from heavy rains, or the invasive hydrilla, but high levels of nitrites—causing algae bloom and reduced oxygen in the water. Studies now showed that the sewage spray field from the fast growing city of Tallahassee—about 16 miles to the north—was believed to be one of the major sources of pollution.

As I listened to the talk, I recognized the same one could be given all over North Florida—where similar problems existed in springs, lakes, and rivers. It was becoming a human health hazard as more people reported allergic reactions to being in these waters. The job I recently had at an environmental organization taught me there was still time to heal these polluted bodies of water, but that it depended upon citizen awareness and action.

When I arrived back in town, I noticed that Mike's car was gone. I wondered if he went out on his boat, and I was sorry I had rebuffed him the night before. It would be nice to have his companionship for dinner and tell him about the Wakulla boat tour. Instead, I fixed some cheese and crackers, broke open a bottle of Merlot, and called Delcie.

"Lorelei, how are you? We haven't talked since last week, before Thanksgiving."

"How was your holiday, Del?"

"Don't ask."

"Something wrong?"

"Oh, the family dinner was fine, but…Luke never showed. Didn't call, just didn't come. Can you believe it?" she sounded more discouraged than angry. "It was so embarrassing."

"Oh, Del, I'm so sorry. Did he finally call you and explain?"

"When I didn't hear anything, I called him. Took two days before he responded."

"And?"

"Oh, he apologized all over the place—said he'd been working the entire holiday on a big real estate deal, and…"

"Forgot."

"Pretty much."

"I'm so sorry, Delcie."

"No, it's my own fault. This is just the kind of behavior we broke up over before. He keeps me dangling like a bungee jumper. Men!" There was a long pause before she continued. "And then, after giving me that lame excuse, he just carries on his business. Asks me what more I've learned about Fairport."

I could hear the disappointment in her voice. "No, 'I'll make it up to you' or any sweet talk?" I asked.

"You got it," she said. "It was like a minor issue for him. Well, I'm over it. I'll keep working with him as a client, but my days with Luther T. Williams are going to be all business."

"Sounds like a good idea, Delcie." I said, feeling saddened by my friend's hurt and disappointment.

"I don't want to talk about it anymore, Lor. Tell me about your holiday. Was it tough without Bill?"

"It was. I woke up so depressed on Thanksgiving morning I almost tried to drown myself in the bathtub."

"Lorelei! Why didn't you call me?"

"And ruin your holiday? Of course, I didn't know it was already ruined. At least, we could have commiserated."

"Did you go to that dinner with your cast?"

"That was a perk. Got me over the hump. I've been okay since then. Actually, I went back to Cape San Blas yesterday."

"You once told me about that place."

"Delcie, I swear, it was like Bill was with me the entire day. I felt so peaceful..."

She said, "I'll bet he was with you, honey. I truly believe our spirits in love hang out with us when we need them to."

"That's a comforting thought." I said. "On another note, I have a report for you."

"About Fairport?"

"Yes. Things have happened since we last talked."

"What things?"

"Another homicide," I said.

There was a sharp intake of breath, before she asked, "Who was it?"

"Buster Stigler had what looked to be an accident. But McBride doesn't think it'll turn out that way."

"You've seen McBride?"

"We had lunch together at the Wakulla Lodge today."

"You two seem to be meeting quite a bit."

"I guess it does seem that way."

"This keeping me in the loop deal I had with your detective friend doesn't seem to be working." She sounded annoyed.

"In fairness, Del, McBride's been spending a lot of time in Tallahassee. Maybe that's made it difficult…"

"To call and let me know what's going on? Oh, well, you know McBride and I never have been what you'd call colleagues. He probably still thinks of me as a dumb rookie deputy."

She probably was right, so I changed the subject. I said, "Anyway, this thing with Buster Stigler…McBride thinks it's related to Hadley's death. He told me he thinks the case is heating up."

"I'll bet it is—two homicides in two weeks? Do they have any solid leads?"

"I don't think so—none he's mentioned to me. There's the same list of suspects—minus one. Homer thinks the research dispute over Graham Springs is pivotal to the killer or killers motivation."

"Guess I'd better get on the phone to Luke. If the report I gave him earlier didn't chill his interest in the springs deal, I think this will definitely kill it."

"I'm sure. Anyway, I'll be attending the funeral service on Wednesday. Homer seems to think I'll be able to pick up some vibes or I'm not sure what."

"And I guess he warned you to be especially careful."

"Uh huh," I replied.

"When a second homicide occurs in a case, you know someone's gettin' desperate. You've been too close to this, Lorelei. It makes me nervous. You think I should come up there and watch your back?"

I laughed. "Oh, here we go again with the Kevin Costner bodyguard routine you did after the Prairie murder. That's really sweet of you, Delcie, but I'm going to be in rehearsals most of the time. The show opens Saturday. I can hardly believe it. So much has happened. Anyway, I won't be alone very much."

She sighed, "If you say so. But I plan to be at the opening anyway. I could just come a few days earlier. There's nothing much going on around here right now. A couple of divorce jobs…"

"No, thank you," I said, firmly. "I'll be very careful. Nothing bad's going to happen to me…I promise."

185

After talking to Delcie, I turned off my cell phone. I decided against calling Jeffrey or my mother. It was better to let them think I was busy with the play. They both knew I often turned off my phone during rehearsal, and when I was preparing for a role. They could always leave a message.

I poured another glass of wine and got settled on the couch with my new books. I decided to start with the Alam mystery which used Wakulla as the inspiration for the fictitious Palmetto Springs. Alam's heroine, Luanne Fogarty, was a professional cave diver. Within the first few pages I was engrossed in the story. It began with the sheriff's department calling upon her to help them find a woman's body reported to be in one of the spring's caves. I thought about my own diving lessons and wondered if I was qualified to venture into a cave. It was scary to think about it, but I was curious. I would ask Rick Lucas more about cave diving when I saw him on Friday.

Suddenly, I remembered McBride's warning to cancel my diving lesson with Lucas. I picked up my cell phone to call Lucas, but decided to wait until after the funeral on Wednesday when I'd have a better feeling about the situation. To my surprise—despite the phony reason for my enrolling in the lessons—I found myself wanting to develop diving skills. And now that I was almost a certified diver, I was eager to follow Luanne Fogarty's dive into the deep and mysterious caves of Palmetto Springs.

Chapter 23

I arrived at the church a little before eleven. The day was overcast and gloomy—a perfect setting for a funeral. The parking lot was already full, so I drove around to the back and parked on the grassy field next to other cars. When I got out of the car, I looked around and remembered this was the field Horse and I had traveled on the dark night we broke into Hadley's house. It seemed like months ago now.

I started toward the front of the church. "Mrs. Crane," I turned, hearing the familiar voice, and saw big Mona climbing out of her baby blue Mercedes. "Wait up," she said.

I waited as she almost skipped along toward me. She wore a large brimmed navy hat, and a flowered navy dress with a wool bolero jacket.

She sounded breathless. "I'm surprised to see you here, Mrs. Crane...Lorelei. You haven't returned my calls, and..."

"I'm sorry," I said. "I keep my phone turned off when we get this close to opening night." We started walking, side by side, toward the entrance to the church.

"Understood," she said. "Isn't this just terrible? Buster...so young. And poor Pete. I don't think he'll ever get over this."

I couldn't resist the opportunity to pry and said, "It's too bad they didn't get along very well."

Mona looked offended. "Lots of fathers and sons don't get along, but they still love one another. You should know that."

It was a rebuke, and probably well-deserved. Before I could respond, we had joined a group of people entering the church and Mona left me to greet others.

I chose a seat in the rear of the small church. It was packed, and I guessed the turn-out was more for the mayor than for his son. As I looked around, I noticed Mona seated in the second pew next to a man who looked familiar, but I couldn't place him for a moment. Finally, I realized it was Deputy Henderson in civilian clothes. Their heads were close together, and they were chatting with occasional sidelong glances. Curious combination, I thought, and continued scanning the crowd.

"Morning Lorelei," I turned and felt the warmth of McBride's body settle next to me in the pew.

"Homer? You didn't tell me you were coming to the funeral."

"Didn't I?" he said, as he took out his cell phone and turned it off.

The service began, and I surveyed the chapel again. Pete Stigler was sitting in the front pew, opposite Mona. I wondered about that. Seated alongside him were a red headed young woman with a pony tail and an older woman who kept a reassuring arm around her. I guessed them to be Buster's girlfriend and her mother. I didn't recognize anyone else.

"Are you going to the graveside?" I whispered to McBride as we stood up for a hymn.

"No," he said. "I still have some interviews here, but they'll have to wait. I think it would be good if you went. See if you can make some casual inquiries among Buster's friends. Find out anything unusual that's been happening to him."

"Okay," I said, eying some young people who were seated directly behind Pete. "Have you talked to the girlfriend yet?" I asked.

"Yes, and...

"Sssh." A woman in the pew in front of us turned and gave us a look.

We stopped talking. The minister invited friends and family to come to the podium to say something in memory of Buster. An old woman with a cane slowly walked down the aisle and patted Pete's shoulder as she passed him on the way to the lectern. I recognized her as the woman I met outside the theatre on my first day in Apalachicola. She wore the same cardinal red suede hat with matching bag. I was interested to hear what she had to say about the sullen Buster Stigler.

McBride motioned me to go outside with him.

Reluctantly, I slid to the edge of the pew and followed him outside.

"I think we should stay and listen to what people are saying," I said. "We might learn something about Buster."

"I doubt it, but you go back in. I've got to leave. I've got a meeting in Tally at one. I just wanted to check on you and see who showed up."

"I asked before about Buster's girlfriend. Have you talked to her yet?"

"Briefly, but she was pretty hysterical. We'll get to her some more after the funeral."

"And?"

"I didn't get much out of her. Just that she tried to call Stigler on his cell around the time we think he died. When she got no response, she was worried."

"Maybe he had it off while he was working."

"Way off," McBride said, as he took a pack of cigarettes from the pocket of his jacket and held them in his hand. "We didn't even find a phone at the scene. The girlfriend said he always wore it. Anyway, I'm putting a check on his calls."

"That's all?" I asked.

McBride glanced around and took a deep breath. "For now. Do I need to remind you again to be careful? Watch everything, but do nothing. Do you understand?"

"Yes, Homer," I said. I was getting irritated by all his warnings. "I'll be careful."

"Okay then," he lifted my chin and winked at me. "Don't let anything bad happen to you, Lorelei. Remember, you owe me a dinner."

When I returned to my seat, the old lady was just finishing her talk.

"...a lot of people thought Burton was just another angry young man. But I believe he was only trying to find his place in the world. He was nothing but kind and courteous to me, and I'll miss him dearly." She brought out a tissue from her sleeve and sniffed into it before slowly walking off the podium. Pete jumped up to help her down the steps and gave her a hug.

189

About half a dozen more people got up to talk about Buster. Most were friends of the mayor's who extolled Pete's behavior as a single parent. A couple of young men and women spoke haltingly, on the verge of tears, about knowing Buster since grade school. One described him as "a good old boy." I wondered if he was in the passenger seat the day Buster tried to drive me off the road.

I didn't learn anything about Burton "Buster" Stigler that I couldn't have predicted about a young man growing up in a small town with an important father. He was likeable but spoiled and had several life-long friends. I certainly didn't hear anything to suggest the kind of nasty and aggressive behavior I had witnessed. But then, it was only his friends who spoke.

I stood on the front porch of the church and watched as everyone paid their respects to the minister, Pete, Buster's girl friend—who barely contained herself—and her mother. When Mona came through the procession, there was a noticeable coolness between her and Pete. It made me wonder what had happened since I last was with the pair.

After everyone else had gone through the line, I went up to Pete and expressed my condolences. He gave me a cursory "thank you," excused himself, and walked down to the limo waiting to take him to the cemetery. *Stigler Funeral Home* was painted on the hearse which was parked in front of the limo.

At the gravesite, I stood near a few of Buster's young friends. They kept their heads bowed and were silent during the brief service. When the minister finished speaking everyone watched the casket lowered into the ground. I overheard one of the girls whisper to the boy next to her.

"His daddy and that Lavender witch should feel real guilty now...keepin' that land away from him. It wasn't right."

The boy nodded and put his finger to his lips warning her to be quiet.

The service was over, and people started drifting back to their cars.

I caught up with the girl. "Excuse me, I wonder if I could ask you a question?"

She stopped and looked at me as though she were trying to figure out if she knew me.

I explained, "I met Buster at the Fairport Diner a couple of weeks ago. You were close friends, weren't you?"

The girl looked to the boy, who had also stopped, before responding. "Yes, I am...was."

"I couldn't help but overhear you say something about the mayor and Mona Lavender..."

"You bet," she said. "I don't mind tellin' nobody. Them two caused Buster's death."

"What do you mean?" I asked.

"If they'd of loaned him the money to buy the springs land he wanted, he'd of been on his own and never would of been working over there at Wakulla." The girl continued, breathlessly, "But his own daddy wouldn't help him out. And that Lavender woman..."

"Why didn't Buster just apply for a loan?" I asked.

The two friends looked at one another, and the young man said, "Guess cause Buster's dad already set him up one business, and it didn't work out."

I couldn't think of anything more to ask the pair, so I stated the obvious, "Buster must have been pretty mad at his father."

"Not just mad...like crazy," the young woman said. "All he ever talked about was getting that springs property. And when Priscilla..."

The boy friend grabbed her arm. "Let's just say Buster had got real desperate to get a piece of that land and start his own business."

She nodded and looked embarrassed as though she realized she had said too much. "We have to go," the boy said, ushering the girl toward the parking area.

So Buster's desperation had escalated. Why? The girl mentioned Priscilla. Was she pregnant? And what was the young woman about to say regarding Mona Lavender before I cut her off? I knew there was only one place I could get more information. I returned to my car and headed to Herb's Diner hoping to find Linda Mae.

Chapter 24

It was after one o'clock by the time I pulled up in front of the diner. I hoped the lunch crowd had thinned to give me a better chance to talk with Linda Mae.

I slid into the front booth, and realized I was hungry. I looked over the menu until Linda Mae appeared.

"How you doing?" she asked, brightly. "Haven't seen you in a bit."

"I just came from Buster Stigler's funeral," I said, curious to see her reaction.

Linda Mae's face fell. "I ain't never had much good to say about Buster, but neither did I wish him dead."

"Do you know of anyone who did?"

She looked shocked. "Why, no, what a question."

"Just curious," I said.

She said, "I still can't believe it—Buster killed in an accident like that. It's creepy to think he's gone. I knowed him forever."

"I guess it would be a strange feeling," I said, looking over the menu. "He was so young."

Linda Mae pointed her pencil at the turkey loaf special on the menu. "Everybody says it's pretty good."

"Okay, I'll take it but with the vegetables on the side." She wrote it down.

"Have you been seeing any of Buster's friends or family in here today?"

"No, I hear they's all been invited back to the mayor's house."

"Mona Lavender, too?" I asked, replacing the menu behind the napkin holder.

She gave a half smile that verged on a smirk and said, "Don't think that was going to happen."

"What do you mean?" I asked.

She glanced at the register where a man was waiting to pay his bill. "Scuse me, got a customer," she said, and left. She returned in a few minutes. "I put your order in. Did you say what you wanted to drink?"

"Just iced tea. So, what's with Ms. Lavender and the mayor?"
She looked uncertain, as if debating whether or not to confide
anything. Then she said, "Now I only know one side of the story, but
Mona and my brother Skip—they's been an item for some time you
know—anyway, they had a fallin' out with the mayor over the springs
property."

"Is Skip by any chance Sheriff's Deputy Henderson?"

"That's right. Do you know him?"

"I met him at Wakulla Springs. He seemed to know a lot about
my visit to Fairport," I said.

Linda Mae blushed, "I guess I must of told him. He's always
interested in learning about new people plannin' to move here. You
did say you were looking at property to buy."

After seeing them together at the funeral, I was still surprised to
learn that Mona and Deputy Thompson were in a relationship. But for
the moment, their conflict with Pete Stigler was of even greater
interest. "Do you know what caused the falling out between them and
the mayor?"

After making sure there were no waiting customers, Linda Mae
slipped into the seat across from me, and in a conspiratorial voice she
said, "The way Skip tells it, he and Mona plan to take their acreage
shares out of the BSRC. They've already got a developer who wants
to put golf course homes on the property. Kind of like what St. Joe's
doing down by the coast."

"I thought the BSRC had a bid on that land from an Atlanta firm
for a water bottling plant."

She looked toward the kitchen and moved to the edge of the seat.
"Just a minute, your dinner's ready."

"What about the bottling plant?"

"Oh that," she said, getting up. "Skip's got a friend at the water
management district who told him they'd never get a permit. It was
something about not being able to use the land for a trucking
depot...to haul the water out, you know. Skip told Mayor Stigler, but
he didn't think it was true. He wanted to fight for it. My brother and
Mona disagreed and decided to make a deal for their share of the

land. I don't know exactly what all's been happening. I just listen and don't say nothing."

Linda Mae walked back to the kitchen. I was grateful that Linda Mae regarded me enough of an outsider that she could talk freely about the feud. And, the great irony in what she had told me, was that I was certain—if Hadley's research turned out to be true—no one was going to get their dream land deals. In a few minutes Linda Mae returned with my order.

"Hope I didn't tell too much," she said, looking worried.

"No, of course not. You've done me a real favor…you know, since I have been thinking about buying out there myself."

"I feel real sorry for Mr. Stigler," she said, tucking her order pad in her apron pocket. "Losin' his boy like that. Terrible thing. And with Priscilla pregnant and all."

God bless Linda Mae, I thought. She just confirmed my hunch. I said, "Oh, yes. It certainly is terrible. Priscilla's your friend, as I recall. I'm sure she's devastated. "

"I haven't spoken with her since the accident, but she was just crazy about Buster." She rolled her eyes as if to say she didn't see the attraction. "Her people will be a real comfort, and she's got good friends, too. We'll be there for her." Linda Mae took in a deep breath and her face brightened. "Well, let me know if you need anything else."

While I ate, I considered the implications of the Lavender and Thompson alliance. I thought, wasn't it Deputy Thompson's idea to let the press believe that Alex Hadley's death was an accident? Was it good for the investigation, as McBride seemed to think, or did it serve a private interest to avoid souring a development deal? Knowing Thompson had a vested interest in Fairport affairs added an extra piece to the murder puzzles, and one McBride was not going to like.

My imagination brimmed with new possibilities. Could Thompson have been involved in the Hadley murder? Could it have been Thompson who mugged me at Hadley's house and later broke into my apartment? My negative first impression of the man was largely based on his cavalier reaction to Buster's abusiveness toward his sister and his condescending attitude toward me. Besides, I thought, Thompson wouldn't be the first officer of the law to get caught up by greed. What I couldn't figure was how it all played into Buster's death? If he really was desperate—as the girl at the cemetery seemed to think—did his desperation lead to his murder? The questions were dizzying.

I finished lunch and went to pay my bill.

"How was the turkey loaf?" Linda Mae asked.

"Quite good," I replied. "By the way, you said your brother and Mona Lavender have been together for some time. Since I'm doing business with her all...what do you think of her? You seem to be a good judge of character. Can I trust her?"

She shrugged noncommittally, and said, "Alls I know is she's a lot smarter than Skip. Shrewd, kind of. Has him wrapped around her little finger, but he seems real happy with her, and that's good enough for me."

"Thank you, Linda Mae. I always enjoy talking with you." I laid down a tip larger than my bill, and she gave me a big smile as she picked it up.

"I like talkin' to you, too, Ms. Crane. I hope you decide to settle around here. It'd be real nice to have you in town."

"Thanks," I said, and left feeling a twinge of guilt for having pried so much information from her. She seemed genuinely nice, and I was glad Buster Stigler would no longer be around to terrorize her—or anyone else.

On the drive back to Apalachicola, I called McBride.

"Is it anything important?" he asked, sounding rushed.

"Actually, I have interesting news."

"Spill it," he said, "but give me the quick version. I'm standing outside FDLE building. I've got a meeting in a few minutes."

"Okay, first, Buster's girl friend is pregnant. According to their friends, Buster was desperate to get in on the Graham Springs property."

"So he needed to raise some fast cash," McBride added.

"At least fifty thousand to buy one acre." I recalled the amount Mona had quoted.

"Next," McBride said.

"This one's really going to surprise you. Mona Lavender and Deputy Thompson are in a land deal together. Apparently, they split off from the BSRC, and the Stigler's angry about it."

"Interesting. How'd you find out?"

"Linda Mae, the deputy's sister. She's the waitress at the Fairport Diner. I've talked with her before. She's my 'deep throat'."

He chuckled, "Lorelei, you do have a real talent for investigation."

"And that's not all. Mona and Skip—that's what his sister calls him—are a romantic duo as well."

"My, my," McBride murmured, "Sounds like the fox may be guarding the chicken coop. I had a hunch Thompson might turn out to be something of a rogue."

"A rogue? What a quaint word for a detective to use." When he didn't respond to my teasing, I continued, "It did strike me as a conflict of interest. Of course, once Hadley's research is made public..." I paused hearing a sharp intake of breath and understood why Homer was standing outside—he was smoking.

McBride said, "Speaking of which, I've had another interview with Dr. Matos at FSU—hey, did you hear the Gators whipped their sorry butts at the Swamp?"

"I thought FSU was your alma mater?"

"It is, but my son Bobby's a big Gator fan, and I've lived in Gainesville so long..."

"So you're now a citizen in the Gator Nation?" I said, intending it as a joke. "What about your meeting with Dr. Matos?"

"I'll have to tell you later. Let me just say, I finally got the guy rattled. Gotta go now. Let's touch base again tomorrow."

I put the phone down and tried to enjoy the scenic trip back to Apalachicola. Soon enough I would need to focus on the play. I had a final costume fitting, and the last rehearsal before the technical which would take place tomorrow night.

My thoughts turned to Mike, and the question he had raised. *"Isn't one drama enough for you?"* Mike even seemed angry about it. Maybe he was jealous of the time I was spending away from

Apalachicola, or maybe he just worried about my association with Rick Lucas.

I pulled over to get some water, at the Quick Stop in Eastpoint, and had one of those rare flashes of insight—an epiphany of sorts. I suddenly understood the reason I continued to work with McBride on the Hadley case. It was the same reason Delcie wanted me to join her agency. I had a knack for getting people to confide in me. I found myself as fascinated by figuring out the motivations of real people as I did fictional ones. Sometimes, like now, even more challenged by it. I liked putting together pieces of the puzzle that led to solving a crime. It was intellectually stimulating, and it made me feel alive in a way the theatre didn't always do—perhaps because it was also sometimes dangerous. I thought of Rick Lucas and shivered. It was not an altogether unpleasant feeling.

Chapter 25

I spent the next couple of days studying my script, doing yoga, and I even took the time to look at the scuba video Rick gave me. When I needed to get out of the apartment, I walked around the small downtown. There were so many interesting shops, and the people were invariably friendly. During mealtimes, Mike and I met at Sophie's and worked together on our lines. He didn't invite me back to his apartment which was fine with me. It avoided any awkward situations.

On Friday, I awoke with a start realizing tonight was the final rehearsal. Rehearsals had seemed to go on forever, yet here it was almost opening night. It was an oddly shocking thought. I got up, glad to have had such a good night's sleep, and opened the windows. The morning air was cool and fresh, and I inhaled deeply.

While I was doing my yoga postures, I watched the almost motionless roosting birds on the pier below. They had been a continuous source of amusement, and today they reminded me of a theatre audience awaiting the performance to begin. There must have been thirty or forty of them, but the only sounds I heard were the drones of marine engines from the small boats heading out from the bay into the gulf waters. Later, I returned McBride's call.

"You are one tough lady to get a hold of," he said, sounding annoyed.

"Now, Homer, I told you when opening night gets close, I have to focus everything on the play."

"Oh, the play. That's this weekend, isn't it?"

"Tomorrow night, actually. Will you be coming to Apalachicola?" I asked. "I've reserved a ticket for you."

"I'll try, but no promises. Depends on whether I have to be in Tally or not. Our murder investigation has gotten hot."

"What now?" I asked. "By the way, you never did finish telling me about your conversation with Dr. Matos. Something about throwing him off his guard."

"I would have told you if you'd have picked up my call last night."

"Well, I'm here now, so get over it." I surprised myself by using the exact same phrase that Renee had used with me the night before when she chided me for flubbing my lines.

"What?" he said, sounding surprised.

"Sorry, Homer. It's my nerves showing…I get tense close to opening. I apologize."

"Accepted."

I asked, "What did you learn from Dr. Matos?"

"I showed him a copy of Hadley's research, and the interpretation Waterman had gotten at the University of Florida. I also had it checked out with another source."

"What did he say?"

"At first he just acted surprised we that we had it, then he got belligerent. Demanded the original drive. "

"On what grounds?"

"Oh, some bullshit thing. Academic privilege," I think was the phrase he used.

"I never heard of it," I said, with the authority of a professor's wife.

"Me neither, but he claimed he was the expert on springs hydrology and had done earlier research on Graham…"

"Did he acknowledge that his conclusions were wrong, according to Hadley?"

Homer let out a snort and said, "You kidding? He made it clear that he—and not the University of Florida—was entitled to have the original Hadley file."

"Yeah, to file it away, no doubt."

"I informed him it was evidence in a criminal investigation and couldn't be released. He asked for the rights to it after the investigation. Ballsy."

"What did you say to that?"

"Believe me, he didn't like my answer. I said it was intellectual property that would revert either to Hadley's heirs or the organization that sponsored the research. He didn't have a comeback for that one."

"Oh, boy."

"Yeah, when I left I could tell he was really pissed. I'd hate to be his secretary, or whoever he took it out on."

"So, are you any closer to sorting through the suspects?"

"Yes, and no," he replied.

I moved to the couch, put the cell on speaker phone, and stretched out. "Explain, please." Listening to McBride's voice had begun to make me feel more relaxed.

"I hate doing this on a cell phone, but I'm not giving away state secrets."

"Homer, what else have you found out?"

"Buster's girlfriend says he always wore his cell phone on his belt. Forensics didn't find any cell holster or phone on him, or in the vicinity of the body. I did manage to get a copy of the detail of his calls. You'll never guess who our boy Buster was in touch with."

"Tell me," I said.

"Both Deputy Thompson and Rick Lucas," he replied.

I was stunned. "Thompson and Lucas? What on earth would the two of them have in common with Buster Stigler?"

"Good question. I've asked myself that, as well."

"Did you come up with an answer?"

"I'm not sure. I have some hunches, but I need to do more checking. In the meantime, you stay clear of Lucas. You did cancel your dive lesson with him, didn't you?"

I hesitated.

"Lorelei, tell me you don't intend to go diving with Lucas."

"I haven't canceled yet. I put if off until Buster's funeral. Are you suggesting he's behind the murders?"

"I'm not suggesting anything, except there's something not right with the guy. He had a motive for wanting Hadley's research hushed up, and now we know he was somehow connected to Stigler. I don't like the idea of you being alone with him in such risky circumstances."

I considered his point. "Look, Homer, maybe I could find out about those calls to Buster. Rick opened up to me last time, and..."

"Lorelei, I can't make you do anything—you definitely have a mind of your own—but please don't pursue him. I'll find out what I need to know without putting you in jeopardy."

"I guess you're right. So what's next? Do you need me for anything?"

"Like you said, you've got your opening night to think about. I'll try to get over there. If not, let's meet on Monday—at Wakulla. That's still your day off, isn't it?"

"Yes, the theatre's dark on Mondays, but do try to make it over here. I think you'll find the play very interesting, in a lot of different ways."

"I'm sure anything you're in will be interesting. What'd they say, uh, 'break a leg?' Where's that come from anyway?"

I giggled. "Probably from some ambitious understudy. No, I've read it refers to the curtsey—bending the leg—the actors take at the end of the performance. I like my version better, don't you?"

"Your version's more violent, I'll give you that," and in a more sober tone, he added, "Just take care of yourself, Lorelei. Remember what I've said before…stay out of deep water."

McBride's warning made me think about Rick Lucas, until I was interrupted by another call. It was one of those eerie coincidences.

"Hello, Lorelei, this is Rick Lucas. I'm checking to make sure we're still on for tomorrow."

I sat up, and said, "Hi, Rick. I was just thinking about you."

"Oh?" he said. "I hope it was something nice."

"In fact, I was about to call you. I'm afraid I have to cancel for tomorrow."

There was a long pause.

"That would be too bad, Lorelei. I'm going away, and I may not be back before you leave Apalachicola."

Rick was leaving? McBride needed to know.

"Where are you going?" I asked.

"I have a conference out west, and I may stay there for a while. It would be a shame if you had to start all over with a new instructor."

"What about your father?"

"Oh, he'll be fine. I've arranged for a caregiver—a grad student—to live in. It'll be a good change for both of us. Are you sure you can't make it tomorrow?"

I had to think fast. Should I finish my dive lessons, and find out more about Rick's plans and his connection to Buster. I didn't know what to do.

"I'd love to finish with you, but my play opens tomorrow night. I guess I didn't think it through when I scheduled the lessons."

"Hmm, I understand," he said. "But maybe I can entice you by telling you we can finish your lessons at Graham Springs. You did say you were interested in buying property there, didn't you? It'd be kind of nice for you to get a view of the springs from below, wouldn't it?"

Graham Springs, I thought. It would be exciting to see what Hadley had seen when he went diving there. Perhaps it would help me understand all of the interest, the fighting, and even the murders that may have taken place because of it.

"Rick, your offer is very tempting," I said. McBride's warning was still fresh in my mind, but I couldn't imagine why Rick would want to harm me.

"What about it?" he said. "We can meet around ten—that should give you enough sleep time—and you'd be back in Apalachicola by midday. Early enough to rest before your evening performance. It might even energize you. Diving always clears my head."

"You're very persuasive."

"So, is it a date?"

I inhaled, breathing deeply, "Okay, it's a date."

He said, "Good. Meet me at the springs. You do know how to get there, don't you?"

"Yes, I do."

"I'll bring all the equipment. I'm glad you're going to do it."

"Yes," I said. "So am I."

I flipped the phone shut and wondered aloud, "Lorelei, I sure hope you made the right decision. Diving with Rick Lucas at Graham Springs could be a great experience, or....McBride worries about me too much," I said, finishing my thought.

I was proud of myself for taking a risk by deciding to complete my dive lessons with Rick. It was almost noon, and my stomach started grumbling. I decided to get dressed and head over to Sophie's for lunch. I hadn't talked with her in a while, and I was hungry for one of her tasty Mediterranean wraps.

I stood in the doorway of Sophie's and inhaled the aroma of freshly made coffee. The cafe was crowded, but I saw an empty chair at the small table near the store room. It was where Sophie did her paper work, and she had let me sit there once before. I looked around, but I didn't see Sophie. Instead there was a dark-haired young woman working behind the counter. I hadn't seen her before. She had the olive-skinned Mediterranean features that made me think she might be related to Sophie…a daughter, or a niece, I wondered?

"Lorelei, how good to see you," Sophie said, coming out of the storeroom, as I approached her table.

"I hope you don't mind my sitting here," I said. "Looks like you're really busy."

"No problem," she replied, and looked around the café, before sitting down opposite me. "Good. Everyone seems to be happy, and the girl can handle the counter."

"She looks a bit like you," I said, in a questioning tone.

Sophie glanced toward the counter, and smiled. "I should only look so good. She's a nice girl. Her name is Idris, she's Palestinian. Just showed up one day, and needed a job for a week or so. She's starting university. We talk a lot."

"Trying to solve all the problems in the Middle East?"

Sophie gave a helpless shrug, "We share a dream of peace, and worry that it will never come to pass, but, she's a survivor…like me." Her face clouded over with sadness, and she said, "Lorelei, unless you've experienced being a refugee, you can't imagine how torn we feel. We long for our homeland yet know we are better off here."

"I hadn't thought of it that way," I said. "I'm sure it's how people displaced by Hurricane Katrina must feel, and all first generation immigrants to this country."

Sophie nodded, "Exactly so. But, let's talk about something more pleasant. Tomorrow's the big night—how does it feel?"

"I'm a bit jumpy—like always—but I'm ready. More than ready. I feel like I've been saying the same lines for years! Thank goodness we're having the final rehearsal. I need all the props, and a live audience to get me excited again."

"Is it always like that for you?"

"Not all the time. But this time..."

She gave me a puzzled look, inviting me to explain further.

"I guess you know I've been working on a murder investigation."

"Mike's mentioned it. He doesn't approve, you know."

"Uh huh," I said, rolling my eyes.

"This case, it's the one over in Wakulla? 'The Creature-Feature murder?'"

"Is that what they're calling it?" It struck me as an entirely too whimsical name for such a tragic event.

"I don't know," she replied. "I've heard some young people call it that. It's about the man who did the research at Graham Springs, isn't it? You mentioned him at Thanksgiving."

"Yes, it is about that, and now there's been another death. The two may be related."

"Really?" she asked, as her eyes scanned the room again.

"It's complicated, but the detective I'm working with is an old friend, and..."

Sophie flashed a knowing smile, and said, "Mike mentioned something about him, as well. Is he the reason you're involved?"

"No...yes, I guess so. We're just friends. But I have to say that, so far, I'm finding the investigation more exciting than the play. Don't tell Renee I said that."

"Hmm, a nice girl like you involved in such a nasty business." She shook her head, and let out a soft "Tsk, tsk."

I could imagine Sophie and Mike talking about how foolish I was to get involved, and speculating on my relationship with McBride. It was time to change the subject.

"You do know I'm thinking about buying some property around Graham Springs. When everything is resolved, that is. It's quite a beautiful place."

She looked wistful for a moment and said, "And living near the water is very healing...it has unique powers."

"Powers? Like we talked about before?"

"Good hado," she said.

"Hado?"

"Yes. Have you never heard of the Japanese water researcher, Masaru Emoto? *The True Power of Water* is one of his books."

"No. What does he say?"

She paused, held up a glass of water and said. "Hado refers to the vibrational energy in all things. See this water? When it's frozen it forms crystals. According to Emoto's research, the crystals behave differently depending upon the quality of the water. And—this is the most remarkable thing he discovered—the crystals also respond to our own interactions with it."

I said, "Is it like the thing about talking to plants? I remember reading somewhere that an Indian scientist discovered plants respond to human threats and to compliments. But water? It sounds far-fetched."

She frowned, "Don't be such a skeptic. In a way, it is similar to what you said about plants. All living things have sensitivities, yes? Everything is comprised of energy molecules." She glanced at the unopened menu in front of me. "Did you order yet? I didn't mean to keep you from your lunch."

"No, and I am hungry, but I'm fascinated by what you're saying. Can I get a Mediterranean wrap and coffee?"

"Of course," she said and got up to fill my order.

While she was gone, I picked up *The Franklin Chronicle*. I idly looked through it to see if there was anything about Buster Stigler's accident or the funeral. I didn't expect to find anything since he lived in a different county, but I was happy to see a large article about our play. My name was among the cast listing, and there was a fairly lengthy plot synopsis. When Sophie returned with my lunch, I closed the paper.

"Do you want me to save the article about the play?"

I thought of my mother. "I'd like that. Thanks."

She sat down again and said, "Eat, and I'll tell you some more about the properties of water and Mr. Emoto. He is quite an extraordinary man. Even though he has had no formal training, he is asked to give lectures about his water research at some of the most prestigious scientific meetings in the world."

Sophie described the water crystal experiments performed by Emoto and his assistant. She said, "You know our bodies are made up mostly of water. When water changes, we change. Hado, this vibrational energy, responds to positive attitudes. That's why Emoto's research caused him to believe we must show gratitude, love, and respect not only for water, but for all natural things in order for us to live in a healthy world."

I thought, not exactly a novel conclusion. Nonetheless, I was intrigued by the idea of water crystals actually changing their shape based upon human intentions. It was something to think about.

"Did you know the year 2005 was declared by the United Nations to be 'The Beginning of the Decade of Water?'" Sophie asked. "I don't think most Americans realize just how critical the situation is...more than the politics, or crime, or even terrorism. What will happen when there isn't enough usable water—when water, and not oil, is the dearest commodity? And don't tell me you'll just drink cola. That's the answer I get from some young people. They don't understand there is no alternative to water—it's the foundation of life."

I listened, while munching on my wrap. It surprised me to learn that Sophie was so passionate about water—more than food.

"Frankly," she continued. "I sometimes have to smile when I read about water problems in this country as though it were some new threat. All this has been a fact of life in the Middle East since....why since Biblical times, actually. Did you even know some of the problems in the Middle East are related to water rather than oil? Israel, Lebanon, Syria, and Jordan all have to share water from the Jordan River system, and..." she paused.

My thoughts had begun to drift away from Sophie's discourse, as I followed her eyes to the counter. A tall well-dressed man was purchasing a coffee. He didn't appear to belong in this laid-back fishing and tourist community. Dressed in a dark suit and tie, he had the appearance of someone who had just flown in from a Miami courtroom or business meeting.

"Do you know him?" I asked, finishing my sandwich. Without looking at me, she replied, "Yes, that's Mr. Rinehart. He's been in here before."

Rinehart, I thought, that's the name of Hadley's father-in-law.

"Is he from Tampa?" I asked.

"Yes," she said. "He's an attorney of some sort. I forget what kind. He happened to be in here one day when I was having trouble with a customer who'd had a bit too much tequila up the street. He talked the guy into leaving quietly. I'll be back in a minute. I don't want him to pay."

As I watched Sophie walk away, I remembered it was Rinehart who found Hadley's body, but who had hurried away from the lodge without reporting it. Some lawyer, I thought. I've got to meet him.

Sophie was still talking with him when I approached. She tucked her arm in mine, and introduced me.

"This is Lorelei Crane," she said. "She's in the play at the Dixie Theatre. Will you be in town this weekend?" she asked Rinehart.

He gave me a friendly but disinterested glance and replied, "No, I'm afraid my business is completed. I'm heading back to Tampa this afternoon."

"Uh, Mr. Rinehart," I said. "I wonder if we could talk for a moment. I'm Jeff Waterman's friend…he was a friend of your son-in-law."

Rinehart was startled and didn't seem at all pleased by this information. He said, "Just what have we to talk about? My son-in-law is dead. Surely you know that."

Sophie excused herself, and Rinehart turned to leave—coffee in hand.

I touched his sleeve. "Please, sir, if you'll give me just a moment. Maybe we could sit on the bench outside. It's a beautiful day, and I'm sure you'd enjoy your coffee more than driving with it."

He shrugged. "As you wish. But I don't have much time. It's a long drive back to Tampa."

I looked over my shoulder to see if Sophie had returned to the table. She motioned to me it was okay to go, and we walked out the door. He led the way to the bench. I had to think quickly about what to ask him.

After we sat down, he said, "Now, Mrs. Crane. What exactly is it you want from me?"

Good question, I thought. Just get him talking, so I said, "How are your daughter and granddaughter doing since...?"

"As well as can be expected, thank you."

Oh boy, this isn't going to be easy. Of course not, he's a lawyer more used to asking than telling. And he had put on his dark sunglasses, effectively blocking me from reading his reactions.

I went on, "My friend Jeffrey told me a lot about your daughter and Alex. He was very fond of both of them...and little Clare."

"Hmm," he said, sipping his coffee.

"I think Jeff was the one who introduced Alex to your daughter."

He turned and gave me a tight smile. "No thanks to him—she's been miserable ever since."

I doubted it was true. Everything I'd heard suggested they were a happy couple until Alex challenged the status quo. "I guess Alex was pretty much of a hard nose—especially when it came to his politics."

"That's an understatement. You have no idea what he put my daughter through with his self-righteousness." He sighed adding, "Well, that's over now. I just put their house on the market. Thank goodness Jennie won't have to return to that God forsaken town of Fairport."

Idly, I wondered if he had placed the listing with Mona Lavender, but I didn't want to get onto that topic. I gave him a side long glance and noticed his body had become more relaxed. I took a chance on a direct question. "Do you know of anyone—beside yourself—who might have had a grudge against your son-in-law?"

He reacted with a quick look and said, "You sound like a detective. Are you sure you're just an actress?"

I laughed. It was a question I was becoming accustomed to. "It's just curiosity. You know, for my friend—he's very distressed about the murder."

Rinehart seemed lost in thought, until he said, "If only Jennie had married that smart young scientist friend of Alex's instead of ..."

"Who's that?" I asked, knowing exactly what he was going to say.

"Oh, a young man on the faculty at FSU. Actually, he and Alex were dive buddies."

"You mean Rick Lucas?"

He said, "Yes, Rick Lucas. Do you know him? Alex and he were best friends until Alex's jealousy put a chill on the relationship. Jennie told me about it."

"Alex was jealous over your daughter and Rick Lucas?" I asked.

"She swore there was nothing between them. Claimed it was just Alex's paranoia, and I believe her. Jennie's a one man woman—like her mother was. She could never have cheated on her husband. She's pregnant with his baby, for God's sake."

I began to reel with this new information and wondered if McBride knew any of it.

He offered me his hand and said, "I've got to be going. It was nice talking with you. Best of luck in your play." He looked up at the marquee. "*An Enemy of the People?* Alex would have liked that all right. Goodbye, Mrs. Crane."

Cliff Rinehart walked across the street, and I watched as he got into a white Jeep and pulled onto the main highway heading east. I sat on the bench for a few minutes trying to sift through what he had told me. Rick Lucas and Jennie Rinehart? Had Hadley's suspicions about the two of them been true? If so...oh, the possibilities.

Chapter 26

"I'm catering the cast party here. You'll be coming?" Sophie asked, when I had returned to the table. She peered at me more closely, and said, "How about some more coffee? Are you upset? Was it Mr. Rinehart?"

"No. I've just got a lot on my mind right now. You were saying...about the cast party?"

"Yes, I said it's going to be here...at Sophie's. I've already begun baking for it." She tipped her head in the direction of the young woman at the front counter. "Idris is helping me."

"I expect I'll be here," I said, trying to tuck my conversation with Rinehart into a mental compartment for later review.

Sophie gave me a kindly look and said, "I know it's none of my business, but tell me, are you and Mike together? He seems so unusually cheerful lately."

Sophie the matchmaker I thought. "I'm glad he's happy, but, no, we're just good friends, Sophie."

She appeared disappointed by the news. "Too bad, I know he's younger than you, but I hoped..." Her voice trailed off as she noticed a line of customers waiting to pay their checks. "Excuse me, Lorelei."

I left Sophie's and went directly to the theatre. The excitement was palpable. The women's dressing room was like a New York subway at rush hour. The actors, the costume designer and her helpers were crammed together, bumping into one another in the small narrow space. The air was filled with the scent of colognes mingled with perspiration. There was a lot of nervous giggling and laughing, until we were given the cue for the opening of Act I. I had butterflies in my stomach as I descended the stairs to the wings. As always, I prayed to Dionysus—god of drama—that I wouldn't block or dry-up once I hit the stage. People don't realize how devastatingly common is the stage fright that afflicts actors...no matter how experienced we may be.

The rest of the rehearsal passed in a blur. I found my stride, didn't miss any cues, and said my lines perfectly. When it was over

Mike and I walked back to the apartment together. It wasn't quite eleven o'clock when we approached our building.

"I'm hungry," I said. "I can't believe all they fed us were pastries, doughnuts, and coffee."

"Calculated to keep us cranked up. As if we needed it," he said. "I think I've got some ham and cheese in the refrigerator. Want to come in for a sandwich and a nightcap?"

"Yes. That sounds great."

We each made our own sandwiches. Mike got a beer and did a microwave brew of Chamomile tea for me. We sat on the living room couch and set upon the food as though we were ravenous.

"I think I have some Oreos someplace. Want some?" he said, washing down the last bite of his sandwich with a Corona.

I nodded, "More sugar? But, yes, I need all the comfort foods I can get at this point."

When Mike returned with the package of cookies, I said. "You know, Sophie was asking me about you today."

"Really? I see her almost every day. What'd she want to know?"

"If we were 'an item.' Said she hadn't seen you so cheerful in quite a while, and thought I must be the cause."

He flashed an arch grin, and said, "Would that were true, my dear Mrs. Stockman. Did you tell her our relationship was, how shall I put it…chaste?"

Chaste? Well, except for one night, I thought. His choice of the word made me picture Mike as an actor in the seventeenth century. Indeed, since I believed in reincarnation, I guessed he probably once was.

"*Chaste as ice, as pure as snow,*" I declared, and saw his lips part in a small smile recognizing the phrase from Hamlet. "I played Ophelia in college—and, yes, I assured her we were simply good friends though she seemed disappointed."

"Ah, Sophie. She desperately wants me to take the cure."

"The cure?"

"You know. The cure for a broken heart—falling in love again."

"Ah, the cure. Yes, I know it only too well," I said, thinking about my susceptibility to Bill Crane's courtship after my divorce from Jeffrey.

We sat in companionable silence. I sipped my tea while he held the neck of his beer bottle to his lips without drinking.

"Oh well," he said, at last, giving me his sweetest smile. "To quote our mutual friend, Will—*If it be not now, yet it will come: the readiness is all.*"

It was my turn to smile, and I raised my cup. "Touché. What a great Zen attitude. If you really believe it, no wonder Sophie has found you so cheerful lately."

Mike shrugged, "You might take it to heart as well and lighten up a bit. You've seemed distracted all week. Want to talk about it? On second thought, do I even want to hear about it?"

I placed my cup of tea on the coffee table, checked the digital clock on the credenza and said, "No, but thanks for the food and words of wisdom. I've got to get some sleep. I'm going for my last dive lesson tomorrow morning."

Mike let out a gasp. "You're not still working with Lucas, are you?"

"Actually, yes. We're going to Graham Springs." Fortunately, Mike didn't know about McBride's warning, or what I'd learned about Rick Lucas.

"He's taking you to a spring for your lesson? That's pretty risky, even for Rick. People die all the time going cave diving. It's not for amateurs."

"We're not going into the caves," I said, though I didn't know that for sure. "He's just going to show me what Graham Springs is like, and let me complete my certification there. I told him I intend to buy property in the area. Anyway, I'm excited to see it from the water."

Mike looked worried. "What time do you think you'll be back? Frankly, I'll feel a lot better when I see you here."

"About two o'clock. I'll have plenty of time to get ready for the opening. The diving is good exercise. It'll relax me...help me avoid my opening night jitters."

"Uh huh," he said, absently. "Well, just be careful, Lorelei. I'm not a scuba diver, but I have a healthy respect for what can happen when we venture out of our natural element."

I knew he was thinking of his experiences on the open water. As I walked to the door I said, "Don't worry so much, Mike. I know what I'm doing. The next time I see you I'll be a certified diver. I'm rather proud of myself for doing it."

He gathered our plates and walked me to the door. "I'll just be glad when you don't have any more reason to see Rick Lucas. Sleep well, Lorelei. I'll see you tomorrow."

I slept surprisingly well and awoke early enough on Saturday morning to do some yoga breathing exercises before getting ready to meet Rick. When I got into my car, I checked my messages. There was one from Homer—wishing me good luck on the play. Another was from my mother saying she couldn't fly up for the play as she had gotten a bad cold, but she insisted I call her after the opening, no matter what time I got home. There was also a call from Delcie, but no voice message. As I pulled on to Highway 98 toward Fairport, I decided not to return any calls until I got home.

It was a sunny, cloudless day, and the weather prediction called for temperatures in the seventies...pretty much the way it had been for the past week or so.

As I drove along the coast, I started reflecting on the jealousy angle mentioned by Rinehart. If there was a basis for Alex's suspicions, it might explain why he so closely guarded his research findings even from his friend.

A jealous Alex Hadley might have cut both Lucas and Matos out of the loop and decided to go it alone. It proved a fatal mistake. And who made it fatal I asked myself. Surely not Dr. Matos, a scientist of international renown. He appeared to have no obvious connection to Buster Stigler, and I still believed the two crimes were related.

So, if not Matos, then how about his assistant? Rick's motivation for killing his former friend might now have an added dimension—to get Hadley out of the way so he could have Hadley's wife. But what about Buster? Where does he fit into Lucas plans? I couldn't come up

213

with any link between them despite the fact that McBride mentioned Lucas was listed in Buster's phone log.

I turned on the car radio. I wanted to be upbeat and not preoccupied when I met with Lucas. I definitely didn't want to emit any aura of suspicion. Listening to a smooth jazz station, my mind drifted back to the question of motivation which led to the twin murders. I considered yet another possibility...Deputy Skip Henderson and his girl friend, the deceptively charming Mona Lavender—violet flower, or black widow spider? Their interest in the Graham Springs property connected them to both Alex Hadley and Buster Stigler. Hadley threatened to thwart their development plans if he made his research findings known.

But why kill Buster Stigler? That was a bit more mystifying. Unless they enlisted Stigler to help them. Buster worked right on the premises at Wakulla. He could have easily placed the ants in Hadley's costume. Who would notice a groundskeeper bending down to collect some sand? It was a clever, well-conceived crime—something I could picture Mona concocting.

Or perhaps they only employed him to find the damning research at Hadley's house, and later my apartment. They would have known how desperate Buster was for money. Then maybe he tried to get too much from them, and they killed him to stop the blackmail. Certainly Mona would be happy to get rid of Buster. She had said as much the day we went to the spring, and a law enforcement officer, like Thompson, would know how to commit a crime and leave no incriminating evidence.

I was eager to talk this over with McBride, but I didn't dare call him on my way to meeting Rick. Besides, I reminded myself, I needed to focus on the here and now. I took several centering deep breaths and soon found the small marker for Graham Springs. I turned onto the sandy track and started getting excited about diving in one of the most serene places I had ever been.

Chapter 27

I pulled alongside Rick's pick-up truck. He waved from his perch on a tree stump near the water. As I walked toward him, I saw he had all the dive equipment neatly laid out on a large tarp, and he was working on a regulator attached to a yellow air tank.

"Beautiful morning," he said. A dour expression belied his greeting.

"Hi, Rick," I replied, and stooped down at the edge of the blue tarp. The ground was covered with fallen leaves and looked like a red and golden colored shag carpet. I sniffed the early morning air and said, "I've really been looking forward to this. I just hope it's not too chilly."

"Water's a perfect seventy degrees—about the same as the air temperature this morning. Shouldn't be too bad. Why don't you suit up and we can get started."

After I got into my wet suit, I found him seated on his cooler at the shallow end of the spring. He motioned me next to him. "Sit here and put on your fins."

I dutifully plopped down. "Can we just hang out for a few minutes?" I said. "I want to take in some of this atmosphere before we get into the water."

With the same sour look he said, "When you buy your property here you'll be able to look at this all day. Right now, we need to focus on diving."

"Is something wrong?" I asked.

He made a dismissive gesture. "I've just got a lot on my mind, that's all."

"Well, as for buying property here, I'm not sure I'll be doing it."

"Changed your mind already?" He picked up a small branch and started idly drawing lines in the ground.

"I don't know. It's beautiful, but I feel like there's a lot of bad karma." It was the opposite of how I felt, but I hoped the lie would provoke him. "I mean, first there's Alex Hadley's murder, and now I understand the springs are connected to Wakulla. In a few years, they might both be badly polluted." I paused, hoping for a reaction.

215

Getting none, I continued, "But you know that, don't you?" I said, in a matter of fact way—baiting but trying not to sound accusatory.

He stopped doodling and looked at me sideways. It was a curiously intense look as though he were studying some odd insect he was about to stick with a pin. It made me squirm inside, though I held his gaze.

"Yes, I know about his findings," he said after a moment. "Some detective brought a copy of Hadley's research to show to Dr. Matos. Matos was very upset by it. We wondered how the detective got a hold of Hadley's research in the first place. Any ideas?"

Uh oh, I thought, how much does he know? I felt nervous. "No, why should I?"

"You tell me, Lorelei," he said, giving me a chilling look. "Horse mentioned you were doing some investigating for friends. Investigators sometimes work with the police, so I figured you might know this detective from your hometown."

Damn Horse. What else did the blabbermouth tell him? Think fast, Lorelei, this is beginning to feel dangerous. "As it happens, I do know Detective McBride. He's a theatre buff, and he attended some of my performances in Gainesville. He heard I was playing here, and he looked me up."

"And that's all?" he asked.

"Yes," I replied, and bent over adjusting the fins. When I regained my composure I said, "Anyway, why would your boss be so upset? As a scientist, I'd think he would welcome new evidence about the springs."

Rick emitted a cynical grunt, and got up to bring the red tank from the tarp to where we were seated. When he returned he said, "You don't know Professor Matos. He's not very nice when he's been proven wrong—especially when one of his grants comes up for renewal, and he's just presented a paper on the subject at a major conference. When that research got into your detective's hands—to confront my boss—it caused me a world of trouble."

Uh oh, I thought and wondered if that was what caused Rick to decide to leave town. Or if Matos was pushing him out of his position at the university. Then a more important question crossed my mind and I asked, "If your Dr. Matos is such an expert, why didn't he make the same discovery that Hadley made?"

"We did," he said, flatly, and at that moment a ray of sun, reflecting off the water, gave his eyes an eerie gleam.

I shuddered, and my mouth became dry. He returned to the tarp, and I watched as he briefly checked the valve on the yellow tank before putting it down next to the red one. Regaining my composure, I asked, "What? You're telling me you knew all along that Alex was right?"

The sharp call of a crow unnerved me. Yet, I couldn't stop myself from pushing Rick for more information. It was too fascinating to let it go.

Rick stood in front of me, legs apart and arms folded over his chest. He was watching my reaction. "That's right. I did the dye tracer study myself...just like Alex," he said.

He gave me a challenging look. It was as though to say, *Okay, you've opened the door, now deal with what I'm telling you.* This was becoming curiouser and curiouser, I thought, in the vernacular of the Cheshire cat.

"Then why didn't you tell Alex? Why let him take all the heat for his discovery? I mean, it even broke up his marriage."

A slow smile crossed Rick's face. Yes, I thought, there's definitely could be something there. Sweet revenge in disrupting Hadley's relationship, or thinking of his own plans with Hadley's wife? Maybe both.

Rick grabbed the stick he had been drawing with and tossed it far into the woods. Turning back to me he said bluntly, "Matos lied about the connection between the two springs. He dummied the research for his paper. And now he's making it hell for me. Among other things, he thinks I should have kept you from getting the log of Hadley's findings." He paused and once again studied me, before adding, "You are the one who gave the computer file to the detective, aren't you?"

Though he said it without malice, I couldn't hide my nervousness. "Me? But I told you...?" My voice trailed off, my stomach muscles tightened, and I turned away from his penetrating stare. Okay, so he thinks it was me. This was not going well. Best to keep him talking. "You said he dummied the research. Why would he do that?"

Rick tensed. I hoped it was a reaction to his problems with Matos, and not directed toward me. I definitely didn't want to ask why he thought I had the flash drive. The name that came to mind was Horse.

He said, "It's complicated, but I'll tell you this much, there was a lot of pressure to make people believe this isn't really a spring." He looked out over the water, and added, "The very eminent Dr. Matos had reasons for wanting everyone to believe it was of no major value or ecological consequence."

"What pressure? From whom?"

So Matos was just another in a recent string of scientists who lied about their research for personal gain. Despite a warning voice that told me to stop, I persisted.

"You said it was Dr. Matos who falsified the research, but I heard that you made a presentation to the Fairport council supporting his claim. Why would you collude with him and perpetuate the lie?"

He looked at his watch. "I've told you enough already," he said, and began collecting the rest of our scuba gear. "If you want to get back to Apalachicola in time, we've got to get started." He helped me on with my tank. "Get your hood on and let's go."

I wondered why he'd admitted this startling news to me now? His barely suppressed anger was disturbing, and yet I didn't believe his mood was entirely because of me. If it were, why make the confession he did?

I followed him into the shallow water where my feet sunk a bit into the sandy bottom. "What about all this algae or whatever," I said, pushing the green mat of plants away from me. "Won't it be hard to see anything underwater?"

"Don't worry about it, just follow me," he said, moving closer. "You mentioned pollution? It isn't only from industry and septic tanks. Wait till you see some of the human debris at the bottom— tires, car batteries, stuff like that. Some people still like to use the water as a dump site."

"That's just disgraceful," I said. "Don't they get it? Whatever they dump into springs or on the ground winds up in our aquifer and eventually pollutes everyone's drinking water."

"Yeah," he said, "Maybe we should give everyone an ecology handbook and test when they apply for a driver's license. Now, let's get back to diving. I've checked the gear, but ordinarily you would want to check your own regulator. Don't forget to clear your mask. I want to do a quick safety review under water."

I knew he meant a buddy sharing drill—making sure if either of us ran out of air, the other one could provide it from their tank and the spare regulator, or octopus, we both wore. He also wanted to check me out on hand signals essential for communicating underwater.

I nodded, cleaned my mask, and we ducked under the water.

Despite the algae and tall grasses at the edge of the spring, there was a surprising degree of visibility as we moved toward the middle. When the safety drill was done to his satisfaction, Rick gave me thumbs up, and we both slowly ascended to the surface at the same time.

We removed our mouthpieces and were standing in shoulder deep water. He asked, "Do you have any questions? Anything you're unsure of?"

His voice sounded even and more relaxed since we got into the water. Yet, I had an instinctive urge to stall until I felt more at ease. I said, "You know this whole diving experience has been so accidental. If I hadn't gone to the dive shop looking for Alex Hadley..." Watch out, Lorelei, I thought, don't get him agitated again. "In Gainesville, it never occurred to me to take scuba diving lessons. I didn't know a single person who did cave diving, or any scuba sports. Even my first husband pleaded claustrophobia at the mention of snorkeling."

"But you did finally get to do it."

"Yes, with husband number two," I said, hearing myself sound like a quiz show announcer. "But I do have one question before we begin."

"What?"

"Are there any caves here? I know it's more dangerous to dive in caves than in open water." It was Mike who had warned me, as though I needed it.

Rick paused thoughtfully before answering, "Look, Lorelei, now's not the time to be worrying about caves. Yes, there are some, and it can be dangerous to dive in them. But only if you're alone or inexperienced. I'll be with you all the way. Anything else?"

"So there are caves?" I persisted.

"A few. Most are shallow, only one of them is deep—probably two hundred feet or more."

"That deep? How about the spring pool? How deep does it get?"

He bit his lip, again he seemed to be trying to decide the best way to answer my question. "It's not all that deep," he said. "Just enough for you to practice diving and using the equipment. It's natural to be a little nervous on your first real dive, but like I said, there's nothing to worry about. I'll be with you. Now let's go."

Rick inserted his mouthpiece, adjusted his mask, and motioned for me to do the same. As we both ducked under water I thought, not all that deep? Pete Stigler told me the spring pool was probably fifty or sixty feet deep, and Rick had just told me one of the caves might go down two hundred feet. That was pretty damn deep.

As I began swimming alongside of Rick, McBride's warning popped into my mind: *"Don't go into any deep water with Lucas,"* he had said. Jesus, Homer, I sure hope you're wrong.

Chapter 28

We slowly swam, side by side, and the sun sent shimmering shafts of light into the water. It was quite spectacular. For a while, I could see the sandy bottom and the areas of pale green colored grasses, alive with small fish swimming in and out. They were crossing paths in a kind of aquatic traffic pattern. I also saw some of the debris Rick had mentioned.

Then the spring pool became deeper, and seeing the bottom was more difficult. Rick swam slightly ahead, and I followed along what appeared to be the edge of the pool. We passed by the mouth of a cave, and he pointed out some interesting limestone rock formations. I noticed several small eels swimming in and out of the cave. I was beginning to feel more relaxed, paddling behind him. Except for the shushing sounds of my own breathing, it was wondrous and silent world. I looked up to the blur of trees above the clear water, and I felt a rush of gratitude at the chance to have this unique experience.

Rick motioned me to follow him deeper. I focused on his red tank. When he leveled off, he veered left toward the entrance to another small cave. He was treading water.

He gestured, asking me if I wanted to explore the opening.

Uh oh, I thought. He told me we weren't going into any caves. I signaled back, "I don't know."

He gestured we would go in only a little way, and to reassure me he pointed to the staked line at the entrance. I thought of the diver heroine in the mystery I was reading, and felt a strong temptation to see even a bit of the interior.

I signaled okay with a thumbs up.

What the hell, I thought, nothing ventured...but it was the staked line that finally decided me. It alleviated my worry about not finding my way back out of the cave if anything happened. I knew I could swim along the line back to the cave entrance. I silently thanked the divers who conscientiously attached safety lines deep into underwater caves. I had first learned about the lines from an account by Wes Skiles, whose team had laid almost two thousand feet of line at Wakulla Springs.

Rick led the way into the cave. It had a narrow opening, just a couple of feet wider than my body, but the roof was high—about the height of my apartment ceiling—and filled with sunlight. It's okay, I thought. Nothing scary—especially with Rick ahead. His fins were kicking in a very slow steady rhythm. The light followed us for a short while, and I noticed tiny floating specs of material.

Turbidity. I remembered the term from one of the manuals Rick had given me. The tiny particles looked like the snow in one of those glass balls that you shake up to simulate a winter storm.

Just as I became aware of the light dimming, Rick made a quick turn around, motioned that I should follow him out and swam above me. Despite my pleasure at the adventure, I was aware that my body had become tense the moment we entered the mouth of the cave. I wasn't claustrophobic, just a bit unnerved by being in such a confining space. Now, looking ahead, I saw why Rick had turned around. The cavern sloped downward, and looked completely dark—a frightening black hole.

I maneuvered my way around to follow him out. As I completed the turn, I was shocked by a thunderous explosion.

My heart threatened to beat right out of my chest, and I had to remind myself to keep breathing. Treading water, I was enveloped in turbulence.

Oh, God, did the cavern collapse?

Was it Rick? Did his tank blow up? I'd never heard of that happening.

I couldn't see anything. Rick had completely disappeared in a murky cloud of bubbles and silt.

I began swimming very slowly, hoping the water would clear up, and I could find him. Maybe he needed help. I touched my extra regulator. It was still attached.

What now?

In a moment of panic, it hit me that a small amount of water was dripping into my mouth.

Holy shit, I thought, there's a leak in the mouthpiece, or in the regulator.

I went totally blank.

What was I supposed to do?

Don't panic! Just don't panic.

I knew in a panic, I could breathe too fast and use up too much air. I've still got enough air coming through to get out of here, I told myself.

What if the crack expands and I start sucking up water? I could drown.

Where's Rick? Why I can't see him yet? If he's all right, why hasn't he come back for me?

The damn water's still muddy. I don't know where I am.

Should I hit the power inflate button? My hand started toward it.

No, dummy, don't hit the power inflate. Buoyancy will just make you to bump into the top of the cave. Wait till you're sure you're outside.

Of course, find the safety line at the wall.

Slow inhale. Slow exhale. Conserve your air.

I groped for the line...running my hands up and down the wall of the cave. Nothing. I can't even see it. Of course, the damn thing looked so flimsy it's probably floating around from the explosion. Maybe broken.

I swam a bit higher—toward the roof of the cave—then pushed myself lower along the wall. Still no line.

Where the fuck is it? I was counting on it. God, I'm breathing too fast...slow inhale, slow exhale.

Maybe I got turned around. The sandy water's still blurring my vision.

Oh no, don't tell me I'm disoriented...losing track if I'm high or low in the cave. What direction am I moving in? Twisting around so much looking for the damn line. Am I swimming back into the cave?

If only I could see where I'm going!

Tread water, Lorelei...try to get calm. Remember what to do. We went over all the safety stuff, dammit.

Not about caves. Rick didn't talk about cave diving.

"Slow exhale!" It was a voice as though spoken by someone else.

That's it. Rick said I had natural buoyancy. Zen breath. Float to the top...slow exhale, just like he taught me.

Take it slowly...slow, slow exhale.

Lorelei—think! You're still in the damn cave. No surface except the roof.

Okay, what else? What else?

Damn you, Rick. You said no caves. You didn't teach me what to do if we got into trouble in a cave.

If I don't get it together soon, I could damn well die in here. Ridiculous.

Mike warned me. McBride warned me. Was I really that pig headed? Why didn't I listen to them? Where's Rick when I need him?

Slow your breathing. Do you want to run out of air?

I inched my way along the cave wall again. Numbly hoping it was in the right direction. Hoping to feel the staked line, and just taking slow and steady strokes with my arms.

Speckles of light appeared ahead. What? Are there mirages under the water?

Thank God. The damn cavern didn't collapse after all.

I'm swimming out.

It's the right direction

My heart throbbed like someone hit it with a cattle prod. Can a heart burst underwater? Not good.

Slow, Zen breath.

Rick's warning...breathe too fast use up too much oxygen. Rise to the surface too fast risk an embolism.

Do I have less air, or is it my imagination? Water still trickled into my mouth.

Please, please dear God, let it hold up. Don't let my air run out now.

Shit! What am I thinking? The extra regulator...the octopus.

Feeling around my body, I moved my arm in slow motion...my fingers groped around the device.

Brain's gone to mush. Don't panic! Zen breath. Zen breath.

Oh my God—sunlight. The water's not murky anymore.

Swim out...everything's okay.

Slow, slow exhale—just like you've been taught.
Sunlight overhead.
Out of the cave. Free at last.
Exhale slowly
Up, up, up…

*How peaceful…walking through an orange grove. Bright sun
sending shafts like beacons through the dense leafy trees. Ah, the
aroma of orange blossoms so sweet. Nauseating. Strange, now I feel
sick. There's the crunch of fallen leaves beneath my feet. The air's
damp and cool. Must have been showers. Summer. There's a
presence…a man with me. He's walking a little way ahead. Wearing
a large straw hat. Daddy? Is it really you? Oh, wonderful. Hurry.
Catch up. He's always the same distance ahead of me. I can't reach
him. Calling to him, but I have no voice. I want to hug him. Have him
hold me in his arms. I'm crying. Deep mournful sobs. He turns, and
calls my name…he sounds harsh. No, no, Daddy, that hurt.*

"Lorelei! Lorelei!"
The voice is familiar, so distant. Daddy? No, it's a woman.
"Lorelei, come back. You hear? You come back!"
Not mom's voice. Delcie? How could it be Delcie?
"Open your eyes, damn you. Don't go on actin' like you're dead
or anything," the voice said.
*I struggle to get my eyes open. I don't know if it's working or
not. I can't be sure I'm seeing anything.*
"Lorelei! You hear me? Wake up! Open those eyes of yours."
*I'm trying really hard to do what she wants. Why does she sound
so mad? It's such a strange feeling—my body's becoming heavy—as
though I haven't been in it, and I'm just pulling it on. I feel my eyes
open—just a crack—and see a blur of green.*
"That's it. That's it. I knew you could do it."
"What…?" The raspy single word was all I could get out. My
throat burned.
"That's it, that's it, baby. Oh, you had me so worried. Thought
I'd lost you."

"Del?" I said, looking up at the trees. I was lying on my back. Delcie was crouched down beside me. She gave me her biggest smile.

"What happened?"

"Don't you worry, Lor. You're going to be all right."

The ground was wet. I reached up and touched my face...my cheeks felt sore. I wasn't lying on the ground, but on the blue tarp Rick had used to lay out all of our equipment. Rick's red tank and mouthpiece lay nearby. I started to get up.

"No, not just yet," Delcie said, and pressed her hand on my shoulder. "Just stay there 'til I can get some help, and you get your bearings. You must of drunk a lot of water. Thank goodness you were able to get your pants unzipped. Your belly looks bloated. When I found you, you were like a pregnant mermaid that'd been dragged ashore."

I lay my head back down...relieved by her touch. I saw my yellow tank nearby, and I glanced down to see my fins had been removed.

"Where's Rick?"

Delcie gave a disgusted grunt. "You mean the dude in the truck who looked scared shitless when he drove past me? He's your instructor?"

"He left? I can't believe he'd do that."

"Believe it. I saw him driving out of here just as I was turning in. The way he looked, I would've chased after him, but it was you I came to find."

"Where was I? Last thing I remember I was trying to get out of the damn cave...and I had this dream."

"Cave! He left you in a cave?" She jumped up and kicked a small tree limb. "Damn his bones. After I get a call in to 911, I'm calling McBride. That's pure negligence—maybe criminal. Was he tryin' to kill you?"

"Please, Delcie." I wanted her to speak softly, to soothe me, but her words resonated. Was he trying to kill me?

She flipped her cell phone closed and grumbled, "I've walked all around, but the damn thing doesn't work in here. We're in the middle of nowhere."

"Delcie," I pleaded again. "Tell me what happened? How did I get out of the water?" I tried pulling myself up into a sitting position. It made me feel dizzy and nauseated. I hoped I wasn't going to throw up.

"For goodness sakes," she said, pushing me back down. "You've got to stay put. I don't remember much about treating dive accidents, but the safest thing is for you to stay still. I'm going to have to go out to the road to use the cell. I'll be back in a few minutes."

She disappeared from view, and I followed her advice. I still couldn't believe that Rick Lucas had left without rescuing me. Did he know I was in trouble? Did he intentionally lead me into the cave hoping something like this would happen?

Chapter 29

I heard the crunch of tires before I actually saw the EMS truck. A uniformed woman and a man soon hovered over me.

The woman asked, "What's your name, dear?"

"Lorelei. Lorelei Crane" I replied, wondering why Delcie hadn't told them. She was standing behind the paramedics, with a worried look on her face.

"Lorelei, we're going to take your vital signs, and then get you to the hospital. How are you feeling right now?"

"I feel nauseated, and a little dizzy," I said.

"How long were you under? Did you run out of air?"

"I have no idea. I can't remember much about the last part of the dive."

The man said, "I see two tanks here. Where's the other diver?" He looked very young, and his face was tanned. I thought he might be a diver himself.

Delcie replied, "The other diver took off."

The woman said, "You're going to be fine, Lorelei." She had a calm and reassuring voice. I tried to place the accent—it wasn't Southern—maybe Midwest.

They placed a small oxygen mask over my face.

The man said, "This'll make you breathe easier. He was tugging on the top zipper of my wetsuit. "I need to get you unzipped so we can take your vital signs." His large brown eyes looked down at me with sympathy as he finally got the zipper down, and the two of them were able to pull off the top of the suit. He connected me to some monitoring equipment.

"I can't go to the hospital," I said, now fully aware of my situation. "I'm opening in a play tonight…at the Dixie Theatre in Apalachicola."

The paramedics looked at each other, and the woman spoke again. "Well, let's not worry about that right now."

The man was talking into some device and calling out numbers…my pulse rate, blood pressure? What else? All I could think about was getting back to town and resting before the play.

"Okay, Lorelei, we're going to roll you onto this stretcher. You don't have to do anything but follow our instructions."

"All right," I said, hearing my voice sounding wimpy, like a scared child.

They managed to get me onto the stretcher and into the EMS truck.

"I'll meet you at the hospital," Delcie said, from the rear of the truck.

After they got me strapped in, the man left and the woman squatted by my side. "How are you feeling now?"

"Still nauseated," I replied. "and itchy."

"Yes," she said, "I noticed you have some rashes on your feet and neck. We'll take care of it when we get you to the hospital." I felt a stick in my arm, and saw I was attached to an IV pole.

The truck bumped along until the ride smoothed out, and I knew we had hit the pavement. The oxygen mask on my face provided a stream of cool air that was refreshing, but it didn't quell my nausea.

- I glanced around. The compartment was packed with equipment, some of it bulging out of pouches attached to the walls. The man must also be the driver. It was just me and the woman paramedic who sat on a bench next to me. It all seemed very cramped and very brightly lit. For some reason, it made me think of the inside of a space capsule...self-contained and functional.

"So you weren't diving alone?" the woman asked.

"No, I was with my instructor."

"He must have been the one who called us."

"I don't think so. I think my friend—the woman—called you."

She patted my shoulder, and said, "Don't worry about that now. You're going to be all right."

I struggled to focus on the play. How long would they keep me in the hospital I wondered. If I couldn't make the opening, who would stand in for me? Would they have to reschedule? It would be so disappointing for Renee, and the actors.

"Lorelei, what are you thinking about right now?" She was checking my pulse rate.

"Uh, I'm worried about how the play will go on if I don't get out of the hospital today...and I really feel very itchy."

In a soothing voice, she said, "Dear, right now you need to remain calm, and avoid thinking of things that are upsetting. Do you understand?"

Just then, I heard the siren begin to wail. As if that's not upsetting, I thought. But, she's right. Zen breath...slow inhale; slow exhale. Wherever the hell did Rick Lucas disappear to?

Our arrival at the hospital in Crawfordville was as dramatic as any scene I had ever played in. Between the paramedics and the emergency staff, I felt encased in a human medical cocoon as they hurried me inside and put me in a dark examining room. One nurse managed to get the rest of my wetsuit off—no small feat since it fit me very tightly—while another attached me to an array of machines. Everyone kept asking how I felt. Soon a white-coated woman with a sweet smile and a stethoscope around her neck, appeared at my side and introduced herself.

"Lorelei, I'm Doctor Bransky. How are you feeling?"

"I'm still nauseated, and I've got some kind of rash. It feels like chiggers," I said.

"Let me take a look," she replied. She listened to my heart, had me take some breaths, and examined my body. "From the looks of your belly, you've taken in a fair amount of water. Fortunately it doesn't seem to have entered your lungs. And, by the way, the rash on your body looks like hives. Looks like a mild case. Have you ever been treated for allergies?"

"No."

"Well, it could have been induced by something in the water— some kind of aquatic toxin. We've had a couple of similar cases in swimmers at Wakulla. I'll give you something to take care of it," she said, and instructed the nurse at her side.

"I don't remember what happened...how I got out of the water."

"From the amount of water in your stomach, I'd guess you probably experienced an epiglottal spasm that caused your windpipe to close as you were surfacing. I've seen this happen once before to a diver. You were taking too few breaths—I think they call it "skip breathing." It resulted in a build-up of carbon dioxide in the blood which caused you to pass out. Did you have a panic attack during your dive?"

I couldn't begin to describe the terrifying thoughts her question evoked, but I said, "Yes."

"Well, we're going to keep you under observation for a day or so. We don't want to risk the chance of an embolism, or anything else. Did you lose consciousness?"

"I'm pretty sure I did," I replied. "Doctor, do you think I'll have any permanent effects?"

Delcie entered the room and waved hello.

"The best thing you can do right now is not to worry," she said. "You're going to be all right. Whoever got the paramedics there so quickly might have saved your life."

I cast Delcie a grateful look.

"You got oxygen right away—and they got you here in time," she said, as she continued gently probing my abdomen and legs.

"Any chance I can leave by tomorrow?" I asked. "Will the rash be gone?' I said, reaching up to scratch my neck.

"The hives will subside pretty quickly once the antihistamines kick in. Let's wait and see how your blood gases and other tests come out. Your body's been through a lot, but you seem to be in good shape. We'll transfer you to another room in a little while. Just take it easy for now." She gave me a kindly smile and left.

The nurse stuck me with a needle and said, "That should take care of your nausea, and we'll get after the hives as well." He followed the doctor out of the room.

Delcie stepped up to the gurney, and took my hand, and looked relieved.

"Wow, Lorelei. You're one very brave or crazy woman."

"Did McBride tell you about Rick?"

"He didn't have to. I knew about him from talking with Mike Foley."

"Oh, so it was Mike."

"You bet," she said. "Mike's the one who told me where you'd gone. I came in to Apalachicola, and I was looking for you. When I asked at Sophie's Café, the owner introduced me to Mike. Nice guy. Told me he was your lead."

"That's right," I said, feeling the nausea begin to diminish.

"You've been holding out on me, Lor. Mike's a handsome guy. He was real concerned about you diving with Rick Lucas. Enough to make me worry, as well. He told me how to get to Graham Springs, and I took off."

"Well, thank goodness you found me, Delcie. I still can't get my mind around the fact that Rick just left me…"

"To drown," she added, shaking her head in anger. "Fortunately, the EMS truck arrived minutes after I called 911. They must have been nearby to have gotten there that quickly."

"Have you called McBride?" I asked.

"Called him right after I called 911. He had some choice words about you diving with Rick Lucas. Asked me to keep him posted. He sounded upset—like he really cares about you, Lor. He said he was going to try to get over here sometime tomorrow."

"Do me a favor, Del."

"Anything."

"Call the theatre and talk with Renee. Tell her I had a slight accident, and I can't make tonight's opening. Tell her I'm going to try to get there for tomorrow's performance."

"Slight accident? I'm sure she'll ask what happened."

I was feeling very tired, and struggled to think what to tell to Renee. "Tell her everything," I said, as I began drifting off. I squeezed Delcie's hand with my last bit of energy and heard myself mumble, "Thanks for being here, Delcie."

When I awoke, I found myself neatly tucked into a bed in a small room with one window looking out onto a large Magnolia tree. I turned my head to see Delcie sitting in the chair next to the bed.

"Hi there," she said. "Have a good nap?"

"They moved me?"

"Yes, you never even blinked."

"What time is it?"

A North Florida Mystery

She looked at her watch and said, "It's five fifteen. How's the nausea?"

I answered, "I think it's gone," I reached up and felt my neck. The welts had receded and there was no more itching. "Did you call Renee?"

"I did. She was very nice. Told me to tell you not to worry about tonight. Said she's going to stand in for you."

"Really?" I was surprised. I'd never heard of a director acting as an understudy. But then, who else would have known the role better than she? And after all, Renee had started her career as an actress.

"Bravo," I said. "Rick Lucas didn't call by any chance did he?"

"Will you give up on that low down piece of white trash? Lorelei, he left you. You weren't even conscious when I found you. If you didn't need me to stay with you now, I'd be out huntin' for him myself."

I decided not to argue with Delcie about Rick. I thought of a different strategy. "I think I'd better let the dive shop know that their equipment is still at the springs. Will you get me the number of Horse's Dive Shop in Carrabelle?"

Delcie found a phone book in the nightstand, looked up the local number, and dialed it for me. An answering machine picked it up.

"Hi, Horse," I said. "It's Lorelei Crane. I had an accident today with Rick...at Graham Springs. Anyway, I'm in the hospital at Crawfordville. I feel okay, and I'll probably get out tomorrow. Did you hear from Rick? If so, will you ask him to call me? Oh, some of your equipment—a tank, and some gear—is still out there. I'll make good for any damage. Thanks, Horse."

Delcie said, "I don't think you'll hear from your so-called instructor. Anyway, McBride's probably got someone out looking for him already. They'll find him, and bring him in for questioning."

"Can you at least get McBride on your cell for me? I want to talk to him," I said.

"Why don't you just relax...remember what the doctor told you. I'm sure he'll be here tomorrow."

Relax? I thought, how can I relax knowing that Rick Lucas might have abandoned me, and worse—arranged an accident that

233

might have caused me to drown. What did it mean? Did he murder Hadley and Buster? Why would he want to kill me? Because finding Hadley's research and turning it over to the police put him in so much trouble?

I thought of the confession he made. I'd seen killers in the movies tell all before they murdered their victims. They thought they had nothing to lose. I wondered what McBride was thinking. It had been almost a week since we talked. Drowsiness blunted further speculation, and I slipped back into a dreamless sleep.

Chapter 30

I awoke the next day to find Homer McBride sitting in the chair next to my bed. He was reading *The Wakulla News.*

"About time you woke up," he said, not unkindly, and looked at his watch. "It's almost noon."

"Homer, I'm so glad to see you." And I really was. There was something reassuring about his presence.

"I thought I might have to eat your lunch if you didn't wake up soon." He stood and lifted the cover off the food tray on the stand next to my bed. "On second thought..."

"I guess I dozed off. You know how it is in hospitals...they're always waking you up for something or other."

He sat down again, and leaned closer to me. "How are you, Lorelei? You gave Delcie quite a scare."

"I know. Actually, I'm feeling pretty good...considering. I guess Delcie told you everything that happened."

He nodded. "They say you'll be out of here by tomorrow."

"So they told me. Apparently my tests came out all right. The doctor is just being careful. Thank goodness I can be back in the play by Tuesday."

"Oh yes, the play. I'll try to get over for it next weekend. That is, if my ticket is still good."

I laughed, "Don't worry, I'll get you another one."

The day nurse, whose name was Gwen, came into the room.

"You doing all right, gal?" she asked, and with a big smile gave McBride a once over. "Well, I guess you are," she said, fiddled with the monitor behind my bed, and exited with a chuckle.

McBride's face flushed.

"Why Homer, I don't think I've ever seen you blush."

He ignored my comment, ran a hand through his hair, and said, "Look, Lorelei. I don't want to upset you while you're still recuperating, but I have some questions."

"Rick Lucas?"

"Yes. Tell me what happened yesterday. I need to know the details."

I took a roll off the tray, spooned some jelly on it, and poured a cup of tea while I tried to organize my thoughts.

"Take your time. It's important that you try to remember everything." McBride had his little red notebook out.

How different, I thought, from the first time I had been interviewed by Detective H. "Mac" McBride. It was at the office where I used to work, the Center for Earth Options, and just after Jeffrey had been shot near Paynes Prairie. I recalled the detective's brusque, almost insulting manner as he grilled me about my relationships with both Jeff and Bill. Delcie had warned me that McBride didn't like women very much, but as time went on I found her to be very wrong about that.

"Lorelei? Are you thinking about yesterday? I need you to concentrate on what happened."

"Sorry, Homer, I drifted off. I've been doing that."

"All right, let me ask you some specific questions. First, what made you decide to go diving with Rick Lucas after I warned you not to?"

I sighed and bowed my head, unable to look directly at him. "I know you did. And I meant to cancel the lesson, but Rick said he was leaving town...did you know that?"

"Yes, go on."

"I wanted to complete my certification. I was intrigued when he said we'd be going to Graham Springs, and..."

"Yes, I'm listening," he looked up from his notebook.

"Homer, you know I have an intuitive sense about people. I really didn't think he would harm me in any way. He's been very professional."

"Is that what you think now?"

"I don't know what to think. Have you talked with him? Has he asked about me?"

"Yes to both questions."

At last, I thought, some answers to the mysterious disappearance of Rick Lucas. "So, tell me. What did he say happened? Where did he go?"

"No, first I want you to describe how you wound up in a cave with him, and the events that followed."

Damn him, I thought, Homer just loves to control information. Spitefully, I took my time responding. I lifted the cover of the luncheon plate and decided to skip it. They say most of the taste in food is its appearance. In this case, everything was an unappetizing shade of brown. I continued sipping my tea while he waited me out.

"Look, Rick knew I was interested in the springs," I said. "I had even told him I might buy property there. When I arrived yesterday morning, he seemed to be in a rotten mood, but he was very open with me. He told me how Dr. Matos had falsified the springs research, and how upset Matos was with him for not getting Hadley's notes before I did. Anyway, Rick intimated he knew I was the one who provided you with Hadley's findings. I think it's Horse Stern who had the loose lips, and..."

I began coughing.

McBride poured a glass of water. "Here. Now take it more slowly. I'm not in a hurry." He waited until I seemed to recover. "So after everything you just told me, you weren't even a little bit wary about going underwater with Lucas?"

"Like I said, he seemed very professional. He had our gear carefully laid out. He checked everything—he's quite anal about it. As for his foul mood...well, he's moody anyway, so at first, I didn't think much of it.'

"Go on," McBride said, still frowning.

"He was very tense when he told me about Matos. I'll admit it gave me second thoughts, but when we got into the water, he settled down. Then I talked to him and asked a bunch of questions until I felt it was okay to go on with the dive. Homer, you wouldn't believe how magical it is underwater. It's..."

"Did you know he was going to take you into a cave?"

"Not at first. In fact, he distinctly said we weren't going into the caves. But, when we came to the second one, he asked if I wanted to have a look inside, and..."

"You agreed?"

"Yes, I mean, by that time I was feeling comfortable with him and the equipment, and being underwater was so dreamlike. Anyway, he showed me the safety line attached to the cave wall. Did you know they did that?"

"So you went in. What happened next?"

"I followed him in. We had to swim in single file because of the width of the opening. When the cave light started to fade, he motioned me to follow him out."

I felt my heart pounding faster as I began to relive the scene. I stopped talking and sipped from the glass of water.

"Lorelei?" Homer placed his hand on mine and looked concerned. He said, "Are you all right? You look pale."

I took several deep breaths, until I felt able to go on. "What happened next was one of the most frightening experiences of my life. As I turned to follow Rick out of the cave, there was this incredibly loud explosion—I can't even describe it. Such a roar…like a rocket going off. It was terrifying. Suddenly the water was filled with bubbles and went dark. I couldn't see anything ahead of me. I didn't know what happened. I worried about Rick."

"That was a waste of energy," McBride said.

I continued, "As if the explosion wasn't scary enough, I realized I had water in my mouth. The mouthpiece, or the regulator must have had a small crack."

"I thought you said he checked the equipment before the dive?" McBride was angry now.

"He did. I saw him do it."

"Yet there was a crack in your breathing equipment. Okay, what next?"

"I was blinded by the turbid water, so I started feeling along the cave wall for the safety line. I couldn't find it. It was about then I began to feel disoriented, and I lost my sense of direction. Imagine, my first real dive, and here I was—in the midst of an explosion—from God knows what. As far as I knew, I was alone. I struggled to keep from hyperventilating, because I worried about running out of air. Homer, it was a pure nightmare!"

I shivered at the memory.

238

The nurse returned, looked at the monitor again, and said to McBride, "What on earth are you doing to this woman? She's supposed to be resting." Gwen was no longer smiling at him.

He started to get up, saying, "Sorry, Lorelei. Maybe this can wait until tomorrow."

"No, no. I want to finish telling you. Otherwise, my imagination will keep making it worse. Please, Gwen, I promise I'll stay calm."

She cast a doubtful look at both of us but nodded and left the room.

"I must have blanked out. I'd spent what seemed like hours trying to find the damn safety line. I never did lay my hands on it."

"How did you get out of the cave?"

I strained to recall the next sequence of events, as I had done over and over in the last hours, but reached the same conclusion. "I don't know. All I recall—now don't laugh—is hearing some angelic voice reminding me to breathe slowly. By that time, the water had cleared enough for me to find the opening."

"So you swam to the surface?"

"Like I said, I don't remember anything from then on—except the strangest dream about my father." Why was he so angry in my dream? Had he hit me?

"Lorelei?"

"Next thing I knew, I heard Delcie calling my name, and I found myself lying on the shore. I must have passed out after I got out of the cave."

"Hmm," McBride said, thumbing through his notes.

"Now, you promised to tell me about Rick. What did he say?"

He sat back, crossed his legs, and looked at me with a mixture of admiration and annoyance.

"Basically, his story checks with yours until the time of the accident."

"Accident?"

McBride consulted his notes and said, "The way he tells it, when he turned and started out of the cave, his first stage regulator hit the roof of the cave and got knocked off the tank. That's what caused the explosion."

"Oh, my. If his regulator broke off the tank, he lost all his air."

"Right. Said he hadn't intended to take you into the caves, and didn't bring proper equipment." McBride was reading from his notes. "When this piece broke off the tank, he was close to the cave entrance so he began to free dive to the surface. Said he was sure you'd be all right getting out as soon as the water cleared. He swam back to the shore to get his small emergency tank and by the time he returned to look for you…"

"Wait a minute," I said. "He could have turned back, and shared my tank. There's something called an octopus for buddy breathing. Why didn't he do that?"

"I don't know. Ask him," McBride said, and continued reading from his notes. "Lucas says he found you outside of the cave. Your legs weren't moving, and you were drifting to the surface—obviously unconscious—so he pulled you to the shore."

I listened with fascination to Rick's explanation.

McBride went on, "He removed your equipment and tried to bring you to. He says he shouted at you and slapped your face a few times to wake you up."

My hand automatically went to my cheek. It was still sore.

McBride flipped his notebook closed, and concluded, "He got you breathing on his emergency tank. When he was satisfied you were okay, he took off to call 911. That's the gist of his story."

I had listened to McBride's rendering of Rick's story with a sense of disbelief. How could both of us have had accidents with our equipment at the same time? And whatever happened to the safety line? I began to wonder if Rick had concocted this story for the benefit of the police. Certainly the explosion was real. Would he have intentionally arranged for the regulator accident to create a storm of debris causing me to panic and use up all my air? When I first arrived at the spring, he had been fiddling around with the tank. I shuddered at the thought.

"What did you say his excuse was for leaving me?"

McBride, returned to his notebook, and said, "Lucas says once he had you breathing, he left to go for help. Said his cell phone wouldn't work, so he had to drive out to the highway to find a live spot."

"So was it Rick who called 911?"

"That's what he says. We haven't checked the recording yet."

"If he did call, why didn't he come back after he made the call?"

McBride shrugged. "Said he was scared and exhausted. He saw the woman drive in, and knew she'd find you and take care of you until EMS arrived. He just took off."

"Just like that?"

"Just like that," McBride said pausing to study my reaction, and looked down at his notes again. "Oh, he gave me an excuse—he's been under a lot of pressure and not thinking straight. Said he's sorry and wants to see you to apologize in person."

"Do you believe him?" I asked, feeling a new hostility toward my so-called professional instructor.

"Hell, no. I don't know much about scuba diving, but I do know you don't take a novice diver into a cave her first time out."

"So what now?" I asked.

"I'm going on with my investigation. I'm closing in on some answers about Hadley's and Stigler's deaths."

"Want to share?"

"Not now, Lorelei. You need to rest. I'll stay in touch," he checked his watch and stood.

"Will you be here for the performance next weekend?"

"Wouldn't miss it," he said, bent down and gave me a full kiss on the lips.

I gasped, "Why Detective McBride, you sure know how to close an interview."

He patted my hand. "You just concentrate on getting out of here." He tapped the covered dish on my tray and added, "I'm sure you'll be craving decent food soon enough." He waved and left.

I touched my lips and smiled. Talk about an investigation that was heating up. I wonder what Nurse Gwen would say if she checked my monitor right now. And then my thoughts returned to Rick Lucas and two big questions—why did he take me into that cave, and why did he leave me there?

Chapter 31

I felt like a diva when the flowers began to arrive on Sunday afternoon. Delcie came back to the hospital to check on me before leaving for Gainesville. Mike and Renee came along with her. Mike brought a beautiful orchid-like butterfly plant, and the cast had chipped in on a large spray of fall flowers. Shortly after they arrived, a Carrabelle florist delivered a generous bouquet of red roses with a note that read, "Sorry. Glad you're okay. See you later." It was signed Rick Lucas.

Renee asked who sent the roses. I replied, "Just someone I know."

After he placed the plant on the window sill, Mike handed me a brown paper bag. "From Sophie," he said. "Her assistant left, and she couldn't get away to come see you. She said you'd need some soul food."

I peeked into the sack and saw what appeared to be a wrap—my favorite Mediterranean sandwich—and a carton of soup. Jewish chicken soup, I predicted.

"Bless her," I said. "I'll call and thank her later."

Gwen came in and told my guests they couldn't stay for very long. "She's already had quite enough excitement from that hunk of a detective who was here all morning," she said.

Mike was not amused, and Delcie glanced at the flowers and gave me an inquisitive look.

"Thank the goddess, I'll have my leading lady back," Renee said. "I never dreamed you'd be performing a more dramatic role off stage. Everybody's glad you're doing so well, but I'm still very angry with you for taking such a risk on opening night."

There was a nervous silence while I weighed my response to her unexpectedly hostile tone. "I'm truly sorry, Renee."

Mike jumped in and broke the tension. "Ask her how she liked stepping into your shoes as Mrs. Stockman."

Renee laughed, and replied, "Dear boy, I can act and I can direct, but directing is my métier—it is who I am. However…all things considered, I did passably well as Lorelei's stand-in. At least, we didn't have to cancel. It's such a short run as it is."

"Don't be so modest," Mike said. "She did more than passably well, though each of you is distinctly different. It gave me the pleasure of having two wives. A provocative experience."

"What a little politician you are," I teased. "Poor Dr. Stockman could have taken some lessons from you and avoided becoming everyone's enemy."

Renee, Mike, and I chimed in together, "...but there wouldn't be a play." It was Sophie's line that had given us all such a good laugh during our Thanksgiving dinner.

Delcie came over and took my hand. "It's fun being with all you theatre folk, but I've got to get back to Gainesville." She bent down to kiss my forehead, and whispered to me, "I've got a late night surveillance gig...someone's zooming someone's wife, and my client wants details."

Delcie left, and Nurse Gwen reappeared. She shooed Mike and Renee out of the room, saying the practiced line, "She needs her rest."

Mike said, "I'll call you in the morning to see when they're letting you go."

Renee blew a theatrical kiss and said, "See you at the theatre on Tuesday. Call if you need anything. I'll send your husband right over," she smiled at Mike and patted his arm.

After they left, I realized Gwen was right. I did need a rest. The last two days had been harrowing, and I still hadn't fully digested the close call I'd had. I was disturbed by not having heard from Rick or Horse, but I let it go, as I dozed off.

I opened my eyes when I heard someone whispering my name. I turned to find Rick sitting next to my bed. The shadows in the room told me it was late afternoon.

Despite my drowsiness, I pulled myself up in the bed. I must have given him an furious look, because Rick put his hands up as if to protect himself.

"What the hell happened?" I blurted.

He pulled the chair closer, and giving me an anxious look, said, "Please, Lorelei. Let me explain."

"Do you realize I could have drowned in that damn cave? Why didn't you come back to me when your regulator broke off? Isn't that what you taught me about buddy-sharing?" My anger ballooned.

"I swear I thought you'd be okay—that you were right behind me. We weren't even that far into the cave."

"Didn't you realize I couldn't see anything? Did it occur to you I would be terrified by the explosion? You never warned me anything like that could happen. On top of it all, there was a crack in my mouthpiece or the regulator. I thought you had checked everything."

"I did check the equipment. Apparently it was only a hairline crack. It happens."

"It happens? Is that all you have to say. Two accidents in one dive. Quite a coincidence, I'd say."

He shook his head and nervously cracked his knuckles.

"Honestly, you've got to believe me. Nothing like this has ever happened before. As for leaving you, I just panicked when my air went."

"Panicked? You?"

"I am human, Lorelei," he sounded prickly, as though he were the injured party. "Even professional divers can panic."

"When did you finally realize you'd left me behind? And by the way, where in hell was the safety line. I could never find it."

"You couldn't?" He appeared taken aback. "Maybe it broke when I was dragging my tank out the last few feet of the cave. It was damn awkward struggling to ..."

"Okay, I get it that you were in a life-threatening situation when the regulator broke off your tank. But dammit Rick, you're a professional instructor. Why didn't you come back to use my octopus like you've taught me to do in emergency situations?"

He shrugged helplessly. "What more can I tell you? Like I said, I panicked. Haven't you ever blanked out—like stage fright?"

I ignored his question. "Tell me what made you run off like that after you got me out of the water? What if I had been in trouble, and my friend Delcie didn't know what to do? She's no diver."

"I know. I know. Truthfully, I can't explain it. After I called 911, I…I felt like—I don't know—like it was all I could do to keep from driving my truck into a tree and ending it all. It's been building for weeks, and then the whole incident with you and the faulty equipment. I felt rotten about everything. It sent me over the edge."

I began to feel exhausted by my angry cross-examination but I pressed on. "Well, you should feel more than rotten. I still can't believe you enticed me into a cave and left me there! Where the hell did you go when you left the springs?"

"I drove back to the dive shop. I wanted to kill Horse. He's done this to me before. He's so goddamn careless about the equipment. You can't risk people's lives like that."

Rick's assertion that he wanted to kill Horse was not comforting. Was Rick's near breakdown related to the murders? Were guilt and remorse finally getting to him?

"Did you see Horse?" I asked.

"No, would you believe it? The shop was closed up tight. I don't know where the hell he was. It was a Saturday. He's never closed on Saturdays. Unless he's off on one of his buying trips." Rick sneered as he made the last statement.

"Buying trip?"

He said, "You don't want to know about it, but he isn't buying new dive gear, that's for sure."

"I don't understand," I said.

Rick shook his head. "Anyway, when the shop wasn't open, I just went home. By that time, I had regained some degree of control, but I was too ashamed to go back. And I thought you'd be long gone."

"Gone is right. I nearly was a goner. How could you even have gone into that cave without proper equipment to get us both out safely?"

He bowed his head. This was not the self assured or sometimes surly Rick Lucas I knew. Yet I was finding little satisfaction in continuing to berate him. He seemed already too beaten down.

"I explained it all to that detective friend of yours."

"Detective McBride."

"Yes. He tracked me down at home. My Dad was very upset when a policeman came to the house. He's always worried about what the neighbors will think. The detective brought a Wakulla Sheriff's Deputy with him."

"Was it a Deputy Thompson?"

"Yeah, that's his name, Thompson. He has a real attitude problem. I can see why Horse gets bent out of the shape at the mention of the guy's name. Thompson likes to throw his weight around."

"Has Horse ever explained their connection to one another?"

"I can only guess. The man stops in at the dive shop from time to time. Always, gets Horse crazy."

"Really," I said.

"How are you feeling?" he asked. "I mean, are you okay? Does everything check out? Blood work and all?"

"Yes, thank goodness, I survived. Thanks for the roses," I said, suddenly feeling weary. "I'm not sure I'll ever venture into a cave again."

"Can you forgive me, Lorelei? You'll get your certification."

"Frankly, I'll have to think about it, Rick. I still don't understand how you could abandon a student like you did."

"It's very complicated," he said, sounding almost annoyed at my persistent accusation. "All I can do is apologize and tell you I'm glad you're okay."

I'll bet, I thought since it lets you off the hook for a law suit. I was no longer angry but not in a forgiving mood.

"Why do you think Horse hasn't called? I left him a message about the gear we left out there."

"I'm going to drive by today. I wanted to make sure you were all right before I did. I'm quitting. Horse will have to find another dive instructor. I can't work for him any longer. Not after this."

So it was all Horse's fault, I thought. How convenient for Rick to lay blame on Horse's equipment.

He got up to leave and said, "Thanks for letting me explain, Lorelei."

"Sure," I said, thinking I should have thrown my lunch at him.

246

I had a lot to think about after Rick left. His behavior during our dive could have been premeditated. But his attitude today was so different. Maybe he was bi-polar or something, I thought. That would explain his mood swings. Could it suggest he was a killer as well? From what I had read, people who were bi-polar were more likely to commit suicide than homicide—which, according his story, he had considered after our dive.

C'mon, Lorelei, it's best to stay in the present and focus on your performance. Besides, haven't you already damn near risked your life for this case?

I reached for the bag of food Mike brought and opened the Mediterranean wrap. "Hmm, delicious," I said, catching the aroma of feta and herbs. I happily took my first bites, flicked on the television and found my favorite diversion…the Food Network.

As promised, Mike picked me up at the hospital around eleven o'clock on Monday morning. I spent the next 24 hours in my apartment where I did yoga, napped, and reviewed the script. I left my cell phone off, but returned some calls when I needed a break.

The cast welcomed me back to the theatre for Tuesday night's performance. I stumbled over some of my lines, but everyone was very patient—even Renee. Being away from it for several days, I felt as though I was hearing the play for the first time. Mike's portrayal of Dr. Stockman caused me to revise my opinion of the character. Yes, he did seem obsessed, but I now saw a certain nobility in his defense of the scientific truth he had discovered. I was able to bring more admiration and kindness to my role as his wife. And I thought of Alex Hadley's trials and ultimate death as a result of defying some greedy landowners. By the end of the performance I realized I had experienced it on two levels, and I had a bittersweet awareness of its timely truth.

Delcie called me every day, and I felt I owed her a daily update. I checked in with my mother, and was reminded why she hadn't been able to come to my opening night. She had contracted a virus on her cruise. She sounded hurt that I hadn't returned her earlier calls but accepted my explanation about how busy I was with the opening.

Mother was a theatre devotee who accepted any excuse in service of the dramatic arts. If she only knew what I was really up to, I thought.

I returned Jeffrey's calls, but I didn't tell him what had happened to me at the springs. I planned to give him the full story when I returned to Gainesville. I kept trying unsuccessfully to reach Horse at the dive shop. Where was he?

It was Thursday before I finally heard back from Homer. I hadn't talked with him since Sunday morning.

"How was your first night back at the theatre?" he asked.

"Homer, where have you been? I waited to hear from you."

"If you'd left your phone on more often, you would have. So how was it...your first night?"

"It went very well. Frankly, I gave a better performance than I had given during rehearsals. Maybe it was the rest I had in the hospital. So?"

"What?"

"Homer McBride, please do not put me through this," I said with emphasis on each word. "I've practically risked my life to get you information in this case. Don't you dare cut me out of the loop at this stage of the game."

"I specifically warned you not to take any risks, Lorelei. But okay, I'm just teasing."

"Very funny. When we last spoke, you said you were making progress. Are you?"

"I'm waiting for a final forensic report, but I've had a couple of lucky breaks."

"Great. Tell me."

"You know we can't talk on the phone. Anyway, you'll know soon enough."

"Are you going to come here this weekend for the play? I've saved you a ticket."

"I'm sorry, but much as I want to see you on stage, I can't. There's too much I'm trying to put together right now."

"So when?"

"Monday at the lodge."

"Lunch on Monday?"

"No, actually, I'm hosting a little gathering in one of the meeting rooms at eleven in the morning. I want you to be there."

"What kind of gathering?" My antenna was up. Homer was not likely to be throwing any parties at the Wakulla Lodge, or anywhere else for that matter.

"I've invited—no, to be honest—strongly urged all of the persons of interest in the two murders to show up for it."

"How'd you get them to come?"

"A little gentle persuasion," he chuckled. "I told them I had some compelling new evidence that linked the two murders, and that they wouldn't want to be the only ones not there. I think they got the message."

"You mean it would look suspicious if they balked about being there?"

"Uh huh. That, and natural curiosity."

"So you've solved the two murders?"

"No comment, but it should be an interesting meeting. That's all I'm willing to say for now."

"Sounds fascinating. I wouldn't miss it for the world. You know Rick finally visited me in the hospital." I told McBride the gist of Rick's story. "He sounded genuinely sorry."

"Yeah, I'd guess he'd play it that way. By the way, it checks out that he did make the 911 call. Look, I've got to go now, Lorelei. Sorry I can't be there this weekend. Maybe later."

"I understand," I said. "See you on Monday. I can't wait."

It was true. I was looking forward to Monday's drama at the Wakulla Lodge. It promised to be even more exciting than the one at the Dixie Theatre.

Chapter 32

I arrived at the lodge around ten fifteen on Monday morning and spotted McBride's car in the parking lot. I was eager to see him before everyone else arrived. I scanned the lobby as I walked toward our usual meeting place—the restaurant. He was seated at a window table having coffee with a man in uniform. The man's back was toward me, but I could tell it wasn't Deputy Thompson. McBride looked up and waved me over.

He pulled another chair up to the table and introduced me to a fifty-something man with graying sideburns and a kind face. "Lorelei, this is Lieutenant Cary Anderson. He's with the Park Patrol. Cary will be around for our little meeting today."

The Lieutenant gave me a warm smile.

McBride said, "Lorelei is an actress—stage actress. She does some P.I. work on the side, and she's been helping with the investigation."

"An actress?" Anderson looked surprised.

"I'm in a play at the Dixie Theatre in Apalachicola."

"Oh, yes. The wife mentioned something about that play. Wanted to get me over there to see it with her. Said it's some sort of classic...about a mad scientist."

I smiled at his description. "It's called *An Enemy of the People*," I explained. "It's about a physician, actually. I guess some would call him mad—he tries to force his town to accept a truth they don't want to hear."

The Lieutenant chuckled, "Oh, so that's why it's a classic. Been down that road myself a time or two."

The two men gave each other knowing smiles.

McBride said, "Wakulla Springs is on Lieutenant Anderson's beat."

Anderson's badge identified his service as Florida Park Patrol Northwest District.

I said, "So you're also working on the murder case?"

"Yes. We've been working with the Wakulla Sheriff's Office and Tallahassee. You know, we've never had a murder here at the park. There've been other kinds of crimes, but never one this serious. We'll be mighty glad to see it all over, and Detective McBride here thinks he's going move things quite a ways in that direction today."

"He does?" I said, casting an admiring glance at Homer. "Detective McBride is a master sleuth. I'm sure his meeting will be fascinating."

McBride stood up. "Well, folks, it's almost time to greet our guests." He put a hand on Lieutenant Anderson's shoulder and said, "You've got the room covered as I requested?"

"Yes sir," the Lieutenant replied, getting up from the table. "Between us and the sheriff's deputies, no one's going to leave without your say so."

"Excellent."

I started to rise, McBride gestured me to stay seated and said, "Lorelei, why don't you stay and have some coffee. Nothing's going to happen until eleven."

I remained seated and watched as the two men walked out of the restaurant. I waited a few minutes and followed them to the lobby. I sat down facing the long hallway which led to the conference room waiting for the parade of characters who had already given me a season of intrigue. In the meantime, I studied Old Joe—the massive alligator shot by a poacher in the 1960's. The gator was honored by being preserved in a glass display case outside the gift shop. Old Joe was a Wakulla Springs legend.

When I glanced at the front door, I spotted Horse Stern standing at the entrance, looking around the lobby. I called him over.

"Horse, why haven't you returned my calls?" I stood up. "You knew I was in the hospital, didn't you?"

He cast a furtive glance around. He looked haggard. "Sorry, Lorelei. My life...well, it's a nightmare. I heard you were okay. I just couldn't call. Is the conference room down that hallway?"

"Yes," I said. "It should be the last door on the right."

"Excuse me," he said, and with no further explanation hunched his shoulders and walked away.

I stayed in the lobby until I saw Mona Lavender, Pete Stigler and a couple of men I didn't recognize. They all came in through the side entrance nearest the conference room. It was time for me to join the group.

I entered the room and caught the aroma of burnt coffee as though someone had left an empty carafe on the hotplate. There was a large oblong wooden conference table surrounded by a dozen or so office chairs. As I took a seat at the far end of the table, I nodded to Mona who returned my greeting with a quick nervous smile. Pete Stigler, who sat on her right, glanced my way and gave me a blank look.

No one was talking, and the tension was palpable. Rick Lucas came in with a tall bespectacled man who looked irritated, as though he didn't want to be here. Dr. Matos, I assumed.

Rick left Matos, came over, sat next to me, and whispered, "What's this all about?"

"Don't know," I whispered back.

He arched his eyebrows as though he didn't believe me.

Alex Hadley's father-in-law, Cliff Rinehart, entered, looked around, and seemed surprised to see me. He nodded a solemn greeting and sat down.

Finally, McBride entered the room, stood at the head of the table, and placed a folder down in front of him. He was followed in by Lieutenant Anderson, Deputy Thompson, and another man. The other man dressed in suit and tie appeared to be an official of some sort. He took a seat alongside Anderson, next to the door. Thompson sat on McBride's right, next to Mona Lavender.

McBride looked around the table and said, "Thank you all for taking time in your busy schedules to come here today. I think you'll find what I have to tell you to be very enlightening. It is, of course, in the matter of the two recent deaths here at Wakulla."

He paused, opened his folder, and seemed to be reviewing some notes. The drone of the wall air-conditioning unit filled the otherwise quiet room. McBride looked like a business executive trying to dress down at a resort conference. He wore a navy corduroy jacket, red plaid shirt, and jeans. I thought him quite attractive.

Looking up, he said, "The deaths of Alex Hadley and Burton Stigler, also known as "Buster," are what has brought us here today.

Pete grimaced at the sound of his son's name. Mona placed her hand on his arm and gave him a consoling look. I guessed the two had made up. Death does that sometimes.

McBride continued. "Let's begin with the death of Alex Hadley. Forensic evidence has it that Dr. Hadley's costume was intentionally salted with red ants. Small apple fragments were found in the feet of the costume. Placed as they were, they would keep the ants busy—and not obvious to the costume wearer—until the costume was pulled on.

"Every one of you has admitted knowledge of Dr. Hadley's extreme allergy to insect bites of any kind. Yet, oddly and uncharacteristically, Hadley's belongings revealed no Epi Pen syringe. Hadley's wife told us he never failed to carry one in his suitcase. We concluded it was intentionally removed by his killer. The cause of Dr. Hadley's death was anaphylactic shock."

McBride paused.

"It was you, Mr. Rinehart, who discovered the body and determined your son-in-law was dead. Instead of immediately notifying anyone, you fled the scene. Only later did you call the authorities."

Rinehart bristled and said, "I told you, I wasn't thinking straight—I was horrified."

"Yes, we have your statement." McBride said, with a dismissive gesture. "Let me proceed."

McBride slowly looked around the table at each of the suspects and said, "It's a curious fact that all of you were at the Wakulla Springs Lodge during the time Dr. Hadley walked around the waterfront, registered at the front desk, and eventually made his way to his room on the second floor. With the exception of Mr. Rinehart, you've all said you were here for the Creaturefest."

McBride paused and looked down at his notes before resuming. "As stated, Dr. Hadley's death was intentionally engineered by ingenious and simple means—red ants found everywhere around the lodge. Hadley was known never to lock his car so his costume and overnight case were easily accessible."

Dr. Matos removed a small notebook from his pocket and began to write in it. He was the only one in the room who appeared inattentive. I suspected he had slipped into his typical university meeting mode.

"TV shows about criminal investigations are very popular these days, so you probably are aware that means and opportunity are key elements in determining suspects. Each of you had both in the case of Dr. Hadley's death."

The air in the room, already heavy, seemed to shift into an escalated sense of anxiety, and I saw big Mona squirm in her chair.

"Excuse me, Detective McBride," Rinehart spoke, his voice resonant. "As an attorney, I find this meeting a bit on the dramatic side. You're not in a court of law. Why don't you simply get to the point and tell us who you believe killed my son-in-law and this other fellow? That's what we're all here to learn, isn't it?" He looked around the table for confirmation. None came. Faces remained blank.

McBride looked away for a moment, and then he said, "This is a criminal investigation involving two related homicides. You're right, it is not a courtroom, but if you'll allow me to continue, you'll see I am simply trying to lay out the facts of the case. And for that I need the cooperation of everyone in this room."

Rinehart sat back and nodded. "All right. I've come all the way up from Tampa. I might as well go along with you."

"Thank you," McBride said. "As I was saying, everyone here had both opportunity and the means to murder Dr. Alex Hadley. The critical question then goes to motive. What person or persons had a need to permanently silence the man?"

I had never seen McBride conduct a session like this before, and I was impressed by his cool and commanding presence—it was sexy. I thought if the décor were more like an English cottage, this could be an Agatha Christie play with Homer as Hercule Poirot.

"As to a motive for the crime, let's just go around the room."

There was more squirming…crossing and uncrossing legs, folding and unfolding arms, and Dr. Matos continued scribbling in his notebook. He couldn't have appeared any more aloof.

"First on the list is you, Ms. Lavender."

Mona's eyes widened, and her body froze as though she were told to hold her breath for a mammogram.

Why had he skipped Deputy Thompson, I wondered.

"Is it true, Ms. Lavender, that you and members of your Resource Council—or BSRC, as you call it—were trying to sell springs property, first to an Atlanta water bottling plant and next to a housing developer?"

"We did intend to sell our holdings," she said. Her voice was weak, and she paused to glance at Pete Stigler. "But no deal's been made. Members of the council had pooled their properties. We wanted better control of the kind of development that would occur."

McBride said, "Please tell me the names of the major property owners in the BSRC."

Mona looked again at Pete and next at Thompson before answering.

"The major land owners included me, Mayor Stigler, and several other citizens who held smaller parcels of land."

"I didn't hear you mention Deputy Thompson's name," Homer said. "Wasn't he also part of the council?"

Mona looked distinctly uncomfortable, but Thompson maintained a mask of disinterest.

"You could say that…but, Skip, I mean Deputy Thompson was really a silent partner."

"Thank you, Ms. Lavender. You've answered my question. Members of the BSRC knew of Dr. Hadley's allegations about the relationship between Graham and Wakulla Springs. You must also have known, if the connection had been confirmed, you would have had regulatory problems, and the environmentalists would have kicked up a stir as well. In short, Hadley's findings—if confirmed— would have greatly interfered with your plans."

Mona's body tensed, and she got her voice back. It was sharp and indignant as she replied, "You're wrong, Detective McBride, Alex Hadley was not justified in spreading those rumors. Dr. Matos had already proven that Graham Springs was independent of Wakulla. Ask him. His assistant there, Dr. Lucas, even came to one of our meetings to assure us there was no problem. "

Matos suddenly became engaged by the proceedings. He sat straight up, closed his notebook, and neatly folded his hands on the table like a student caught not paying attention when his name was called. I glanced at Rick, who rolled his eyes.

Homer persisted. "But if Dr. Hadley's assertions were proven, you and your co-investors stood to lose valuable flexibility in selling the property. Isn't that true?"

She paused before responding, and finally said, "Possibly."

McBride said, "Thank you, Ms. Lavender. You've been very helpful, as usual."

Mona helpful? I was surprised by Homer's remark, since in my experience she had not exactly been forthcoming. But Homer was a man, and I'm sure that made a difference with the dramatic Mona Lavender. For my part, the most fascinating outcome was learning that Thompson was on the BSRC.

My next surprise came when Homer's focus returned to the attorney who sat opposite Mona. I had expected him to question Thompson next.

McBride said, "Mr. Rinehart. You never approved of Alex Hadley's marriage to your daughter. You also were known to express strong feelings about his reaction to her and your granddaughter's safety when things heated up in Fairport. After she moved back to Tampa to live with you, you phoned Hadley repeatedly demanding he abandon his public fight over the springs, so he could bring his family home. You advised him your daughter was being treated for severe depression as a result of it. Hadley refused, and you allegedly came up to find him. Isn't that when you…"

Rinehart's face flushed in anger. "I came up to reason with him. To try to persuade him to do the right thing. Any father would have done the same."

I felt sympathy for Rinehart. Once again, I was reminded of the resemblance between Hadley and Stockman in Ibsen's play. Hadley, too, was willing to sacrifice the well-being of his family in order to pursue his passion for the truth.

McBride remained silent.

Rinehart slumped in his chair, and the anger seemed to drain out of him. He said, "Alex killed my girl's spirit. Yes, I hated him for it, but I didn't kill him. Christ, his death sent my daughter into an even deeper depression. I don't know if she'll ever recover."

I turned to Rick to see his response, but he seemed unaffected by Rinehart's statement.

"I'm sorry," McBride said in a soft voice and looked down at his notes.

I was starting to think this was like a group therapy session. I wondered where McBride's next probe would be.

He looked up and turned to Matos. "Dr. Matos, have you had a chance to review the Hadley research I left with you during our last visit?"

Matos nervously adjusted his glasses and replied, "I have."

"And what did you think when you found that it completely contradicted the assessment you made about Graham Springs?"

Matos frowned and took a long breath as though preparing to make simple, something too complicated for a class of students. "Scientific knowledge is always changing, Detective McBride," he intoned. "Naturally, what Dr. Hadley found will have to be confirmed by more research. It's too early to tell."

"I'll be more direct. Didn't you actually falsify your research to make it appear that Graham was nothing more than a sinkhole lake? That assertion would protect the upstream forest products company from any closer scrutiny about pollution. You knew there was pending legislation that would affect North Florida wetlands. You get a lot of research money from the forest industry, don't you?"

Matos flushed, started out of his chair, thought better of it, and sat down again. "Those are very serious allegations, detective. Do you have any proof, sir?"

McBride responded, "I do, actually. Your own colleague, Dr. Lucas, gave me a statement to that effect. I'm sure we'll find other experts who would confirm his testimony."

I understood why Rick had chosen to sit next to me and away from Matos. If looks could kill, there would have been a third murder to deal with. The faces of the three BSRC members, seated across from Matos, were set in non-committal expressions. Did they know the truth, I wondered.

"By the way," McBride said, addressing the Fairport group, "Dr. Hadley not only found a connection between the two springs, but he had tested the water at Graham Springs. It contained traces of a toxic organic solvent—like turpentine."

Jeffrey didn't tell me that, I thought. McBride must have learned about it when he had Hadley's research checked by one of his experts.

"I don't have to sit here and take this rubbish," Matos said, as he got up and started for the door. His exit was blocked by McBride's colleague who tried to soothe him and suggested he retake his seat. He complied...with smoldering stares at Rick Lucas.

"It's evident that several of you had a strong interest in seeing that Dr. Hadley's research findings were suppressed. Dr's Matos and Lucas had funding and reputation issues at stake; members of the BSRC—Ms.Lavender, Mr. Stigler, and you, Deputy Thompson—had land deals to protect. Hadley had stirred up quite a hornet's nest."

McBride paused, as though thinking through the implications of what he had just exposed. He continued, "So you can see how complicated our investigation became with such a long list of people who had a motive for murder. Then matters became more complicated when Dr. Hadley's death was followed by that of Buster Stigler. That's where you come in, Mr. Stern."

Horse? I had almost forgotten Horse was in the room, and I was surprised to hear McBride mention the dive shop owner. Horse Stern was slouched in his chair at the far end of the table—an empty chair between him and Rick on one side, and him and Pete Stigler on the other. He didn't look at anyone and seemed totally out of it. When Homer spoke his name, all eyes turned to him—yet he continued to stare down, as though to will himself away.

"Mr. Stern," McBride said, using a more forceful voice to get his attention. "Initially, I was puzzled at where you might fit into this case. But it all fell into place when I pieced together your relationship with Deputy Thompson."

Wow, I thought. At last, an answer to the riddle of Horse and Thompson. McBride does seem to have put it all together. I had wondered about their connection from early on. There was always something strange about Horse's reaction to the mention of Thompson's name—even Rick couldn't explain it.

I was practically on the edge of my seat waiting for Homer to continue, when a uniformed deputy sheriff came into the room and told McBride he had a phone call.

Homer said, "Please remain exactly where you are, I'll be back in just a few minutes."

As soon as he was out the door, the room burst into a buzz of private conversations. Thompson, Lavender, and Stigler huddled together. I overheard Matos asking Rinehart what kind of law he practiced and something about handling academic law suits. Lieutenant Anderson and the plainclothes man sitting next to him talked quietly. Next to me, Rick fidgeted with his cell phone. Horse remained fixed in the same position, as though in a fugue state.

Chapter 33

McBride returned and withdrew the red notebook from his jacket pocket. He placed it on the table and said, "Sorry for the interruption, but I had to take that call from Tallahassee." He shot a meaningful glance toward the man sitting next to Lieutenant Anderson.

Cliff Rinehart checked his watch and asked McBride, "How much longer do you think we'll be? I may need to make a call or two."

"Not very much longer. Let me pick up where I left off. I was about to ask Mr. Stern about his relationship with Deputy Thompson."

Horse's slumped down further, but he didn't look up. McBride turned to Thompson instead.

"Deputy, maybe you'd care to respond," McBride said. "What is your relationship with Mr. Stern?"

Thompson shifted nervously in his seat, considering his response. "Do you mean the investigation?"

"Yes," said McBride. "Please describe the sheriff's office investigation—led by you—of Mr. Stern and his dive shop."

The deputy looked annoyed, as he glanced around, and said, "That's confidential. I don't think it's appropriate for me to discuss it here."

"Don't worry, deputy. I've cleared it with your superiors at the sheriffs office. Please, speak freely."

Thompson frowned, wiped his hands on his pants legs, and said, "I don't know what relevance it has to this matter."

He was clearly stalling, but McBride waited patiently for him to answer the question.

"Oh, all right. You probably know about it. I was investigating Mr. Stern for drug related offenses."

Horse showed no reaction.

"Please describe your investigation. For example, how long had it been going on?" McBride prompted.

Thompson cleared his throat, looked around for a glass of water, and seeing none, responded directly to McBride. He said, "We had evidence that Mr. Stern was dealing drugs from the dive shop. Informants told us they knew persons who, from time to time, purchased methamphetamines, cocaine, and marijuana at the shop. I'm sure you've already learned Mr. Stern was incarcerated for possession and sale of heroin in California."

I knew that Horse had a record in California but I was amazed that he had continued dealing drugs since moving to Florida. I looked at Rick to see his reaction. There was none.

"Deputy, I asked you how long you knew about Mr. Stern's activities?" McBride sounded like he was losing patience.

"Uh, I don't know. Maybe a year or more." Thompson replied.

"A year, or more? For at least a full year you had evidence of illegal drug trafficking at the dive shop in Carrabelle. Yet—despite repeated questions about the case from your superiors—you made no arrest. Isn't that a bit unusual, Deputy Thompson?"

By this time, Thompson was sitting bolt upright in his chair and had a frozen, defiant look on his face. "Just what are you implying Detective McBride? It was a complicated case...there were unusual circumstances."

McBride waved aside his attempt to explain. "The fact of the matter is you were blackmailing Horse Stern. Isn't that right?"

Thompson half rose from his chair, but when he saw Lieutenant Anderson stand he sat back down again.

Mona looked distressed, but made no attempt to calm her boyfriend. If I had to describe her, I'd say she was trying to pull as far away from him as she could without actually getting up and moving her chair.

"Now, let me ask Mr. Stern about your so-called complicated case." McBride addressed his question to Horse. "Was Deputy Thompson blackmailing you with the threat of arrest and certain imprisonment?"

Horse didn't look up, but nodded yes.

Deputy Thompson said, "Of course he'd say anything to discredit me. He knew I had the goods on him. You can't possibly believe a drug dealer and addict."

McBride silenced Thompson with a disdainful glare and said, "Let me finish, please."

By this time McBride had everyone's full attention...the room felt electrified.

McBride opened his folder, looked at his notes, and said, "Horse Stern was seen in the parking lot near Alex Hadley's car during the time Dr. Hadley was at the waterfront. FDLE's forensic lab has just notified me there is physical evidence of Mr. Stern's entry into the back seat of Hadley's automobile where both Hadley's costume and overnight case had been left before he checked into the lodge. We expect DNA evidence to further confirm this."

All eyes were on Horse Stern. He raised his head and gave McBride a pleading look. "I swear, I hated doing it to Alex. He was my friend, but I was desperate. I couldn't do prison again. I nearly got killed in there." Horse stood, and pointed to Thompson. "He drove me to do it—he's been blackmailing me for months—I should have killed him instead!" His body shuddered and he looked about the cry.

The man in the suit got up, quickly went over to Horse, whispered a few words to him, and—taking him by the arm—led him out of the room. On his way to the door, Horse stopped, looked at McBride, and in a broken voice said, "You got to understand, I didn't have a choice. Thompson was driving me crazy. And after Alex died...what could I do?"

Horse was ushered out of the room. Everyone must have been holding their breath during the exchange. When the door closed behind Horse and the officer, I could hear the sound of almost simultaneous exhalations.

Rick look at me in disbelief.

I, too, was thoroughly shocked. Horse did seem to be Alex's friend. He had defended and helped Alex with his problems in Fairport. He had apparently been to the Hadley house with some frequency and even knew their daughter's birth date.

Mr. Rinehart broke the silence. "My God, I never would have guessed…" He didn't finish his sentence.

McBride stood, with arms folded, and once again stared at Deputy Thompson who looked pale, and uncharacteristically submissive.

"Before we go into the matter of motive, I want to discuss the death of Buster Stigler." McBride gave Pete Stigler a sympathetic look, and said, "I hope this isn't too rough on you, Mayor Stigler, but I'm sure you want to know about your son."

Pete waved a hand in the air, "No, no. Please continue detective. If you've learned anything about my boy's death, I want to know. Hard as it will be."

Mona—who by this time had actually moved her chair away from Thompson and closer to Stigler—put her hand on Pete's arm. She gave him a look that dripped with concern.

"Then I'll continue. Earlier, I mentioned my puzzlement over the connection between Stern and Thompson. Mr. Stern has admitted the deputy was blackmailing him. But how did this fit in with the mayor's son? Buster Stigler's cell phone record only showed calls from you, Dr. Lucas, and Deputy Thompson."

I looked at Rick who began cracking his knuckles again. I could see beads of sweat on his forehead.

"Why did these men have any contact at all with young Buster Stigler? After all, Buster was simply a lawn maintenance employee here at the springs. We do know, however, that his girl friend was pregnant, and he was desperate for money."

McBride looked my way, and I was glad to have uncovered those facts for him.

"Still, there didn't seem to be any obvious reason for him to be the center of these contacts—until our investigation revealed his death was no accident. It was murder."

I looked at Pete Stigler and saw him wince and brace himself.

"Bruises on his neck, the position of his body, and that of the small tractor indicated someone had broken his neck before the tractor landed—was pushed—on top of him. We found other supporting evidence at the scene."

McBride paused, looked at his notes again and continued, "As I said, the cell phone calls were baffling. But as sometimes happens in an investigation like this, a witness comes forward to reveal significant information. More about that later."

McBride gave me a look to say he was going to ask me some questions, and I felt tension creeping along my neck and shoulders.

"Mrs. Crane has been assisting with aspects of this investigation, and I want her to tell us about a certain computer drive she discovered."

"I'm not sure what you want me to say, but I..." Should I tell them about the break-in to Hadley's house? I sent an inquiring look to McBride.

"Tell them everything, Mrs. Crane. It's okay."

I said, "There was so much conflict related to Dr. Hadley's findings at Graham Springs. So I thought if I could locate his research findings it would aid the investigation into his death. I persuaded Horse Stern to help me look around Dr. Hadley's house. Horse was reluctant at first, but he finally agreed to help me. He said he was a friend of the family and that Jennie Hadley wouldn't mind if he looked around."

I paused, reflecting on the irony of Horse's recent confession, and wondering how much I should say about that night.

"Go on, Ms. Crane," McBride said.

"We went in the house late one night and started to..."

Deputy Thompson interrupted, "That's breaking and entering." He looked puffed up with indignation.

McBride gave him a withering look, and the deputy slumped back in his chair.

"Anyway, I found a hidden flash drive. I suspected it contained Dr. Hadley's research. It was apparently overlooked by the sheriff's deputies when they searched the house. I took it back to my apartment with the intention of turning it over to Detective McBride. While I was at the theatre that evening, someone broke into my apartment and took it. Fortunately, I had sent the contents earlier by email to a friend at the University of Florida."

McBride nodded and asked, "Do you have any idea who it was who broke into your apartment and took it? Did you notify the local authorities?"

"I did, but they couldn't help. Frankly, my first suspicion was Buster Stigler." I looked at Pete and gave him an apologetic smile. "I thought it was Buster because just a week or so before I think he tried to run me off of the road when I was returning from Fairport. We'd met at the diner and had words."

"How would Buster Stigler know you had this drive? And why would he be interested in it?" McBride asked.

"I don't know...unless someone told him I'd found it. As you said, he was desperate for money, and he was angry with his father for not letting him have property at the springs. Maybe he thought he could sell the research to get money for the property."

McBride gave me a wry smile, and said, "Close to the truth, Mrs. Crane. I believe you have the right thief."

It was Dr. Matos's turn to express impatience with the proceedings. "Detective McBride. This is a fascinating story, but I've got to get back to the university. So unless you plan to charge me with some crime, I'm going to leave. You know where to find me." He rose to leave, and McBride signaled Anderson to let him go.

McBride rubbed his hands together, and said. "All right, it's time to close the gaps. Thanks to Ms.Lavender, the puzzling connections between these two crimes can be resolved."

Thompson looked apoplectic. He face flushed with a combination of anger and dismay as he turned to Lavender. "Mona," it was almost a groan. "You didn't..."

She put her hands to her face...maybe to shield her from his look of betrayal.

McBride said, "Ms. Lavender has given us a statement that explains much of what has happened in these two cases. She and Deputy Thompson had pooled their resources for a land sale. If Hadley's findings about Graham Springs proved to be true, they threatened to stand in the way of the deals BSRC had hoped for. Thompson, who was already blackmailing Horse Stern, got him to agree to get Hadley out of the way."

Thompson sat with his head in his hands. At McBride's prompting, Lieutenant Anderson moved behind the deputy and quietly asked for his holstered gun. Thompson gave it up without protest.

"As we know, the plan succeeded, and Alex Hadley died." I was stunned to hear Horse's confession confirmed. McBride said, "With Dr. Hadley's death, Mr. Stern was already facing a murder charge. So Thompson used the crime as additional leverage to rid himself of another impediment to his plans...Buster Stigler. We eventually would have found Stern to be the perpetrator of his death. We found evidence linking Stern to the crime—one of the rangers identified a man fitting Stern's description on the trail at about the time of Buster Stigler's so-called accident, and there were footprints along with other physical evidence that tie him to the crime scene. I suspect Mr. Stern will make a full confession to this crime as well."

Deputy Thompson appeared to pull himself together and sat straight up, with a grim look on his face. He stared at Mona Lavender who had averted her face from him.

McBride resumed, "Apparently, young Stigler himself had become an artful blackmailer. When Horse mentioned the computer drive to Thompson, the deputy paid Buster to get it by breaking into Ms. Crane's apartment. Buster recognized he had something of value and started bidding it up to Thompson. I also suspect he was offering it to Dr. Matos through his assistant, Rick Lucas. That would explain the record of cell phone calls to Dr. Lucas."

Rick looked impassive.

"Is that true, Dr. Lucas?" McBride asked.

Rick responded, "It isn't against the law to buy someone's research. In academic circles, it can be freely given or sold...faculty sell their research in one way or another all the time."

"You're right," McBride said. "One question, how did you know Buster had it?"

Rick replied, "Buster heard me speak at the council meeting. He knew I worked with Dr. Matos, and I guess he thought we'd be interested. He called me."

McBride nodded, looking satisfied with the explanation, and said, "Deputy Thompson didn't like being held hostage in his own game. With his control over Stern—who had already committed one murder—he was able to persuade him to stage Stigler's 'accident'."

Mona grabbed Pete's arm and cried, "I didn't agree to it. It was all Skip's crazy scheme. I didn't find out what he was doing until later. That's when I went to the police. I swear, Pete. I didn't know."

Pete threw off her hand. His face contorted with anger, and he looked as though ready to get up and beat Thompson to a pulp. It was Mona's pleading, and grabbing hold of his arm that held him back.

McBride walked to the door, opened it, and ushered in a uniformed sheriff's deputy. The deputy walked over, and stood behind Thompson, along with Lieutenant Anderson.

"Richard Thompson," McBride intoned. "These officers will accompany you to the Wakulla Sheriff's Office, and you will be read your rights."

Except for Mona's sniveling, the room remained in stunned silence as Thompson was led out. He made no protest, but he stopped and gave Mona a hard look before leaving the room.

McBride checked his watch, and said, "Unless any of you has something more to add, our business here is concluded. Once again, I thank you for coming. Naturally, those who have material knowledge about the two cases will be called upon as witnesses by the county prosecutor."

McBride closed his folder and jerked his head at me to join him as he left the room.

I turned to Rick and said, "You knew Buster had stolen Hadley's file from me, and that's how you knew I was the one who found it."

Rick pushed himself away from the table, "Yes, I knew. Horse told me you had found something that might be valuable. Then the kid called about it."

"You didn't tell me," I said. "Why?"

He stood and started to walk around me to the door. "It didn't matter. I've got to get back to Tallahassee. Good luck, Lorelei."

It didn't matter? That was his answer? I stood there for a moment, watching as the room emptied. No one looked my way, and I walked out to join McBride.

I found him standing outside the exit door. He was smoking. I stood next to him and shivered in the chill wind.

I said, "You know, you really need to quit. I can't keep meeting you outside all the time. Anyway, that was quite a performance, detective. Masterful and dramatic. You'd make a good actor."

He smiled—a grim smile. "I hate it when the bad apple turns out to be one of our own. I knew the deputy was up to something. I never really bought his argument for giving the press that story about Hadley's death being accidental. But I never figured him for blackmail and murder."

"You sure got a lucky break with Mona Lavender. I've got to give her credit for having a bit of a heart."

"Yeah." He ground the cigarette out under his heel, picked it up, and put it in the trash can nearby. He chucked me under the chin, and said, "Got lucky with you, too, partner."

Was he going to kiss me again, I wondered.

He bent toward me, but stopped. "Lorelei, I…"

"I understand, you're still on duty. How about lunch. Do you have the time?"

"Naw, sorry. I owe you more than a lunch, but I've got to get over to the sheriff's office."

"Okay, but call me as soon as you get a chance. I'm totally knocked off my feet by what just happened, and I still have questions."

"I will," he said, and walked toward his car. He turned and waved.

I hugged myself to stay warm, and walked back into the lodge. I decided to treat myself to lunch before driving back to Apalachicola. It was a perfect day for the Wakulla Lodge restaurant's famous navy bean soup.

Chapter 34

All the way back to Apalachicola my head was spinning with questions. Who finally got Hadley's flash drive? What about the incidents McBride never addressed—my car accident, for example? With Buster dead and apparently no evidence on his truck, I'll probably never know if he was the one who pushed me off the road. And, who mugged me in Hadley's bathroom? Could it have been Horse? But I felt sure there was someone else in the house that night. Finally, I thought about the question of a romantic relationship between Rick and Alex's wife? It might have been what spawned the paranoia that divided the two former friends.

It was almost four o'clock when I got back. I stopped at Sophie's for coffee. I needed some diversion to clear my head.

"Lorelei, Mike was just here asking for you."

"He was?" I said, plopping down at a table by the window. "I thought I'd mentioned I was going to Wakulla Springs."

"Oh," she said, sliding into the seat opposite me. "After all you've been through, you're still involved in all that meshugass with your detective friend?"

I nodded and looked out the window, my thoughts still anchored in the scene at Wakulla. I was like a dog chewing on herself to get rid of a flea. I couldn't seem to stop picking at it.

Sophie put her hand on my arm and asked, "What can I get you? I just finished baking some Mandelbrot. Have you had lunch?"

Dear Sophie, I thought, always the Jewish mother. I looked at her strong care-lined face and felt a rush of affection for her.

"Sophie, I'm really going to miss you when I leave. You've been so…" I began feeling teary.

"It's not for a week yet. So don't be in such a hurry with the goodbyes," she said. "So, what can I get you?"

I laughed, "After what I've heard today, I'll take a double espresso, and some of what you just baked. It smells delicious."

"Coming right up," she said, and left to get the order.

My mind reverted to the pesky questions that continued to distract me. Rick tried to buy Hadley's research from Buster. If he wanted it that badly, could Rick have been the intruder at Hadley's house the evening we broke in? Horse may have told him we were going to the house that night. Maybe Rick planned to get there ahead of us. He wouldn't have known—at the last minute—I got Horse to meet me an hour and half earlier. Remembering the encounter, it did seem possible Rick was the mugger. And if I fully painted him as villain, it would fit with his taking me into a remote cave springs. Or now that I knew Horse was a murderer, maybe he tried to kill both Rick and me by giving us faulty diving equipment? That was a whole new scenario to chew on.

"Hi gorgeous."

I turned to see Mike standing beside my table.

"Can I join you? You looked deep in thought. What happened at Wakulla?"

Before I could respond, he planted himself in the seat Sophie vacated, re-arranged his ball cap, and sat there—elbows on the table—grinning at me. He looked so cute—and so young.

"Exciting? It was unbelievable. If only I were a writer."

"Tell me about it."

I thought a moment about what I could tell him without violating McBride's confidence. "I really shouldn't, but watch the newspapers. In a few days, I'm sure you'll read about a couple of indictments in the Alex Hadley murder, and another one related to it."

"Wow," Mike said. "Let me get some coffee. I'm glad I ran into you."

He went to the counter where Sophie was arranging a tray for me. Mike paid her and brought back my order, along with his coffee. "May I?" he said, picking up one of the pieces of mandel bread. "I love this stuff. She doesn't make it very often."

"It is a treat," I said, and took a piece of the stubby sugared cookie. Lifting it to my mouth I could smell the combination of butter, nuts, and cinnamon.

Mike asked, "So did they get the man who killed Hadley? It wasn't Rick Lucas by any chance was it? I wouldn't put something like that past the bastard—especially after what he did to you at the springs."

I shook my head. "No, it wasn't Rick Lucas. Although a part of me thinks he's seriously mixed up. I'm going to ask McBride..."

"McBride. The guy who got you mixed up in all of this intrigue? I still don't get it, Lorelei. You're an actress, not a sleuth."

"There's not as much difference between the two as you think, Mike. We actors are kind of like detectives, aren't we? A homicide detective uses a process not unlike ours. We have to sort through evidence—given us by the playwright—to uncover our character's motives, their conflicts, and obstacles. We explore the events that logically led up to their behavior and deconstruct the scenes. We create a back story. And we collaborate with others to achieve our goal. You see, there are a lot of similarities."

"I'll give you all that, but acting is still a creative art form. It takes place on stage, not in the real world."

"All art mirrors the real world, doesn't it?"

"Oh, don't start quoting Aristotle."

"C'mon Mike, you know very well that plays explore universal themes. They give us new perspectives. The best theatre brings the audience to the edges of truth and makes them think."

"So you and your detective friend are going to do Dragnet: The Musical?"

"Oh, you're hopeless." I threw my paper napkin at him.

Sophie came over, "Now, now children."

Mike and I looked at each other and burst out laughing.

"What the hell was that all about," he said.

"I don't know, but laughing sure feels good."

"Of course," said Sophie. "Next to eating and making love, laughing is best. Look, it's been very slow here today. I think I'm going to close early. Take your time, but I'm going to lock the door."

"How about having dinner with me tonight, Lorelei? There's something I want to tell you."

I pictured myself spending a long, lonely evening in my apartment waiting to hear from Homer, but I was curious to learn what Mike had to tell me. "Yes, I'd love to."

"Fine," he said, getting up. "I've got to get back to the dock and do some things on my boat. How about my place for drinks at seven?"

Where would you like to go—Tamara's Café Floridita, or the
Apalachicola Seafood Grill for fried oysters?

"The Grill is always great, but I feel like having Tamara's
paella."

"I'll make a reservation. Hold the door a minute, Sophie," he
said, and left.

I finished sipping my coffee and ate the last of the cookies. I
carried my plate over to the counter where Sophie was cleaning the
grille and asked, "Anything I can do to help you close up?"

"No, darling, thank you. But if you want to stay and talk for a
while, that'd be nice."

Something in her voice caught my attention. "Is anything wrong,
Sophie? Anything special you want to talk about?"

She turned and gave me a wistful smile. "Just a few minutes
while I finish this, and put some things away. We'll go in back where
no one will bother us."

"Okay," I said.

I looked through some magazines while Sophie finished closing
up.

"There," she said. "Would you like something to drink? Take
anything you like from the cooler."

"No thanks," I said, and followed her into the small storeroom.

There were two straight back chairs, and a table squeezed amid
boxes of various restaurant items...table settings, baking and cooking
ingredients. A ledger on the table had invoices sticking out of it.

"So," she said, settling into the chair with a mug of tea. "You're
finished now with your detective work?"

"Yes, I'm finished."

"How are you feeling? Have you recovered from your accident?"

"Yes, I'm fine," I replied, wondering where the conversation was
going to settle.

We sat in silence while Sophie sipped her tea and looked
troubled.

"Sophie?" I said, "Is there something you want to talk about?

"Yes," she replied, with a sigh. "Did you know I have a great
love here?"

I was startled by her unexpected revelation. "No, you've never talked about anyone. I guess I just assumed…"

"He's a Greek. Older than me."

"Wait a minute. Didn't you buy this place from a Greek man?"

"That's him. The Greeks were no good for Jews…but that's history. Ari's a good man. A very passionate man."

"I'm glad for you, Sophie."

She closed her eyes, put her hands on her cheeks and took another deep breath.

She seemed distressed, and I reached out to touch her.

"He's dying…cancer." She said, in a soft voice, and raised her thick eyebrows in a plaintive expression.

"Oh, I'm so sorry, Sophie."

She looked at me, her blue-green eyes watery. "Ei yi yi—life. It can kill you."

"I know," I said. "But what can we do?" I thought of Bill.

"Do? There's nothing. We just go on, don't we?" She gave me a tender look and patted my hand. "I'm sorry to burden you. But, today, well I'm feeling a bit overwhelmed. He told me about it this morning…when we woke up. Of course, I'll be strong, for him, but it opens old wounds. I've lost too many loved ones." She shook her head in one of those universal expressions of grief and dismay.

I sat silently in respect for her anguish. I knew the losses Sophie referred to had taken place during the Holocaust. I couldn't think of any comfort for it.

Sophie looked at me, and smiled wanly. "Not to worry, Lorelei. I just needed a moment. I thought it would help to tell someone who could understand."

"I do," I said, thinking of myself and others who were suffering similar loss…Pete Stigler and Jennie Hadley. Murder isn't a tragedy for the victim, Delcie once told me, it cuts a swath of pain across many relationships.

Sophie said, "Tell me, what will you do when the play ends next week?"

I took a deep breath. "Honestly, I don't know. I'll go back to Gainesville, of course." To do what, I wondered?

"Maybe you need to take some time for yourself and think about your life. Why don't you stay here awhile after the play closes?"

"Stay here?" I mused, half to myself. "So much has happened. I know I need to make some changes in my life."

"Stay here, by the water," she said, with intensity. "Remember what Mr. Emoto said about its vibrational energy? You'll find out what you need to know if you stay—without the play, and the negative energy you've been involved with.'

I chuckled. "Negative and fascinating. But you're right. I need to just hang out for a while. Maybe Mike will let me stay in the apartment."

"Oh, I'm sure he'd be thrilled to have you there."

"No entanglements though...I'd have to keep it real simple," I said, as much to myself as to her.

"Good," she said, lightly slapping my knee. "Now, let's go. I'm beginning to feel claustrophobic. I can't stand the storeroom for very long."

I felt a weight lifted from my shoulders at the prospect of remaining in Apalachicola. Talking with Sophie seemed to help me sense what I needed. I only hoped I had helped her, as well.

"I love you, Sophie," I said, and gave her a big hug. "Did I ever thank you for the wrap you sent over to the hospital? I swear, it's what got me well enough to get out of there—you wouldn't believe the food."

We walked out of the room, arm in arm, and I said, "Look, if there's anything I can do—for you or your friend—anything at all, just let me know."

She patted my hand. "You're a good girl, Lorelei. Thank you, you've already helped."

"Margaritas and guacamole...sound festive enough for you?" Mike said, greeting me at the door to his apartment that evening.

"Why you're a real cheerful fellow today," I replied, draping my jacket on a chair near the door.

"Why shouldn't I be? The play's a hit. We've had a bigger house every night than anyone expected."

"And...what else?" I asked, settling in on the sofa. I knew there had to be more to his mood than just the play.

He handed me my drink and sat down. He had the same big goofy grin on his face he'd flashed earlier at Sophie's.

"Oh, wait a minute. Let me guess." I had been so self-absorbed over the past few days, it was only at this moment I recalled seeing Mike and the young actress who played my daughter making eyes at one another. It seemed like the kind of harmless flirtation that's common among cast members. "It's Emily, the girl who plays Petra, isn't it?"

"Yes, Emily. We were out on the boat all day, and..."

"Don't tell me—you're in love."

Mike glanced at the photograph of his deceased fiancée and said, "Not in love, but we really clicked. There's definitely something there, Lorelei. She's feeling it, too. We've kind of been hanging out together—you know, after rehearsals. Anyway, we have so much in common."

"I'm happy for you, Mike, and it helps that you're both around the same age," I said, taking a sip of my drink.

He looked embarrassed. "Oh, c'mon, Lorelei. You know that doesn't matter to me."

"No, I mean it. People who are similar have a better chance at happy relationships. Opposites may attract, but they often wind up in a tug of war. Tell me about her."

His voice held a note of restrained excitement as he talked about her. "I guess you haven't spoken with her much. She's very bright, and funny, and she likes the out of doors. Her folks are from around here...her dad's a contractor."

"She has a young child, doesn't she? I've seen her...a pretty little girl."

"Yes, she does."

I sipped my drink and thought how perfectly the gods sometimes plot our lives. His news gave me a sense of relief—no worry about disappointing him—but I also felt surprisingly jealous remembering the excitement of a new romantic relationship.

"Will she be joining us for dinner tonight?"

"No, she can't make it," he said. "She had to go into Tallahassee for some family celebration. She'll be back by tomorrow evening."

"And she didn't take you with her?" I asked.

"Hey, we're not officially a couple or anything. I just wanted to let you know…well, that it's cool between us…you and me."

"Mike, you've been a great friend. It will always be cool between us."

"Good, now how about digging into some of my special hot and spicy guac?"

I followed his advice, and devoured several scoops of the delicious avocado dip.

"How about you, Lorelei? Any plans after the show closes?"

"Funny you should ask me that. I was just talking about it to Sophie. I wonder if it would be okay for me to stay here a week or so longer? I want to spend some time at the beach—just hanging out— before I return to Gainesville."

"No problem," he said. "Stay as long as you like. I haven't got the place rented until March."

"Thanks, Mike. I'll be happy to pay rent."

"No, Lorelei, friends don't pay." He looked at his watch. "Time to go. We've got a 7:45 P.M. reservation at Tamara's."

A full moon lit our way along the wharf to the restaurant. Mike chatted about his day with Emily, and how he was feeling a renewed sense of hope about his life. In a mystical mood, I suggested it may have been his fiancée who had sent someone to fill the emptiness in his heart. Even as I said it, I wondered if my Bill would do the same for me. I, too, was feeling hopeful.

Chapter 35

I didn't hear from McBride until the next day. My dinner date with Mike ended early, and I decided to allow myself the luxury of reading until the early morning hours. It was 8:00 A.M. when my cell phone went off with an annoyingly cheerful tune.

"Lorelei, I hope I didn't wake you."

"Homer? Yeah, you kind of did."

"Sorry, but I'm driving back to Gainesville, and this might be the only time I'll have to talk to you today."

"Okay, I'm waking up," I said, and swung my legs off the bed to sit up. "What's happening? I've been waiting to hear from you."

"The short version is Horse Stern's booked into the Wakulla County Jail... charged with murder. Thompson's already out on bail, and he's been suspended from the sheriff's department pending his trial. Get a copy of *The Wakulla News*. It'll have the story."

"It's a weekly, Homer, and I don't think it comes out until Thursday. Can't you give me some details?"

"Details? I can tell you Horse signed a confession, and—of course—implicated Thompson."

"Did he mention anything about the night we entered Hadley's house?"

"Only in connection with how Thompson learned about the flash drive. Why?"

"I really think it was Rick Lucas who mugged me that night. I'd like to know if Horse told him about our plans."

"I see. You haven't had much luck with that diver of yours. A professional, I think you said?"

"I guess I deserved that."

McBride said, "Your hunch could be right. We know he and Matos needed to suppress Hadley's findings. Horse could have been the one who told him about your plan to search the house. For someone dealing drugs, he had pretty loose lips. Buster Stigler wasn't even involved at that point. Yeah, Lucas could have been there. It makes sense."

"That's what I've been thinking," I said. "For a while, I suspected the deputy and Mona Lavender—even Horse himself."

"Thompson would know better than to get directly involved like that. Hell, he didn't have to."

"I agree. And I don't think it was Mona, either. She always wears such strong perfume. I don't remember there being any fragrance in the bathroom."

"We may never know for certain. Lucas sure isn't going to be making any confessions. He and his boss will have enough problems with the university once they find out about the falsified research."

"Speaking of Big Mona, has she been charged?" I asked.

There was no response.

"Homer? Are you there?" I thought he ran into one of the dead spots where the cell phone doesn't work.

"Homer?"

"Yeah, I heard you. Some college kids just passed me. They must have been doing at least 90-95 miles an hour. This damn I-10 is dangerous. I shouldn't even be talking to you while I'm driving."

"So pull over at a rest stop and call me back," I said, putting my cell on speaker phone while I got out of bed and slipped on a pair of jeans and a shirt.

"There's not much more I can say. I'm going to try to get over to see you this weekend. I'm supposed to be back in Tallahassee on Thursday."

"What about Mona?"

"Don't know yet. It's up to the prosecutor."

"Did you ever learn who wound up with the actual flash drive?"

McBride said. "They found the drive among Buster's things. What else?"

"Now that we know it was Horse who committed the murders, I've been wondering if he intentionally gave Rick faulty scuba equipment—you know, to get both of us out of the way?"

"Sounds a bit far-fetched. Didn't you tell me Lucas inspected all your gear before the dive?"

"Yes, that's true," I said. "Well then, if his equipment really did fail maybe Rick took advantage of the situation to let me drown."

McBride said, "That's a lot of speculation, Lorelei. There are some things we just never will know for sure. I suggest you just get on with you life and let me wrap up this case."

"Just one last question, I promise. When you interviewed Jennie Hadley, did you get any hint that she was having a relationship with Rick Lucas?"

"Lucas? Why would you think that?"

"Something I put together from conversations with both Horse and Cliff Rinehart. It would help explain the bad blood between Hadley and Rick."

"Nope, she didn't even mention Rick Lucas, as far as I recall."

"Thanks, Homer. I do want to stop thinking about this case."

"Good. You should be enjoying what you're doing there. Gotta go now, Lorelei. See you Friday night?"

"Friday's fine. Our last performance is Saturday evening."

"Maybe we can get a bite to eat after the show? I'll probably stay over in town."

"It'll be good to see you when you're not being a super detective."

"I know what you mean. I'll be glad to see you, too," he said. Did his voice sound huskier just then?

I put the phone on the nightstand and went into the kitchen to fix a cup of tea. As I waited for the kettle to come to a boil, I thought about Homer, and wondered if the spark of attraction between us would ever ignite into something significant. "No entanglements now," I said aloud, chiding myself for the thought. Yet, I couldn't help but think, what if?

The week passed quickly. I was disappointed that neither Homer nor Delcie was able to make it back to Apalachicola to see the play. Delcie had an investigation that took her to Dallas. Homer was assigned to a double murder in the city of Alachua.

Saturday night we struck the set and had a cast party at Sophie's. Mike and Emily were obviously absorbed in one another and left early. I left shortly after them. As I think about it now, except for the night I returned after being in the hospital, I never was fully engaged in the play. Renee knew it, but didn't complain as long as I gave a professional quality performance. Mrs. Stockman wasn't exactly the pivotal role.

It was a rainy cold week leading up to Christmas. I was glad not to be home for my first major holiday without Bill. Mother told me I could come down to Davie to stay at her condo and even asked me to join her on another cruise she was taking. Neither idea appealed.

I spent the week reading, sleeping late, and taking walks along the bay. I toured the beautifully restored antebellum homes and visited the small John Gorrie State Museum. In the mid 1800's, Doctor Gorrie was treating victims of yellow fever when he concluded his patients would recover quicker if they were cooler. I was fascinated by the exhibits showing how he constructed a machine believed to be the forerunner of modern air conditioning and refrigeration.

Several afternoons I treated myself to massages and took some yoga classes in town. In short, I did everything I could think of to center my thoughts and spirit. Each day I stopped by Sophie's for coffee and conversation. I saw little of Mike since he was spending the holiday with his family and with Emily in Tallahassee.

One morning, while Mike was away, I heard Clarence meowing loudly at his door. By the time I opened a can of tuna and brought it out to the landing the cat had gone. Clarence's visit made me think of my own cat, Maynard, and added to my growing feeling of homesickness. I guessed by this time, Maynard would have adjusted to living at the neighbor's.

The afternoon of Christmas Eve it was drizzling and cold. I had my usual seat at Sophie's, and I was feeling sorry for myself.

As I looked out the window I saw Delcie pull up to the curb. My heart leapt at the sight of my friend, and I rushed to the door to greet her with a big hug.

"Take it easy, girl. You're holdin' on to me like a drowning woman," she said, "and I know you know what that means."

"Delcie, I couldn't be happier to see anyone."

"You didn't think I'd let you be alone on your first Christmas Eve without Bill, did you?"

I took her hand and drew her to the table where I was sitting.
"But what about your mama and family? Shouldn't you be with
them?"
She took of her jacket and draped it on the back of the chair.
"Oh, they won't even miss me…there's so many kids running around.
You know how I feel about kids." She gave an exaggerated shudder.
"Well, I'm not going to complain about your being with me. You
can stay a couple of days, can't you?"
"Till Sunday. I've got a meeting with a client first thing Monday
morning."
"Great, Delcie. We'll spend Christmas together." I clapped my
hands and saw Sophie headed our way with a big smile on her face.
"Hello," she said to Delcie. "Nice to see you again. You seem to
have made Lorelei so happy. I think she's had a difficult week, and I
haven't been much help."
"Oh, Sophie," I said. "Just being able to come here every day
and talk with you has been wonderful."
"What can I get you?" she asked Delcie.
"Just coffee, thanks."
Sophie left.
"I hope you've been taking care of yourself this week. How are
you feeling? Any insights you want to share?"
"It's hard to pin down, Delcie. Sometimes I've felt really
scattered, but I have made a couple of decisions."
Sophie brought Delcie's coffee and left us alone.
"I'm all ears," Delcie said, leaning on the table with her hands
wrapped around the coffee mug.
"First of all, I've definitely decided to sell the house in
Micanopy and move into Gainesville. Without Bill there…well, I
need to be in the city at this time in my life. I want to be closer to
friends…you, Jeffrey, and Homer."
"Homer, huh? Whatever," Delcie said, giving me one of those *I
still don't see what you see in him* looks.
"You don't know him the way I do," I said. "He can be very
sweet. Actually, I'm hoping to see more of him when I get back."
"You mean romantically?" she asked.

"Maybe...yes."

"Whatever rocks your boat. Personally, Homer McBride wouldn't be my choice," she said taking a sip of coffee and adding, "But I like it that you'll be in town. We can do more fun things together and maybe you'll finally come to work with me."

"Ah, that leads me to my other decision. You're not going to like it."

"What?"

I said, "I'm not going to make a career of private investigation."

"But Lorelei, you're so good at it," she protested.

"That may be, but I've been thinking about a discussion I had with Mike Pardo. You remember my actor friend here. He's been after me to start focusing my energies on my real profession, the theatre. I've decided he's right. I gave a pretty mediocre performance here, Del. My heart wasn't in it from the moment McBride let me get involved in the murder investigation."

"And you loved that. Be honest."

"Yes, it was an exciting distraction while I was trying to get my head together after Bill's death. But I'm not cut out for the kind of day to day stuff private investigators do...spying on adulterers, setting up security systems. I'm an actress. It's what I set out to be, and it's my first love."

"Yeah, but try making a decent living out of it," she said.

"Thanks to Bill, I don't have to worry about finances."

"He left you that well off? On a professor's salary?"

"Remember, he did a lot of lucrative consulting work. Anyway, I've got his university pension and quite a stock portfolio. Don't get me wrong, I don't plan to just sit around, or join some volunteer organization or anything."

"What if McBride asks you to help on a murder investigation again. Would you do it?"

I had to smile at the thought. "Work with Homer again? I might consider it."

"Got ya. I thought you enjoyed the sleuthing business too much to give it up totally," Delcie said, with a satisfied look.

"I am going to audition for more acting roles and not just in Gainesville. Then there's a ton of other things I'd like to do and places to go. Maybe I'll spend a season in New York or San Francisco. I'd like to take a course in set or costume design. I want to do something creative with my hands."

"Pottery?" she asked. "I've always wanted to do that."

"No, but I've been remembering I once took a course in art metal welding. I don't really know yet. I'm going to experiment."

Delcie leaned back, and smiled. "Follow your bliss? Isn't that what they say?"

"I remember a quote from Suzuki's *Zen Mind, Beginner's Mind.* It was the first book I ever read on Buddhism, and it made a big impression on me. The quote was something like, 'Your work is to find your work.'"

Delcie smiled, "And you're sure you've already found it in the theatre?"

"Let's say I've rediscovered it. Now, how about you? Anything more going on with you and Luke?"

Delcie stared out the window. It was becoming dark as the winter evening clouds moved in. It felt so cozy in the small cafe and a wave of gratitude swept over me. How blessed I was in so many ways, I thought.

Delcie said, "Luke? No, that's a dead end—again. But I guess I've found my work, too. I like helping people. Even if it gets a bit risky at times."

"Sorry, friends, but it's time to close," Sophie said, removing the cups from our table. "Christmas Eve...I'm spending it with Ari." She gave me a soulful look, and I stood to hug her.

"I'm glad," I said.

"What are you going to do this evening?"

Delcie cast a questioning look at me as we both donned our jackets.

I said, "I think we're going to go to my apartment for a glass of wine and celebrate our friendship and good fortune. After that dinner reservations—it'll be oysters," I said, looking at Delcie's smiling face.

The Monday after Christmas I packed my belongings into the car, left a thank you note for Mike, and headed back to Gainesville. I had a feeling of closure as I drove along the beautiful coast. So much had happened in such a short time. I felt stronger and better able to cope with whatever came next—I would open my arms to it. I knew the experiences I'd had—the intrigue and threats to my life—and the characters I'd met all added to my creative reservoir. I also had two new friends, Sophie Vatine and Mike Pardo, and I intended to stay in touch with them. As for my relationship with Homer? I decided not to over-think it.

I drove past Tate Hell's Forest and the cut-off to Fairport and Wakulla Springs, and I made yet another decision. I was going to contact one of the realtors, whose signs peppered the roadside, to see about buying property in Wakulla County. It would have to be something within walking distance of the water. I had grown to love this area of Florida, and I hoped at least some large part of its natural beauty could be preserved.

A North Florida Mystery

Printed in the United States
116484LV00002B/40-87/A